Six

Six

The 11th Percent Book 6

T.H. Morris

Copyright (C) 2019 T.H. Morris
Layout design and Copyright (C) 2021 by Next Chapter
Published 2021 by Evenfall – A Next Chapter Imprint
Edited by Fading Street Services
Cover art by CoverMint
This book is a work of fiction. Names, characters, places, and incidents are the product of the author's imagination or are used fictiously. Any resemblance to actual events, locales, or persons, living or dead, is purely coincidental.
All rights reserved. No part of this book may be reproduced or transmitted in any form or by any means, electronic or mechanical, including photocopying, recording, or by any information storage and retrieval system, without the author's permission.

This book is dedicated to Louis Morris, my "Uncle Blue," for always illustrating that the focus should never be on the numbers, but just living life one day at a time. Miss you, sir.

Contents

1	Creatures of the Night	1
2	The Crowded Stage	9
3	The Traveler	23
4	Changeable	31
5	Family and Felon	43
6	Giving Thanks	61
7	Rapport	77
8	Memory Lane, Etcetera	90
9	The Seventh at Seven	95
10	Pine, Needles, and Roses	108
11	Independent Studies	124
12	Yuletide Tales	136

13	New Year's Revelations	156
14	Spirit Puzzles	166
15	Patience, (Once Again) Not the Virtue	181
16	An Old Friend and an Old Place	191
17	Smacks and Cracks	214
18	Six	227
19	Karma	235
20	March Madness	246
21	Madness, Continued	262
22	Prom Nights Present, Prom Nights Past	276
23	Biblio-Informant	286
24	Ai	291
25	Six-Fruition	308
26	Time-Honored	344
Acknowledgements		374
About The Author		376

1

Creatures of the Night

The woman lit a cigarette and stood with her weight slightly against a brick wall, calmly watching the individuals walking this way and that. A couple shuffled past her, giggly and jovial as though they were children, with the woman's hair slightly disheveled. The observing woman shook her head in disgust as she brought the recently lit Marlboro to her lips, pulled heavily, and let the smoke escape her mouth and nostrils.

These night lifers had no class. No sense of self at all. She had been waiting here no less than forty-five minutes, and she'd seen a great many people during that time, dressed like the characters they would play that night. There was a man with a silk shirt and leather pants, who clearly aimed to make himself out to be more man than he truly was. There was another man who she had seen take a receipt from a nearby A.T.M., and then "accidentally" drop it when he neared a group of women in line at the club. Predictably, one of them snatched it, read the bank balance on it, and then approached the man with a sly smile that matched his own when he saw her. The smoking lady took another draw from the Marlboro and shook her head. She wondered when the lady would be more disappointed; later tonight, or early tomorrow morning.

Clearing her nostrils of the cigarette smoke, she wondered if the person she'd been ordered to find would even show up tonight. She focused her intent and took a rather meditative sniff of the air. If some bystander happened across her at that moment, they'd likely be puzzled, wondering if she could decipher one scent from another. But such concerns were challenges for Ungifted trash, and she certainly wasn't one of them.

She was Charlotte Daynard. She was a Deadfallen disciple. She was as superior to these meat-hunters as a spider was to a housefly.

She also had the gift of not only deciphering odors through her olfactory senses, but also people's essences. Once she caught that "scent," she'd fixate on the one she waited for.

And there it was.

She opened her eyes, and her ethereality sense hadn't betrayed her. There was the woman she'd hoped to find.

She looked right at home as the centerpiece of some gaggle of female flesh-flaunters. She was perhaps the most convincing character of them all; her costume consisted of a red halter top, a black and extremely short miniskirt, and French-tipped nails. Charlotte watched her as she laughingly conversed with her counterparts. She played her part well; there was no point in disputing that. But if her little buddies knew of her true allegiance and capabilities, maybe they wouldn't be so keen to be around her.

Charlotte's eyes narrowed. There was an addition to her quarry's evening costume. It was a strategically placed choker at her throat. Hmm...

"Well, hello there," said a falsely low voice.

With a frown, Charlotte turned. Mere feet away from her stood a member of this crackpot nightlife. He was a bane to her eyes and nose. He wore an ill-fitting muscle shirt, which was oxymoronic, and, judging by his smell, seemed to have baptized himself in cheap cologne and aftershave.

"What's a fine—well, you don't look all that young, but nobody's perfect...why are you out here and not in there?"

He nodded in the direction of the club.

"Since I am on official business, you get one chance," murmured Claudette. "Go on in there, find some way to boost your clearly low self-esteem, and leave me be."

The idiot man tilted his head with a smirk. "Spunky," he commented. "Maybe what you lack in youth, you make up for in personality."

Charlotte glanced at the club entrance. The woman and her clique were about to be let in...

She took a step forward, but the wannabe Casanova grabbed her arm.

"Now, don't be that way—"

Charlotte whipped around and clamped his chest with her other hand. He gasped in shock, and then immediately cried out. Charlotte focused her ethereality into her fingers and watched as her fingertips turned black. When that occurred, the bones in the man's chest where she touched him cracked, his eyes rolled up into his head, and he collapsed on the ground.

"I did warn you," Charlotte muttered as the man's body fell.

When she looked at the door once more, she saw the lady had gone into the club.

Charlotte swore in frustration, kicked the corpse across the face for delaying her, and hurried across the street to the back of the club. When she was assured of her privacy, she stuck out the index and middle fingers of her right hand, tapped her throat, uttered, "*Per Mortem, Vitam,*" and then lit another cigarette while she waited.

Exactly eight minutes later, a click of heels told her that her quarry hurried her way. The woman rounded the corner, wide-eyed and furious.

"What the hell are you doing here, Charlotte?" the other woman demanded.

Charlotte grinned. "And a mighty fine evening to you, too, Jessica," she said in a sweet voice.

Jessica Hale had little patience with the pleasantries. "I asked you a question," she snapped.

Charlotte took a pull off her new cigarette, then extended it to Jessica. "You're too aggravated," she observed. "Here. It'll calm you down."

Jessica's gaze remained wintry, but she took the cigarette, puffed it twice, and handed it back. Charlotte smiled.

"Isn't that better?" she asked. "Hopefully, you didn't get ashes on that outfit of yours. I've always wondered how you seamlessly bounced between wearing this mask and your true self. It's commendable. The outfit alone is most—"

"Why are you here, Charlotte?" asked Jessica once more. "I won't ask again."

"It's been ten months, Jess," said Charlotte, who filled her voice with false hurt. "Almost a year. You don't call, you don't write—how am I supposed to feel?"

"The Transcendent mandated I detach myself," snarled Jessica. "You heard what he said, because you were standing there when he said it. He desired that I reintegrate—"

"Because he didn't want to look at you," drawled Charlotte. "You failed him, Sweetpea."

"I followed the Transcendent's instructions to the letter," said Jessica angrily.

"And yet, Jonah Rowe didn't abandon his conscience and turn to the dark side," said Charlotte.

"I was not in control of how he succumbed to his impulses!"

"Controlling men is something you brag about, Jessica," said Charlotte. "Or, at least, it was ten months ago."

"At least I didn't flee the scene," spat Jessica.

"You hitched a ride with the Transcendent only because he showed you mercy," dismissed Charlotte.

"What's the deal, Charlotte?" Suddenly, Jessica's lips curled into a cold smile. "The Transcendent didn't make you his right hand in my absence? It's not my fault your abilities are pennies to my own—"

Charlotte invaded Jessica's personal space, so their faces were only inches apart. "Now you look here, missy," she growled. "You may think you're the most wonderful thing since pecan pie, but I recall a time when you were a broken, confused girl the Transcendent pulled from the gutter. And, just so we're clear, were it not for your little pretty-talking ability, you'd still be in said gutter."

Jessica hadn't flinched. Charlotte's eyes lowered to the choker. Without an invitation, she hooked it with one of her fingers and lifted it which revealed an asymmetrical, two-inch scar at the base of her neck. A smile lit her own face.

"He didn't heal it," she breathed. "Rowe marred your perfect image, and the Transcendent didn't heal it. He left you with your very own mark of Cain."

Jessica had remained stationary through all of this. When she finally spoke, it was soft and deliberate. "Charlotte, if you don't take your hands off me and back off, I will drop you where you stand."

Charlotte looked at Jessica for a few moments, then released Jessica and distanced herself from her.

"I am willing to play ball because the Transcendent has commanded it, and thus, it is law," she said. "He told me to find you and tell you you're wanted back into the fold."

Jessica's hard look morphed to curiosity. "What is going on?"

"The Curaie and all the nonbelievers have been led to believe the ten months which have passed means they have braved the worst," said Charlotte. "They are in a false sense of security. That fool Jonathan has been desperately trying to convince them otherwise, but they still don't want to take him seriously, even with their decision to respect him and those idiots at the estate. And all the while, the Transcendent has been making moves in the background that no one can see."

"False sense of security?" said Jessica. "The Curaie is buying that? Since Jonathan has gotten off the Curaie's shit list, there has been a laundry list of deaths, so-called 'accidents', and disappearances."

Charlotte raised an eyebrow. "You've been out of the loop," she said. "You've spent almost a year keeping up with the Ungifteds. Case in point—" she pointed at the nightclub.

Jessica leered at her. "You continue to sell me short, Charlotte. Dace Cross' car going into the ravine back in back in July? The bitch wasn't fond of Tenth Percenters and hated their traveling even more. She didn't even own a car. I'm guessing Kendrick rendered her heart useless then put her in the driver's seat. And the multi-car pile-up on Highway 220? It had Kevin Tooles written all over it. And, oh yeah—the girl who took over the Curaie's Gate Linkage after the Ocean waif resigned? Phoebe Linkletter, or whatever? That was you, wasn't it?"

Charlotte shrugged. "If she had linked up a Gate to the weapons Spectral Law confiscated from our brothers and sisters they arrested, I would have let her live, at the very least."

"No, you wouldn't have," said Jessica.

Charlotte grinned. "Okay, fine. No, I wouldn't have."

Jessica made a face. "I know the work of our brothers and sisters when I see it," she said. "And…I miss it. I miss the killing, the torture. I suppose some gratitude is in order because you told me I'm back in."

"Don't thank me." Charlotte shrugged again. "It was the Transcendent's call."

"When am I to be summoned?" asked Jessica.

"Not so fast," said Charlotte. "I want to know two things. First, how did Rowe break your C.P.V.?"

Jessica blinked, and then her expression hardened. "Apparently, the rage he felt over losing his boss brought about an eventuality I hadn't foreseen," she muttered. "It was a one-time thing, and it will never happen again."

"Good to know," said Charlotte, who sounded matter-of-fact. "Because if you can't do your little fancy-schmancy power-talking, you're not much good to the cause, you know."

Jessica tightened her knuckles until they cracked. "Any other stupid questions?"

"You were supposed to be out of the loop," Charlotte's voice was slow, "but you've obviously been paying attention. That said, how much do you already know about the Transcendent's plan?"

Jessica's eyes narrowed. "Where are you going with this, Charlotte?" she demanded. "We answer only to the Transcendent. He wants me back in, and his word is law. Why, then, do I have to bother with your third degree?"

Charlotte took a calm draw from her cigarette. "Too timid to share? Just say so!"

Jessica cast a murderous glare on her. "I know enough to know when the Cut comes, it will be what signals Omega, and it will be a glorious time for us all."

Charlotte nodded. "Damn right, it will."

"Is the Transcendent getting one created right now?" questioned Jessica. "In prep for when it happens?"

"Yes," said Charlotte. "Just one, though. Too many would raise red flags."

Jessica nodded. Charlotte regarded her with a neutral expression.

"We don't have to be friends," she said, "but we will always be Deadfallen. Always among the Transcendent's chosen. *Per Mortem, Vitam.*"

She extended her hand. Jessica shook her hand once and withdrew.

"*Per Mortem, Vitam,*" she said.

If Charlotte was offended by the terseness of Jessica's handshake, she didn't show it. "You'll have to give your little girlfriends the slip," she told her. "Now that you have been informed, the Transcendent is expecting your presence."

She tossed Jessica a twig to use for a portal, which Jessica caught reflexively.

"I'll see you there," said Charlotte as she began to back away.

"What will you be doing?" asked Jessica.

"I've got to clean up a mess," Charlotte replied.

"Mess?"

"An Ungifted playboy was interested in more than conversation," Charlotte explained. "We had a disagreement. I lived. Now, go. You know the Transcendent doesn't like to wait."

2

The Crowded Stage

Jonah was antsy.

He stood a few feet away from the theatre, which was located in the center of an ostentatiously artsy district in Seattle. A light rainstorm had ended just a few minutes prior, and on this mid-November evening, it made the air clean, fresh, and gave the night an overall pleasant feel.

As he surveyed his surroundings, he took the time to adhere to all of the precautions given to him and his friends by Jonathan. He had seen the list so many times, he could recreate it, practically verbatim. His other friends had been mandated to do these things as well, but he himself had to be doubly vigilant, being as he was the Blue Aura and all.

No. He was the *other* Blue Aura. The Light Blue Aura. As such, he had to watch his back more than anyone else.

First, he had to make sure he hadn't been followed. He hadn't.

Second, he had to make sure there were no portals near him, and if there were any twigs within walking distance, then he had to break them. Twigs functioned as portals, used specifically by Creyton and his Deadfallen disciples. It was their transportation of choice because twigs couldn't be regulated or supervised. That was one of the reasons why the Curaie had forbidden usage of them. They were powerful tools when stealthy travel was needed. But they were utterly useless after they'd been broken.

Jonah looked around and spotted three twigs near him. They were innocent enough at the moment, but he knew what could happen if they were left unchecked. A forceful stomp cracked two of them, but the last of them, which was slightly thicker, required Jonah to pin it down with one foot, while breaking it with the other. There. Now they were gone.

The third and final task was his own, personal thing. He focused on the area around the theatre, inhaled deeply, and activated Spectral Sight. When he opened his eyes, he found himself deeply relieved.

The spirit count around this place was pretty high. Spirits and spiritesses of all ages were around the physically alive beings. Some looked focused and determined; they were probably the ones who guided children. The rest looked happy, serene, and content. All good things.

All of the tasks Jonah had just performed were simple, but they did very little to assuage his nerves.

But Jonah wasn't nervous or tense because of threats concerning Creyton and the Deadfallen disciples. It was because he was going to see Vera. He hadn't seen her since late February, the night they'd had sex, and she'd left him in the middle of the night. That had been over nine months ago if anyone was counting.

And unfortunately, Jonah had been counting.

A great deal had changed since then. For Jonah and Vera both.

Vera had experienced a true blessing. It turned out that her theatre friends had been dead-on with their hypothesis. The minute Vera re-established ties with them, and *Snow and Fire* got rolling, things took off. Jonah began his own research, because getting second-hand information from Liz got old very quickly. Jonah hadn't ever seen Vera act, but, by all accounts and reviews he'd read online, she was a natural. He'd seen rave reviews about *Snow and Fire,* and he was on the website regularly for a while, but he had since stopped.

Because it had stopped being enough.

They toured all over, but finding tickets was a nightmare, because they were almost always sold out in every city. Then Spader came out of nowhere, having scored a ticket—coincidentally—to a showing in Seattle. After having toured all across the United States, they were doing a two week-long production in Seattle, where they'd gotten their start. As usual, Jonah didn't know how Spader did it, but he'd learned a while back simply to not ask behind Spader's practices. Then it was a simple matter of using the *Astralimes* under Jonathan's supervision. Because of the ethereal travel, a trip from Rome, N.C. to Seattle barely took thirty seconds.

It was times like these when Jonah loved being an Eleventh Percenter. But with the perks and bonuses that came with ethereality, there was also a flip side.

While Vera had been flying high all this time, Jonah had spent the past months helping to keep fires at bay. He and his friends had been at work helping Jonathan with improving defensive measures for the ethereal and non-ethereal humans around Rome and the surrounding areas. Jonathan and the Phasmastis Curaie had come to an understanding in the early spring of that year, but beyond that, not much had happened. The Curaie had ceased in clamping down on Jonathan and the estate residents, but, in many ways, they still didn't take Jonathan seriously. In the time that had passed, things had been, to the untrained eye, relatively quiet. The Curaie knew better, but denial and fear colored most of their actions. Jonathan, however, had no such inhibitions.

The Protector Guide had informed them all that after failing to manipulate Jonah into succumbing to the darker aspects of his nature, Creyton was going to make absolutely certain Omega would happen without a hitch. While the Curaie handled matters in their own way, Jonathan was proactive in many other ways. He had every resident of the estate invite their families there to be briefed. He made sure people were on their Ps and Qs, with regular destruction of twigs, understanding Eighth Chapter crimes, and knowing what they could do to keep their families safe. He spent time Off-plane, but never for long stretches. Jonah understood—now—that there was a point to all of Jonathan's absences the previous year. There had been good reasons for it. Great reasons, even. But even the Protector Guide himself had been the first to admit he wasn't perfect. And now, he probably wanted to make it up to them.

All of it was all great, but it did come with one snag. As the Light Blue Aura, Jonah's well-being was given more attention than ever before. Even Terrence and Reena were involved in it.

Terrence was never bold enough to invite himself to functions Jonah attended, but he didn't hesitate to invite Jonah to all of his. Family dinners. Fishing. Football games. Reena did her damnedest to make sure Jonah stayed in shape and vigilant, ethereal and otherwise. The private training he did with his informal brother and sister had increased tenfold. Reena was even watching Jonah's food intake again. That had a silver lining: Jonah was practically being forced to eat right during the day, but it motivated him to go to every Decessio family dinner he was invited to. So, a day of garden burgers on gluten and wheat-free bread would end in meatloaf, mashed potatoes, and French bread. Everyone was happy, Jonah included. Especially after Terrence and Mrs. Decessio's savory meals.

The crazy things going on in the ethereal world were compounded by the fact Jonah, Terrence, and Reena had gotten themselves in trouble out west several times in the past nine months, too. Eva McRayne, their dear friend (and another person they referred to as family), was a celebrity with an open secret. The secret got her into one Hell after another, and sometimes Jonah, Terrence, and Reena assisted in putting those fires out. Those encounters were stories all by themselves.

Suffice it to say, there were some truly wild things happening across the board.

But tonight wasn't about any of those things.

Tonight was about Jonah finally having the chance to see what he had been reading about for all of these months.

* * *

The ticket Spader got for Jonah was third row, center. Jonah had a perfect vantage point of the entire stage. There wasn't an empty place he could see, and there was such a buzz of excitement from everyone in the audience. Plays weren't really Jonah's thing, but in this particular situation, it was next to impossible to be in this environment and not have the excitement rub off on him.

But there was one bit of anticipation he didn't share with the rest of these people.

The play began.

And there she was.

Jonah blinked. Vera wasn't even dressed to impress. It was a scene where her character had just assassinated someone, and she stood over her target, with equal amounts of satisfaction and doubt. Jonah took in the lines and curves the confusion made on her face. The slight pout at her lips when she had to struggle with her thoughts. She had a facial profile which said *I am in complete control of this situation,* while, at the same time, said *What the hell am I doing here?*

Even dressed in black and wielding garroting wire, she was unequivocally the most beautiful woman Jonah had ever seen.

There was one difference. Well, two.

The first was they had covered up Vera's facial scar with make-up. To Jonah, this seemed to do her a disservice. Vera was a beautiful woman, inside and out. Her scar was insignificant. It's like how a tire mark on a driveway didn't take away from the beauty of the whole house, or how an apple pie didn't suddenly stop tasting delicious because part of the crust cracked and fell away when you pulled it out of the oven. Some things simply didn't need glossing over.

The second thing was, with a face absent of the scar, Jonah could definitely see the family resemblance between Vera and her older sister, Jessica Hale.

Who happened to be Jonah's mortal enemy.

Jonah had known Jessica from his first job out of graduate school. They'd run afoul of each other the first day they met and had hated each other from that day on. A couple of years later, though, that hatred had taken on a new dimension: After a protracted ruse, Jessica revealed herself to be one of Creyton's Deadfallen disciples. One of his most loyal—Inimicus. She'd aided Creyton in achieving Praeterletum. And then later on, she murdered Bernard Steverson, Jonah's boss and one of his mentors. The action nearly sent Jonah over the edge, and Jessica had attempted to save her physical life by revealing she and Vera were sisters. Vera had attempted to detach herself from her family ties, but Jessica undid that with her revelation. It made Jonah and Vera's relationship, which wasn't the clearest to start with, more complicated than ever. It also played a part in Vera's leaving the estate.

Jonah had no trouble seeing the resemblance. They had the same fire in their eyes when they were focused. They had the same side profile. The same hardening of features when they were pissed off.

But Jonah could see a difference between them, too, apart from the obvious, of course. Having not known the two women were family had allowed him to see Vera as her own woman. She was intelligent, funny, brave, and had a sassy, sarcastic streak. And she had come a long, long way from the woman she was when Creyton was hunting her for being the Time Item. Jonah was sure of it. And she had definitely come a long, long way since the fight with Jessica which scarred her face. Vera was naturally everything her older sister could only be through evil, deception, and manipulation.

It was evident on the stage. Jonah couldn't tell where Juliette Nightingale, her character, ended and where Vera began. She looked to be in complete control of the entire stage, and her counterparts fed off of that. As he watched, he saw, beyond a shadow of a doubt, this was where Vera needed to be. She was completely in her element: comfort, conviction, and poise radiated from her.

It was a bittersweet realization.

If life were fair, there would have been no complications. No Creyton. No blood ties to a crazy bitch whose head Jonah very nearly sawed off. And Vera wouldn't have left him in bed while he was asleep, with a note in her place that declared the two of them had gotten what they felt for each other out of their systems with a very intense, passionate night of sex. He wouldn't have had to struggle with himself to find some place of understanding concerning Vera's actions…find some way to file away the hurt, confusion, and stress she'd caused him by leaving Rome. But life wasn't fair. It had to always have its strings, complexities, and—in a word—shit. It seemed to be so for Jonah, anyway. If his life was a stage, it'd be crowded from wall to wall.

He gave his head two harmless raps. "Task at hand," he murmured. "Enjoy the show."

He didn't even have to work hard to do so. The play was outstanding, and at the end of it, there was a standing ovation. Vera had been pushed to the forefront, and Jonah could tell she was reluctant, but her smile was sincere and radiant. He'd hoped she noticed him, but she didn't. He saw her look up higher, and her smile widened somewhat when she did. He felt a smile on his own face as he applauded. She must have been looking skyward, thinking of her mother.

Jonah had no doubts that Mrs. Haliday would be proud of her youngest daughter.

No. Mrs. *Hale.*

After the raucous applause, people began the slow, arduous dispersal. Jonah had no plans to go with them.

He was going backstage to speak to Vera.

Unfortunately, that required getting past a rather large guy, who regarded him suspiciously. Jonah wasn't bothered, though. With the things he'd seen, a burly Tenth Percenter wasn't likely to intimidate him.

"And where do you think you're going?" the guy mumbled.

"I would like to speak to the star of the show for a bit," replied Jonah.

The guy's expression didn't change. "Fanboy, huh?"

"I am a fan, but I haven't been a boy since I became a man," said Jonah calmly.

The guy's eyes, already low, narrowed further. "Alright, smartass," he grumbled, "are you trying to say you're a close, personal friend?"

"Yes."

"Then you would know her given name, then."

Jonah frowned. Surely, Rent-a-Guard wasn't privy to such information? "Her given name is Altivera Irene—" he paused for just a second, "Hale."

The man looked stunned, then sheepish. He stood aside.

"Sorry, man," he mumbled. "Fans can be crazy sometimes."

The hold-up was annoying, but Jonah got it. The man was doing his job.

But now, his only job was to move.

Jonah walked past him, his mind already on what he could say to Vera. He'd already made up his mind to not mention their last night together. Thinking about that would make him stammer like an idiot. He'd just improvise. According to all of his friends, he had a way with words, after all.

He wondered which dressing room was hers, but he didn't have to go far. Hearing bits of a conversation led him straight to it.

"—they love you, V!" gushed an ecstatic voice Jonah remembered. Eden Bristow.

"They love all of us, Eden," corrected Vera.

"Stop being modest," Eden chided. "You were the missing link, V. You truly have a knack for this. Everyone says—"

"That's because they see the end product, Eden," said Vera. "They didn't see how much time it took to get this right. They didn't see all those plays where you and I got paid in roses. They didn't see all the effort you put in to bring me back here with you all—back where I belonged."

Jonah closed his eyes for several moments. Yeah, he knew Vera belonged here. He understood; he had even admitted it to himself. But to hear her co-sign it was a different matter.

He decided the head games were unnecessary. So, standing tall, he walked in the door.

Eden was working a shirt over the one she was already wearing. Vera was seated in front of a mirror, with her fingers over her eyes. She was slowly massaging them in a clockwise manner. This just might be fun for Jonah.

"Hey, Vera."

Her fingers froze. Eden forced her head through the top of the shirt and stared at him, wide-eyed.

"Is this...are you—?"

"Yeah, I'm Jonah," said Jonah, whose eyes narrowed slightly. "It's nice to meet you, Eden."

Jonah wasn't high on this woman. He'd overheard her telling Vera she ought to leave him and the estate behind because he was a distraction. She didn't know he knew that. Or perhaps Vera had told her. There had to be some reason why she looked so terrified as she made eye contact with Vera, who looked beyond surprised herself.

"Vera—" Eden began, but Vera shook her head.

"It's cool, Eden," she said hastily. "Give us some privacy."

Eden didn't move. "But Vera—"

"It's fine, Eden—"

"But you know—"

"Did you hear Vera, Eden?" asked Jonah, who wasn't too interested in kindness. Which one of them was a distraction now? "She can talk to me."

Eden's eyes narrowed, but only slightly. She must not be used to being owned. But, thankfully, she walked out of the dressing room and closed the door.

Finally, Jonah and Vera were alone.

"It's good to see you, Jonah!" Vera rose and gave Jonah a hug but backed away before he could really hug her back. Odd. Then again, given how they'd parted, he couldn't be surprised this was a bit awkward. All things considered, maybe it wasn't odd after all.

"It's great to see you, too, Vera," he said. "Or should I call you V?"

Vera waved that aside. "You shaved off your beard! When did that happen?"

"For a red-carpet event," murmured Jonah, "but never mind—"

"Oh, right." Some of the nerves left Vera's face. "You have been rubbing elbows with the world-famous Sybil! What's she like?"

"Eva is something else," was all Jonah could say. "But you were incredible in the play!"

At Jonah's praise, Vera blushed slightly. "Jonah, we're all good. When the unit is on all cylinders, the projects are stellar—"

"Bullshit." Jonah's response was instant. "You are the chain on this whole bike, Vera. You keep things in motion. You are an amazing actress."

Vera still looked slightly uneasy but pleased at the same time. Maybe she was pleased because Jonah's opinion of her mattered. That had always been the case for him.

"I did tell you that when I am on the stage, I lose myself, Jonah," she said.

"That you did," said Jonah, determined to not let this conversation travel into tricky waters. "I've kept up with things on the website, and everyone raves about you. I know you've been touring all over the U.S., and you're only gonna be here for two weeks. Any idea if the play might make its way to N.C.? Charlotte or Raleigh, maybe? Everybody else needs to see this play!"

"I couldn't tell you, Jonah," said Vera, "but from what Liz has been telling me, you guys already have full plates. Did Jonathan really invite the families of every resident to the estate five months ago?"

"He did and more," said Jonah, "but trust me, I'd be doing you no favors talking about that stuff. On my way here, I saw a nice little Chinese restaurant, only a few minutes walking distance. Want to catch up over chow mein?"

"Uh—," Vera began indecisively, but then there was a knock at the dressing room door, slightly less than casual. Jonah turned, assuming Eden had returned.

She hadn't. It was some guy. He was taller than Jonah, bearded, with every hair in place. Truth be told, he looked like a critic.

"You take your job seriously, don't you?" Jonah asked with a frown. "Don't you people usually put reviews online, or something?"

"I beg your pardon?" said the man, who frowned himself.

"Jonah," said Vera, who shook her head, "this isn't a critic. It's East."

Jonah raised an eyebrow. "East?"

The man named East looked Jonah over, looking much more intrigued when he heard Jonah's name. With a sly smile, he walked past him to Vera and kissed her.

Jonah felt his entire face sag. He wondered if he'd ever be able to make another facial expression again. Now he understood why Eden had looked so worried. It wasn't because she was leery of Jonah's opinion of her, it was because she knew East was on his way to the dressing room.

Vera's boyfriend.

In that moment, Jonah realized Vera hadn't been looking upward, smiling at thoughts of her mother at the end of the play. This guy East had been who she'd turned her eyes up to, grinning so hugely.

Well, that was just swell.

East backed away from Vera, who looked discomfited, caught off guard, and a little aggravated by what he'd just done. To Jonah, it hadn't looked like a sincere kiss so much as a dog on two hind legs, marking territory.

"You were wonderful tonight, baby," he said to her.

"Thanks, East," murmured Vera.

East turned his attention to Jonah, trying not to look triumphant as he extended his hand. With reluctance, Jonah took it.

"East isn't actually my name." East continued his Alpha Male shtick by clamping Jonah's hand more tightly than necessary. "Full name is Marlon Eastmoreland, Jr., son of Marlon Eastmoreland, Sr."

"Obviously," mumbled Jonah under his breath.

"Sorry?" asked East.

"Nothing," said Jonah.

Jonah was trying to keep his temper under control, but this punk guy was purposely crushing his hand. It would be only too easy to conjure ethereal strength and snap this man's bones like a pencil.

Vera grabbed East by the arm and pulled him away from Jonah. She'd likely figured out the thing Jonah was contemplating in his mind. She wasn't stupid. "I think that's enough handshaking," she said, sternness in her voice. "Wouldn't you two agree?"

East shrugged. Jonah was mildly annoyed, regretful he missed his chance to hurt the bastard.

"It's nice to meet you, East," he managed. The name was imbecilic, no matter how many times he turned it over in his mind. He turned to Vera. "So, um, how long have you guys been together?"

Some of the annoyance left Vera's face, and she licked her lips. "Six months," she answered.

"Six months tonight, actually," added East. "This is our anniversary."

"Really, now?" asked Jonah, trying to hide his surprise. Or maybe surprise wasn't the word.

The word was *shock*.

Six months? That meant they started dating three months or so after Vera left the estate. It also meant they'd obviously met before that time, because reaching the dating stage took time to reach.

Or maybe that was only true for some people.

It didn't seem to have taken Vera long to figure things out for herself and move on. She was the Time Item, after all; perhaps she didn't have to do things as long as lesser mortals.

Suddenly, this dressing room was as crowded as the stage Jonah had conjured in his mind during the play.

East turned to Vera and took both of her hands. "Darling, since Chinese food is your absolute favorite, I got reservations at P.F. Chang's China Bistro for tonight."

All the tension left Vera's face, and she looked at him. "The one in the Westlake Center?" she breathed.

East nodded eagerly. "The very same."

Jonah looked on, feeling more and more like excess baggage with each passing second. He swallowed. "Congrats on you guys' anniversary," he murmured, "and I wish you a safe and great night." It actually sounded sincere when he said it. Nice. "And Vera, once again, you were great tonight. Kudos."

"Thank you, Jonah." Vera sounded apologetic about the awkwardness of the situation, but it was a hard thing to file away when Jonah saw her hands in East's. "I'm so honored you came to see my play. And it was great seeing you again."

"Likewise," said Jonah quietly, and he left the dressing room.

Before he left the door, he glimpsed East's face. When Vera looked away, he had the audacity to wink at Jonah, with a smug smirk.

Jonah barely acknowledged it. He had plans as well.

The fact they were the next morning and didn't involve a date was immaterial.

3

The Traveler

Jonah used the *Astralimes* to step directly into his room. He wasn't interested in talking about the night.

Had the play been good? No, it was great.

But Jonah hadn't expected Vera to be in a relationship. He hadn't expected the new guy. Then again, after six months, East wasn't exactly new, was he?

And once again; what the hell kind of name was East?

He stared at the ceiling, his mind full of just about everything under the roof before he realized sleep wasn't going to come naturally. Whatever.

He braved downstairs and went to the kitchen. Reena wouldn't mind if Jonah took one of her melatonin. It did the trick. After maybe six hours of sleep, which included a weird dream where Vera, in character as Juliet Nightingale, sat him down on some stage and explained to him in detail why East was better for her than he was, his alarm woke him up at 7 AM. He'd slept with all of his clothes on, but, given where he was going, that probably wasn't the biggest deal.

Next to his phone was a note which certainly hadn't been there when he'd gone to sleep the night before. Grabbing his reading glasses, he opened it, and read the golden, cursive letters:

> Use the Astralimes to Candler. Focus on the truck stop at
> Exit 37, right off I-40 West.

Puzzled, Jonah did as the note instructed. Two steps later, he stood in front of the truck stop off of Exit 37 in Candler. It was at that moment he'd realized he'd forgotten his coat. Candler was in the mountains, right outside Asheville. This was November, so to call this Candler morning brisk was an understatement. Before he ran into the truck stop to get some breakfast, he noticed a neatly folded note underneath his shoe. Picking it up, he read:

> Use the Astralimes to Edenton. Focus on the waterfront that
> overlooks the Chowan River.

Jonah frowned. Edenton? That was clear on the other side of North Carolina! Why did he have to come to Candler, when he was going to be whipped off to Edenton?

With a sigh, he focused, stepped onto the Astral Plane, then stepped onto the waterfront in Edenton. There were only a few folks there this early in the morning, but all looked out to the Chowan River. It was shaping up to be a nice morning here, provided those grayish clouds on the horizon stayed tucked in their little corner.

Jonah didn't bother taking in many sights, because he spotted another note nailed to a bulletin board near the waterfront. He snatched it down, tore it open, and impatiently read:

> Wilmington. The Battleship North Carolina.

The destination triggered a memory, and Jonah laughed, despite his impatience. When he was in the eighth grade, his class had taken a trip to that very spot. But Jonah had to miss the trip—plus an entire week of school—due to conjunctivitis.

And now, nearly fifteen years later, he was finally going to go there...as part of Jonathan's ethereal wild goose chase. He couldn't call it a treasure hunt, seeing as how there was no treasure.

He crammed the note into his pocket. There had better be a good reason why he had just had to jump between three different corners of the state. Jonathan seemed to be taking the whole "From Manteo to Murphy" thing a little too seriously.

He took the two ethereal steps and now stood on the battleship. It was long before touring hours, so he wasn't expecting to see anyone.

But he did.

A fully dressed naval officer walked right past him and gave him a smile and a half-nod as he did so. The gesture was kind, but the guy was neither shocked nor alarmed when Jonah stepped out of thin air. Why would that be—?

Oh.

It was a spirit. Duh.

"Brilliant, Jonah," he murmured to himself. "You didn't think about the spirits at one of the most haunted areas in the whole state."

"Now, you know better than that, Jonah," said a familiar voice.

He turned. Jonathan strolled towards him, his hands in the pockets of his duster. He greeted the naval officer as well then turned to Jonah.

"Spirits and spiritesses don't haunt anything," he said. "The spirit count is high here because many of the officers find it familiar and, therefore, comfortable. Haunting is an entirely different matter."

Jonah sniffed. "Right, sir," he said. "Now, what was the deal with the spot-hopping across the state?"

"First things first, Jonah," said Jonathan. "How was last night? How was visiting Vera, and seeing her at her creative best?"

Jonah looked away from Jonathan, out to the ocean. "It was what it was," he mumbled. "Now, why did I have to go from Candler to Edenton, and then Edenton to Wilmington? It only took a couple minutes, sure, but it was still quite a trek."

Jonathan raised an eyebrow, no doubt curious about how quickly Jonah had changed the subject from Vera. That made Jonah curious; it wasn't like Jonathan had ever known how Jonah had felt about Vera. Or had he?

Not that it mattered now.

Thankfully, Jonathan didn't pry. Though he did flash a quick, knowing grin.

"The strategic bouncing around was a necessary measure, Jonah," he said. "A little disorientation couldn't be avoided, and one must perform a bit of misdirection before going to The Plane with No Name."

Jonah took a deep breath. Jonathan had approached him with this task about three weeks ago. Many Eleventh Percenters in the ethereal world had taken the past few months as a good sign and figured Creyton had decided going up against Jonathan was too much. No one involved with the Grannison-Morris estate was that naïve, however. Jonathan had seen to that.

He had informed them the quiet they'd experienced was merely the calm before the storm. Eighth Chapter crimes had popped up here and there, expertly spaced out, so they appeared to be random. But Jonathan had taught them all to see the signs.

There had been a multi-car pile-up on Highway 220, which had ended the physical lives of fifteen Tenths and three Elevenths. Survivors swore there had not been a crash to trigger the pile-up; but a car, in front of everyone, simply stopped.

The driver, they recounted, stepped out of the car, holding a twig in their hand for some reason, and vanished right before the vehicular carnage. Tenth authorities had written these claims off as hysterics. Eleventh authorities knew better.

In the middle of July, Dace Cross, a Spectral Law practitioner, and world-class bitch, had been found at the bottom of a ravine, in a car that had been registered to no one. Tenth authorities hypothesized she'd fallen asleep at the wheel. Spectral Law, posing as the FBI, took over the case and determined in no less than three minutes that not only had Cross been physically lifeless before the crash, but there hadn't even been any evidence she'd driven the car at all. Jonathan told them Dace Cross hated Tenth means of travel, and, as such, hadn't even bothered learning how to drive. Jonah hadn't liked the woman, but to be killed in such a way was nightmarish.

But last month, about a week before Jonathan approached Jonah with this task, something rattled people even more than what had occurred with Dace Cross.

The girl that had taken over the Gate linkages when Katarina Ocean had resigned from the Curaie had headed home after work one day. She didn't go to work the next day, which was immediately taken as a bad sign, because such behaviors were not suffered lightly by those employed by the Phasmastis Curaie. Spectral Law was sent to her home and had made a most grisly discovery. She had been bound by ethereal fetters, tortured, and then murdered. Jonathan told the estate residents a source of his revealed the girl had been ordered by her killer to link up an unauthorized Gate to the weapons the Networkers had confiscated from the tattoo parlor earlier in the year. Jonah found out her name had been Phoebe Linkletter. Katarina had said she was growing more and more into her role every day. It wasn't fair or right that had happened to her. Jonathan put a marker in the cemetery near the Glade in her honor.

But there was one Jonathan had learned about that even the Curaie didn't yet know. After what happened at Blood Oath's tattoos, Jessica had been ordered to re-integrate back into Tenth Society completely, for an indefinite amount of time (Terrence had jokingly likened it to leave without pay). Three nights after Phoebe Linkletter's murder, Jessica got reactivated. Her reactivation also coincided with the disappearance of some slovenly Tenth who was a regular at a club she frequented on the weekends. Jonah took this to mean the calm was nearing its end and had become more proactive than ever.

Jonathan hadn't even looked impatient as Jonah stood there, going over events in his mind. He simply looked out over the ocean, so reverently, so majestically, he almost seemed one with it. Jonah was grateful for the task, but he had requested it happen after he had gone to watch Vera's play. He'd figure it'd be a nice balm, seeing her beforehand.

Well, it hadn't quite worked out like that.

And that was the thought which pulled him out of his own mind.

"I'm here, Jonathan," he said, so as to acknowledge his internal thoughts had quieted.

Jonathan seemed to come out of his own trance and nodded. "Now, Jonah, the random locations I had you use were done for two reasons," he said. "The first, as I said, was misdirection. The second one was necessary to build up your ethereality…power you up, if you will. The greater the distances, the better. I figured going from the mountains to the Tidewater to the ocean would more than suffice."

Jonah didn't really know how to respond to that, so he nodded.

"I want you to understand The Plane with No Name is not for the faint-hearted Elevenths," Jonathan went on. "I know you are not that at all, but it's necessary to let you know the place is uncivilized, sadistic, and, in a word, dangerous."

Jonah couldn't remember the last time he scared easily. One couldn't be a Blue Aura and be timid. But Jonathan's words did cause anxiety.

"The focus is a little different," said Jonathan. "Since this is The Plane with No Name, you can't really focus on a location. Therefore, you need this."

He gave Jonah what looked like a pager. Jonah's eyes narrowed; he'd seen this before.

"This is a Tally," he said. "Why do I need this thing?"

"Tallies keep your ethereality on file," Jonathan explained. "They also work well with locations where you first put them, meaning they can function as a homing beacon."

Jonah's brow furrowed. "So...once I'm on the Plane, the Tally will assist in getting me back?"

"And actually help to get you there in the first place," nodded Jonathan. "They are quite useful items, when they're not being used for bullying."

"I imagine so," said Jonah. "What else do I need to know?"

"Walk proudly," said Jonathan at once. "Be confident in who you are, and what you're capable of doing. Appearances are a mask, but true strength is a state of mind. The Plane with No Name is a place of base-level emotions: anger, despair, hopelessness. You have done no wrong, and you get to leave when you have completed your task. Therefore, there is no need to succumb to such damaging emotions."

Jonah was of two minds on that. Despair and hopelessness? He got the pointlessness of those. But anger? That had saved his life a few times. But it had also caused him to be quite an asshole to some of his loved ones. Double-edged sword, much? "Anything else?"

"When you reach the Gatekeeper, tell him you are there on official business from Jonathan," said the Protector Guide. "He'll have something for you."

Jonah nodded, ready to get started. Jonathan stepped aside.

"Peace and blessings, son," he said.

Jonah saw Jonathan's Infinity medallion on his neck. It was a good thing to focus on... something infinite. What was more positive than that?

He clamped his finger on the Tally, and saw the blue sheen flash up and down the thing. Taking a deep breath, he placed his attention on The Plane with No Name.

Wherever the hell it was.

In two steps, Jonathan, the Battleship *North Carolina*, and the ocean were gone.

4

Changeable

Jonah had to squint. Not because of sunlight, because there wasn't any. The sky was a defiant, rainy gray. It was because the place seemed to be permanently shrouded in fog. He could barely see in front of his own face.

Wait.

Why the hell was he putting himself through this? He was spiritually endowed. He had control over fog!

He placed his hands in front of himself, and concentrated. Almost instantly, the air began to clear. But right after that happened, a voice shouted from another clouded place.

"Hey! Stop! Are you not playing with a full deck?!"

A hand gripped Jonah from the shadows and pulled him into the mist. Jonah had no idea where he was being taken, as he could barely make anything out, but then, his captor pushed open a door, and pulled him inside.

The place resembled a hermit's hut, or the like. There was obviously very little need for material possessions; the place had some broken furniture that appeared to have been rigged to hold weight, a wood heater, and books that looked older than the earth on which they lay.

The person who had brought him inside looked to be in his forties, and with his hardened eyes and stance, it was clear he did not suffer fools lightly.

"Why the hell were you practicing ethereality?" he demanded, throwing off his coat and glaring at Jonah in disbelief. "Do you realize you could have gotten an arrow or a javelin through your face?"

Jonah stared at the guy, not knowing how to proceed. "I—I couldn't see through the fog," he said jerkily. "I couldn't see the entrance—"

"This Plane is entirely shrouded by fog and mist, boy!" snapped the man. "What were you expecting? A gilded palace? An oasis? That was irresponsible, boy. Rank amateur—"

"Look here, old man," said Jonah, who'd tired of the heckling, "I am here on business from Jonathan, and I really don't have time to sit here and have you breaking my balls—"

The man's entire demeanor changed when he heard Jonathan's name. He didn't smile—his face didn't seem wired to do such an action—but his scowling features relaxed. "Jonathan sent you?" Even his voice was friendlier. "You're Jonah, then. My name is Elijah Norris, Gatekeeper of the East of the Plane."

Jonah scowled himself. Had to be the East, didn't it? "Yes, sir. I'm Jonah."

"Then your mistake is forgiven," said Elijah. "You can never be too careful 'round here. I thought you were trouble. Or one of them Spectral Law fools trying to come here and prove their mettle by doing something rash and stupid."

"You don't like practitioners of Spectral Law?" asked Jonah.

"The Networkers are superb," said Elijah, deference in his voice. "It's them dummies ranked below them who chap my ass. The Curaie always keep the Networkers polished and sharp, but it seems like with the other units...anybody with a trace of Eleventh blood in their veins can carry one of them ethereal steel badges."

Jonah found himself agreeable to his assessment. He had had some less than wonderful experiences with practitioners of Spectral Law himself. The common ground he'd found with Elijah over this subject allowed him to overlook their initial misunderstanding. "Amen to that one," he said. "So, what's wrong with trying to look through the fog?"

Elijah carefully lowered himself into one of his jerry-rigged chairs and sighed. "No one but Gatekeepers and guards can be spiritually endowed, strictly speaking," he explained. "If I had allowed you in, and you'd unknowingly practiced ethereality in front of inmates, they wouldn't hesitate to use you to try to get them out. Any attempts like that are futile, and never end well for the hostage. There was also the possibility you could have been a threat. So, your manipulating the fog like that could have been interpreted as a decoy tactic. One of the archers could have gravely injured you, or worse."

Jonah nodded. "I won't be brazen like that anymore," he promised. "Now, Jonathan said you had something for me?"

"I do." Elijah rose from his chair and went to a closet that was about waist-high then pulled out a poorly patched and darned shirt along with a drab, gray hooded coat.

Jonah stared at them dubiously. "I'm cool with my current clothing," he murmured.

"Unacceptable, son." Elijah shook his head. "This is standard wear for prisoners. The pants are fine, but the waist up needs changing. If you go in there looking the way you do, you will be apprehended, and quite possibly killed. Besides all that, Jonathan has placed some type of ethereality in the fabric which will blunt the fact you're spiritually endowed."

Jonah grimaced. Yeah, he understood, but he still didn't like it. He removed his shirt and put on the patched one. Surprisingly, it was a bit too large. Then, he put on the hooded coat.

He walked up to a piece of broken mirror in the corner and inspected himself. The clothes vastly altered his appearance. The hood didn't blind him, but it obscured his face. At the very least, he didn't look like he was playing a character.

"That'll work fine," said Elijah after his own brief inspection of Jonah. "I wish you'd have had a beard or some stubble, but ah, well."

Jonah snorted. He'd just had a beard recently but shaved it off for a friend. That was another matter.

"The batons stay as well," said Elijah, who reached out for them.

Somehow, Jonah had expected that, and dropped them into the Gatekeeper's hands without protest.

"Finally," said Elijah, "the prisoner you're looking for is EC #—"

"EC?"

"Ethereal Convict," clarified Elijah, "EC#571976. You will find him in dwelling 3034."

"Wow," Jonah commented, "that's a lot of numbers."

"You're the Blue Aura, son," countered Elijah. "You can retain information, even if you don't recall it at all times."

"How do you know that?" asked Jonah. He had always known that about himself, but he didn't know it was common knowledge.

"I just do," said Elijah. He looked neither discomposed nor awkward when he said it. For that reason, Jonah wasn't suspicious. Everyone possessed knowledge of some sort, after all. "Now, Jonah Rowe, it is my great pleasure to, at least for the next couple of hours, welcome you to The Plane with No Name."

* * *

When Elijah let Jonah inside the border, Jonah paused, stunned.

Being as this was a prison, he expected bars, cells, and stairways.

Not true here.

The Plane with No Name was a shanty town. Or more accurately, shanty city.

As far as Jonah could see, there were crudely erected huts and dwelling places everywhere. So, spots consisted of thatched fabrics propped on sticks. Further away, it seemed as if some of the prisoners had made loftier attempts at houses, but they were laughable attempts. One or two looked as though they'd collapse if someone blew on them the wrong way.

Then there were the prisoners themselves. Jonah thought he had seen people suffering in the past. He thought he had seen people who were worse for wear. He remembered those sazers he'd met in Dexter City, and recalled Felix and Prodigal's stories of the sazer underground.

Those sazers were top-tier citizens compared to this.

The best way to describe what Jonah saw was to describe it as Creyton's Desert of the Ethereal, come to life. The Elevenths looked sick, woebegone, wan, and in some cases, enraged. There was a man about Jonah's age who stared in a corner some feet away, with a rather fractured look in his eyes. In another direction, some prisoners were playing some type of baseball game using a human leg bone for a ball bat, and a skull for a baseball.

"Don't feel sorry for them, boy," said Elijah, who hadn't left just yet. "Not a single Eleventh or sazer here is innocent. Hell, with the crimes that a few of them have committed, some of these psychos deserve worse."

"I…I get it," murmured Jonah. "It's just that…Jesus."

"Jesus?" scoffed Elijah. "He ain't got nothing to do with this place. Now move along, and remember, no ethereality."

He left, and the portion he'd opened was resealed. Jonah had work to do.

"3034," he said to himself, "3034..."

He looked at the nearest shanty. A well-worn decal on the side of it read 2081.

He took a deep breath and choked. The place stank with every foul smell imaginable. The sooner he did his task, the sooner he'd be out of the place.

He started to walk, remembering Jonathan's warnings to not look sheepish or afraid. The good news was that he was on the right track; the numbers looked to be sequential. The bad news was...well, everything else.

It became clear to Jonah the numbers denoted different areas, or different—for lack of a better term—districts. Each one had different attributes. Where he'd begun was 2080 through 2090. With the exception of the ones playing the sick baseball game, all the prisoners were too busy being depressed to hurt anyone. 2090 through 3000 was a different matter. There were fights almost every five feet. Some were minor; just simple reminders of who was the top dog. Others were bloody. Some people who Jonah saw get taken down in those duels...never got back up again. 3010 through 3020 was pretty much the same. 3020 through 3030 was a district of horrors, and for Jonah, that was saying something, after watching those fights. From what he could gather, the place was in the middle of a Greek style *Pankration.* Jonah had spent enough time with his Greek friends in California to know what a *Pankration* was. Basically, the last one standing was the winner.

No. The last one alive was the winner.

Apparently, the prize was a big pot of something that looked edible only by the loosest definition. Then Jonah saw the two men who were battering everyone.

Knoaxx Cisor, and Iuris Mason. Two men that were on The Plane with No Name because of him and Gabriel Kaine. No, scratch that—they were on the Plane because of their schemes, plots, and attempts to incite a war.

Head lowered, Jonah hurried on. He had a feeling that if they saw him, they would not quibble over trivialities.

It was with profound relief that he reached the dwelling 3034, another one of those attempts at building an actual house. He'd scowled at it before. He wasn't scowling now.

Jonah raised a fist to knock but paused. This wasn't the suburbs! And after the things he'd seen over the past two hours (it shouldn't have been that long, but Jonah was forced to waste time here and there due to ducking, hiding, and, once or twice, throwing some rights and lefts), he was full of a rashness that kind of clouded his judgment. Jonathan had told him to remember who he was.

Those were cute words for a spirit who he'd left standing on the deck of a damned tourist attraction.

He lowered his hand and kicked the door down.

The one-room shack had a handmade chair, pots and pans, a pair of boots in the corner that had dried blood at their tips, and strips upon strips of cardboard, all covered with writing. Jonah wondered where this guy got his hands on writing utensils.

He walked in, still feeling reckless adrenaline, and sat on the chair. It was comfortable enough. When he relaxed somewhat, the adrenaline began to wane, and with its decrease came a surge of logic and reason.

He had just kicked in someone's door. A criminal's door, which had probably been created by trial and error. And he'd destroyed the end product.

He started to miss his batons.

The inhabitant of the dwelling walked to the doorway and paused, looking at the remains of the door itself. Jonah stared at him, ready for anything. The man must have felt eyes on him, because he slowly rose his head, and looked in Jonah's direction. He slowly lowered his hood, looking livid.

If Jonah had to age him, he'd have said early fifties. But even though a half-century had put a little wear in the man's face, he didn't look weary by any means. His arms weren't muscular, but he looked pretty durable, like he could hold his own in a fight. His eyes were very dark and looked as though they'd seen everything there was to see.

"You better have a good goddamn reason for being in my house," he said in a brutal voice.

Jonah decided a façade was the best thing to have here. "I didn't do it out of spite," he said coldly. "I needed someplace to hole up because I wasn't interested in that *Pankration*."

The man hissed and looked outside, in the direction of the previous district, where Cisor and Iuris were probably still wreaking havoc. "Upstart panty waists," he grumbled. "Still trying to prove they are dangerous. It'll be their undoing soon enough."

Jonah frowned. Panty waists? Maybe this man was older than his fifties.

He looked back at Jonah. "Even so, I ought to kill you," he said. "But you aren't off the hook. You're going to pay for that."

"What?" said Jonah. "There's no money around here."

"Favors are currency, boy," said the prisoner as he walked in. "I'm coordinating a border attack tomorrow, and you're going to take part."

"A border attack?" said Jonah.

The prisoner looked at Jonah with curiosity. "You must be new," he said. "Border attacks are carried out when districts in other borders are breached for supplies. This is the East, but hopefully, that old Gatekeeper already told you that. We're going to the West border at first light. The Networkers dropped iodine, painkillers, and blankets there. I heard that it was between district 1200 through 1210. And we're going to take it all. If the EC's resist, then we'll kill every living thing there. You're coming. If you survive, then we're square for my door."

Jonah felt numb. The man was a mad criminal, talking about theft and murder like they were notches on a daily schedule. Steal supplies—check. Murder the people we stole them from in the first place—check. Jonah wasn't about to kill anyone. It was about time to get to the point.

"I'm afraid that's not happening," he said calmly.

The prisoner zeroed on him. "I'm sorry?"

"I said it ain't happening," said Jonah, not sure where this bravery was coming from. But Jonathan had coached him well. He knew what to say, and when to say it. "I'm not participating in your attack."

The prisoner rose and removed a crudely made shank from his boot. "You owe me, EC," he said. "I have given you a pass for defacing my property. You will accompany us, or I can tear your throat out, and leave you out there for the sazers to eat."

Jonah's eyes were on that shank, but he counted on his balancing powers to keep his nerves in check. "I'm not an EC," he said slowly. "And if you kill me, you'll miss out on a golden opportunity."

The prisoner tilted his head to the side. "And what the hell is that?"

Jonah rose himself. "I have a way off this Plane, EC# 571976."

The prisoner's eyes widened. Using the hand holding the shank, he pointed at Jonah. "Lower your hood," he said. "I want to talk face to face."

"Fair enough," shrugged Jonah, and he lowered his hood.

The prisoner's eyes hardened, and then relaxed. He sat down. "I don't know where you come from," he said, "but Luther Coy is your father."

Jonah was so stunned, he actually flinched. "How the hell did you know that?"

"You look just like the bastard," said the prisoner. "Who'd have thought that good for nothing piece of shit had a son? Are there any more of you?"

Jonah didn't answer. "How did you know him?"

The prisoner dropped the shank, and spit into the corner. "The dumb fuck owed me money. That's how I knew him."

Jonah's eyes widened slightly. He remembered Felix telling him his father had been killed over a gambling debt. "Are you the one that killed him?"

"Wish I had been," murmured the prisoner, "but he owed others, too. One of them got to him before I could. But Luther was Ungifted, and you obviously aren't. Who are you?"

Jonah was reeling. This Eleventh criminal had known his father, and he'd hated him. He couldn't but wonder whether or not Jonathan knew that information. But the prisoner had asked him a question.

"My name is James," he answered.

Another bit of advice from Jonathan. *Maintain anonymity as long as humanly possible,* he'd told him. *This man is smart; he'll figure it out eventually. But don't help him along.*

"Alright, James," said the prisoner. "Laban Cooper's the name. Now, how did you get here if you're not an ethereal convict?"

Jonah still hadn't yet gotten over the fact this man knew his father. "That isn't important," he said, forcing himself back to center. "I told you I have a way off The Plane with No Name."

Laban tilted his head. "Impossible," he said flat-out. "No member of the Curaie would give me freedom. What's your angle, boy?"

Jonah manufactured a look that showed more composure than he actually felt at the moment. "The offer isn't from the Curaie. You will be in someone else's custody."

Laban snorted. "I don't know how interested I am in trading one prison for another," he admitted, "but you've got my curiosity. Who, pray tell, is this generous, risk-taking benefactor?"

Jonah paid close attention to Laban. Jonathan had warned him what might happen once he dropped the Protector Guide's name. "The Overseer of the Grannison-Morris estate."

Jonathan had called it perfectly; Laban did a complete one-eighty. His eyes widened, and he performed the hugest gasp Jonah had ever seen. "Jonathan is doing this?" he whispered. "Then the Season of Omega has yet to begin!"

Jonah frowned. "What? Season of—"

"You must be Jonah Rowe!" exclaimed Laban. "You told me your name was James…The scumbag Luther Coy…he sired the Light Blue Aura!"

Jonah didn't know what to think. This man knew his dad, knew about Jonathan, knew about Omega…and he knew about him being the Light Blue Aura. What was going on?

He meant to ask just that, but then Laban surprised him by chuckling, like he'd figured something out.

"Clever, Jonathan…really clever…then again, you always were…"

"Um," said Jonah, baffled, "what are you talking about?"

"Never mind, never mind," Laban murmured. "I accept. I surrender myself to Jonathan's custody."

Jonah raised his eyebrows. That was quick as hell. But he was also curious about something else. "Begging your pardon, but why exactly are you on The Plane with No Name? What was your charge?"

Laban smirked. "I was charged with being a Deadfallen disciple."

"You were falsely accused?" demanded Jonah. "Why didn't you ever say you were innocent?"

"Because I'm not innocent," said Laban as though it were obvious. "I'm guilty as sin."

"What?" Jonah's eyes bulged. "You're a known Deadfallen disciple, and Jonathan wants to work with you?"

"Cool it, Rowe," said Laban. "You needn't worry. Although I am an instrument of Hell, the Devil would never have me back."

"What are you saying?" asked Jonah, more leery of this man than ever. "Creyton betrayed you?"

Laban's face hardened. All traces of the mirth and humor vanished. "Hell yeah, he betrayed me. He's the reason I'm in here."

"Why did Creyton betray you?"

Laban clamped the shank once more, which put Jonah on edge once again. "He viewed me as too changeable," he growled.

Jonah blinked. Then he got a truly sick feeling in his stomach, because, in this particular instant, he actually agreed with Creyton.

Then, just as sudden as the mask of rage, Laban smirked again. He rose and tossed away the shank. "But that's water under the bridge now. Get out your Tally—"

"You know about that?" said Jonah.

"You aren't a prisoner here," said Laban. "And how else would you be able to alert Jonathan? But go on ahead, alert him. Tell him I accept, and you're good here."

5

Family and Felon

The next events seemed oddly quick. The second Jonah clicked the Tally, two guards appeared via the *Astralimes,* commanded both he and Laban don their hoods once more, and then the four of them used the *Astralimes* to reach the border. Jonah felt two emotions about this situation: amused these guards were leery of walking through the shanties, and secretly relieved he wouldn't have to do it himself a second time.

At the border itself, Elijah released them all, looking at Jonah with newfound respect as he did so. The look he gave Laban, on the other hand, was a combination of disdain, caution, mistrust, and maybe a little fear.

"Great work, boy," he told Jonah. "I have to admit I had my doubts. Kinda felt like I was throwing a mouse into a snake pit."

Jonah didn't want to show how much The Plane with No Name had unnerved him, so he nodded shortly. "Glad I could get Jonathan's task for me over and done with," he said.

Elijah tilted his head to denote private conversation, and Jonah obliged him, stepping into the dwelling behind him.

"Do you know who E.C.#57-19-76 is?" he asked.

Jonah nodded. "Laban Cooper. He's a Deadfallen disciple."

"He's an old-school Deadfallen disciple," corrected Elijah. "One of the elites, up there with T.J. Rivers, the 49er, Billy Askew, Monty Raines...but they'd all be before your time. That man there has committed atrocities you cannot imagine. Why does Jonathan want him out? Please tell me."

Jonah looked at Elijah a bit hopelessly, which the man didn't like. "I don't know, sir," he was forced to admit. "I was practically a foot soldier in all this, just following orders."

Elijah looked at the door, as if he could see Laban through it. "Jonathan's always handled business by his own rules," he mumbled. "But he's always gotten the upper hand, one way or the other. All we can do is trust him."

He offered a hardened worker's hand which Jonah took without hesitation.

"Take care of yourself, boy," he said. "It's getting cold out there, and I ain't talking about the weather. Do what you got to do to survive out there, because Creyton..."

He pretty much let the sentence hang there, but it wasn't necessary to finish it.

"I'm not worried, sir," said Jonah. "I'm on Jonathan's team."

Elijah gave him a small smile, but still looked concerned. "Ain't we all, son," he said softly. "Ain't we all."

Jonah, still following his instructions, returned to the *Battleship North Carolina*, where Jonathan still stood. Jonah was so glad to be back in his own shirt and jacket, he walked to the Protector Guide with a pep in his step. Then, he realized what he had just done.

"Jonathan!" he said in a low hiss because the ship actually had tourists aboard now. "Why didn't you tell me I was springing a Deadfallen disciple?"

"He is a *lapsed* Deadfallen disciple," said Jonathan calmly. "And you were successful in swaying him? Beautiful work, son."

"I didn't sway anyone," muttered Jonah. "He heard it was you behind the deal, and then his whole demeanor changed, just like you said it would. But lapsed or not lapsed, that man is bad news, Jonathan. He is crazy, and completely cool with it! He was plotting to slaughter inmates over painkillers and blankets. He only abandoned that plan because I showed up with your offer."

Jonathan returned his gaze to the water. "I know what Laban is, Jonah," he said. "But war makes for strange bedfellows. I will need you to trust me."

Jonah looked at the spirit. Jonathan had been an enigma from the moment they'd met. He had run the emotional gauntlet with the Protector Guide. Confusion. Joy. Pride. Frustration. Anger. Awe. Respect. But through and through, Jonathan had always emerged victorious. He'd always had that ace up his sleeve. His methods may have been unorthodox, but he got the job done. "You have my trust, Jonathan," he said. "You know that. I just don't get a great vibe off of this guy. Just because Creyton gave him a pink slip doesn't make him a saint."

"True," said Jonathan, "but in some cases, the enemy of my enemy... is my secret weapon."

Or your secret enemy, thought Jonah to himself. But he had to give Jonathan credit for being a mystery through and through. If nothing else, he was consistent. "What's going to happen to Laban now?"

"Have some last-minute arrangements to make, and then he will be moved to a new location, where he will remain for the foreseeable future," answered Jonathan. "But you needn't worry, Jonah. You have done wonderfully today, and you ought to go on and get back to the estate. You've got Butterball or Bust with Terrence and Reena later, yes?"

Jonah blinked. "Oh yeah," he said. "I do."

"Well then, go get yourself some rest then, son," said Jonathan. "See you this evening."

* * *

Butterball or Bust was a program done through the Brown Bag Charity, where Jonah's good friend Douglas Chandler was a volunteer. He'd always enjoyed it, but when his girlfriend, Katarina, started doing it along with him, it became one of his favorite things to do. Jonah, Terrence, and Reena got on the bandwagon this holiday season, after hearing Mr. and Mrs. Decessio being openly critical of people who only aided folk on Thanksgiving and Christmas, and then bragged about it like it changed the world. In their opinion, doing two good deeds two days out of the whole year wasn't very helpful in the grand scheme of things. So, things such as Butterball or Bust helped provide holiday meals to the needy and elderly but did so in a way that was respectful and considerate of people's dignity.

It also required a good set of legs and lungs.

"Box ready, Terrence?" Jonah asked his informal brother later that afternoon.

"Applying the finishing touches as we speak," muttered Terrence, who placed some last-minute items into the big box. "Turkey, ham, A-1 sauce...bunch of sides...it's good and ready. So, where are we going?"

"The Beckers," said Jonah, who glanced at the house surreptitiously. "I wish we could use the *Astralimes* for this. It would make things so much better."

Terrence scoffed. "Where is the fun in that? Let's go."

They crept to the front door, balancing the box between them. With a nod to each other, they carefully lowered the box of food on the stoop. Terrence braced himself. Jonah placed his thumb on the doorbell.

"Count of three," he mumbled. "One...two...three."

He rang the doorbell, and he and Terrence hightailed it, racing down the road as fast as they could.

"Last one to the van has to eat Reena's tofu casserole," said Terrence after he'd gotten a little bit ahead of Jonah.

"Oh, you bastard!" Jonah hustled a bit harder, but Terrence still beat him. He even had the audacity to rest his weight on the van while Jonah caught up, clutching his side, and leering at him.

"Punk..." he gasped, but he wasn't angry.

"Hey, man," said Terrence, who raised his hands, "I don't eat Reena's health shit if I can help it."

"Just for that, Terrence," said a disapproving voice from around the van, "you're delivering the next box alone."

Reena was with them, not looking worse for wear at all, despite all the running they'd been doing. She wasn't all that spent at all, and her black and scarlet hair was still in its ponytail. Her oversized clothes made her look like such a slouch, but Jonah knew his sister was probably more comfortable than he and Terrence were.

Terrence's gloating smile faded at one. "Aw, Reena, you know I didn't mean—"

"I know you don't mean the lie you're about to spew," interrupted Reena. "Now go. Celia Crane, 162 Eagle's Crossing. You don't even have to run all that hard back; she's probably napping at this time."

With a scowl, Terrence reached into the van and hoisted the box out of it. "Just because you're engaged and everything doesn't mean you have the right to delegate shit."

He went off down the road. Reena smirked.

"Shouldn't have been badmouthing my casserole," she muttered, but there was no annoyance at all. Jonah shook his head at her.

"You are awash with glow," he observed. "Are you really still that elated? After a week and some days removed?"

Reena was unfazed. "It could have been a month removed, and I'd still be as happy as I was when Kendall said she'd marry me," she told him. "You have no idea, Jonah."

Jonah clapped her on the shoulder, happy for her. "Have you two set a date?"

"Nah," said Reena. "We left it open-ended. I want some of these storms to pass first; you know what I mean. For the moment, affianced is great. But I have to ask you something."

"Sure," said Jonah.

Reena focused on him, in that way that only she could. "You told Terrence and me all about The Plane with No Name, and from the sound of it, I wouldn't even wish that place on Trip. You told us about the psycho Laban. But you didn't say one thing about Seattle. How was *Snow and Fire?* How is Vera doing?"

Jonah felt his smile fade somewhat. While Reena was soaring high off of her engagement, he was flying low, and at the risk of clipping trees. "The play was excellent," he admitted. "And Vera is going as strong as you are, with companionship and all."

Reena raised an eyebrow. "She's got a new guy friend?"

"Friendship was passed a couple exits back," muttered Jonah. "Six months' worth of exits, actually."

Reena's eyes widened. "Gotcha."

"Yeah," said Jonah. "So, you see why I went more into detail about that godforsaken Plane than I did about Seattle. She's moved on."

"So have you," said Reena. "You can go work out some of that frustration with Lola."

Jonah lowered his face to his hands. Lola Barnhardt was a classmate of his, who'd had the hugest crush on him, but he didn't like her in that way. Once crap got crazy in the ethereal world, though, Jonah re-established many ties with his Tenth friends, just to have time and space from things ethereal. Lola was one of those ties. To his surprise, she was actually a cool woman to hang around, and they became better friends. To the surprise of no one who knew them, however, that friendship became physical. No one judged him, but Reena saw fit to tease him about it every now and then. "Lola is not my emotional substitute, Reena," he said. "We're just two consenting adults, having some fun. That's it. But I won't go visit her just because something Vera is doing aggravates me. Not now, or ever."

"I can respect that," said Reena, "but I can also trust you to know you didn't believe it when you said she moved on."

Jonah blinked. "And why do you say that?" he asked.

Before Reena could reply, Terrence was back, breathing heavily.

"Your casserole is delicious, Reena," he panted. "God's gift... salt of the earth. Now, can we please do the last box together? Pretty please?"

Reena smirked. Jonah remembered these acts they were performing are not about him, and he filed Vera away.

"Yeah, we can do it together," she told Terrence. "It's right over there. Francine Mott."

"Ms. Mott?" Terrence seemed to forget his fatigue. "I love that lady!"

"Who is she?" asked Jonah, who dropped a couple of extra side dishes into the box.

"Nicest woman you'll ever meet," said Terrence with fondness. "Mom used to help her with flowers when she was a kid."

"When your mom was a kid?" said Jonah. "How old is Ms. Mott?"

"Hundred, I think," said Terrence.

"Hundred and three," corrected Reena. "As of last week."

"Wow," commented Jonah. "That's a lot of living."

"Physical living, anyway," said Reena. "When she passes on into the next phase of living, she will have earned the rest."

Jonah thought about it. His own grandmother had passed into Spirit at ninety-two, which was ten years younger than this woman was. He wondered whether or not things would have been different for him had his grandmother remained a physical being a little while longer. Would he have been a better man? It would have been nice to still have her advice from time to time. That alone would have been a blessing. But the more he thought about it, the more another side of that coin came into focus. If Nana had still been physically alive, she would be over a hundred herself, or very near it, anyway. She would almost certainly have needed assistance with activities of daily living. And Jonah would have done that for her, no questions asked. What would have happened then? Would he have gone to college? Would he have tried for better? Would he have even left Radner?

There were always going to be things that people wished had happened and wished hadn't happened. But every happening, or not happening, had its ripples and consequences. Positive and negative. Life was never just "Because Thing A happened, Thing B happened." That wasn't the case for Jonah's life, anyway.

Reena had likely gleaned from Jonah's essence that his mind had wandered, and she'd engaged in a joking debate about holiday food with Terrence, who had probably simply looked at Jonah, and figured out where he'd gone mentally, so he played along with Reena. Jonah loved them more than they probably knew.

"I'm good," he told them, and the fact that their conversation immediately ended let him know that he was right. "Let's get Ms. Mott her stuff, and head on home."

They returned to the estate at about six o'clock, so it was already dark, and many of the lights were on outside. Jonah liked the fact that the residency was at full capacity again. It gave him comfort knowing that so many of his friends were close by. It had almost become a necessity for him to be cognizant of his loved one's safety. His Eleventh friends, Nelson and Tamara, Lola, everyone... particularly after Mr. Steverson.

The smell of cigarette smoke, along with Terrence murmuring, "Oh, great," reined his thoughts back in, and they looked over and saw Trip, in the shadows of a birch tree. He welcomed them with his usual scowl.

"Well, if it isn't the Mod Squad," he grumbled. "Done your part for the needy and the elderly, and now your life's complete?"

Jonah's eyes narrowed. "You know, Trip, there are two types of people in this world: Quality, worthwhile folks, and you. Nothing you say matters. Not now, not ever. So why don't you keep that cancer stick in your mouth, so it continues to prevent you from speaking?"

Even though the cigarette looked only recently lit, Trip tossed it away in defiance.

"Got some hair on your chest now that you've been on The Plane with No Name, huh?" he spat. "Don't get it twisted, Rowe. You still ain't shit. You never were, and you never will be."

Terrence looked at Jonah with apprehension, but Jonah successfully blew it off.

"And I'm sure those last words you just said are the words you hear every time you submit a demo," he said. "Goodbye."

Trip looked furious, but Jonah walked on. Reena clapped him on the shoulder.

"Well done, Jonah," she said, impressed.

"Better than anything I could have said," said Terrence.

Jonah shrugged. "We've got too much going on to be sweating the small stuff," he said, legitimately indifferent. "And if Trip isn't small stuff, then I don't know what is."

The scene inside was lively, but that wasn't a problem in the slightest. Spader was owning Douglas in spades, while Maxine had roped Malcolm into a sci-fi debate. Ben-Israel was animatedly conversing with some people on the sofa, while Alvin and Bobby were arm wrestling, with the loser being stuck with dish duty. Nella was teaching guitar again, and Magdalena was still having trouble. But Nella's new student, Themis Fields, took to it like a duck took to water. Themis was a classmate of Nella's; they'd known each other since kindergarten. But Themis had had no idea she was an Eleventh Percenter until she began passing out at school the previous school year as a result of Creyton's Mindscopes. According to Nella, their homeroom teacher thought Themis fainting was due to dizzy spells, and automatically wrote her off as another teen pregnancy, but Nella had volunteered to take her to the nurse's office, and after five minutes' conversation, confirmed her friend's status as an ethereal human.

An ethereal human who now sat in the chair Vera always had while practicing guitar.

That thought prompted Jonah to zero in on Liz, who stood nearby, absently stroking a herald's ears.

"Hey, Jonah," she greeted him in her usual sunny voice.

Jonah disregarded her words and beckoned her into the kitchen. Brow furrowed, she carefully lowered the herald, and followed.

"What's up?" she asked once they were alone.

"You knew about East, didn't you?" Jonah asked her at once.

Liz, who'd likely been expecting something earth-shattering, frowned. But then, her features smoothed out as she sighed. "Yeah, Jonah, I did."

Jonah looked at her in disbelief. "When were you planning on telling me?"

"It wasn't your business, Jonah!"

"Are you still playing that card, Liz?"

Liz contemplated Jonah with an expression on her face that looked akin to disappointment. "Jonah, why do you care? Don't you have Lola Barnhardt?"

Jonah's eyes narrowed. Liz rolled her own.

"Jonah, look," she said, "you already know it wasn't fair of you to expect Vera to wait around for you to screw your head on straight. So what if she's got a boyfriend? She's living her life. *Snow and Fire* is doing great, and she is happy. So why aren't you happy for her?"

Jonah stared at Liz. "You're joking, right? Do you expect me to grab some pom-poms and jump for joy?"

Liz placed a hand on Jonah's shoulder. He wasn't hateful or spiteful enough to shrug it off.

"I didn't expect that, Jonah," she said. "What I expect of you is to remove yourself from the equation, and be happy that, after everything Vera has been through—parents, sister, Time Item mess, all of it—she's got her life finally moving in the right direction. Even if that includes her having a man in her life. It's no slight to you because it was never about you."

Jonah took a deep breath. Liz was telling him things he didn't want to hear. And the reason why he didn't want to hear them?

Because, damn it all, they were the truth.

Vera's life had been full of strife, much like his own. Even after he'd saved her from Roger, her life still hadn't been peachy keen. She was safe, made new friends, learned to control her ethereality, but she had still been dealing with unresolved trauma from her past. She'd probably been in Hell the second Jonah had returned from that accursed house and revealed her older sister as Inimicus. Maybe it had been torture for her, living with that secret. And now, she was free. Free of everything. And with someone who had no baggage, and whose life was obviously working out.

East, unlike Jonah, had something to look forward to besides a monster Eleventh who'd made it his life's ambition to destroy him. And he made Vera happy. That was good. Didn't change the fact that he was a territorial dick, but it was good.

"I see your point," he murmured.

Liz nodded, looking stubborn yet sincerely sympathetic. Only Liz could pull something like that. "I'm sorry you had to find out about him in such an embarrassing way," she said. "But I'm not sorry my best friend's happy."

"Me either," mumbled Jonah, but he was proud to realize that it was mostly true. Mostly.

"Let's move on," Liz's voice was back to its usual sweetness, but she looked at Jonah long enough to ascertain whether or not he was game. When she saw his expression didn't change, she continued. "Did Jonathan really make you go to The Plane with No Name?"

"Yes, he did," said Jonah, thankful the kitchen's pleasant smell was a far cry from that dystopia of a Plane. "He gave me information, and he apparently paroled some guy. I'm not so sure—"

The door flew open. It was Bobby.

"You gotta come outside," he said. "Quick."

Jonah and Liz followed him without hesitation and joined the throng of people heading out of the door. Jonah couldn't help but think of the last time they'd all barreled out into the yard as a collective like this. That time had consisted of the unpleasant surprise of Sanctum Arcist, who had invited themselves. Tonight, there was also a collective in front of him and his friends, but only one in their number was unpleasant.

The group consisted of eight people, with Jonathan in the front. Behind him to the left were Reverend Abbott, Patience, and Felix. Behind him to the right were Daniel, Prodigal, and Raymond. The two groups of men flanked the last person Jonah expected to lay eyes on ever again.

Laban Cooper.

He stood there in clean gray clothing. His face had been shaved, and his hair had been trimmed and washed. He looked like a completely different man.

But Jonah knew better. The guy's sanitized visage still radiated something that was inherently wrong. And evil.

"Who's that?" Liz asked Jonah.

Jonah swallowed. "That's the guy," he answered. "From The Plane with No Name."

"What?" croaked Liz. "But—"

Laban saw Trip, who had still been outside and was probably on his fortieth cigarette, and grinned as widely as Cheshire cat.

"As I live and breathe!" he exclaimed. "If it isn't Titus Rivers, Third Edition! I knew your father and grandfather well, you know! And you came out of your mother's womb looking just like 'em both!"

Trip dropped the cigarette and looked at the man with eyes of iron. "Don't you ever mention my mother, Cooper. Or my family. I won't tell you again."

Laban looked at him with mock offense. "Why do you take that tone with me?" he asked innocently. "*I* wasn't the one who blighted your family. *I* didn't drive your mama insane. Your daddy did that. His poor judgment rendered his physical life forfeit long before the 49er gutted him!"

Trip wrenched a pocketknife from his jeans, which immediately gleamed with the red of his aura. He pushed past the ranks, and grabbed Laban by the throat with one hand, pocketknife held aloft with the other.

"Say one more thing about my family," Trip whispered. "One more goddamned thing."

"Titus," Jonathan's voice was forceful and cold as he grabbed Trip's arm. "You will not commit murder right in front of us."

"I'd be doing the ethereal world a favor, Jonathan." Trip's tone, though quiet, was vicious. "It'd be so easy to forget you brought him on the estate grounds if he were lying in a pool of lifeblood."

"Titus, you are not cold-blooded," insisted Jonathan. "And I refuse to allow you to taint yourself. Especially with the blood of Laban Cooper."

Trip still looked bellicose, but he closed the pocketknife, and returned it to his jeans. Before Jonathan could say anything else, Laban affixed an icy glare to Trip's face, looking as wrathful as he did.

"That's right, you little fucker," he growled. "Being all vengeful... you're nothing more than Jonathan's little bitch."

Jonathan belted Laban in the midsection. People in the crowd jumped in shock. Felix blinked at the Protector Guide like he had become another person. Jonah had seen his mentor in a fight or two before, but he'd never seen him straight-up assault someone. Even if it was Laban.

Laban coughed, and fell to his knees. Jonathan motioned with his hand for the men around to fall back for a second and knelt down with Laban.

"Make no mistake," he whispered, "I did indeed get you off the Plane for a reason, but you need me a whole hell of a lot more than I need you. Any further antagonism, and I will personally dump you back there, with specific instructions to leave you, bound and gagged, in the middle of the very district you were planning to pilfer."

Laban coughed again, but Jonah saw something like fear flash in his eyes.

"I—I'm on board, Jonathan," he said politely. "We're good."

Jonah looked at Terrence, then at Reena. He had already shared the story with them, so he knew by their expressions that they were in complete agreement: When Laban described himself as changeable, he couldn't have trivialized himself anymore if he'd tried.

Jonathan gave him one more glare, and then signaled to Patience to lift him up. Then he faced the group of estate residents.

"Eleventh Percenters," he said to them, "the man you see before you is former Deadfallen disciple, Laban Cooper. He has been placed into my custody."

Many people stopped hearing words after *former Deadfallen disciple*, which Jonah hoped Jonathan knew would happen. Reena stepped forward.

"Why have you brought him here, sir?" she asked, trying very hard to keep emotion out of her voice. "Is he a threat to us?"

"The answer to your first question is because Laban, despite previous affiliations, has no love for Creyton," responded Jonathan. "We have reached an understanding. As for your second query, Laban is no threat. I can personally vouch for that."

Jonah saw Felix, Raymond, Daniel, and Reverend Abbott didn't seem to agree with that. He was with them. It prompted him to step forward himself, but he did take the chance to turn over the words in his mind before speaking.

"Sir," he said, "I'm not trying to be contentious, but I think it's a bad idea to have this man in our home."

"He won't be, Jonah." Jonathan looked appalled at the very notion. "Certain accommodations have been made."

"Jonah!" Laban's voice was almost expectant. "How nice to see my new friend again! Why don't come along with us, see these new accommodations Jonathan speaks of?"

Jonah frowned at the odd request, but Terrence murmured, "Go, dude. Find out what you can. He might let something slip."

Jonah hated everything about it, but curiosity was eating at him. Ever since he'd heard Laban say that whatever Jonathan was doing was "clever," and then saw the man practically bend over backwards to surrender, a strange feeling had lingered inside him. A feeling that just wouldn't be abated by any number of reassuring words from Jonathan.

He walked to the group. "Yeah," he murmured. "Alright."

Jonathan waited for him, and then looked back to the residents. "Please, people, return to the warmth of the indoors," he said. "We will discuss this in more detail later."

He jerked his head, and the group flanking Laban began walking again. Residents began to slowly return indoors; the apprehension among them was almost tangible. Jonah found himself next to Prodigal.

"Hey, Prodigal," he said quietly.

"Hey, friend," said Prodigal back.

"How do you feel about this guy?" he asked the sazer boy without preamble.

Prodigal, aware of the close proximity, lowered his voice even further. "While he's locked in Jonathan's ethereal chains, I feel just fine about him," he replied. "But left to his own devices, he frightens me. There, I said it."

Jonah didn't consider it to be cowardice on Prodigal's part to be afraid of this guy, but they could speak no further, as they'd reached the garage. Felix flipped a switch, illuminating the place, and Laban laughed.

"You trust me to bunk in the garage, Jonathan?" he asked.

"I don't trust you period, Laban," said Jonathan. "I don't trust you; I don't respect you, and I don't like you."

Laban's smile faded. Reverend Abbott actually snorted.

"And no, I do not intend to leave in the garage," said Jonathan. "Daniel, Raymond, please."

The two men broke rank and walked over to an area near the wall. They grabbed at a portion of the floor and lifted it, like they'd done it a million times. Once the floor piece had been moved, Jonah could see a wide opening, complete with stairs leading downward.

"The Grannison-Morris estate was an integral cog in the Underground Railroad," Jonathan explained as he beckoned them all to follow him. "There are tunnels underneath our home in all directions, but a great many of them have been sealed off by age, and simple passage of time. Others, however, remained intact. With the proper fortifications, and a healthy dose of ethereality, many things can be done."

After a great deal of walking, Jonathan held up a hand to get them to halt. Jonah could see nothing in front of them except darkness.

"Jonah, you have been endowed," said Jonathan, and Jonah gasped as the endowment overtook him. "Now, kindly use that control over electricity you spin so well."

Curious, Jonah stretched his ethereality, willing whatever electricity might be around to become active. It complied, and his eyes widened.

He had just lit up a twenty-by-twenty room directly in front of them. It seemed to be made of a glass that couldn't decide whether or not it wanted to be liquid or solid. The interior of the room was sparsely furnished with a futon, a coffee table, and a bookshelf.

"This will be your new home for the foreseeable future, Laban," he said to the former Deadfallen disciple. "The glass is unbreakable, courtesy of the Protector's Proximity I've placed in its very being. If you attempt to use the *Astralimes* to leave, you will be sidetracked, and deposited right back onto The Plane with No Name. And don't bother trying to destroy the bookshelf to get pieces of wood for twig portals. They are indigenous to these grounds, and all nature here is under my supervision. They will not cooperate with any illicit activities. Now, get inside."

Laban calmly shuffled into the glass cage, where Jonathan willed the ethereal bonds to fade from his hands and arms. He casually seated himself on the futon and looked as serene as could be. Reverend Abbott looked openly worried. Apart from the earlier snort when Laban got owned by Jonathan, he'd had the same expression the entire time.

"Jonathan, are you sure about this?" he asked. "I remember what this man was like before Creyton betrayed him. Evil does not fall away like dirt. I don't trust him on these grounds."

"I understand your concern, Cassius," said Jonathan softly. "But you can rest assured that I have taken every precaution necessary to ensure everyone's safety and well-being. I will know Laban's actions every minute of every day. If he so much as coughs the wrong way, either me or the heralds will know."

Laban looked at the collection of men on the other side of the liquid-esque glass, flashing what he must have believed to be an innocent smile. "I have no intention of causing waves," he said. "You've already got plenty of those from my ex-patron."

"Shut up," muttered Raymond. "Jonathan, are we done here? This place gives me the creeps."

Jonathan nodded, but said nothing further. To Jonah, he seemed to be deep in thought, like his mind was a thousand miles away. He was even running his fingers idly across his infinity medallion. Jonah wondered what his mentor was thinking about, but then, movement from Laban caught his attention.

The man stretched, like his muscles were stiff. But that wasn't what was strange.

What was strange was that he looked straight ahead, staring at no one in particular, and clearly whispered, "One."

Jonah glanced at the group. Of course, no one else saw it; they were all heading back upstairs.

What the hell did that mean?

6

Giving Thanks

Everyone was in the family room the second the group returned. Jonah could tell, just by the feel of the room, the wait had not been a patient one.

Jonathan gave Daniel a quick look, and then stood in front of the fireplace, fully prepared to address the more than curious crowd.

"I know you all have many questions," he began, "but I implore you to let me explain without interruptions—"

"Why the hell is Laban Cooper here?" demanded Trip. "Why did you spring him from The Plane with No Name?"

"Did you not just hear the part about no interruptions?" demanded Felix, but Jonathan threw him a quelling glance, then turned his attention back to Trip.

"If you can find it in yourself not to speak over me, Titus," he said, irritation in his voice, "then I will gladly tell you."

In spite of himself, Trip shut his mouth. Daniel, Jonah saw, had loosened his grip on his bow.

"Now, then," said Jonathan clearly, "I have made an arrangement of sorts with Elijah Norris, the Keeper of the Eastern Gate of The Plane with No Name. Laban Cooper has been released into my custody."

"Sir, pardon the interruption, but I must ask you," said Reena, puzzlement all over her face, "you said you made an arrangement with this Elijah Norris guy. You didn't mention the Curaie. Does that mean they are not...um...involved in this transaction?"

Jonathan looked at Reena, neither sheepish nor awkward. "They are not."

Trip made a choking sound. "Great day in the morning," he snapped. "If it's not one thing, it's another."

"Tell me something, Trippy," said Raymond suddenly, "I don't have to be as nice as Jonathan does. What have you done for the cause lately? Seems the only thing you've been working out is your mouth."

Trip glared at him, and then stood up. Jonathan shook his head.

"Sit, Titus," Jonathan's voice was stern. "You're leaving for a smoke, I'd wager? Those things won't help you. When you're done smoking, the status quo still will not have changed."

Trip took a long, heavy inhale and exhale through his nostrils. Then he lowered back down. Jonathan returned his attention to the rest of the residents, smoothing out the anger and frustration on his face while he did.

"I made this decision independently of the Curaie, simply because they have made it clear they plan to go their own way, despite their acceptance that we have a common enemy," he told them. "They have their methods; I have my own. No better, no worse...just different."

Jonah heard the displeasure in Jonathan's voice, and he agreed. He didn't understand why the Curaie still chose to stand apart from them. He thought it might have something to do with the way he'd owned them, but they had made the arrangements that got him out of his lease at Cremo Ridge, as well as lifted his exile from the estate. Why would they have done those things if they were still pissed about that?

One would have thought they'd have pulled their heads out of their asses after what had happened to Phoebe Linkletter, but her death only made them more aloof.

"Do you think Cooper's presence gives us an advantage of some kind?" asked Bobby.

"This is not meant as conceit," said Jonathan, and he sounded sincere enough when he said it, "but I don't see the Curaie having lapsed Deadfallen disciples who are willing to divulge information."

Reverend Abbott piped up. "Jonathan, I have to say something. It's great that you've got someone with insider's knowledge on Creyton, but I'd bet Faith Haven that Cooper would have sold out his mother to get off that Plane. Now that he has achieved that, are you sure he'll honor your agreement?"

"I have no doubts that he will," answered Jonathan, "because non-compliance will result in him being placed right back on that plane."

"Why did Creyton betray him?" asked Terrence.

"I can answer that," snorted Jonah. "He told me Creyton said he was too changeable."

"That's an oversimplification—" began Felix, but Jonathan waved a hand.

"Unnecessary, Felix," he said quickly.

Felix swallowed. "Right. Sorry, sir."

Jonah looked at Terrence. They were of the same mind. Laban had already proven his changeability; he'd flip-flopped between half a dozen emotions in the past day. But there was more to the story than Jonathan wanted them to know. What might that be? He kind of wished Jonathan had been more forthcoming. The last thing he wanted to do was ask Laban himself.

"There is something I want to tell you all," said Jonathan. "Creyton will know I have sprung Laban. He will have not been sitting quietly. Look at these months and months of pseudo-silence. Over eighteen people have lost their physical lives."

Jonah shuddered. Creyton had ordered acts of horror so strategically, they didn't appear interconnected, and he'd fooled even the Curaie, at least until what happened to Phoebe Linkletter. Thankfully for the estate, Jonathan hadn't ever bought the randomness, and kept a number on the toll. Eighteen people... that number prompted him to look around the room at his friends. Reality told him not all of them would make it through all of this. That still didn't stop him from having the crazy impulse to hide them all in a bunker somewhere.

With a jolt, he forced himself to refocus on Jonathan's words.

"—I think Creyton is moving his pieces onto the board," he was saying. "No more games or runarounds."

"Does this mean Omega is about to happen?" asked Liz in a small voice.

Jonathan looked at the floor. He clutched his infinity medallion once again, an action which gave Jonah a ripple of uneasiness whenever he saw it.

"No," he said finally. "That particular fire has yet to be lit." He sighed. "I beg all of you to continue placing the safety precautions I've taught you into effect. Stay in populated areas, be mindful of strangers—all of the things you usually do. Just continue to do them with further vigilance. Felix, Prodigal—you are our ear to the sazers. Their cooperation and support are necessary. Obtain it for us. Do the absolute best you can."

"No pressure," murmured Prodigal, but he nodded. Felix began to leave, and his path was "accidentally" blocked by Maxine.

"Oh, so sorry!" she exclaimed. "But since I'm here, I just wanted to say good luck, and be safe."

Felix contemplated her. "Thank you, Max," he said. "To you, the same. And by the way," his eyes narrowed, "something's different about you. You look more grown up. It's a great look."

He passed her, leaving her about ready to faint. When Jonah actually bothered to pay attention, he noticed something was different about Maxine. She'd finally done something about her overly frizzy hair. It was as straight as could be. But as marked as that change was, it wasn't the biggest one: Max also wore contacts.

Or that had to be the case because she didn't have her glasses on yet wasn't bumping into everything in the room.

"It took Felix saying something for you to notice," said Reena, with mock sadness in her voice. "And you men wonder why women have body image issues."

"Oh, come on, Reena," said Terrence before Jonah could respond. "Max...we don't look at her as a woman. She's just...she's Max."

Reena transferred her gaze to Terrence. "I rest my case," she said. "Let's get out of here and go down to the studio."

The three of them detached themselves and went downstairs. Jonah was always amazed when he entered Reena's studio. She was either painting, or—when she was stressed—sketching.

There were five new sketches on her table: one was a fruit basket, one was of steepled hands, one was of the estate itself, one was of an artist painting, and one was of the engagement ring she'd just given Kendall.

"Been sketching a bit much, eh?" said Jonah unnecessarily.

"Of course I have," said Reena. "A lot of things are going on right now."

She seated herself and grabbed some of her rice cakes but didn't actually remove one from the bag.

"I don't like this," she said flat-out. "Rarely do I question Jonathan. You both know that. And I know he said he was using this man Laban as a source of information. But I don't trust him, or this situation."

"If it's any comfort to you, Jonathan doesn't like or trust him, either," said Jonah. "He just told him as much to his face."

"What was going on in the garage?" asked Terrence.

"There is an underground place," responded Jonah, who still had trouble believing it. "You can get to it through a section in the floor. Jonathan's got some kind of liquid-glass...I don't know, cube-thing for a cell. He claimed it was impossible for Laban to escape."

Terrence frowned, but Reena nodded.

"The passageways from the Underground Railroad," she said. "They're still good, though? And one of them was large enough to construct a jail cell?"

"I'm sure Jonathan helped matters along," said Jonah. "But here is something odd. Right before we left him down there—and of course no one noticed it but me—Laban looked off into space and said, 'One'."

Terrence and Reena stared at him.

"That was it?" said Reena. "The number one?"

"Yep."

"Maybe he was happy to be off The Plane with No Name," suggested Terrence. "Maybe he was thankful to be alone after being around those legions of prisoners. He was happy that now, he was the only one."

Jonah heard the attempt at hopefulness in Terrence's voice, but couldn't bring himself to humor him. "Do you actually believe that, Terrence?" he asked. "Honestly, now."

Terrence rolled his eyes. "'Course I don't," he muttered. "But the positivity was worth a shot, right?"

It was so foolish they all got a laugh out of it. Reena was the first one to sober.

"At the present time, I don't think we can even entertain the notion of finding out what that means," she said. "But Trip pulling a knife on him? I haven't seen him act like that since Felix."

"Trip was almost nicer to Felix," snickered Terrence. "He at least had the decency to threaten him; but he was gonna kill this guy outright for mentioning his family. I doubt he had any reservations about doing it in front of all of us."

"No doubts at all," replied Jonah. "But he made mention that Trip's father drove his mother insane. Was he being a dick? Is Trip's mother insane?"

He had figured Terrence and Reena might know something, since they'd known Trip longer. To his disappointment, however, they both shook their heads.

"Couldn't tell you anything about Trip's family, Jonah," said Terrence. "Hell, we didn't even know his father had been a Deadfallen disciple until a couple years ago."

"Cooper said Trip's dad's poor judgment over something was bad enough to put him on Creyton's list," said Reena. "It almost makes you think Creyton had the 49er kill the man for a different reason than just trying to move his family away. Seems like that 'loose end' thing was bullshit."

"The whole thing gets even better," said Jonah, suddenly tense. "It just so happens that Laban knew my father, too."

Terrence and Reena both regarded him with surprise.

"Laban knew Luther Coy?" said Terrence.

"Yeah," said Jonah. "Apparently, my father passed into Spirit owing Laban money. When he saw me on The Plane with No Name, he flat out told me who my father was; called him by name. It wasn't a question. He was also shocked that my poor excuse for a father could have produced a Blue Aura."

Reena idly twirled a paintbrush, speechless. Terrence shook his head.

"All that talking they do about aliens and outer space," he said, his voice pensive. "But it seems like the craziest things happen right here on Earth."

* * *

Thanksgiving Day was on them before they knew it, and although several people left the estate to celebrate with their families, the estate was still a bustling place. Kendall proudly showed off the ring Reena had given her to the people who hadn't yet seen it, Bobby had to beg his mother to allow him to eat dinner in the family room so as to watch the game (she shot it down), and Douglas was aiding Katarina in navigating through all the savory foods that were available.

"I was raised pescatarian," she explained to Jonah. "It's only been in the past six months that I've started eating other meats. I have to slowly do it, or I could ruin this day for everyone."

"You spent twenty-seven years eating just fish?" Terrence was wide-eyed. "Woman, you have to eat some of my mother's bacon mac and cheese! And the sausage stuffing! And the honey-baked ham! And you ain't lived 'til you—"

"Okay, carnivore," interrupted Reena as she pushed Terrence away from Katarina, who looked mildly nauseated from the thought of so much meat. "You obviously don't grasp the concept of the word slowly."

"She'd be fine," said Terrence, oblivious. "One variety plate. What's slower than that?"

Finally, everyone had a plate, and was situated at tables. Of course, no one was allowed to touch anything until Reverend Abbott blessed the food. He even had everyone join hands.

"Instead of prayer this year," he told everyone, "I thought, in light of the present climate of the ethereal world, we could each talk about what we're thankful for. I'll start, no problem. I am thankful for…"

Fortunately, no one was particularly long-winded, but the combination of not having breakfast that morning and the truly wonderful smells at the table made Jonah just a bit impatient. Reena, who wasn't wearing her dampener, gave his hand a tight squeeze, and narrowed her eyes. Jonah sighed. He was so busy willing his stomach not to growl, he missed some of the things that people were thankful for. He was able to focus when they reached Terrence.

"Easy," he said, "I'm thankful to have a place where I can rest my head, call home, have my parents and brothers always there for me no matter what I do, and have people appreciate my cooking."

The last bit elicited some laughs, but they desisted for Reena.

"I'm thankful for all of you guys," she said. "Thankful to have this place of refuge. Thankful to be surrounded by people who can all say they have something precious to give to the world, Earthly or ethereal. Thankful for the beautiful woman who has agreed to be my wife," she shared a smile with Kendall, "and I'm thankful for my artistic expression through painting."

Now, all eyes were on Jonah. He knew it'd reach him eventually, yet he was full of inexplicable anxiety. Why was that? He knew these people. Trusted them. Why would he have a reason to be nervous?

Another squeeze from Reena's hand got him out of his thoughts. He had a way with words; he had to say something.

"I'm..." he was acutely aware of all the eyes on him, "I'm thankful for the routine. It's a calming thing, knowing that some things in this world aren't ever going to change. No matter what has happened, no matter what mood we've been in—we can always come back to this estate. There will always be friends, always be family, and always be routine. Since this town is called Rome, I suppose we can be thankful for the little empire we've got. In essence, I'm thankful there are things that will stay the same."

His words got some looks, smiles, and nods. Not bad at all.

Now if they could only indulge in the food—

"Wait a second," said Magdalena hastily, and Jonah shot her a hard look. Surely, he wasn't the only person at the table who was hungry? "We left out Jonathan."

Many people turned because Jonathan hadn't been present earlier. He smiled at Magdalena's acknowledgment.

"I'm thankful for life," he said. "With all of its complexities, hurdles, triumphs, and revelations. Even though life never ends, there are always ebbs and flows, risings and settings. The valleys strengthen, the peaks allow appreciation. Life provides the most wonderful sensations there could ever be. That's what I'm thankful for. Now, by all means, dig in."

No one hesitated, but Jonah couldn't help but realize some of his impatience faded as he thought on Jonathan's words. It was not in his nature to be so concise. But by Jonathan's standards, that was terse. Maybe he was respectful of the hungry folks. Maybe there was more to what he said. But once a couple dishes started passing under his nose, he successfully pushed the thoughts from his head.

It was delicious, as usual. Terrence had actually smoked a few turkeys, and his mother had provided a couple Cornish hens. There were the usual dressings, hams, and sides. Jonah had developed a partiality to Mrs. Decessio's green bean casserole, as well as her succotash and chive mashed potatoes. When he hailed for them, Nella passed them gladly. He noticed her sleeve had lifted somewhat, which revealed the rose was still tattooed around her arm. She saw where he was looking, and disdain colored her features.

"I know," she muttered. "I don't want to think about any of it anymore but letting go is all but impossible because of this tattoo."

"What do your friends at school think of it?" he asked her.

"Are you kidding, Jonah?" scoffed Nella. "They love it! Clarissa thinks it makes me the girl's leader or something, since I was the first to get ink. If they had any idea..." her voice trailed off, and she smirked. "But Liz told me she'd get it off of my arm if it was the last thing she ever did. We're shooting for getting it off before my prom, so we've got some time!"

Jonah smiled right along with her, but he was amused at her naiveté. The fact that she was seventeen played a huge part in it, he knew that. It was November now, and her prom was in May. Not even seven full months to go. To her, it signified a bunch of time left. To him, it was the blink of an eye. Yet and still, a lot of things could happen in the span of a few months. Vera was a perfect example of that.

With some effort, he wrested his mind from thoughts of Vera, and re-engaged himself in conversations around the table. Kendall and Katarina were laughing at something Douglas had just said, while Spader was regaling Alvin and Benjamin about the finer points of slots over roulette. Raymond, Sterling, and Bobby were deep in conversation about the football lineup for that day. Mr. and Mrs. Decessio were talking with Daniel, Reverend Abbott, and Jonathan (Jonah was sure he would have no interest in that one). Liz, Maxine, and Magdalena were gossiping about things at L.T.S.U., while Nella shot the breeze with Themis. Just seeing them all made Jonah smile. No matter what happened outside the estate, the inside of it would always be a blessing.

"How come you aren't talking, Jonah?" said Terrence, who was on his fourth plate. "This ain't the time to be lost in your own head!"

"I'm not," murmured Jonah. "I'm just thinking of the fact that it gets no better than this."

Reena declined a bowl of Hawaiian rolls which had just been offered to her by Ben-Israel and looked Jonah's way. "I was thinking along those lines as well. It just makes me want to ignore everything that's going on, and just focus on stuff like this. These things are the things that I never want to change."

Before Jonah could respond, a pawing at his leg got his attention. It was Bast.

"What's up?" he said to her.

Bast locked eyes with him, and words splashed across his mind: *"Jonathan requests your presence,"* she intimated. *"He's in the back."*

Jonah rose—he'd had three plates, so he wasn't lacking—and followed the calico out into the hall. Voices in the room off of the hall stopped him in his tracks. He moved closer to listen.

It was Trip talking. Jonah started eavesdropping when the man was near the end of a sentence.

"—no regard from anyone," he was saying in his trademark cold tone. "They sit there in that huge dining room, being all festive and oblivious and shit, while Hell itself is seeping right out of the ground."

Jonah frowned. What?

"What exactly are you saying, Trip?" asked a voice that Jonah recognized as Karin's. "Do you know what's coming?"

"Somebody blind, deaf, and dumb would know what's coming, Karin," said Trip. "The issue is the response to it... or lack thereof."

"But Jonathan has been making moves behind the scenes that neither we nor the Curaie know." That was Grayson talking. "Is it so wrong that he hasn't—I don't know—militarized us, or whatever? He has never been wrong."

"Jesus, man." Jonah recognized the scornful voice as Markus. "When did you develop such a boy crush on Jonathan?"

"Drop that, Markus," snapped Trip. "Jonathan has done more for this place than you could ever know."

Jonah widened his eyes. Did Trip just say something positive?

But the man was still speaking.

"You saying Jonathan is never wrong, Gray?" Trip's voice was sardonic. "I've been here longer than any of you. I can assure you, that's a falsehood. Besides, think about what went down with Sanctum Arcist. Yeah, he was aware Kaine and his pack of shits weren't above board, but he was ass-backwards concerning the involvement of Inimicus and Creyton."

Anger trickled through Jonah's insides. That was beyond unfair. Jonathan didn't know Creyton would come back from the grave. He wasn't some all-knowing deity!

"So, what do you plan to do?" asked another crony. "With Jonathan doing his own thing, and Laban Cooper on the premises?"

Trip was silent for a few seconds. "There is something my mom used to say back before that home deemed her mentally unstable. She used to say things always change once you're tired of something. Well, I'm tired of this shit."

Jonah's eyes narrowed. Then—

With a jolt, Jonah saw Bast stood near him. He could swear her feline eyes were heavy with rebuke.

"It's very rude to eavesdrop," she intimated, *"particularly on people who have so many things wrong."*

"Wh—?" began Jonah, but then he realized he hadn't actually left the door. Trip and the others would hear him.

With a silent nod, he let Bast know he intended to follow her to the back to speak with Jonathan, like he was supposed to all along.

They found him waiting patiently, staring out onto the lawn with a look that carried just a trace of concern. Or was Jonah reading him wrong? He could never tell.

"Hello, again, Jonah," he said. "You did take your time. Was the food that good?"

"What? Oh." Jonah's mind had sort of slipped from the food after listening to Trip. "Yes, sir. The food was excellent."

Jonathan raised an eyebrow, as though he knew Jonah withheld something, but he opted not to pry. "I'm glad to hear it. Son, I called you out here because I wanted no one else's opinion to muddy up decision-making."

That was an odd way to preface something. "Okay," said Jonah slowly.

Jonathan turned, and gave Jonah his full attention. The gray eyes were as piercing as ever, and, as usual, it was unsettling. "Jonah, I see now where I've made mistakes in the past," he said. "One such mistake was leaving you out of the loop last year. I'm sure you can at least understand why I did, even if you don't agree."

Jonah wasn't fond of thinking about that time. It had been a very conflicting period. His sanity was pushed to the very brink, and his emotions back then felt like they hadn't been his own. Admittedly, he did still feel justified in the anger he felt due to chafing under rules and regulations, but he'd taken his anger out on undeserving people. Even the emotional strain he'd undergone hadn't been an excuse for that. It had been a very messed up situation because not only had most of the people he'd gotten angry with got angry right back, but the situations that had caused the anger in the first place had been orchestrated to worsen, which ultimately resulted in Jessica Hale murdering his close friend, Mr. Steverson.

He tightened his eyes at the thought. It had been almost a year, yet the passage of time had done little to help. Yes, Katarina had confirmed Mr. Steverson was at peace in Spirit, and didn't blame him for anything, but it didn't change the fact he was gone because of Jonah.

"Continue, sir," he practically blurted out to Jonathan.

Jonathan wasn't stupid, but thankfully, he obliged Jonah, and continued.

"Due to the current status quo, being tucked away is no longer an option," said the Guide.

"Sounds like you got another task for me," commented Jonah.

"For the time being, it is one thing only," said Jonathan. "And it concerns Laban."

"Laban?" repeated Jonah. "Has he already begun giving you information?"

"No," said Jonathan, who sounded perturbed. "He has requested a specific go-between."

Jonah blinked several times, as though the action would make this less surreal. "Me."

Jonathan nodded.

"Any particular reason?" asked Jonah.

"Apparently," said Jonathan, "he has made it his goal to familiarize himself with the Light Blue Aura, since his dealings with the Dark Blue one proved so disastrous."

Jonah glanced at the garage, like he expected to see Laban through the ground, or something. "Do you buy that?"

"Hardly," said Jonathan. "But we do have an opportunity. Were it not for that, I wouldn't entertain this at all."

"What makes you think he'll tell me anything of value?" asked Jonah.

"Because he doesn't want to go back to The Plane with No Name," said Jonathan promptly. "If there is one thing we can take as gospel, it's the fact indecent people are nothing if not selfish. If there is something that assists Laban in looking out for Number One, you'd best believe he will do. And I've made it clear that cooperation will be the most helpful thing to him at this time."

Jonah looked away. He didn't like this. At all. He hadn't been able to read Laban Cooper, and those mood shifts didn't help matters. And those things that he heard about Trip's mother being insane…which he'd just heard Trip confirm himself…

He was struck with sudden inspiration. He would turn the tables on Cooper if that were possible. The guy wanted Jonah to be a go-between? Then, damn it, there was going to be something given back. And if he happened to get information that could work against Creyton out of the deal, wonderful.

"Did you know Laban knew my father?" he asked Jonathan at random.

"I did," said Jonathan, "and they didn't appear to be bosom buddies. That was one of the reasons why his desire to get acquainted with you for being the Light Blue Aura was off from the start."

Jonah nodded. He was relieved he and Jonathan were on the same page. "I'm in," he said.

"Good man," said Jonathan. "But I must warn you, Jonah. Laban is highly skilled in craftiness and deception. He is a master at it; Creyton had him in his inner circle for a reason. But I know you have had dealings with insecure people in the past and know how to guard yourself. I implore you to lean heavily toward the experiences if Laban tells you something that causes you unease."

"I'll bear that in mind," said Jonah. "When does this start?"

With a dark look, Jonathan grabbed a box and placed it into Jonah's hands. Jonah saw two snugly wrapped platters of Thanksgiving food, as well as two bottled waters. "Now," he answered. "He has said hearty meals have always made him most verbose."

7

Rapport

Jonah trekked to the garage, not bothering to rush. He had to be careful with the food because it was hot as hell.

But that was hardly a bother.

Jonah knew there would be unbreakable glass, designed by Jonathan himself, between him and Laban. He knew that.

But his batons were in his pocket, full-sized, just in case.

That sudden inspiration he'd had about this arrangement being mutually beneficial had gleamed so brightly in his head mere minutes before. Unfortunately, it seemed to be losing luster with each passing step. Laban bothered Jonah. He didn't know if it was actually fear, but Laban had a bothersome effect on him. Something like critters on the skin. Couple that with the fact the son of a bitch was messing with his Thanksgiving.

He lowered the food to the floor once he reached the groove that marked the underground opening. When he lifted the hatch, he grabbed the bundle and began the descent. The temperature, brisk on that November afternoon, elevated underground. Jonah registered somewhere in his mind that a chthonic dwelling place would actually be warmer, but part of him associated the temperature spike with the visit.

When he reached the glass room, Laban was on the floor doing pushups. He must have registered another presence nearby because he paused and looked at Jonah. For some reason, he stared at Jonah for a full minute, his face an impassive mask. Jonah stared back, not knowing whether to be awkward or impatient.

"You look so much like your father," said Laban at last. "So much so that when I look at you, I catch myself getting angry thinking about how he stiffed me."

Jonah was instantly furious, which bullied away the apprehension. Three times he'd seen this guy, and two of those times, he'd mentioned Luther Coy. Jonah didn't know his father, and barely knew how he'd lived his life. He was a long way from wanting Laban's acceptance, but he would be damned if he was going to be judged for the actions of a man who was now a corpse.

"I ain't Luther, man," he snapped. "So, do us both a favor, and forget his name. Now stay right there while I deposit this food."

Laban smiled. He was far from the derelict specimen he'd been on The Plane with No Name. He had been shirtless while doing pushups, and though he wasn't a hulking figure, he looked durable and scrappy. The t-shirt he put on was immaculately white, much like the sweats and sneakers he already had on. In the couple weeks he'd been there, he'd kept his face shaven. But despite the gear and getup, there was nothing even remotely presentable about him. Especially that damned smile. It didn't reach his eyes at all. He simply looked like a man who enjoyed disaster, chaos, and doing bad things. It seemed as though all the things wrong with the ethereal world were the things that brought a smile to his face.

He made no movements except to raise a hand to invite Jonah to do the deposit. "By all means," he said.

Jonah cut his eyes from Laban and looked to the corner of the glass. He'd almost forgotten what he needed to do, but then he recalled Jonathan's instructions. He walked to the corner of it, near a part of the wall Laban couldn't see. Embedded in the wall was an unremarkable sheet of ethereal steel, about the size of a card deck. He touched it with his thumb and forefinger, and it began to hum, awaiting his next action. He cleared his throat.

"Food," he murmured. "Two platters, plastic silverware, and a water bottle."

The square of ethereal steel gleamed the golden of Jonathan's aura, and a portion of the glass, just the right size for a parcel, melted away. Jonah pushed the package into the opening, and hurriedly withdrew his hands. When the deed was done, the opening sealed itself.

Laban waited patiently throughout the whole process, only moving when the food was available to retrieve. He then seated himself on the futon, inspecting his dinner with interest.

"Ah, now," he murmured, "this looks exquisite."

He tore off the wrapping of one of the plates and went to town on some bacon mac-and-cheese, honey-baked ham, and smoked turkey. He practically inhaled one of the Hawaiian rolls; Jonah barely even saw him chew the thing. He frowned at the gluttony.

"I ain't about to go in there to perform the Heimlich if you choke on that food," he told him. "You act like you never had food on The Plane with No Name."

"This food is nothing like that shit," said Laban after a hefty swallow. "Besides, I haven't celebrated Thanksgiving in years on top of years. And given our location, I figured when in Rome, do as."

Jonah scoffed. The crazy bastard had probably been waiting to use that one. "Why did you want me as your go-between? Why weren't you willing to talk to Jonathan? He is the one who got you off the Plane, after all."

Laban, who'd been in the process of bringing turkey to his mouth, paused and gave Jonah a calculating look. "You don't believe—?"

"Hell no, I don't believe what you told Jonathan, and he doesn't, either," said Jonah. "But something tells me you didn't expect anything less. So, what's the deal?"

Laban smirked. "Simple, really," he said. "I know exactly where I stand with Jonathan. We've got a history, see. One that is checkered, antagonistic, and in a word, unpleasant. But you, my friend…"

His voice trailed off as he put pieces of turkey and ham on one of the Hawaiian rolls. He took two bites off the sandwich, chewed in a meditative sort of way, and then swallowed. Jonah found the protracted pause maddening.

"You don't know me, Jonah," he said finally. "You are not so prone to cloud my words with the same doubts Jonathan would."

"Wait," said Jonah, incredulous. "Wait. You're expecting me to trust you?"

"I expect you to listen," said Laban. "Like a war veteran would say…I've seen some things, man."

Jonah made a wry face. He'd known two military veterans in his life; Mr. Steverson, and Reverend Abbott. And neither man had ever uttered words that were such a crock. "So…what? Your word is supposed to be gospel, then? Pardon me for not hiding my skepticism, but dude, you worked for Creyton. What kind of fool do you take me for?"

"Not taking you for a fool at all," said Laban. "I merely take you as a man with a sense of morality I don't have."

Jonah stared. "Excuse me?"

Laban took another one of those infuriatingly slow bites of food. "I'm not innocent like you, Jonah," he said. "I've hunted, I've killed, I've betrayed, I've screwed over…and I loved it. I couldn't get enough of it. I'm an opportunist, amoral, self-serving...all of those things. And I freely admit it. I am who I am. But you, son? You probably believe that the experiences you have had have hardened you. That is folly...you still have decency. You have a conscience, so let's not bother debating the contrary."

Jonah wasn't sure where Laban was headed with this, but he also was unsure how to respond. Laban saved him the trouble.

"What that means, boy, is I couldn't care less what you do with my information," he said. "But *you* might. Say I tell you something that you don't trust, and therefore take for granted. Say you ignore it, and your ignoring me resulted in someone up there," he pointed upwards, indicating the estate, "getting hurt or killed? What if some heralds got wiped out? Or some spirits and spiritesses got usurped, or forced to the Other Side? Or, God forbid, something was to happen to...loved ones far away?"

"What the hell are you talking about?" said Jonah, his voice sharp.

Laban's smile vanished, replaced by an expression of heavy impatience. "Not exactly quick on the uptake, are you, boy?" he snapped. "I'm talking about the younger sister of Inimicus, of course. You're sweet on her, aren't you?"

Jonah felt blood recede from his face and finger. An icy know of alarm sprang fully formed in his guts. How did Laban know about Vera? He'd been on The Plane with No Name for years, or so Jonah had been told. His alignment with Creyton was long over. How the hell would he be informed? Jonah knew no one and nothing mattered to Jessica, but was she really so far gone she'd kill her own sister?

He knew the answer to that question. It sickened him.

If Creyton sent someone after Vera, she'd stand no chance. And her little boyfriend would probably be killed first.

"You're far off about me being sweet on her," he managed. "Besides, she's out of the game. She's done with us. Long gone from here."

Laban chuckled. "You don't think that Creyton doesn't have ways and means to track those that he's designated as prey?" he asked. "You think once he has decided someone will die, they will be in this world much longer?"

Jonah felt confusion. "I thought you hated him?"

"I do." Laban's response was prompt. "The mere thought of the bastard makes my insides blaze. But my personal feelings don't prevent me from appreciating what he is capable of doing."

Jonah was silent, but his face must have spoken volumes. Laban burst out laughing.

"Calm yourself, boy," he said. "No one's plotting anything against the girl. If you could have seen your face! But I believe I've made my point. It would be very wrong for you to dismiss or disregard any information I might give you, don't you agree?"

Jonah almost scorned the relief that settled in his body. In that moment, it became crystal-clear why Laban had requested him as his go-between. Jonathan would never be swayed by Laban's bullshit; he'd barely bat an eye before he put the bastard in his place. Not so with Jonah.

Reena had told him some time ago that he was predictable, and often wore his heart on his sleeve. At the time, he took it for the friendly jab it was, but now, he thought Reena may have been more truthful than he realized.

He was suddenly ashamed of himself. He had thought, with all the things he'd seen and done, he had grown some resolve. Maybe had developed some inner steel. He could actually admit that after his experiences as an Eleventh Percenter, there weren't many things in the Tenth World that scared him anymore.

But that was the Tenth World.

This was a whole other situation.

And Laban was a whole other monster.

"Why does Creyton hate you?" Jonah asked quietly. "Why exactly did he betray you?"

Laban's face, full of savage mirth, hardened. "That's another story for another day, Rowe," he rasped. "You don't get that kind of information just yet. We are merely establishing rapport right now."

"Fair enough." Jonah was pleased his voice was full of coldness. "Trip, then. Why does he hate you?"

Jonah expected Laban to look even crueler, but Laban surprised him by scoffing. "Ah, Titus the Third," he said in a musing tone. "He doesn't hate me. He hated his father. As his father is dead, he had to find someone to transfer it to. And since I happen to be in the area...well, what better place?"

"Death ain't real," snapped Jonah.

Laban snorted, and looked away. "Right," he said. "I forgot how you guys were all about that 'round here. But anyway, Rowe, if I were you, I would believe anything and everything I said. Non-compliance could very well get you the wrong attention. Well, more of it than you already have, I should say. You think eighteen people is a high death toll? It's table scraps compared to what can truly happen."

"What the hell is that supposed to mean?" demanded Jonah.

Laban stood up. "Take this back to Jonathan, okay?" He said it as though they were touching on final points of a business meeting. "Tell him if he wants to get ahead of Creyton, he will need to spread his ethereal dragnets farther than Rome. And he will need to tell all of his sources, and your little buddies up there," he jerked his head upwards, "that if they hear the phrase *Per Mortem, Vitam*, there is no need to even fight. They will be completely at Creyton's mercy."

Jonah's eyes narrowed. He'd heard those words before, more than once. But he didn't appreciate Laban writing them off, like easy meat.

"Don't underestimate me," he grumbled. "Or my friends."

"Just callin' it like I see it," shrugged Laban. "But I think that's enough for now. Thanks for the food, and of course, Happy Thanksgiving."

* * *

When Jonah returned above ground, he saw people dispersing. Douglas had Katarina so tightly in an embrace, he didn't think the guy would let her go. Malcolm and his mom laughed with Kendall and Reena. All seven Decessios plus Terrence were outside. Raymond and Bobby engaged in playful roughhousing, while Liz and Mrs. Decessio shook their heads, but grinned, nonetheless.

Jonah was in no mood to smile, but he also wasn't in the mood to be downer-guy, either. He ducked back into the garage and left through one of the back windows. He then entered the estate through a side entrance and made a beeline for Jonathan's study.

Before Jonathan could say a word, Jonah blurted out the first sentence that popped into his head.

"Jonathan, I can't do it."

Jonathan looked neither surprised nor disappointed. He didn't even ask for clarity. He knew exactly what Jonah meant.

"May I ask why?" was all he said.

He motioned for Jonah to seat himself. Jonah hardly even felt the seat when he did so.

"Laban Cooper has no spirit, Jonathan," he told him. "He sat there and told me he enjoyed being evil. He said the words as lovingly as Nella talking about music! He...touched on a sore subject—"

"Vera," said Jonathan for him. "He made an empty threat to Vera, yes?"

Jonah shook his head. So much for pulling the wool over his mentor's eyes. "The point is that he was able to get inside my head within a few minutes. Even after you warned me, he still got in my head. I won't do it, Jonathan. Give him Felix. Or Raymond. Or Patience. Hell, even Reverend Abbott. Not me."

Jonathan sat forward in his chair. "I apologize, Jonah," he replied, "but those options are out of the question."

"What?" Jonah sat forward himself. "Why?"

"Because you are the person who was requested, Jonah," Jonathan answered. "I don't agree with it, and never did, but there it is. Besides all that, you're the best person for the job."

Jonah narrowed his eyes. "Did you not just hear what I said, Jonathan? The exact opposite of what you prepared me for happened…within minutes. He suckered me in—"

"Which makes you perfect, Jonah," was Jonathan's immediate response.

Jonah stared. "Sorry, Jonathan," he said slowly, "but I'm afraid we aren't on the same page. I doubt we're even in the same book right now."

Jonathan smiled. "Allow me to explain. We have established Laban Cooper is evil. He is guilty of more than you know. I warned you he was ruthless and manipulative, and you fell victim to his skills. This shows your strength, Jonah. Not your weakness."

"Strength?" Jonah made zero effort to hide his incredulity. "Jonathan, he just made a complete ass of—"

"Were you ashamed of yourself?" interrupted Jonathan. "Thought that maybe you had developed an impregnable sort of armor now that you've been through the fire and all?"

Jonah blinked. *How did he do that?*

"Let me tell you something, Jonah," said Jonathan. "If I were still in the flesh, I'd be a hundred and ten years old."

Jonah felt his eyes widen. And he thought that Mrs. Mott up in town had done a lot of living at a hundred and three. But a hundred and ten?

"I was in my mid-thirties—thirty-six, to be exact—when my physical life ended," Jonathan continued. "And I immediately became a Protector Guide shortly after I went into Spirit. I've seen many things, Jonah. When I was physically alive, and afterward. Yet, I still can look at this and have concern."

He pointed at the Vitasphera. Jonah felt his mouth tighten.

In its original state, the Vitasphera, which was the property of the current Master of the Grannison-Morris estate, was a brilliant, gleaming dome the size of a softball. Its interior was a vibrant amber color, with a golden infinity symbol suspended in its center. The color inside reflected the state of the ethereal realm.

And right now, it was bleak.

The amber was almost nonexistent, and the infinity symbol was only visible because the bright gold it was made of gleamed somewhat through the dark interior. The interior looked as if someone had taken a handful of black soil and unceremoniously dumped it into clear water. Basically, the Vitasphera was no more than an unnecessary reminder of facts that no one at the estate could ever forget, anyway.

Jonah pulled his eyes from it and looked at Jonathan, who had been looking at the object himself, while clutching his medallion. When he saw Jonah had raised his gaze, he acknowledged the mutual worry with a slight nod.

"Despite the horrible things I've seen and experienced, I never once stopped caring," he said. "You never want to lose your empathy, son. The heart is much like the spirit. Through experiences, it can be bruised, hurt, strained, but it can never actually be broken. You've been to Hell and back, Jonah; I won't dispute that. But that should never turn you into a cold, unfeeling bastard. Why would you ever want to be a person who can hear heinous, unconscionable acts, and have no emotional reaction whatsoever?"

Jonah was silent. He had indeed felt weak and inferior, but after Jonathan described it like that...

He could see now that he wanted nothing to do with heartlessness or indifference. What Laban had said, with his stupid little mind games, had bothered Jonah. But that was only because, unlike Laban, he hadn't abandoned his conscience and moral compass.

Because, unlike Laban, he was not a Deadfallen disciple.

The revelation chased away the shame, and his mind was much clearer.

"Point," he said to Jonathan, his voice lighter and significantly less tense.

Jonathan nodded. "Now that that's over and done with, what else did Laban say?"

Jonah told him the gist of the conversation, however vague it ultimately turned out to be. He wondered if Jonathan would find any relevance in the filler parts, but he took no chances. Jonathan looked engaged the entire time, so Jonah had no idea if there were any devils in the details. But it was near the end that the Protector Guide's unflappable mask wavered.

"He said any information he gave us had better be treated as valid and credible," Jonah was saying. "He said if we thought eighteen was a high death toll, it would be 'table scraps' compared to what could truly happen."

That was the part when Jonathan's expression wavered.

"Did you ask him to elaborate?" he asked.

"Not in so many words," said Jonah, momentarily defensive. "But it wouldn't have mattered, anyway, because he kind of skated over it to tell me to relay one thing to you, word for word."

"And that was?" asked Jonathan.

"He said to tell you if you wanted to get ahead of Creyton, you'd need to spread your ethereal dragnets farther than Rome," recounted Jonah. "He also said you need to make sure everyone knows if we hear—" Jonah had almost forgotten that he couldn't say the phrase, "—those words no one but Deadfallen disciples can say, we needn't even bother fighting, because we'd be completely at Creyton's mercy."

Jonathan's face was unreadable. But then he spoke.

"He wants us to be afraid of Creyton, then," he said. "After all this time, all the hatred he has towards Creyton—he still defers to his damn power."

Jonah regarded his mentor. "I thought the phrase they say when they tap their throats was a means to identify one another as Creyton's disciples."

Jonathan closed his eyes. "You're half-right," he told him.

That didn't settle well with Jonah. "So, they say that after they kill people, or something?"

For some reason, Jonathan's face looked to be made up of several emotions. Sort of angry, sort of fearful, and strangely, sort of regretful. "No," he said eventually, "they say it beforehand." He sighed. "The first time I ever heard *Per Mortem, Vitam* was right before the Decimation."

Jonah's eyes widened. "You mean—?"

"Yes," interrupted Jonathan softly. "If you hear that, it typically means that your time is up."

* * *

Jonah felt almost heavy when he left Jonathan's study. It wasn't the first time he felt like his mind had been saturated by things he'd heard.

But he wasn't ready to unload everything with Terrence and Reena yet. Besides, they'd still be flying high from the holiday. Terrence was having fun with his family, and Reena was with Kendall.

Jonah needed to file things away as well.

He pulled out his phone and sent a text to Lola. He knew she hadn't done much of anything; she had been raised Jehovah's Witness, and wasn't big on holidays.

Lola, I'd love to hang out with you tonight. Not after your virtue, I swear. I just want to get away from festivities and hang out.

Jonah received a response from her within two minutes.

I always treasure your company, Jonah. I'll never say no to hanging out with you. And if we just so happen to have sex before the night's through, so be it.

Jonah smirked when he saw that. Thanksgiving didn't have to end on a crappy note, after all.

8

Memory Lane, Etcetera

Jonah and Jonathan were pretty much done conversing after that, although he told Jonah not to go spreading the mind chant story around the estate, as it was Thanksgiving, and he wanted the day to end on a high note. Jonah respected that, and he didn't even tell Terrence and Reena until the next morning. It was hard to focus enough to actually recount everything to them at that time, as he hadn't gotten much sleep after his conversation with Jonathan. If he'd been thinking, he'd have probably snagged more melatonin, because the only thing on his mind was Laban's words.

Terrence surprised them both once Jonah was done.

"Dad told me about that," he murmured. "He used to hear tell of it back when he had a desk job for Spectral Law. When they did, nasty things followed."

Reena had been twirling a paintbrush, like she usually did, but Jonah's words made her cease.

"When I was younger here, I heard some of the older Elevenths say they considered it a blessing if they went a whole day or two and did not experience the mind chant. Did Laban say we'd start experiencing it anew, Jonah?"

"Not exactly," said Jonah. "He said we needed to be on the lookout. But there was something else that bothered me almost as much."

He told them about Jonathan's reaction, as well as the things Jonathan attempted to skate over. Terrence and Reena both looked as disturbed at this as well, which arose curiosity in Jonah.

"Tell me something," he said to them, "both of you have known Jonathan longer than me. What was he like when you were teenagers? I don't think I've ever asked you guys that."

Reena stood up, and slowly walked through her painting, pausing at her depiction of the Roman Goddess, Pompona. "Jonah, you have to understand, when I first met Jonathan, my Uncle Kole had just been killed, and I still wasn't over my family disowning me. And on top of that, I barely understood the Eleventh Percent. Jonathan found me, in my uncle's empty house, right before I was about to be dumped into the foster system. You wouldn't have recognized me then. I had this God awful haphazard braided hairstyle, and I hadn't mastered the red highlights yet. I also dressed like an aimless rocker in search of a band to join."

The image and humor Reena had in her voice actually made Jonah snicker. Terrence did, too. Even Reena snorted, but then she went on.

"I didn't trust anyone then, especially anyone who was an adult," she told him. "So, when Jonathan appeared out of nowhere, I wasn't scared, because I'd seen spirits and spiritesses all of my life. So, in my mind, it was just another adult, and I expected one of those cheesy *Touched by an Angel* moments or something. But he didn't do that. He sat me down in my uncle's favorite chair and explained ethereality to me. He told me I could finally be around people like me, and it was the first I heard 'people like me' and wasn't pissed off by it. It was the first time that phrase had a positive connotation.

He was so friendly to me, but also... like a rock. Unshakeable, always in control. An authority figure I could trust, despite myself at the time."

Jonah nodded, and turned to Terrence, who, in contrast to Reena's standing, had seated himself.

"Like I told you before, I met Jonathan through the Decessios," he said. "He filled in all the blanks Dad and Mama couldn't, in regard to ethereality and everything. I started dividing my time between my new family's house and here after I got my first job, so started seeing more of Jonathan. You asked me to describe him back then... well, like Reena, I didn't have too many good experiences with grown folks, either, not until I got to Rome, anyway. But Jonathan was like the teacher who everyone wants. Like the parent who could have ten kids and still make them feel like an only child. The one who always had an answer, no matter how dumb the question. Next to the Decessios, he was the first to treat me like a person and not a burden." He shook his head. "All that sounded better in my head. I don't know if it was the best explanation—"

"Oh, it was fine," said Jonah hastily. "That was really good. I got the point."

Both Reena and Terrence's experiences, as unfortunate as they were, are walks in the park compared to his own. Jonathan was able to explain what ethereality was to them in serene situations. His indoctrination into the ethereal world had come after his vision turning blue, an overwhelmingly fatiguing spiritual endowment, and nearly getting hit by a truck. But, those thoughts aside, Jonah noticed similarities in his brother and sister's stories. He even saw it in his own story. And it was that thought he spoke aloud to them.

"He had all the answers," he said. "He wasn't worried or concerned, at least not to the point of showing it."

They looked at each other. The realization passed between them.

"Until now," they all said at once.

Jonah sighed in frustration. "I don't get it! Creyton had been active, causing so much hell, for all of those years. Jonathan was always a thorn in his side, so I've been told. Like Reena said, unshakeable, in control. So, what's so different about this time? Why is he worried now?"

"Jonah, can't you see?" asked Reena, anxiety in her voice. "This was never supposed to happen. When you killed Creyton back then, we thought that was it. But Creyton came back. He literally found a way to buck the natural order and return from the grave. The fact that he was able to do that scared even the Curaie, Jonah. It had no precedent whatsoever. This is a new experience, and it's being made up day after day. And I'm sure that right now, Creyton is feeling invincible. Look at how brazen he was with the killings these past few months. Almost like the subterfuge was more out of habit than necessity. If you were Jonathan, wouldn't you be worried?"

Jonah glanced at Terrence, who scowled somewhat. He agreed. Reena had a way of making things so obvious, one could feel downright stupid for not reaching the same conclusion. So yes, Jonathan had reason for concern. They all did. But that didn't change the fact that if Jonathan was alarmed at time, then the shit that was already bad was only going to get worse.

"I have to ask, Jonah," said Terrence suddenly, "did you get around to telling Jonathan about Laban calling out the number one?"

Jonah swore. And he'd had it in his mind, filed away, to tell Jonathan. He had already decided not to withhold things from their Protector Guide and mentor anymore. Too many bad things could happen when everyone wasn't in the know. Too many physical lives could be lost.

But suddenly, there arose in Jonah the urge to remain silent. He knew exactly why, despite the randomness of the urge:

There was already a great deal going on. People at the estate and around it were almost afraid of their own shadows. The status quo was that tense. What if "One" was another cause for concern? What if it was yet another issue to pile on top of the issues they already had?

A part of him didn't actually want to tell Jonathan anything about it at all. Out of sight, out of mind. It was almost like avoiding a voicemail because the person who left had only done it to mention bad news.

"Nah, I didn't," he answered, and then hurriedly added, "but I'm not worried about it."

Reena frowned. "You're not?"

"Nope," said Jonah, who placed as much confidence in his voice as possible. "Because Laban said it. He's a prisoner. And even if it is something significant, there isn't a damn thing he can do while he's locked away in that glass box."

9

The Seventh at Seven

"How many is that, Jonah?"

Jonah pulled a face at the nosiness, but quickly manufactured a grin. "Forty-two, Smith," he answered. "So far, anyway."

Smith shook his head. "That's an interesting habit of yours, Rowe," he said. "Breaking all those twigs every single day. I keep asking you, man, but you never really answer. What do you do that for?"

Jonah took a deep breath as he snapped a dry birch twig in two. "I *have* 'really answered' you before, Smith," he murmured. "I told you, it was personal."

He picked up a couple more, not waiting for Smith's undoubtedly puzzled look. He didn't need to see the look, because he'd seen it almost every day for the past four months.

In the aftermath of Mr. Steverson's murder, Jonah had been at the estate, coasting. That hadn't particularly been a bother, because he was at the estate, not freeloading. But after a few months of no work or school, he'd found himself getting a little stir crazy. Training in the Glade, hanging with his family, and filling up journals could only do so much. So, after a few inquiries about job prospects in Rome, Bobby had gotten Mr. Decessio to put a good work in for Jonah at the one of the two local libraries. Initially, Jonah had been annoyed, as he felt perfectly capable of obtaining employment on his own. But Mr. Decessio quickly schooled him on how things worked regarding jobs in town.

"This isn't the city that you got used to job hunting in, son," he'd explained the day after Jonah had gotten the job. "A lot of townies can be rigid and unyielding in their ways, which I'm sure that you already know. Therefore, the best way to get a job in Rome is to know somebody. Pure and simple."

Jonah was, in fact, no stranger to small town mentality. He'd grown up in Radner, N.C., population, two hundred people, give or take a dozen. So here, in Rome, with its "sprawling" population of seven thousand, it was paradise compared to Radner. But he had had very little experience with strangleholds on job positions. He'd been lucky in that regard; even the job at Essa, Langton, and Bane had come easily, though his sanity had been the tradeoff. Bearing that in mind, he decided to count his blessings. Besides, it was a library. So long as he was around books, he'd be alright.

Except for one thing.

He couldn't bring himself to befriend these people.

They weren't bad people by any means. He saw the same nine or ten folks every day, in one rotation or another. Smith, in particular, had tried to forge a bond since day one. But Jonah wasn't interested. And that was because he could not forge a bond with these people. He'd fail them spectacularly if they became his friends. When they'd later be used against him. He'd already made that mistake, befriending colleagues at S.T.R. He, Harland, Amanda, and Mr. Steverson were quite a quartet. And they'd been Jonah's lifeline when things got tense in the ethereal world. It had been a selfish desire, but he'd appreciated it just the same.

And now, Mr. Steverson was gone.

And things were never the same.

Harland had returned to school and was working on a second degree. Amanda had decided to devote more time to her young son, Zachary, which was understandable. They had pretty much lost touch with each other. Jonah hadn't been all that sad about it. They were probably safer if he were nothing more to them than just a co-worker they had at some job at some time. It didn't matter.

Oh, who the hell was he kidding?

He missed S.T.R. Missed Harland and Amanda. Missed Mr. Steverson most of all.

But his presence had put them at risk, and Mr. Steverson had paid the ultimate price.

Therefore, no more buddy-buddy with too many Tenth Percenters. Nelson, Tamara, and his friends in the city were too far away to be adversely affected by knowing him, so they were safe. Kendall was primarily Reena's responsibility, plus, she was pretty scrappy. And Lola didn't know—obviously—but Jonah saw to it that she was protected through ethereality. And every time he spent the night with her, he bolstered defenses a bit more. Besides that, they were new. He'd had prior ties with them.

But these new colleagues' safety was his responsibility. And he protected them. By putting a wall around himself.

And also snapping every twig—every potential portal—that he could find.

He closed his eyes and shook his head. God only knew what his co-workers thought of him. If only they understood that keeping his distance was to keep them safe... that being in their social circle might not be good for their physical lives...

He tossed the twig fragments on the ground and went back inside. He'd probably stayed longer than his break was, anyway.

"Jonah?"

He turned in the direction of the computer lab area and saw who'd called him.

It was Victoria, a young black woman who was a part-time employee at the library. She had squeezed this job in between her community college courses and could usually be found studying or doing homework behind the reference desk. Though Jonah had known her several months, they'd had less than five conversations, which was a direct result of his reluctant reticence.

Because of that fact alone, she must have had a pretty important reason to call him out.

"Yes?"

"I was wondering if I could ask you a quick question," said Victoria.

"Sure," he said to her. "What's up?"

She beckoned him nearer. "I don't know if you knew, but Mrs. Ernestine is retiring on the ninth."

"I did, actually," nodded Jonah. It was the honest truth. A side effect of keeping to himself at work was being significantly more observant most of the time. "She's been at this library since 1971, right?"

Victoria's eyebrows inclined slightly, which puzzled Jonah. Did she think he was deaf? Mrs. Ernestine hadn't exactly been quiet about her coming retirement. She hadn't been shouting it from the highest mountain or anything, not that Jonah thought that mountain climbing was something Mrs. Ernestine's joints would allow, anyway. The point was, it wasn't a secret.

"You were saying?"

"Oh, yeah," continued Victoria. "I wanted to do something for her."

"A card?" asked Jonah. "You have one that you want me to sign?"

"I do, but that wasn't my question," said Victoria. "I wanted to get a small dinner together at Olive Garden."

"Oh," said Jonah. "Well, that's—" Then he realized the point of this conversation. "And you wanted to invite me, too."

Jonah didn't know what to say. He could only laugh at the self-imposed double life he was living. At the estate, he was Jonah Rowe, friend to all (except Trip), and an overall pleasure to be around. At work, though, he was "that Jonah guy," who snapped twigs and hardly spoke to anyone. He had never shown the slightest bit of interest in activities outside of work, yet Victoria had thought enough to invite him.

It was a good feeling. So, what the hell? One time wouldn't hurt anything.

"I'll be there," he said.

Victoria was no more successful at hiding her surprise than Terrence would have been if Reena sprung a juice fast on him. "I'm... I'm glad to hear it! It'll be the seventh, at seven. I figured that that would be really early for a Christmas party, but we might as well merge the two, since Christmas is so near—"

"Victoria, why were you so surprised just now?" interrupted Jonah. "Did I ever give you a reason to be afraid to approach me? I don't talk very much, but—"

"No, no, no, I wasn't afraid to approach you," said Victoria hastily. "I was just wondering about... other people."

"Really," said Jonah. "I'm not sure I know what you mean."

Victoria looked at him rather guiltily. "Wally and Paula said inviting you might not be a great idea," she confessed. "They said that, with the way you act around here, you'd likely you'd be a downer."

Jonah ran his tongue across the inside of his mouth, the telltale sign of irritation. So, they were back in middle school now? Or worse yet, was he back at Essa, Langton, and Bane? He was trying to help these people, and what was the thanks he got? Deprecating gossip and the promise that he'd ruin things if he was invited to the damned Olive Garden?

He had a half a mind to befriend Wally and Paula now, if no one else. Get really tight with them. And then they might get threatened or attacked—

Wait.

He didn't mean that.

He'd just prove them wrong. Much less extreme than the previous thought.

"Don't worry, Victoria," said Jonah, smirking at her apprehensive face to hide his annoyance. "Mrs. Ernestine will have a wonderful night."

* * *

"You want me to dress you?"

Jonah rolled his eyes, yet again. "For the thousandth time, Reena," he said through clenched teeth. "Yes."

Reena paid no mind to Jonah's consternation. She brimmed with delight. "I'm sorry. Well, actually, no, I'm not. But I want to savor this! You actually want me to help you with your wardrobe!"

Jonah knew he'd be forced to stomach Reena's gloating, but it was getting more and more worrisome with each passing second. "I need your help because I'm obviously hopeless," he grumbled. "But I want to get this right. It would be the biggest middle finger to everyone who thinks I'll ruin the party."

Reena's laughing faded, and she nodded. She strode over to Jonah's wardrobe and looked around.

"Tell me, just for the sake of my knowledge," she said, without looking at him. "What did you have in mind?"

"I don't know, Reena," muttered Jonah. "If I knew that, what the hell would I need you for?"

"Don't give me that shit, Jonah," Reena shot back. "You have to have some semblance of fashion sense, or you'd be going to work nude every day."

"Perish that thought," mumbled Jonah. "Um, I don't know... It's cold, so I was thinking basic black would do me well, so as to trap heat—"

"No good." Reena's response was instant. She actually paused her searching in Jonah's clothes to give him an aggravated face. "Some of your coworkers have already made up in their minds that you're a downer. Why the hell would you co-sign that by going to this dinner dressed in all black like an undertaker?"

Jonah frowned. "Point," he mumbled. "So, what would you suggest?"

"This shirt right here." Reena held a hunter green button-down in Jonah's face. "And those olive slacks there will go wonderfully with it."

"Hang on," said Jonah, pensive, "if I can wear that green button down, why can't I wear that one?"

He pointed to a similarly colored shirt in a heap at the foot of his dresser.

Reena looked incredulous. "Jonah, it's on the floor, balled up and wrinkled."

"Hello? Iron?" Jonah took a page out of Reena's book and made his tone sound obvious.

"Jonah, it's dirty—"

"Dirty?" exclaimed Jonah. "Reena, please! Dirty and clean are fluid terms! I could iron that shirt and hang outside for fifteen minutes, and it'd be perfect—"

"This shirt is the one you'll wear," interrupted Reena loudly. "It's great... you have dark hair, and dark features. Trust me; you go in there wearing this outfit, and you'll knock them on their ass."

Jonah sighed, and took the shirt from her. "Fine. I'll play it your way."

He grabbed the slacks.

"How did you get so good at this?" he asked Reena. "I've been around you a long time, Reena, and I know what type of wardrobe that you prefer. And I haven't forgotten that vegan-punk-rocker getup you described."

Reena snorted, which faded instantly. "From my mother, believe it or not," she answered. "Back when she was still trying to make me a cookie-cutter doll like herself and my younger sisters, she was always giving free advice about wardrobe. My punk and goth looks at the time were a direct rebellion to her, however ridiculous many of those clothes were. But I never forgot her—um, 'tutelage', and I use the term very loosely. It allows me to play the game, should I ever need to."

Jonah nodded in approval. "Way to turn a negative into a positive, sis."

Reena snorted again. "Much like you plan to do this evening," she said. "And besides, it's the holiday season. Maybe they'll all be jazzed for that reason alone."

* * *

Jonah actually got to the Olive Garden early, but not because it was all part of his grand plan to impress. He wanted to check the place out with Spectral Sight beforehand.

Olive Garden was in a lightly busier section of Rome. Several more people to see, doing this, that, and the third. So, it should be a no-brainer to see a bunch of spirits and spiritesses in this part of town.

That was the hope, anyway.

He closed his eyes, inhaling deeply, and willed the curtain to rise, and the actors to perform. It was a rather bittersweet picture to paint nowadays, but it was what it was.

He opened his eyes. There weren't as many spirits and spiritesses as he expected, but there were still a fair few. A lot of the Rome citizens had spirits around them, some as few as one, while others had as many as six or seven.

But there was something odd. Every single spirit looked frightened.

When Jonah had gone into Spectral Sight for the first time ever in his physical life, he'd seen spirits and spiritesses that looked sad, woebegone, and, in a couple of cases, depressed. But that had been because Creyton had been shackling and usurping them. The ones that weren't experiencing the usurping were used to strengthen his minions. Jonah would have expected fear then, but they had been more depressed and sadder than anything else. But now, there was fear. Fear beyond fear, to be honest. The spirits that he saw looked over their shoulders every other second. Some even looked reluctant to be around the people they frequented, as though their desire to be out at night put the spirits themselves at risk. Some spirits weren't with any people, which wasn't unusual. What was unusual was the fact that there were no spirits that were alone. Every spirit and spiritess that Jonah saw not with a physical being was in some sort of group. But the strength in numbers approach didn't seem to bring much comfort to them, either; they seemed more afraid than the spirits around the Tenths. If Jonah were honest with himself, it appeared as though they felt like, since they were a collective, they were at an even greater risk.

Jonah couldn't help but sit back and stare. Creyton had hurt spirits and spiritesses before, and they'd been depressed. Now, they were scared. They weren't even comfortable in each other's company. What was Creyton doing to petrify them this way?

Then his colleagues started to pull up in the parking lot, which forced him to deactivate the Sight, and reattach his game face. When he saw the excited, chipper faces, he almost wished he hadn't seen those spirits and spiritesses. But he refused to let that drape itself over his mind. Not when it was time to be sociable. But he'd be great. Stress was simple enough to file away. It wasn't about him; this was Ms. Ernestine's night. If he tried hard enough to have fun with these people, he might have some by accident. Maybe.

He sighed. It was seven o'clock. Showtime.

The December night was cold, but that was a boon. Jonah always thought more clearly in the colder months than he did in the summer. Weird, considering that he was born in June. Ah, well.

He watched all of his colleagues go inside, and then walked away from his own car. Once he reached the maître d' and was told where the party was seated, he took a deep breath, and headed to the area.

And damn if Reena hadn't been right.

Everyone who saw him was stunned. He didn't know how much of it was wardrobe, and how much of it was shock that he actually turned up. Victoria looked apprehensive; it was clear that she wanted this to be a great night. Smith looked surprised, but pleased. Wally looked like he'd need extra water to help wash down his foot, and Paula even had the audacity to give him an appraisal that almost made him cringe. The woman was not pretty, and years on top of years of sun hadn't helped matters. What genetics hadn't provided, she attempted to compensate for with a massive layer of makeup. Jonah almost snorted. No wonder she was so prone to gossip behind people's backs. That was probably the only time of the day when she felt good about herself. What a pitiful existence.

"Hello, Jonah!" said Ernestine, smiling when she spotted him. "So, Vicky got you to come out here for me, too!"

Jonah smiled, and moved forward to hug her. She wasn't fake like Paula, and therefore, much easier to like. She always kept her iron-colored hair in a ponytail because she didn't like it in her face. After sixty-eight years of living, her joints weren't what they once were, but she still was a very proud woman who was barely stopped by age. She never complained about stiffness or pain. Jonah likened her to Mrs. Souther from his old accounting job, although she wasn't quite as sunny tempered as that. Nonetheless, she was a great person, and well-deserving of the retirement she was headed for.

"Victoria did indeed get me here, ma'am," said Jonah respectfully. "I wouldn't have missed this anyway. I want to be a part of your sendoff just as much as everyone else. You deserve this, and I hope to do all in my power to contribute to your special night."

Ernestine looked surprised and appreciative, whereas the others looked stunned, especially Wally and Paula. Jonah tried hard not to be smug. This was nothing. They ought to see him when he was around people he actually wanted to entertain.

Shortly thereafter, their orders were taken, and the conversations began. To Jonah's surprise, most of the questions were directed his way. When he politely attempted to shift the focus back to Mrs. Ernestine, he discovered that even she wanted to know about him. When he thought about it, though, maybe he shouldn't have been surprised. He was willing to bet cash dollars that everyone was of the belief that they were seeing him in rare form tonight, but when they got back to work, he'd retreat into himself once more. Could he really read people that well? Maybe Reena's essence reading had rubbed off on him a bit.

"I don't think I've ever heard of Radner," said Wally in a conversational sort of way.

"Doesn't surprise me," said Jonah. "Seems like no one actually has heard of Radner, save the people who live there. The nearest town to it that you've probably heard of is named

Elizabeth City." He turned to Mrs. Ernestine. "Tell me, ma'am; what do you plan to do with your new freedom?"

Mrs. Ernestine smiled. "I don't know, sugar. But that's the best part of it all. After forty years of having a routine and set schedule, it will be a breath of fresh air to finally have days that I will have to play it by ear. Maybe gardening when spring gets here, maybe sewing, maybe catch up on all the books that I've wanted to read, or maybe just sit on the front porch and talk to Donald for hours on end. I just don't know. And I'm excited because I don't know."

Mrs. Ernestine continued speaking, but Jonah's attention wandered. Something that she'd said triggered several thoughts. This was a woman who had earned the right to do a lot of nothing. She'd earned it, and she had absolutely no idea how she was going to fill in her time. But the unknown was so foreign to her after forty years of routine that she was actually excited about it. She was absolutely thrilled that she had no idea what was going to happen.

For Jonah, as the Light Blue Aura, the unknown was not a welcome thing. There was nothing thrilling about the prospect at all.

No, he wasn't alone. He would never be selfish or conceited enough to entertain that notion. But Jonathan had made it clear that when Omega descended, it would come down to Jonah and Creyton. He didn't know what would happen. He knew what he wanted to happen, but he didn't know how things would play out. That knowledge, or lack thereof, made him envious of people that were on...clearer paths.

Everyone else was so free. Even his friends.

He knew that Terrence, Reena, Liz, Malcolm, Bobby, Douglas, Spader, and so many others would gladly march into Hell right next to him, even if they were aware it might be a one-way trip. And he loved them for it.

But that was their choice to make. There was no obligation. He didn't have a choice. Fate, life, or whatever it was, had made that choice for him.

Ernestine had paused in her talking, and he was struck with inspiration.

He hopped up, holding his wine glass aloft as he did so.

"I'd like to propose a toast," he said to the table. "To Mrs. Ernestine. To the fact that all your hard work has paid off, culminating in peace, freedom, joy, and continued well-being. Everything that you've done has led to this moment. You came out successful, came out thriving, and poised for the simple action of filling your days with everything that you've been missing. The strife, stress, and duty has passed. To freedom and peace."

Ernestine blinked, looking genuinely touched at his words. Smith was looking at Jonah with something like admiration. Everyone else simply seemed astonished at the fact that he had said more words to them in an hour than he'd said in four months.

"Thank you, sugar," said Ernestine warmly. "I will definitely drink to that."

She took a drink. Everyone else followed suit. Victoria's eyes were so full of gratitude over the fact that Jonah had proven to be the best part of the entire dinner.

Jonah acknowledged her relief but didn't think much more on it as he sipped his wine.

That was because, for them, his words were a profound, thought-provoking end to a delicious retirement dinner.

For Jonah, though, the words were an affirmation.

An affirmation that desired to come to fruition but was unsure of whether or not it'd happen. That answer lay in the unknown.

A place that also included wildly dangerous Spirit Reapers and the frazzled spirits that were frightened of them.

10

Pine, Needles, and Roses

"So then, I ended the dinner with a toast that almost has Mrs. Ernestine in tears, and Wally and Paula were in complete shock and awe. Victoria had no cause to worry. She even came to me after the dinner was over and told me as much. So, all in all, it was a great night."

Reena nodded, approval on her face, and Terrence looked very impressed.

"I swear, Jonah," he said slowly, "you can adapt to any situation. If I ever have to get through a social setting of any kind, I want you on my team."

Jonah laughed. "You'd better get Reena for that," he said. "She's been playing this game longer than any of us."

"Don't remind me." Reena shook her head. "My staff Christmas party has yet to come. So, Jonah, the whole night went off without any hitches at all?"

Jonah felt the slight frown settle on his face. "Not entirely," he said, and he told them about the spirits and spiritesses he'd seen while in Spectral Sight that were so frightened and tense. Terrence nodded.

"I'd noticed that, too," he told Jonah. "I go into Spectral Sight every time I'm at the high school or at my parent's house."

"Do you see a bunch of spirits and spiritesses at the high school?"

"God, are you joking?" said Terrence. "Kids always have more ethereal beings around them than we adults do. I s'pose it has to do with the youth needing extra guidance or whatever."

"Huh," said Jonah, interested. "So, when the kids reach a certain age, the spirits abandon them?"

"Not leave so much as back off a little," responded Terrence. "As kids come into their own and become more independent. The spirits that guide never actually leave completely, though. They just give breathing room. But back to my point, the ones around the kids at school look like the world is about to end, or something. When I tried to ask one of them what was up, he just shook his head and shuffled off. Couldn't make hide nor hair of it."

"Same thing on my end," said Reena. "I do what I can to look out for my coworkers, too, Jonah, like you do with your twig snapping at work. The spirits are afraid and tense around my job as well. No one has actually run from me, but they haven't been too forthcoming with information, either. The most I got was that Creyton and the Deadfallen disciples were making Earthplane very uncomfortable, but nowadays, the Astral Plane wasn't the safest place either."

"That's a cheap answer," said Jonah instantly. "They are withholding something."

"Or things," said Terrence. "Maybe they'd be willing to talk to the heralds. Bast could probably get something out of them."

"Maybe," said Jonah. "I could probably ask her—"

"Or you could go under the garage and talk to Laban," suggested Reena, though there was reluctance in her voice.

Jonah shook his head. "Jonathan has made me feel like I'm built for being the go-between," he murmured, "but it's like—I don't know—I have to get myself psyched up to talk to that guy. He is a master at what he does."

"But he's on a short leash," Terrence reminded him. "He has to be forthcoming, or else he's back on The Plane with No Name. But you don't have to talk to that guy today, man. It's a good time!"

He stood up, grinning at Jonah's and Reena's puzzled expressions.

"Jonathan's putting the tree inside today!"

Sure enough, when they'd left Jonah's room, the gigantic tree that was usually located near the gazebo was now inside the family room, with everyone crowded around it. Liz was barely containing her glee, and Malcolm already had out the boxes of wooden ornaments, which he doled out to everyone, while Nella and Themis handed out the plastic and glass ones. With a smile, Jonah took some ornaments into his hands. He had always loved this tree and was always fascinated by it as well. Jonathan had figured out a way to take a tree that had been battered by fall and discolored, make it lush and green again, and place it inside the estate, void of support or foundation. Jonah was sure that he wasn't the only one that curious about how it worked, but everyone was just so happy that it was Christmas time that they rolled with it without questions. He figured what the hell; he could roll with it, too.

"Spader, I'll do the candy canes," said Magdalena quickly. "You always want to eat the cherry ones."

Spader, with narrowed eyes, withdrew his hand from the huge box. Maxine slid in to help Magdalena, grinning at Spader's disappointment.

Melvin, Benjamin, and Douglas were decking out the fireplace, while Reena, Barry, and Liz laid out the garland and the Christmas wallpaper. Terrence tapped Jonah's arm with a snicker and passed him the box of ornaments.

"Um, pardon me," said a voice.

Everyone turned. It was Grayson.

No one knew how to react. On principle, most folks ignored Trip and his bunch like they weren't even there. It was a very rare thing for one of them to talk to anyone outside their circle.

"I was wondering if you guys had room for one more with putting up the decorations," continued Grayson, who looked so awkward that it wasn't even amusing.

Many eyes widened, and Jonah didn't blame any of them. What the hell had brought this on? Had Trip ordered team building, or something?

Liz was the first to recover. "Certainly, Grayson," she grinned at him. "Alvin and Bobby could use a hand with putting the garland on the staircase."

With a nod, Grayson grabbed some and went to work, while Alvin and Bobby continued their own, looking mystified as they did so. Spader tapped Reena's shoulder, cold surprise all over his face. She glared at him.

"What?"

"She was nicer to Grayson than she's ever been to me," he mouthed. "What the hell is that about?"

"Really, Spader?" said Ben-Israel with a scoff. "Liz calling you by your first name is a giant step; you had better appreciate the gains you've made and stop pining away for the ones you wish you had."

Still sullen, Spader returned to his task. Terrence looked at Jonah with raised eyebrows.

"What the hell?" he mumbled. "Do you think he took a hard fall the last time we trained, and accidentally deactivated his asshole gene?"

"Nah, don't think so," replied Jonah. "We both know that Grayson has been growing a brain, and opinion of his own to match, for a while now. Maybe he took a leap of faith."

"I'll be damned," said Terrence, glancing at Grayson's back. "I guess miracles do actually happen this time of year. Say, Nella? Themis? Slide one of those candy canes over here before Magdalena sees you."

The Christmas decorations took most of the day, but it was a welcome time consumer. Afterward, people dispersed. As Reena had already committed herself to helping Kendall find a Christmas present for her father, Jonah and Terrence were on their own going to the mall two counties over to do their Christmas shopping. The conversation on the highway was pretty uneventful until Terrence posed a rather blunt question.

"You plan on sending Vera anything?"

Jonah's eyes instantly narrowed. There had been no trigger for the question whatsoever. How was he supposed to know that Terrence would bring up Vera in casual conversation? "East will handle her Christmas," he said in a level voice.

Terrence snorted. "Thought you'd say something like that," he said. "You think you're out of the game?"

"Not sure I understand your question, Terrence," Jonah replied. "Vera and I were never like that."

"Were you thinking along those lines when the two of you boned each other?"

Jonah shook his head. "I never should have told you that. But anyway, that was more like a go forth and prosper-type thing. She moved on. I have, too. You ought to hear Liz go on about it. Besides, she clearly made a better choice. I work in a library. That guy is business magnate—"

"Don't tear yourself down like that, Jonah," chided Terrence. "And besides, the dude's *father* is the magnate…he is just the heir. He ain't the man just yet."

Jonah cut an eye at Terrence. "Did you look him up?"

"Nah," scoffed Terrence. "I couldn't care less about the dumbass. Reena did. But hold up—how did you know that he was an executive?"

"Eastmoreland Enterprises has a website that rivals small countries," said Jonah without thinking. Terrence snorted again.

"Thought you didn't care," he commented.

"I don't care about Vera's boyfriend," said Jonah. "But I do care about Vera's well-being. She is our friend, after all. It mattered to me that she was with a guy who was who he said he was. Let's not forget what happened to Nella. It's not her relationship that I bothered with. It was her well-being."

Terrence looked at Jonah for a little bit. It made Jonah feel a bit awkward.

"Why are you looking at?" he questioned. "What are you thinking?"

"Nothing, brother." Terrence returned his eyes to the road. "Nothing in the world. Let's just get on to this mall, so we can do this Christmas shopping."

The mall at Christmastime, no matter where, is a test in patience, a grate on sanity, and a study in maintaining respect for one's fellow man, all at once. Jonah and Terrence had a pact to keep their resolve and attention as focused as possible, but Terrence had rattled Jonah's somewhat, bringing up Vera. But the two of them split up, agreeing to meet in the food court for some nice, greasy mélange of some kind before they got back to the estate, where Reena was once again making veggie burgers on arrowroot buns, and tofu fries. Jonah looked over his list. He had already taken care of Reena, Douglas, Nella, Magdalena, and Terrence. That left Liz, Themis, Malcolm, and Maxine. He wasn't worried about Lola, because she wasn't into holidays and was probably more interested in hanging out than anything else. He wasn't worried about

Spader, either. He'd probably steal or swindle whatever it was he wanted most for Christmas.

Liz was easy. Anything dealing with healing or gardening, and she'd grin brighter than the winter sun. He had surreptitiously gotten the scoop on Themis from Nella. She, like Nella, was an aspiring musician who adored anything to do with makeup or One Direction. Also, easy. Malcolm would love the hammer and chisel that he'd gotten him. That left Maxine.

Ever the tricky one.

At first glance, one would think that a sci-fi geek would be easiest to please. The problem with that was that Maxine already had most of the things that Jonah would get to surprise her. *Star Trek, Watchmen, Star Wars,* Anime. She already had all of those. Action figures were covered, and she made all of her cosplay outfits herself. When Jonah asked Magdalena about it one night after they'd relinquished endowments in the Glade, she'd mentioned that Maxine was also a fan of *The Walking Dead.* Jonah was not about to buy those sets; they cost too damn much. But he'd get her a nice T-shirt from Hot Topic. She'd love that with all her heart and soul.

So that covered everyone.

With a smile, he went up to the food court to wait for Terrence. Three feet away, a hand grabbed him.

"Wh—?"

"Cool it, man," said Terrence hastily, "it's just me. I wanted to catch you before you went in."

"Why?" asked Jonah. "What's up?"

Terrence turned to face Jonah. "Look over my shoulder," he said, "by that Cajun food place. Isn't that Prodigal's girl?"

Jonah did as he was told, and his eyes widened. He recognized the lank brown hair, and the young, but not very delicate features. It was indeed Prodigal's girlfriend. Autumn Rose.

But something was so wrong.

As she walked to a chair, having just partaken in a sample, it was clear that favored one side. When she reached the chair, she didn't sit down in it so much as collapsed into it, which caused her to grimace. When she made that expression, she turned, which gave Jonah a full frontal of her face. His mouth parted in alarm. Her nose had been badly broken. The injury looked recent.

"Dude, her nose has been bashed," he said to Terrence. "Something isn't right."

"Duh," said Terrence, with unrepentant sarcasm. "What was your first clue?"

"Shut up," snapped Jonah. "I mean that it's not in her nature to be a loner. She was in a group ten deep last time we saw her. And on top of that, who or what has she tangled with could break her nose and screw her up like that? Sazers have denser bones and tougher organs than the rest of us."

"Oh, right," said Terrence, who now looked sheepish.

"Come on," said Jonah, who made a split-second decision.

They cautiously approached her. Autumn Rose was a very intense girl, and that was before one got to the part about her being a sazer. Not only that, Jonah and Autumn Rose hadn't had the greatest experience the last time they'd seen each other. Jonah still had shame over that; he had been angry and tense at the time, and his temper and rash actions had put several people at risk, one of them was Jael, Autumn Rose's then-pregnant sister. He had a feeling that Autumn Rose wasn't in the mood to be forgiving.

But there was no time like the present.

"Autumn Rose?"

Unsurprisingly, she sprang up from the chair, and immediately gritted her teeth in pain. A lot of people in the food court looked at them curiously, but they paid them no mind. Jonah was more concerned with the injured sazer in front of him.

"Rowe." Autumn Rose's voice was acidic. "You scared me half to—oh, you get the point."

She winced, and Terrence came forward.

"Back up, Eleventh," she snapped half-heartedly. "I'm good."

"Shut up and get over yourself, girl," Terrence shot back as he placed a firm hand on her shoulder. "I think you've cracked your pelvis. Does it sound like something clicks and snaps every time you walk?"

With another wince, Autumn Rose nodded.

"Sit down," said Terrence. "You don't need to be standing too long."

Jonah looked at Terrence, intrigued. "How did you know her injury?" he asked.

"Happened to my brother once or twice," Terrence replied.

"What? Bobby cracked his pelvis? And Liz didn't heal it straight away?"

"Not Bobby." Terrence shook his head. "Lloyd."

"Ah," said Jonah. "Right." He turned to Autumn Rose. "What happened to you?"

Autumn Rose tried to look angry. Tried to look resentful. But at the current time, her heart just wasn't in it. She sighed. "I'm in Hell," she said.

Jonah looked at Terrence, who mouthed, *"Crazy, much?"* He turned back to her.

"Could you...elaborate?" he asked.

"Before you do that," said Terrence suddenly, "where is your other half?"

Autumn Rose closed her eyes. "That ain't an accurate statement anymore," she said quietly.

"What!" Jonah's eyes widened. "You and Prodigal aren't together anymore?"

"No." Autumn Rose sounded hopeless. "And it's my fault."

"Well, I'll be damned," spat out Terrence. "You can't depend on nothing—"

"Not helping, Terrence," said Jonah. "Autumn Rose, start from the beginning."

She took a deep breath, and then plunged. "About a month ago, I got a call from Jael," she began. "She told me that her adoptive parents wanted to distance themselves from Alexandria, with the ethereal world being a threat to them and the baby and all. They were moving to the West Coast. They know all about the Eleventh Percent; Patience filled them in when he returned Jael to them, with her baby boy, Addington. Anyway, I wasn't cool with my sister moving away. At all. I didn't want her and my nephew on the other side of the country. So, I decided I was going to do something about it."

Jonah glanced at Terrence, who looked to have the same thoughts. They knew where this was going.

"Stella Marie tried to stop me," Autumn Rose went on. "Edwardious... all of them. They told me that it would defeat the purpose of being in a safehouse if we were running all over the place like that. Felix trusted us, and Prodigal would never go for it."

"Where was Prodigal during all of this?" asked Jonah.

"He's off doing what Jonathan asked him to do," answered Autumn Rose. "Getting the feel of sazers, tryin' to get them to join the fight."

"So, I take it that Stella Marie and Co. were unable to stop you?" asked Terrence.

"No, they weren't," answered Autumn Rose. "They moved to Manhattan Beach; when Jael told me they were leaving, it was just a formality. They were gonna leave two days after that. Stella Marie and Edwardious stalled me for those two days, thinking that once they and Jael were all in the air, I'd just let it go."

A prickle of foreboding went through Jonah. "What did you do, Autumn Rose?"

She sighed. "I did an unauthorized *Astralimes* to Manhattan Beach."

Jonah closed his eyes. Terrence buried his face in his hands.

"You didn't," he mumbled through his hands. "The *Astralimes* are being heavily watched! The Curaie—"

"I know that now," said Autumn Rose, "but it wasn't Spectral Law that got on to me. It was Broreamir."

Jonah felt his eye twitch. Broreamir was Daniel's brother who had abandoned his role as a Protector Guide and embraced life as an ethereal human to join the Deadfallen disciples. As he had had a curious affinity with sazers, Creyton had appointed him as liaison with them. "What happened then?"

"I went to Manhattan Beach, and then realized that I didn't know where Jael's new house was," said Autumn Rose, her voice heavy with shame. "I searched and searched, for almost three weeks. Finally, I gave up. I used the *Astralimes*, not knowing Broreamir was on the trail of the stupid sazer girl making unauthorized travels. His means of tracking led him straight to the safehouse. I didn't know what I had done until we heard them outside."

Even though these events had already happened, horror engulfed Jonah as though it occurred in real time.

"Aw, hell," murmured Terrence.

"Go on," said Jonah.

"Broreamir sic'd some vampires on us," Autumn Rose whispered. "We're sazers; we've been fighting vampires all of our lives. But the vampires that Broreamir had with him... it was too much. We vanquished two, maybe three, but it was just too much. They were high on a substance, or something... I don't know. Edwardious got killed almost instantly. Octavian was next. I don't know about Stella Marie. She was fighting a pretty vicious bitch of a vampire... I don't think she'd fed in a while. I hope that she got away. I got knocked out when I hit a TV, damned vampire hit me so hard. When I woke up, the vampires were gone. It was after sunrise, so they had to clear out. They stole a bunch of Felix's equipment—I hope and pray that that wasn't his only one. He never told us. Edwardious and Octavian were there covered in so much blood. There were the husks of the vampires that we managed to vanquish. I don't know what happened to the rest of my friends. Broreamir left a note that said something about the Ungifted and the unworthy needing to get their affairs in order, because One was only the beginning."

Jonah looked at Terrence. One was only the beginning? It was that "One" that Laban had mentioned. There was no way that Jonah would believe otherwise. Autumn Rose wouldn't know, but that wasn't to say that Jonah and Terrence knew anything, either. What had it meant? Or should he keep in the present tense, as he didn't know whether or not it was still significant?

Arduously, Jonah pushed those thoughts to the side, for the moment, anyway. There was still one thing he had to know. "What happened with Prodigal? Was he angry? Did you have a falling out after what happened?"

A tear slid down Autumn Rose's cheek. Jonah had only met Autumn Rose once before, but with that one meeting only, he felt that had accurately pegged her as a person who was never weepy.

Not the case right now.

"I wrote him a note," she murmured. "I told him that what happened was all on me. He and Felix had permission to hate me, because no matter how much they did, they couldn't possibly hate me more than I hated myself. I freed him from having to see me, from having to talk to me, from...everything. That was last week. I think he's checked in by now, and he hasn't contacted me. He couldn't if he wanted to; it's not like I have a cell phone. It's better that way."

Jonah's mouth twisted. That was horrible. He understood why Autumn Rose had done it like that. But still...Prodigal was likely somewhere, crazed with worry, because his girlfriend had just "freed" him, and left. Autumn Rose may have thought that she was helping, but she hadn't helped a damn thing. And that was a week ago?

First Vera, now Autumn Rose. Jonah shook his head. What was it with these notes followed by vanishing acts?

"I got to know, girl," said Terrence. "How did you wind up here, in this mall? You've made it more than obvious that you don't like people outside your circle."

Autumn Rose looked at Terrence. "Prodigal. He told me that before he met you guys and Felix, he used to come here all the time. Bathe in the bathroom, use the water fountain to stay hydrated, eat the samples...all of that. I came here to...I don't know. But I'm here, for the foreseeable future."

"To hell with that," said Jonah, who transferred his purchases to one hand. "You're coming with us."

"Hell no." Autumn Rose's response was instant. "I don't give a damn about you people, and I know that you don't give a damn about me."

"Dispense with the frost, Autumn Rose," said Jonah, who barely even acknowledged her failed attempt at snapping, "you're scared, hungry, hurt, ashamed, and we know that you don't want to be alone."

"Besides," said Terrence, "I seem to recall one of 'our people' saving your sister from some prenatal disease, and then bringing her little boy into the world. Now lean on me, and no, it's not a request."

* * *

Jonah drove as carefully as possible, because he didn't want bumps and craters to further aggravate Autumn Rose's pelvis, but they made good time. Terrence spent the entire time texting Liz, so she'd know what to expect. When they arrived at the estate, Jonah saw to it that the gifts were all in the trunk, and they both grabbed one of Autumn Rose's arms.

"Are you kidding me right now?" she demanded. "I'm a big girl, thank you very much."

"I swear to God if you don't shut up," growled Terrence.

They assisted her to the infirmary. Liz, Ben-Israel, and Akshara were all waiting. Jonathan stood nearby, looking somber and concerned for Autumn Rose's well-being.

"Help her onto the bed," directed Liz. "This won't take long."

Autumn Rose looked at her. "You're the one who helped my sister," she said.

"Indeed, I am," said Liz, "and we're going to help you, too."

"I don't care about me," said Autumn Rose in a heavy voice. "I deserve this pain."

"That is a lie," said Jonathan, instantly stern. "You deserve to be copacetic and whole, just like everyone else."

"Jonathan, you don't know what I've done—"

"I know exactly what you have done," interrupted Jonathan. "You experienced victimization at the hands of Creyton's Deadfallen disciples. Granted, the unauthorized *Astralimes* travels will need to be addressed, but that is not an issue now."

Jonah approached Akshara. "She's going to be okay?"

"Physically, yes." She splayed green-tipped fingers over the lower half of the sazer girl's body as Liz injected some type of tonic into her arm. "But the night's not over."

"What's that mean?" asked Terrence, clearly thinking along the lines of some new fresh hell.

"It means that Prodigal is on his way," said Jonathan.

Autumn Rose sat bolt upright. Her pelvic area clicked again. "Jonathan, no. I can't look him in the face! I've fucked up so bad—it's like needles under my skin—"

Jonathan shook his head. "You will face that boy, Autumn Rose," he said firmly. "After an ordeal like that, a note is just unfair."

"But—"

There was a sudden sharp breeze, and Prodigal stepped into the infirmary, with hard eyes sole affixed on Autumn Rose.

Everyone froze, likely having the same thought. Jonah watched the sazer with apprehension and wariness. Not long ago, he thought that Autumn Rose should have done better than a note. But he didn't factor in Prodigal's vulnerability to the sazer's Red Rage. Were they at the risk of a guy on girl sazer duel?

Liz's and Akshara's fingers ceased gleaming green as they regarded Prodigal, and the latter backed out of his path. Prodigal ignored everyone as he advanced on Autumn Rose, tightly clutching her note.

Autumn Rose looked more resigned than anything else. "I deserve whatever you are about to do or say," she muttered. "But before that, did Stella Marie—?"

"She made it out," said Prodigal in a hollow voice. "Alecksander and Obadiah did, too. Constantine and Ambrose are in Spirit, just like Edwardious and Octavian."

Jonah closed his eyes. Those kids were so young. Damned Deadfallen disciples. With effort, he refocused on the scene in front of him, prepared to restrain if necessary.

Prodigal was now inches away from Autumn Rose. Terrence fidgeted somewhat, like he wanted to intercept, but Jonathan shook his head. Jonah's eyes widened. Was that a good idea?

Without warning, Prodigal dropped the letter and wrapped Autumn Rose so tightly in a hug that she gasped.

"Thank God!" he whispered. "I was going out of my mind. I didn't know where you were. And as for your note...no deal. You ain't gettin' rid of me."

Another tear slid down Autumn Rose's face, which could have been two parts relief, two parts pain. Liz gently tugged Prodigal away from her, while Ben-Israel helped her back down to a prone position.

"She doesn't need to be squeezed like that," murmured Liz to him. "She did experience a television falling on her."

There was relief on every face. No Red Rage tonight. Jonathan nodded his approval of it all, and Jonah looked at Terrence, who raised an eyebrow.

"What's up?" he asked.

Jonah gave a shaky laugh. "You were speaking of Christmas miracles earlier? Well, I agree now."

11

Independent Studies

Jonah, Terrence, Reena, and Liz were pleased to see that Autumn Rose's recovery was rather quick. Not only that, but when Prodigal arrived, he'd brought Stella Marie, Alecksander, and Obadiah with him. They were more or less okay; the most severe injury was Stella Marie's separated shoulder, which Ben-Israel fixed with no problem. Understandably, they were devastated by their losses, but thankful that Autumn Rose was okay.

"I went back after sunrise, because I knew that I'd be safe, at least from vampires, at least," said Stella Marie. "I found Edwardious and Octavian..."

She hung her head. Alecksander took over after draping an arm around her shoulder.

"We didn't know about the rest of you," he said. "Stella had jumped out of the window, and we knew that Autumn Rose was underneath that TV, and Obadiah and I ran. We stole a car and just drove. The vampires gave chase, so we just drove and drove until daybreak when they had to take cover. So, we drove back, met up with Stella Marie, and saw the note that Autumn Rose left, and the one from the Deadfallen disciple. We couldn't use the safehouse phone to contact Prodigal, because the vampires ripped it out of the wall. Plus, if he was in the underground, he probably couldn't be disturbed. Felix was out; he's on the same trail as Prodigal. It never occurred to us to try to contact Jonathan."

"What did you do until you saw Prodigal again?" asked Reena.

"We decided to go to an old refuge of ours from once upon a time," answered Obadiah. "We even used the old signals we had before we had access to a phone. All we could do was pray that Prodigal remembered."

Prodigal shook his head. "Did you really think that I'd forget everything we've been through?"

"It was dumb of me, I know," said Obadiah a bit sheepishly.

Prodigal looked over at Jonah and Terrence. "We didn't even know where to begin to look for Autumn Rose," he said. "It was pure luck that I remembered that mall."

"You talked about it enough," said Autumn Rose, breaking silence for the first time in a long while. "I just went there, thinking about you."

"And you happened to be there when Rowe and Terrence were buying Christmas stuff," said Stella Marie, and she turned to them. "I'm thankful that you both helped Autumn Rose out. And Rowe, maybe you don't suck so bad, after all. I think it's possible that I can forgive you for almost getting us killed last fall."

Jonah didn't know how to respond to that, so he just nodded. It was at that point that Terrence perked up.

"The count's off," he observed. "There is somebody that is missing, and you guys ain't brought him up. The Abimilech boy. What happened to him?"

The sazers all looked at each other. Prodigal was the one to answer.

"He took off," he said. "We tried to talk him down, but we couldn't. He said that we were doing better before we met 'the pampered sazer,' and that he needed to get back to basics, because he was tired of 'skating uphill,' whatever that means. We haven't seen Abimilech in almost a year."

Before anyone could respond, the infirmary door opened, and Felix and Jonathan stepped inside. Once again, the scene was uncomfortable. Autumn Rose had caused untold damage by leading Broreamir and the vampires to Felix's safehouse, after all. Her friends forgave her, sure, but they weren't Felix.

Prodigal rose. "Felix—"

Felix shook his head, and Prodigal reluctantly stopped. Felix threw inscrutable eyes on Autumn Rose, and then at Jonathan, who raised his eyebrows. He sighed.

"We're cool," he told her.

Autumn Rose, who'd braced herself for a warpath, frowned. "Really." The disbelief in her voice was obvious. "You ain't pissed?"

"Oh, I'm very pissed," replied Felix without hesitation. "But the fact that you guys made it out with your physical lives intact is the most important thing. Don't worry about the safehouse—"

Felix paused, clearly angry, but Jonathan cleared his throat. With another sigh, he went on.

"Those things are easily replaceable. I've decided to put you in another one—"

"No," said Jonathan firmly. "I want no repeats of what happened. They will stay here until further notice."

This elicited some stares; even Felix was caught off guard. Jonah saw that Reena had on her dampener, so even she was surprised.

"Um, sir?" said Prodigal. "I don't think that that's a great idea—"

"It's a wonderful idea." Jonathan spoke right over him. "I care about your well-being and will do what I can to secure it."

"But we're sazers," said Stella Marie.

"You're ethereal humans," said Jonathan. "As such, you are welcome here."

"We are *mostly* ethereal humans," said Autumn Rose stubbornly. "And I don't think your guy Trip would be cool with it. Besides, we don't mesh well with normal Elevenths—"

"Titus doesn't have any say over who can or can't rest their head here," said Jonathan. "As for you not meshing with normal Elevenths—tell me something, girl: How far has balancing your lives on that crutch gotten you?"

Autumn Rose was silent. She had no words. Jonathan nodded, as though that was what he had expected.

"Liz, Ben-Israel, and Akshara can show you to some rooms," he said. "If you want to eat, you will go to the kitchen. And by no means will you hide away while you are here." He turned to Felix and Prodigal. "Please get back to your duties, my friends," he told them. "I expect you back here around Christmas Day, with full reports. And Prodigal, know that your friends are under my protection."

Felix nodded, took a step into nothingness, and was gone. Prodigal clearly did not want to leave, but he was loyal to Felix and Jonathan, and he had a job to do. He walked over to Autumn Rose and kissed her, and then nodded to his other sazer friends. Once Jonathan granted him permission to use the *Astralimes,* he was gone as well. Jonah looked Terrence's way, and he nodded.

"Jonathan?" said Jonah. "Can we talk? Now?"

"Certainly," said Jonathan with slightly inclined eyebrows. "Meet me in my study in five minutes."

He disappeared, and Jonah, Terrence, and Reena headed for the door. Reena paused, pulled out her cell phone, and tossed it to Autumn Rose.

"Call Jael," she told her. "She has probably wanted to hear from you since she got to Manhattan Beach. You may not have a phone of your own, but I'm sure you know her number."

Autumn Rose nodded. She and her friends were still a bit stunned by their new accommodations. Still, she looked at Reena with gratitude as she dialed her sister's number.

Finally, they left the room, and were surprised to see Daniel waiting. He looked livid as he sharpened the tip of an arrow.

"Daniel?" said Jonah. "What's up?"

Daniel tossed the arrow back into the quiver. When he spoke, his voice was terse. "I'm about to speak to those kids in there. My dear brother is the reason why they no longer have a home. I want to know everything they know. See if there is something that I can use against him. Goodbye."

He went into the infirmary without another word. Reena shook her head.

"I might actually pay money to see the day when Daniel and Broreamir finally face each other," she said. "Now, what's going on with you guys?"

Jonah told Reena about how Broreamir had left the note at Felix's safehouse, which included the mention of "One" again. Reena's curiosity transformed into mild alarm during Jonah's story.

"Jonah, you said that you weren't worried about this 'One' as long as Laban was in that box," she hissed. "Now it seems that the problem was outside the box all along!"

"Duh," said Terrence. "That's why we're on our way to ask Jonathan about it."

Jonah barely heard them. He was fighting the urge not to beat himself up.

That "One" thing had been in the back of his mind since he'd heard Laban utter it. And he'd meant to mention it to Jonathan, but he'd almost convinced himself that it meant nothing if it were just a number. And now this happened, complete with a note that said that the number was just the beginning. When perceived threats were ignored in the past, it had always been disastrous. Everyone knew that.

So, it was time that things got changed up.

They were in the study in the allotted amount of time, and Jonah was there to meet them. He invited them to sit, and then seated himself.

"Now, please enlighten me," Jonathan's tone was welcoming, "what's on your mind."

Jonah told his mentor the entire thing, from the moments that Laban was placed in that chthonic cell and spouted the number to when Autumn Rose mentioned the same number from the note that was left in the remains of the safehouse Jonathan's face was neutral the entire time. Jonah waited for Jonathan's usual activities when he heard heavy information: the concerned eyes, the index finger tapping on the table, the grabbing his infinity medallion…

But none of them happened. The Protector Guide actually rose from his seat.

"Please forgive me," he said, "but I have no earthly idea what that number means."

Jonah was stunned. "Come again?"

"I don't know, Jonah," repeated Jonathan. "Laban Cooper is an insincere, evil individual, full of nuances, manipulations, and deceit. But calling out numbers? That is a behavior of his with which I am not familiar."

Jonah was disappointed. Maybe a little aggravated, too. In light of what had just happened, Jonathan's lack of information just felt wrong. It was like having an exciting idea or creation that one knew would change the world, only to have it unceremoniously shot down.

"Alright," said Jonah in a careful voice that prevented coldness, or heat, to permeate it. "Fine."

Terrence looked disappointed as well. Reena looked shocked. Jonah couldn't imagine why.

"I wish I did know," said Jonathan. "It would let us know what Laban knew concerning whatever Broreamir was trying to convey with that note. I will go bring the heralds and some of the other Protector Guides up to speed."

Reena nodded before Jonah could do or say anything.

"That's fine, sir," she said. "We will just stay here for a bit. No particular reason…just wanted to relax for a second."

Jonathan waved a hand. "Stay here as long as you like," he said, and then he vanished.

Jonah promptly stood. "Well, that was a whole crock of—" he began, but then Reena yanked him back down.

"Reena, what's the matter?"

Reena still looked stunned as she turned her gaze to Jonah and Terrence. "Jonathan just lied to our faces."

Jonah's eyes narrowed. "What do you mean?"

"It's damn simple, Jonah," said Reena with heat, "you asked for the meaning of One, and Jonathan said that he had no idea. That was a lie."

"Hang on, Reena," said Terrence, who came to his feet. "How could you possibly know that?"

Reena looked at Terrence. "I've known Jonathan since I was fourteen. And I have never seen him answer a question poker-faced. Even at his absolute calmest, he's never done that. Jonathan kept emotion out of his face, and if he were physically alive, I am willing to swear that he would have paled when you brought One up."

Jonah looked Reena in the eye. "Are you implying that—?"

"No, I'm not implying that Jonathan is plotting against us," snapped Reena. "After everything that he has done for us, that notion would never creep up into my head. I don't think he's made a habit of lying to us, or anything. But he lied about One."

Jonah wondered. He thought that it was weird that Jonathan didn't know anything at all. But to flat-out lie?

Suddenly, Reena closed her eyes, and focused. Terrence frowned.

"Uh, what are you doing?" he asked.

"I'm looking for something," answered Reena. "Now, shut up."

A few seconds later, savage satisfaction changed her expression.

"Found it," she said.

She walked past Jonathan's desk, and began perusing a specific area on the bookshelf. Jonah's eyes bulged.

"Reena, are you crazy?" he hissed. "That's Jonathan's stuff!"

"I know," said Reena, who pulled a collection of papers from in between two thick books. They were very cunningly hidden, which made Jonah more suspicious.

"How did you find that?"

"*What* is that?" asked Terrence.

Reena folded the pages neatly, lodged them in her jeans pocket, and then faced Jonah and Terrence again. "They are the files we got from that tattoo parlor back in the winter," she revealed. "The ones that Jonathan told us outlined Omega. If he is uncomfortable discussing One with us, we'll just have to put the pieces together ourselves."

"But how did you know where they were?" asked Jonah again.

"Easy," Reena told him. "I handled the pages that night. Whatever we touch leaves invisible traces of our essence on it. I focused so as to read my own essence and located the pages."

"Neat," praised Terrence, "but if my memory serves me correctly, those particular pages were written in some kind of cipher?"

"If a cipher can be made, it can also be cracked," dismissed Reena.

Jonah, who'd seated himself, rose suddenly. Reena wasn't the only one with an information outlet. Although he'd be the one that took the encoded paper if given the chance.

"What's up, Jonah?" asked Reena.

"I'm going to the source," he said with reluctance. "Are there any veggie burgers left?"

Jonah was out into the night, headed to the garage as quickly as possible, because it was pretty chilly. When he reached the door, he paused when he saw Trip resting against the wall.

Anyone with a fully functional brain would know that he'd be pissed beyond belief when he discovered that Jonathan was lodging sazers. He was out here, presumably attempting to smoke away his anger. But by the amount of cigarette butts at his feet, it wasn't going too well.

"And just what are you doing?" he demanded through clenched teeth when he saw Jonah.

"Sight-seeing," murmured Jonah. "Matter of fact, don't even mind me. Just keep on puffing."

He walked into the garage before Trip could say anything else. When he lifted the hatch to get underground, he shivered. Damn, this idea brought about mixed emotions. And Jonah also felt the same unnerved feeling he felt on Thanksgiving. It wasn't as strong now as it was then, and this time, he had a goal. Maybe that would assist him with this.

He reached the cell, and found Laban cross-legged on the floor, eyes closed. He must have felt eyes on him, because his own popped open.

"Jonah," he said quietly. "To what do I owe this pleasure?"

Jonah activated the opening, slid the bag of veggie burgers inside, and returned to standing.

"I've got questions," he said tersely. "Some people got murdered a couple of nights ago."

"There are always people being murdered, Jonah," said Laban through a bite of veggie burger. "What makes these particular deaths so noteworthy?"

"Death isn't—oh, forget it," said Jonah, appalled at Laban's indifference. "A haven of sazers got ambushed by vampires."

"Vampires and sazers are natural enemies, boy," said Laban, with a maddening tone meant to denote the matter as obvious.

"Look, quit being cute, okay?" snapped Jonah. "These sazers were under Felix Duscere's protection. They were attacked by vampires that were sent there by Broreamir."

"Ah." Laban looked smug, but finally attentive. "That guy. A more recent addition to Creyton's star-studded roster. Wasn't he the Protector Guide who decided being a nice guy was boring?"

"Obviously, you already know the story," hissed Jonah. "The point is that Broreamir left a note at the scene, which said that 'Ungifteds' and the unworthy needed to beware. And it also said that One was just the beginning."

Laban's smugness faded at once. He slowly lowered the veggie burger and swallowed the portion in his mouth. "Is that what it said?" was his quiet question.

"What is One?" asked Jonah outright. He was getting very tired of Laban's demeanor. That quelled the anxiety. Felix had told him in the past that anger was a valuable tool if properly harnessed. And Laban angered people like it was nothing. "I know that you know. I heard you say it that day when Jonathan and the rest of them brought you down here. You looked straight ahead, made sure no one saw you, and said, 'One.' And now, sazers have been killed, and Broreamir said that One was just the beginning. And now Jonathan is lying—"

Jonah paused. But Laban caught it.

"Jonathan lied?" he asked. "He looked you in the face and told you a bold-faced lie?"

Jonah didn't answer.

"So that means that you asked him about One before you asked me, eh?" prodded Laban.

"Okay, so I asked him," spat Jonah. "I wanted to know what it meant, because of that attack on those sazers."

Laban chuckled, and said nothing. Jonah continued.

"You know something, Laban," he said. "I know you do. You were on The Plane with No Name all those years, yet you're remarkably well-informed. I want to know what is happening out there, beyond the obvious. Spirits and spiritesses are horrified. The Curaie chooses to be an island, and meanwhile, their own people are getting killed, too. What do you know? What is Creyton's grand plan before Omega?"

Jonah didn't mean to fly off the handle like that, but he didn't appreciate being played with. It was tolerable up to a point, but that ship had sailed. He didn't know how much more of these games he could take.

Laban remained seated the whole while Jonah spoke. He hadn't even straightened his legs. He neither flinched, nor batted an eye. In all honesty and truthfulness, the only reaction he'd exhibited was a chuckle here and there. If Jonah had stopped to take a breath, he would have realized that Laban had gotten into his head yet again.

All he could do was shake his head. This man was a better nerve-grater than Trip.

"Jonah, you are navigating waters that will only lead to disaster," Laban said quietly. "For you, that is. I would suggest that you look at the big picture, and not allow your heart to bleed for Ungifteds and barely evolved sazers. That type of naiveté could prove very costly for your long-term goals."

"And what's that supposed to mean?" demanded Jonah.

Laban finally rose, eyeing Jonah with incredulity. "Hasn't Jonathan ever told you the reason why Creyton integrated the Deadfallen disciples in the first place?" he asked. "Hasn't he ever told you why Creyton was using minions when you were first introduced to the ethereal world?"

Jonah paused. Just like that, he'd been thrown off. The questions had hit him like cinderblocks to the head. Once again, Laban's eyes gleamed.

"See, now that's the look that tells me everything I need to know," he said with the merest trace of triumph. "Run along to Jonathan and find out those answers. Then, we'll talk."

"I'm not running anywhere," snarled Jonah. "Now, what does One mean?"

"Come back tomorrow," said Laban. "Same time. Bring real burgers, not this veggie shit."

He resumed his sitting, and his silence. Jonah could tell that this conversation was over. It pissed him off so much that he had half a mind to punch the glass, but he didn't know the effect that that might have on Jonathan's security measures. The last thing he needed was to have a hand in Laban trying to escape.

With a leveling breath, he turned and walked away.

And promptly froze about ten steps from the glass.

His eyes were wide; even his frustration had fallen from him.

It was all because of what he had just heard. It wasn't loud or anything, but Jonah had heard it plain as day.

From his pseudo-meditative position, Laban had just quietly uttered, "Two."

12

Yuletide Tales

Jonah sought out Terrence and Reena, but luckily, they weren't hard to find.

They were in the art studio, where Terrence was attempting to dissuade Reena from trying to break the cipher.

"Reena, I don't like this," he said. "Everything about it is wrong."

"People are getting killed out there, Terrence! I'm not flailing around in the dark, even if you're willing to do so!"

"I'm sure Jonathan had a perfectly good reason—"

"—to lie to us?" interrupted Reena. "At a time like this? Forgive me, Terrence, but that is bullshit in the purest form!"

"TWO!" said Jonah loudly.

Both of them jumped and looked over at him. Jonah was glad to have curtailed the bickering but hated having to drop the new information on them like that.

"Yeah," he said in a resigned tone, "you heard that right. I asked him about One, and he spat out Two."

"Great," said Terrence, "just great! Since we all love to have a challenge 'round here!"

"Put that to the side for a second," said Jonah hurriedly. "Do either one of you know why Creyton integrated the Deadfallen disciples in the first place? Why Creyton decided to use minions way back when?"

Reena frowned. "That's a random question," she remarked. "Would this happen to be another bug that Laban put in your ear?"

"Does it matter?" said Jonah. "Do you know?"

Reena shook her head. "Don't know the exact reason. All I know is that one day, Jonathan announced to us that the Deadfallen disciples had gone to ground," she said. "He didn't treat it like a celebration; he said it was cause for suspicion."

"Dad was the same way," said Terrence. "When the Deadfallen disciples were integrated, he and a lot of other people thought that Creyton was making way for something worse. Even Trip thought that it was too good to be true. He said Creyton would never have done that unless he had bigger plans."

Jonah stared. "That's it?" he asked. "Jonathan said what happened, but gave no reasons?"

"If Jonathan knew, he didn't tell us," said Reena. "Many people relaxed, but Jonathan wouldn't let us do that. He figured that such an abrupt change on Creyton's behalf didn't bode well."

"And he was right," grumbled Jonah. "That was when he started sucking Elevenths dry, using them for vessels. So basically, what you're saying is that Jonathan responded through protection and warning, much like he did this time around. But gave no concrete reason as to why it happened?"

"Not that I can recall," said Reena. "But what's up, Jonah? Why the interest in that? Does it have to do with One? Or now, Two?"

Jonah briefly touched on what Laban had told him. Terrence frowned.

"He said that saving the lives of sazers was being narrow-minded?" he demanded. "What the hell is he talking about?"

"Couldn't tell you," said Jonah, "but he also said that asking about One was treading dangerous waters. Can't forget that. That's when he told me to find out why the Deadfallen disciples were integrated in favor of the minions."

"Question, Jonah," said Terrence. "Why did you come to us? Why didn't you just go to Jonathan?"

Jonah was ashamed of himself for it, but his faith in Jonathan had been shaken tonight. When Reena revealed that he'd lied to them, straight-faced, no less, it bothered him. A great deal. He'd overheard Terrence's protest to Reena earlier, when he said that Jonathan probably had a good reason for lying. If that were true, fine. But Jonathan had also been the one who'd said that he'd wanted to keep Jonah in the loop. How the hell would any of them get anywhere is Jonathan continued to withhold information?

Reena seemed to follow Jonah's train of thought, or at the very least, read the shift in his essence. She placed a hand on his arm.

"Don't worry, Jonah," she told him. "I told you before, Jonathan lied about One. But he's on the level with everything else. I don't think you'll have to doubt and second-guess everything he says from here on out."

Jonah allowed himself a small smile. "Is that why you took the encoded files from his study?" he asked her in a shrewd tone. "And why you're cracking the cipher?"

Reena smiled back. "I am merely striving for knowledge," she said innocently. "That's what life is all about, yes?"

Jonah snorted, and left them in the studio, heading for Jonathan's study. When he thought about it, he had to admit that he was tired of all the message relay. At the same time, this whole thing had a certain quality to it that he couldn't fully comprehend. He didn't want to call it a good one; there were too many variables. And due to the variables, there seemed to be an answer that confounded everything else because the paths to get to it were always muddled. Laban knew something but wanted Jonah to hear it from Jonathan. Jonathan wanted Jonah to get information from Laban but warned him to be wary of manipulation. Terrence and Reena wanted to help but acknowledged that Jonah himself had to be the point man. Yet and still, Reena wasn't waiting around to be informed. She was about to work on that file. Jonah could've laughed. The confusion of it all was funny if nothing else.

He ran into Bast as he headed upstairs, who intimated something to him.

"If you need Jonathan, now is a good time. Because after this, he is headed Off-Plane for an undisclosed amount of time."

Jonah looked at the herald. "Does he think it's a good idea to leave the estate for long stretches like that?" he asked.

Bast looked Jonah in the eye. Even in her best moods, those eyes were unsettling. *"The estate will be fine,"* she intimated. *"Jonathan has yet to fail it. Besides, Daniel is here, and we heralds are here. Have no worries, but if you need to speak to him, do so now."*

"Noted," said Jonah. "Thanks, Bast. Stay warm!"

He put some speed in his steps as he headed to the study, nodding at Malcolm and Themis who were in a room nearby, working on Nella's Christmas present. He knocked on the door before he'd even stopped walking, and barely broke stride when he heard, "Come in."

"Hello, Jonah," said Jonathan, with curiosity in his tone. "I'm just about to head out, but I can spare some time."

Jonah nodded, and seated himself when Jonathan invited him to do so. With a deep breath, he began. "Sir, I know that we've already conversed tonight, and you made it known that you knew nothing about One."

He paused right there, watching for a change in Jonathan's expression, but to his disappointment, no such change occurred. He continued.

"So, I decided to seek information from Laban."

"Did you, now?" Jonathan's eyes widened somewhat. "What did he say?"

Jonah swallowed. This was going to get tricky. Especially since he knew that Jonathan knew what One was about. "He told me that I was treading dangerous waters," he repeated for the second time that night. "He said that I should focus on the big picture and not be a bleeding heart—that was in regard to caring about sazer's welfare. He said narrow-mindedness could be costly. He used that bit of advice to segue—"

"—into asking whether or not I ever told you about Thaine's integration of the Deadfallen disciples," finished Jonathan. "Am I right?"

Jonah was taken aback. He made no effort to conceal it. Jonathan grinned.

"Don't be alarmed," he said. "I've known Laban a lot of years. His thinking patterns are quite familiar."

Jonah's eyes narrowed. Was that supposed to be a satisfactory answer?

Jonathan sighed, ran his fingers across his medallion, and then spoke again. "Before I tell you that, Jonah, I feel that some background information is in order," he said. "Thaine, as you know, was initially trained here, as I was. When I first met him, I was eleven, he was nine. I had been here since I was four years old, learning the ins and outs of ethereality. It is not in my nature to be boastful, but I'd like to think that I took to it like a duck takes to water."

He smirked. Jonathan did the same.

"I was eleven, as I said," he went on. "In those days, the Overseer of the estate was a man named Franklin Trent. He brought Thaine here on his ninth birthday. He introduced him to all of us and explained that he was the Blue Aura. It would be decades before you were born, so he was the only one at the time."

Jonathan paused when he saw Jonah's gaze wander off. It was still a shock at times to know that Creyton was a Blue Aura as well. It made him wonder about so many things, the most prevalent being his role in Omega. Jonathan had said that when a Blue Aura turns dark, eventually, a light Blue Aura would be born to come along to restore true balance. If Creyton hadn't gone bat-shit crazy, what aura color would Jonah have had? Red, maybe? Green? White or auburn…no, not auburn. That happened to be the color of Jessica's aura. Granted, he did know some decent auburn auras, but still. It was quite a thing, wondering how he might have turned out if Creyton hadn't ventured to the dark side.

"Anyway," continued Jonathan, "Franklin explained to us that the Blue Aura represented amazing things, like balance, equilibrium, harmony…all of the things Thaine was not."

"You could tell that by looking at him?" asked Jonah.

"No," said Jonathan. "I'm not an essence reader. But I am a pretty good judge of character. I could tell it by our very first interaction. As a matter of fact, I will show you."

Jonathan extended his hand. Jonah looked at it, puzzled.

"Take my arm at the wrist," explained Jonathan. "This expends a great deal of energy and essence, so I don't do it often, and even now, I'll only do it this once. I am going to show you my memory of that moment. It's the thing that, in many ways, told me everything that I needed to know about Roger Creyton. You will see it as though you're inside a movie, or the like."

Jonah wondered, but did as he was told. The second he grabbed Jonathan's arm; he was outside in the courtyard. But it didn't feel as though he had form. He seemed disembodied; as though, since he was in a memory of a time where he didn't exist, he was in memory form himself. It was a weird feeling, but as an Eleventh Percenter, the word "weird" had very fluid meaning. It made it easier for him to roll with it.

So, this was Jonathan's memory of the estate at that time. It didn't look much different, apart the ancient cars, and the fact that more of the estate was covered in nature. This was long before Liz's multicolored gardens and Malcolm's woodshed. Even the gazebo wasn't present yet. But everything else, more or less, was the same.

Then, Jonah saw Jonathan. It was a strange, rattling thing, seeing him as a kid. He was tall, his hair was parted with a distinctive precision, and even then, his gray eyes were piercing. But he looked like a very concerned kid as he looked near the trees. When Jonah followed the gaze, he saw why.

He was looking at another child, who could only be Creyton.

Since Jonah knew what Creyton would grow up to be, his opinion of what he looked like as a kid was already colored by bias. But it was what it was. Although they were two years apart, Creyton looked to be the same height as Jonathan. His dark hair was fuller than Jonathan's, but his features were more angular. Despite that, he didn't look lacking, or malnourished. He had his arms folded across his chest, looking about the estate in a weird way. It looked as though he were gauging fortifications or sizing the place up.

Jonathan seemed to steel himself, nodded once, and headed Creyton's way. Creyton glanced at him when he was en route, but then resumed looking about the place.

"Hello, Roger," he said kindly, extending a hand, "happy to meet you."

"Likewise," said Creyton, who contemplated Jonathan's hand before he took it. "And your name is...?"

"Jonathan."

"Jonathan," Creyton sized Jonathan up. Jonathan gave him a curious gaze. "What color is your aura, Jonathan?"

"It's gold," replied Jonathan.

"Gold." Creyton's eyes narrowed. He looked at the estate, and then back at Jonathan. "Not quite as powerful as blue, but still... you're probably the most talented one here."

Jonathan looked awkward at the assessment. "I, um, I really love to learn," he said.

"You probably take to it easily," said Creyton.

"I—" Jonathan looked as though he wasn't comfortable with the budding competitive nature of this, and he waved a hand. "I just work hard. I really want to get this right."

"Yes," said Creyton. "Failure is a burden."

Jonathan's brow furrowed. "I guess so. But anyway, I'm glad you're here. I hope that we can be friends at this place from now on."

Creyton looked at Jonathan as though he were amused. "I don't intend to stay here forever, Jonathan," he replied. "One day, I will transcend this place."

And just like that, Jonah was out of Jonathan's recollection, and back in the chair, opposite the Protector Guide. Being back in his bodily form was an interesting feel at first, and then he readjusted to his familiar self. But he stared at Jonathan, stunned by what he'd just seen and heard.

"He said that?" he questioned. "At nine years old?"

"Indeed," said Jonathan. "And his proclamation of 'transcending the estate' was his very own self-fulfilling prophecy. Over the years, he became the prominent force among us. He maintained everything he ever learned, saw, or practiced. Thaine... it was all about ambition with him. That was the truth from the very first moment. He was the best of us; there was no doubt about it. The best of us, but not actually one of us."

Jonah raised an eyebrow. It was not Jonathan's way to say things like that. That was the mentality that he expected from Creyton.

"Let me explain," said Jonathan after seeing Jonah's surprise. "I do not say that to say that we were the ones that excluded him. It was the other way around. Thaine was the black sheep, no pun intended. We all treated each other as family. Thaine eschewed such bonds. He didn't care about things such as that."

"Did he have a bad childhood, or something?" asked Jonah.

"Hardly." Jonathan actually scoffed. "His father, Tiberius, was a white aura, and a close personal friend of Franklin's. His mother, Cecille, was from a privileged but very liberal family, which consisted of green, brown, and cerise auras. There were also several Tenths in Cecille's family, but to my knowledge, none of them were shunned. They married, their son came along soon after, and they named him Roger Thaine Cyril. No doubt they hoped for him to be the best of both of them."

Jonathan looked away with a grimace. That expression alone made Jonah almost pity Creyton's parents, who couldn't possibly have intended for their baby boy to grow up and become Armageddon on two legs.

"But back to the point," said Jonathan. "Thaine had little interest in forging bonds. He felt that allies were only as good as what they brought to the table. If I may be so bold, I believe that was why he considered me to be an ally for so long."

"So, the Deadfallen disciples are just disciples?" asked Jonah.

"That's right," said Jonathan. "I assure you that even those among the Deadfallen who are in Thaine's inner circle don't know who he truly is."

Now Jonah frowned. "Are you certain?" he questioned. "After all the years they were around him?"

"Being around a person doesn't mean that you know them, Jonah," said Jonathan. "Trust me, there is only one person who knows exactly what's going on in Thaine's head, and that's Thaine."

Jonah nodded. He thought that he could kind of see why Jonathan had seen fit to give him background information. Kind of. "So how exactly does this translate to the Deadfallen disciples being integrated?"

"To give you a little insight on how easily he can disperse with allies," answered Jonathan. "Remember what I've told you. To him, allies are only as good as what they bring to the table. If that is ever in doubt, then so, too, is that person's worth to him. And consequentially, so is that person's physical life. You yourself are aware of his apathy toward his followers. Remember when he allowed Marla to be forced to the Other Side? You told me that he simply stood there, with nary a word of protest. More recently, do you remember how Jessica Hale, his darling Inimicus, was to be what he sacrificed to ensure you abandoning your conscience?"

Jonah swallowed hard. He wasn't likely to forget that experience. Not ever.

"The same is true for all of his disciples," said Jonathan. "They may think that they are in his confidence, sure, but I believe that, at least on some level, they all know that they have to lobby for their spot every day. Remain relevant, or else."

Jonah's eyes narrowed. It seemed to be coming together in his head. "The Deadfallen disciples were integrated because someone decided to be ambitious themselves," he guessed.

"Ambitious in a way that was not conducive to Creyton's plans," said Jonathan. "He couldn't have that, but he also wasn't about to obliterate his entire following. So, he tucked them away, where they were to wait until he needed them again. Not a second sooner. And he enlisted the minions because—"

"Their sole existence depended on the sustenance that he provided them," said Jonah. "One screw-up, and all he had to do was usurp them."

Jonathan smiled. "I think you now understand why Laban told you to look at the 'big picture'," he said.

Jonah's mouth twisted. "He was also advising me to abandon those around me, and look out for number one," he grumbled. "Laban's the one, isn't he? The one who saw fit to be ambitious. That's how he got on Creyton's list."

"One of three Deadfallen disciples to have that distinction," said Jonathan. "The first was Titus Rivers, Jr., who was killed by the 49er on Thaine's orders. The second was indeed Laban. The third, ironically enough, was the 49er. Woe betide him if Thaine ever locates his body."

Jonathan came to his feet, with a look of determination on his face. "He hooked you, didn't he?" he asked Jonah. "I take it that you gleaned that obtaining that information was a hostage to obtaining more, am I right?"

"Yeah," said Jonah, surprised. "He told me to find out and come back tomorrow night."

"Don't," said Jonathan flat-out. "You are not an errand boy. There are neither slaves nor masters here. Let *him* sit, for a change. Let's see how well the bastard enjoys it." Jonathan retrieved his duster. "I'm heading Off-plane, as you know," he said. "Expect me back maybe Christmas Day. I think that we might see Felix and Prodigal that day as well. Until that time, peace and blessings. Enjoy these next couple weeks preparing for Christmas with your friends."

"One final thing, sir," said Jonah, despite his apprehension.

"And that is?"

"It's concerning...concerning One," Jonah murmured.

Jonathan's eyes narrowed slightly. Jonah felt his own do the same thing. "What about it?" asked Jonathan.

"I only wanted to say that I hope that it's something that we can handle," said Jonah quietly, "because as soon as I told Laban that I'd asked you about One, he said, 'Two.'"

They stared at each other for several seconds. It was now clear to Jonah that his mentor knew what those numbers meant. One hadn't been a revelation, and Two hadn't been, either. But something had changed.

Reena had described Jonathan as being "poker-faced" he heard One. Now that he had heard Two, the expression was...unsurprised? Yeah, that was it. Unsurprised. Jonathan had been expecting that.

Jonah didn't know how to take that reaction. Did the fact that had been expecting it make it less dangerous, or more dangerous?

"Huh." said Jonathan at last. "I'm glad you told me, Jonah. Well, I'm off. See you on Christmas Day, or shortly."

* * *

"What are Lola's plans?" Terrence asked Jonah a few days later at the wood pile. "I know that Christmas is out for her; I remember you said that she doesn't celebrate holidays."

"The news station she works for is doing one final toy drive," answered Jonah as he tossed a piece of wood on the pile they'd carry back up to the estate, "and then she's taking a trip to Vegas, straight to the tables."

"You ought to surprise her there, man," said Terrence.

"The thought crossed my mind," mumbled Jonah. "But the *Astralimes* are being watched, and with Jonathan Off-plane, who could I ask to give me permission?"

Terrence rolled his eyes. "Hello...Daniel was left in charge. He used to be a Protector Guide. He can give you the green light."

"Ohhh..." Jonah felt better about things. "I'll ask him when we're done here. We still got a bunch to keep us busy, but damn, if it isn't fun."

Jonah found the days leading up to Christmas very interesting. Work was actually more enjoyable; he was more vocal, but not by too much. Wally and Paula still wanted to keep him at arm's length, but that mattered so little to him that it required little to no thought. He had one regret, though. Now that Mrs. Ernestine was retired, he missed her. He wished that he had gotten to know her more, spent more time conversing with her in the months leading up to her retirement.

At the estate, of course, the preparations were laced with excitement. Present wrapping was always fun, and when the tree was packed with multicolored boxes, it was clear that the patience was wearing thin. Not in a negative way, though. People were just itching to find out what they'd gotten for Christmas.

There was a rather tense moment five days before Christmas. Katarina had come by to visit Douglas and help with all the fun stuff. Jonah, Terrence, and Reena had suggested involving Stella Marie, Alecksander, Obadiah, and Autumn Rose into their activities. It wasn't like they'd do themselves any favors hiding in their bedrooms waiting for Prodigal to come back. It had been Liz, however, who successfully convinced them. Katarina, who hadn't yet been made aware of their presence, was alarmed and unnerved when she saw them. Jonah could have slapped his own self for not thinking of it before: Katarina had been around the estate residents for months now, having long since warmed up to them while being in a committed relationship with Douglas. But she had heard plenty of horror stories about sazers during her time with the Curaie and hadn't had as much time as the others to become friends with them and realize that they were simply people. She'd discovered a kindred spirit in Autumn Rose, and before anyone knew it, they were on their way to becoming instant friends. Mere hours into it, however, Katarina simply *had* to marvel at a neat-looking Santa-themed basket by looking at Autumn

Rose and saying, "Work like this makes it clear that you're one of the good ones!"

Everyone froze. It was similar to the effect that one experienced when a person abruptly stopped an old vinyl record. The first one to recover, unfortunately, was Autumn Rose, who shot up to her feet in a fury. Katarina had recognized her mistake too little, too late.

"Oh," Autumn Rose growled, "you milk-faced ethereal bi—"

"Cease and desist, now!" commanded Daniel, who had moved between the two women so quickly that it almost seemed as if he'd used the *Astralimes* to move ten feet. "Katarina, that is precisely the ignorance that helps nothing at all! My brother is now a charter member of the Deadfallen disciples and is Creyton's liaison to the sazers. He gets the cooperation of sazers for Creyton by taking advantage of enmity they possess because of words and beliefs just like the ones you just voiced. Would you call me a good one because I abandoned Guidanceship and took a stand? Would you call yourself a good one because you broke away from the Curaie's hard line?"

Smugness permeated Autumn Rose's anger. "I appreciate that, Danny Man," she grumbled. "Glad we got that taken care of—"

Daniel rounded on the young woman, which made her step back in surprise.

"We?" he thundered. "I haven't begun with you, child. Your eternal issue is that it seems that you spend your life reacting and not thinking!"

Autumn Rose scowled. "She called me—"

"I know what she called you, I was right over there," interrupted Daniel. "And you reacted in kind, right? There was no need to label her as ethereal; we all are, yourself included. There was also no need to label her 'milk-faced,' because I didn't think Katarina needed reminding of her pale features.

Did it occur to you to be objective? Maybe say that that statement stung you, and you didn't appreciate it? Or maybe be frank, and say that it made you uncomfortable?"

Now Autumn Rose looked foolish. That was saying something.

"These are the attitudes that need to change," said Daniel to the room at large. "These are weaknesses on which Creyton hopes to capitalize, and you need to check them now. I'm not afraid to tell you this, because I don't have to be as nice as Jonathan is. Dispense with these petty differences post-haste, or you will be lucky to have a snowball's chance. And Chandler," he snapped his glare to Douglas, who had risen to comfort Katarina, "sit down. Your lady friend is not a pup to be babied. She can soothe herself right now."

And then, Daniel resumed his seat, picked up an arrow and a whetstone, and resumed his silence.

Jonah saw that everyone was just as alarmed as he was. It was almost like a character that he switched on and off.

"I hate it when he does that," murmured Spader from nearby. "One moment, he's a lecturer, and the next moment, he's a mute. It's disturbing."

"I don't know about that," said Magdalena. "He came full circle with the monologue."

"What?" said Terrence. "How you figure that?"

"Remember summer before last?" asked Magdalena. "When it was only like twenty of us here and we'd first met Daniel? He told Doug off for that skin tone assumption. Now, he's told off Doug's girlfriend for a sazer assumption. Full circle."

Spader snorted. "You make it sound like a good thing. There is no benefit to having people make an ass out of you like that."

"I wouldn't be so sure, Spader," said Liz from a few inches away. "Observe."

Across the room, Katarina and Autumn Rose had approached each other and begun a tentative conversation. Liz grinned.

"It's a little more than necessary from time to time, don't you think?" she said.

"I've said it a thousand times, and this is once more," said Reena. "With that mercurial tongue and those arrows, I am thankful Daniel is on our team."

Jonah was awakened on Christmas morning by an insistent knocking on his door. The sound jarred him awake, which was a feeling that he did not enjoy.

"What?" he murmured groggily.

His door opened to reveal a beaming Themis, who looked wide awake. "Merry Christmas, Jonah!" she said brightly. "Grab a shirt and come downstairs!"

Jonah looked over at the clock. "Themis, it's twenty-five to six. Can't you wait just a little while—?"

"Nope!" said Themis. "It can't wait! I want Nella's gift to be the first one opened, and I want everyone to see it! This moment will be perfect; Trip isn't even here to ruin it!"

All drowsiness faded from Jonah at that. "Trip's not here?"

"No, he isn't." Themis looked giddy. "He left to go to Orangeburg to spend time with his mom."

Jonah was so pleased at that news that he hopped up, grabbed a shirt, and wrestled it over his head. "Alright, Themis. What's your big surprise?"

Themis practically pulled Jonah down the stairs into the family room, where many other barely awake individuals had already gathered. Nella was at the center, looking at Themis with drowsy curiosity, and Malcolm was nearby, with a gleam in his eye that Jonah couldn't place.

Themis nodded, and Malcolm handed her a huge green box. She then looked at Nella, who was more puzzled than curious now.

"Nella, this is for all the help that you gave me after I passed out in chemistry class and didn't know what to think," she said. "And also for helping me to adjust to the Eleventh Percent, and meeting all of these wonderful people."

She put the box in Nella's hands, and she unwrapped it. When it was open, everyone saw a guitar.

There were several gasps; even Jonah was stunned. The thing was utterly magnificent and seemed to gleam with loving varnish.

Nella lifted it out, awestruck. She looked Themis full in the face. "How did you buy this?" she breathed.

"I didn't!" gushed Themis. "Malcolm made it!"

Heads turned. Malcolm shook his head.

"If it involves wood, I can do it," he said. "But I'm just a vessel; Themis is the one."

Nella didn't hesitate to wrap her best friend in a hug, and everyone applauded. Yeah, it was corny and cheesy, but no one cared. And Themis had her moment.

After that, gift unwrapping began in earnest. In no time flat, Jonah had multiple gifts which he loved, though the thing that he was probably most partial to was the new leather wallet. His current wallet had been stepped on, ripped, washed in the washer, and stretched, so it was way beyond time for it to be retired. He glanced at Reena with gratitude, and she grinned and nodded. Terrence's gift wasn't too shabby, either. It was a brand new cerulean blue polo. As most of his polo shirts looked like nightgowns on him now that he'd slimmed down, this was a welcome change. He made up his mind right then and there that he would wear it later that evening when he used the *Astralimes* to get to Las Vegas to surprise Lola.

Alvin and Bobby sported new watches that their parents had gotten them. Nella and Themis had volunteered themselves as the musical outlet and played while people marveled over presents and conversing. Themis was coming along nicely, but still stumbled with some songs. Terrence and Jonah both laughed at Reena, who inspected one of Kendall's gifts with a frown. It was a scarlet blouse that matched the highlights in her hair. It was clearly intended to be included in Reena's professional wear, but Reena loathed feminine clothing in the extreme. Jonah and Terrence both agreed that she would appreciate it because it was from Kendall, but it'd be far from a favorite.

Douglas had Katarina grinning hugely because of his enthusiasm over her gift, which was a framed Kirie depiction of a Queen's chess piece. Jonah had asked Douglas what he'd gotten Katarina, but he'd been vague and evasive. With a glance at Terrence, he saw that they came to the same conclusion. Either lingerie, sex toys, or both.

"Jonah," said Maxine suddenly, "there's one more for you down here."

Jonah took it from her, frowning. It was a small box, no name tag, but wrapped in blue paper as usual. Shaking it achieved nothing.

He opened it, and his eyes bulged.

It was a Class of 2005 high school class ring. His class ring. There was no note or anything, but that didn't matter. It could only have come from one person.

Jonah had lost his class ring over fourteen months ago, assisting Vera with moving furniture in her living room back at Colerain Place. When she'd sold that house and moved back to Seattle, he'd assumed it was lost forever.

But she'd had it all this time?

Why would she have kept it? Maybe she hadn't done so intentionally. He could have dropped it between her couch cushions, or something. Maybe she'd been perusing her belongings and happened across it.

The ring was nine years old. But seeing it again, it may as well have been brand new.

"What up, Jonah?" asked Terrence. "What is that gift?"

"Oh, nothing," said Jonah, suddenly feeling selfish, and wanting to hoard the moment. He slid the ring on his finger, a sinister grin coming to his face as he thought about what East would think of his girlfriend sending rings to other men.

Then he gave himself a mental shake. He had a woman to surprise.

Jonah used the *Astralimes* to Las Vegas at about 10 PM, which was when Reena left to spend quality time with Kendall. He knew that where Lola was, it was three hours back. He wasn't tired, though; he was spiritually endowed, and still flying high from a great Christmas day with his family. He hated suits and ties with a passion, but knew that he had to be presentable, as Lola was staying at the Bellagio. So, he compromised with black slacks, his new blue polo, and a black blazer.

He was intelligent enough to use the *Astralimes* between two buildings (he'd researched the place, and gauged nice places to use ethereality unseen), and stopped to marvel at a few things. It had to be high eighties; it was almost too warm for his blazer. There were so many people on the strip that no one paid much attention to him, which was great. The Bellagio was an amazing sight in person. Jonah, being who he was—which was to say a person who enjoyed sleep—couldn't imagine how these people could be up all night, gambling and painting the town red. But now that he was here, he couldn't help but feel giddy and ready for whatever.

But first, he had to find his friend.

He readjusted his overnight bag on his shoulder and headed that way.

Courtesy of Spader, Jonah found out Lola's room number. He didn't even want to know how Spader did it. But he had to suppress his smile when he reached the door. As to how he got there, as far as Lola would know, he'd caught a late flight from Southwest.

The door swung open, and when Lola saw Jonah, she froze, surprise and delight flashing across her face. Jonah took her in. She was dressed for a night on the town in a jade dress that accentuated her curves, black heels, and her hair done up in a gorgeous design. Jonah grinned.

"What's up?" he said. "I would say Merry Christmas, but I know you wouldn't appreciate it. So, I'll just say, Surprise."

Lola took him in the same way he'd just done her. "How long can you stay?"

"Till the 30th," answered Jonah.

Lola grinned. "*This* trip just got better."

Jonah regarded her outfit again. "I see you're headed down," he said. "Perhaps after some festivities, we can welcome each other properly—?"

Lola tossed her purse to the side and grabbed Jonah. "Get in here. That casino isn't going anywhere."

13

New Year's Revelations

Jonah had an amazing time in Vegas with Lola and didn't give the slightest thought to anything ethereal. As Jonathan had advised him to make Laban sit and sweat, he didn't give a single thought. There seemed to be a subconscious shift in power. At least it felt as such.

When Jonah returned to the estate, it was December 30th, the day before New Year's Eve. He reluctantly left Lola in Las Vegas, as still had four days left of her vacation, and used the *Astralimes* to his room to drop his bag down. When he went to greet people, he discovered something odd.

Jonathan had told everyone that he'd be back on or shortly before Christmas Day. That hadn't happened; it was one of the reasons why Jonah didn't use the *Astralimes* to Las Vegas until 10 P.M., because he'd waited around for him. As of New Year's Eve, he still hadn't returned. Felix and Prodigal hadn't, either. Jonah knew a fact that the latter's friends were getting worried, particularly Autumn Rose. Felix, to Jonah's knowledge, had no friends, except from the ones he'd made amongst the estate residents. But no one knew what to think. Felix Duscere wasn't the most stable individuals. Bobby had confided to Jonah once he'd returned to the estate that Liz and Magdalena had been going out of their way to distract Maxine from her concern. Jonah was as puzzled as everyone else but decided that visiting Laban was a good a distraction as any.

When he reached the garage though, he saw that some people were already there.

Karin Tanke and Markus Milcaine. They were busily discussing something when Jonah walked in, but all he managed to overhear was the word "illogical." They abruptly ceased when they saw him. Despite usually blowing Trip's friends off, Jonah frowned, suspicious of why they were in here.

"What are you two doing in here?" he asked.

Karin threw her hair over her shoulder. "Minding our business," she said shortly, "and leaving your alone."

"It's thirty-four degrees out here," said Jonah, not even bothering to hide his suspicion.

"Chilliness isn't so bad," said Markus. "It clears the mind."

That reasoning was about as authentic as Karin's hair color. Jonah shrugged.

"Whatever."

He lifted the hatch and descended. He couldn't put a finger on it, but something about seeing Karin and Markus bothered him. He didn't give Trip and his friends much residence in his mind, but it was unsettling. Why was that?

Were they thinking of defecting? No, surely not. Duplicity required cunning. Wit. Solid frame of mind. Karin and Markus lacked all three departments. It seemed like most of Trip's friends were like that. Or maybe Jonah had a bias.

Was *Trip* defecting?

No, that made sense at all.

Trip was the son, and the grandson, of Deadfallen disciples. He harbored a deep-seeded hatred for the father for trying to mold him into a disciple. That hatred was still strong even now, and Trip's dad had long since passed into Spirit.

Although Trip had hated Felix back when he thought the bounty hunter was the one who murdered T.J. Rivers. And when he had discovered that it was the 49er that had done the deed, he had dispatched the vampire most ruthlessly.

And then there was that thing that Jonah had overheard Trip say back in November.

Mama used to say that things always change once you're tired of something. Well, I'm tired of this shit.

It was obvious that there was extra meaning in that. But what the hell was it?

He brought his mind back to center. It couldn't be scattered right now.

He reached Laban's cell, and found him reading a book. When he sensed Jonah's presence, he raised his eyes.

They instantly hardened.

He tossed the book aside and rose, storming toward Jonah with purpose. Had it not been for Jonathan's specially made glass, he might have even grabbed Jonah's shirt.

"You've got some nerve, boy," he whispered. "I distinctly told you to—"

"—come back the day after you withheld information," interrupted Jonah. "Yeah, I remember. But here's the thing. You don't tell me what to do, Laban. You're not my father. Never had one of those anyway. Now, you know how it feels to be left hanging."

Laban eyes widened. "Rowe, did I not tell you that slighting me could be disastrous?" he demanded.

"And did you not remember that you are leashed?" Jonah shot back. "Your assistance is your lifeline, man. Trying to hook me like some old T.V. sitcom saying, 'To be continued' will not fly."

"And where are my damn burgers?"

"I am not your goddamned butler!" snapped Jonah. "Were you thinking you'd be dictating my every move? Who the hell do you think you are, Geppetto? There are no masters here.

And don't forget that I'm the closest thing you've got to a contact. Piss me off, and I'll personally see to it that you on the first thing smoking back to The Plane with No Name."

Jonah wondered if he'd gotten carried away. Laban had pissed off by daring to make demands and being angry when Jonah didn't carry them out. What the hell did he think this was, Culverton Inn and Suites?

But Jonah hadn't actually planned on threatening the man. He didn't have that kind of pull. Jonathan was the one who made those calls. What if Laban saw through that? What if he realized that it was an empty threat?

And then, Laban smiled. "Growing a set now, are we?" His voice was full of a grudging approval. "It's quite refreshing to finally see man standing before me."

Laban seated himself in the center of the room, cross-legged. "Let's talk. Did you find out that information I said, at least?"

Jonah just stared. It had happened again. Again. Laban Cooper had to be one of the most capricious men he'd ever met. He wished the crazy bastard had come with a manual, full of code words that triggered his moods. He grabbed a chair, and sat in it reverse style, propping his arms across the top.

"Yeah, I did," he answered. "Even got some background information on Creyton to go with it."

"Did you, now?" said Laban. "How much?"

Jonah's eyes narrowed. "Enough to know Creyton views on allies," he responded. "Enough to now know that you view me as a bleeding heart for my compassion. And that, well…" Jonah paused, though he wasn't sure why. Maybe he didn't want to bear witness to another mood swing. They were archaic by this point. But he plunged anyway. "I know that when T.J. Rivers tried defying Creyton, Creyton had the 49er kill him. Creyton wasn't around to deal with the 49er's betrayal when he achieved Praeterletum, but he promised to deal with him the moment he found his body. So, by process of elimination, the reason why Creyton integrated the Deadfallen disciples was because of something you did."

Laban actually brought his hands together in mock applause. "Beautiful work," he complimented. "Did you figure it out yourself?"

"Took a nudge or two in the right direction," said Jonah, unmoved by the praise.

Laban snorted. "Figured," he said, "but yes. I was the reason why Creyton integrated the Deadfallen disciples."

"What did you do?" asked Jonah.

Laban cracked his neck muscles and straightened his spine. He seemed to want a more relaxed state. When he was satisfied, he spoke. The jokester voice was gone. "Creyton is dangerous—," he began, prompting Jonah to roll his eyes. Lame, much?

"Oh, is he?" Jonah cried sarcastically. "Never would have guessed."

"You misunderstand me, boy," said Laban softly. "If you were self-serving or a little more open-minded about so-called 'rules,' it might be clearer. Take yourself and Creyton, for example. Light Blue, Dark Blue. One would think that, both being Blue Auras, your endowment powers would be similar, right? This is not true."

Jonah wondered where this was going, particularly since it had nothing to do with his query, but he listened anyway. Also, there was a trace of apprehension within him, given this specific subject matter.

"You have power to kill bulbs of light? That right?"

Jonah raised an eyebrow. Laban smiled.

"Thought so," he said. "Well, you can kill a bulb; Creyton can blackout a city. You can manipulate winds; Creyton can simulate a fatal gale. You can make people lightheaded by withholding oxygen? Creyton can nullify all the oxygen in your lungs, brain, and blood. You've probably realized that you can use electricity to tase people. Creyton can engender a voltage so elevated that if he touched you, your muscles would contract to the point of snapping in two. And all of that was before you 'killed' him. Imagine what he can do now, after Praeterletum."

Jonah hadn't missed the finger quotations Laban placed around the word 'killed,' but his mouth parted. Creyton was capable of all that? When Jonah experimented, he'd done some wild things, but Creyton was capable of all that consciously?

"I'm sure you see now what I mean when I say Creyton is dangerous," continued Laban, seemingly relishing the reaction his words had had. "You are no match for him, and you share the same color aura. What, then, is there for the rest of us?"

Jonah was silent.

"You've said that you are now aware of how Creyton views allies," Laban went on. "Expendable, dispensable, and forfeit. As long as you mattered, you were fine. Stop mattering—"

He performed the cutthroat sign with a smooth flick of his hand.

"Now, T.J., being the fool that he was, thought about spiriting his family away would work when he thought Creyton might dispose of him. Nope. The 49er was two kinds of stupid if he thought *his* plan would succeed, but at least he attempted his plan after Creyton was out of commission and the Deadfallen disciples were all integrated. What was my crime? This."

He tapped his head.

"I was a lecturer when I wasn't assisting Creyton in expanding his base," said Laban. "I spoke to people all across the country. Way with words, move people, yada, yada, yada. Anyway, after I saw the extreme indifference with which Creyton handled T.J. Rivers, I decided that I wasn't going to go the same way."

"By doing what, exactly?" said Jonah.

"By employing an insurance policy," answered Laban. "Certain people I lectured were given a small amount of my essence. Not enough to be noticeable, but enough to make their minds darken to the point of, say, killing everyone within five feet of them."

Jonah stared in horror. Laban smirked.

"Lovely, I know," he said. "And Creyton did *not* want that to happen. It would bring far too much attention to his plans. Generally, he didn't care who got in his way—he simply killed them—but he wasn't a fan of muddied waters. That kind of carnage would muddy the waters utterly. I was sure that Creyton would deem me too valuable to betray."

"But you were wrong," guessed Jonah.

Laban's eyes flickered with hate. "Yes, I was wrong," he rasped. "He found out about what I'd done, as I knew he would, but instead of being impressed at my ambition, he was furious. He was also tired of my 'changeability,' and decided that if I could pledge my loyalty one day, and then put a failsafe in like that the next, then I was no longer useful. He sent Asa Brooks, Whyndam O'Shea, Davis Powell, and Athena Harkness after me."

"How the hell did you get away?" demanded Jonah.

Laban smirked again. "I figured that if my changeable nature sealed my fate, then it would save my life," he replied. "When they used twig portals to get into my home, I did an unauthorized *Astralimes* directly into the Median. I turned myself in. Confessed to forty-seven Eighth Chapter crimes."

Jonah was so stunned that he backed away. He literally rose from the chair and backed away. "You voluntarily snitched on yourself to the Curaie?" he said loudly.

"Sure did," said Laban. "And to think, Athena and her man showed up there as prisoners soon after that. Powell...I hope it hurt when he died—"

Jonah swallowed, but didn't interrupt.

"—and that godforsaken vampire," Laban's eyes flashed. "Lifeblood-looting dumbass."

Jonah shook his head. "What's your angle, Laban?" he asked him. "You wouldn't turn yourself in—"

"For no other reason than saving my own ass?" finished Laban. "I did exactly that, Jonah. You think that I had a motive? The truth is far less complex. I look out for myself, Jonah. My well-being is the most important thing to me. I will advise you, once again, to stop toiling with morality and look out for your own ass. I will do anything to protect myself, even tolerating this."

He indicated the cell.

Jonah shook his head again. "No," he said. "You're lying. You care about where you are, because when they brought you from the Plane with No Name, you told me that you didn't know how interested you were in trading one prison for another."

Laban nodded. "I wasn't all that willing, but I had no problem with it," he said. "It saved me, did it not? Got me off that infernal Plane, right? It all comes back to looking out for me. Look at Trip, example. Idiot had no idea just how much he should hate me."

"Trip—" Jonah's eyes bulged. "You betrayed Trip's dad?" he demanded. "You were the one who sold him out to Creyton? What for?"

"I wanted his spot," shrugged Laban. "We were both in Creyton's inner circle, but Rivers had a bit more prestige than I did. I tired of where I was and sought advancement in Creyton's eyes. Turnabout is fair play, I suppose, but there it is."

It was at that moment that Jonah heard something like a crack. Like a twig, or a spark. He looked here and there but saw nothing. It was subtle, and had the place been any louder, he might not have even heard it. Laban looked at him with confusion.

"What's going on out there?" he asked.

"I—" Jonah frowned. "I thought I heard something. But there isn't anything there. It's just a quiet night is all. Hearing randomness and all that. But that isn't important. Your plan, to turn the Tenths you chose into maniacs if anything happened to you. How were you going to activate that?"

"Not important," shrugged Laban again. "Creyton erased my connection the night he betrayed me—"

Jonah heard a noise overhead. Both he and Laban looked up. Then the hatch open and slammed. Jonah heard someone thundering down the passage, grumbling to themselves angrily. When the feeble lights illuminated the person, Jonah nearly fell backward.

It was Trip. He looked irascible and wielded the longest knife that Jonah had ever seen. It gleamed with the red of his aura.

"What the hell are you doing?" Jonah demanded.

"Fuck off, Rowe!" Trip snarled.

He then began to bang on the glass. Viciously so. "You fucking bastard!!" he bellowed, even trying to cut the blade through the ethereal glass. "You're the reason my mother is insane!!"

Laban spread his hands, moving his head around, and grinning. "Do something about it, boy!" he taunted. "That's right, you can't! Your daddy was a walking crock of shit, and so was that skank he called his old lady!"

"Mother—!"

Trip began to bash the glass in earnest, while Jonah watched, stunned. Restraining him was out of the question...he wasn't going anywhere near that knife.

Then Daniel appeared out of nowhere and grabbed Trip about the arms.

"Titus, no!" he snarled. "What do you think you're doing?"

"He sold out my father!" barked Trip. "What he did drove my mother insane!"

14

Spirit Puzzles

"Titus, stop!"

"Get off me!"

"Final warning!"

"You think I give a f—"

Daniel poked Trip at the nape of his neck. With a grimace, he collapsed to his knees, and fell in the dirt, his knife clattering away. Laban regarded his prone form, grinning from ear to ear.

"Dumb whippersnapper," he said. "Way to teach him a lesson—!"

"Shut up!" snarled Daniel, and then he saw Jonah. "Were you speaking with him, boy?"

"Yes, sir," answered Jonah, "he was talking about being the one that betrayed Trip's father to Creyton. Karin and Markus must have had the tunnel bugged, and they probably told Trip what they heard."

"You're like schoolgirls with all this!" commented Laban. "The boy got what was coming!"

"If you don't shut the hell up," snapped Daniel, "you'll get what was coming to you on the night you got arrested! Jonah, head on back to the estate. Hope you had fun in Las Vegas."

He hefted Trip up into a fireman's carry and headed up the stairs. Jonah followed.

"One moment, Rowe." Laban grinned. "You said there were no masters here. That is not true... there is the Overseer of this estate. Tell me, has he returned from his, ah, travels?"

Jonah hurried away, like Laban was radioactive. He couldn't get away from the bastard fast enough.

"That man makes me sick."

The second that Jonah got Terrence and Reena together in the same place, he told them everything, finishing the story with Laban's last question.

"It's like a chess game, or something!" he exclaimed. "And he knows that I'm not good at it! Every time I think I've made some headway of any kind, he comes from nowhere with a new revelation. Like the fact that he was the one that betrayed Trip's father."

Terrence sought to calm Jonah's nerves by offering him Hawaiian Punch jelly beans. He gave a shaky, incredulous laugh.

"So, Daniel knocked Trip out by poking him in the head?" he asked. "What, did he catch his karate move, or something?"

"Nah," said Jonah. "He hit him with a technique of some kind. But Trip was hot... crazed. Damn Karin and Markus... they bugged the tunnel, and then ran and told Trip everything."

"So, Laban went to the Curaie and turned himself in," he said slowly, "not because it was the right thing to do, but because his own preservation meant more to him than paying the price for getting a big head."

"Can't say it's surprising," said Reena shortly. "You mean can be self-serving that way, no offense."

"None taken," said Terrence and Jonah together.

"It all makes sense," Reena went on. "Now, I mean. Creyton decided to integrate all the Deadfall disciples that hadn't been killed by Networkers or dumped on The Plane with No Name just to be absolutely sure that no one else among them had gone into business for themselves. That explains why he was beyond infuriated when his plan for Praeterletum was hijacked by the 49er."

"He was doubly pissed by that one," said Jonah. "I saw him that night, after all. The 49ers' ambition involved shafting him, the oh-so-mighty Transcendent. If 49er is even partially aware wherever he is right now, I'd bet cash dollars that he's happy to be in the ground, moving every thirty seconds."

"It's a strange thing," said Terrence. "Laban wanted Trip's dad's spot, betrays him to get it, and then tries to rig up a failsafe so that the same thing won't happen to him. It's just strange that he feared the exact same treachery that happened to him."

Reena snickered coldly. "It's not strange when you think about it, Terrence," she said. "People love it when you do well, but not *too* well. The Deadfallen disciples are the same as the rest of us."

"Like hell they are," said Jonah tersely. "We would never set up a failsafe that involves countless people slaughtering each other."

Reena realized what she'd said, and slowly closed her eyes. "You know what I meant. But...all those things Laban said Creyton was capable of doing before you killed him. And he's even more powerful now..."

She trailed off into silence. Terrence's eyes were on his knees. For some strange reason, Jonah was thankful that they weren't putting up a front of bravery, and not trying to hide the fact that they were afraid for him. It gave him a sort of comfort knowing that he wasn't alone in feeling what he was feeling.

"Well, Reena, I can tell you two things that I am sure of right now," he said clearly. "One, I'm ready for Jonathan to get back, and two, I am completely on board with you and damned cipher."

New Year's Eve went by so slowly, many folks started wondering if it was ever going to pass at all. A lot of people had asked their family members to come to the estate. Most said that it made them feel safer. Jonah couldn't blame them. And having all the Decessios around him, including Raymond and Sterling, never hurt. Liz and Nella's family were there, as well. Mr. Manville never spoke too much, but was friendly and likeable, while Mrs. Manville was as sunny-tempered and chipper as her middle and youngest daughters. Sandrine, the oldest Manville sister, was normally not loquacious (a trait that she inherited from her father), but this time, she smiled, conversed, and even danced playfully with Malcolm when Ben-Israel turned on some music. Liz pulled Jonah to the side and explained to him what the deal was.

"She's been offered a graphic design job, and she's decided to take it," she told him. "She's got a pulse tonight because she hadn't cared for being twenty-eight years old and still living in Rome. Now, she's got a chance to leave here."

"Sweet!" said Jonah, who grinned Sandrine's way. "So that's her shtick, then? Graphic design? I thought all of you were all Green Auras."

"Oh, we are," said Liz. "And Sandrine is good, better than me, I think—"

"Oh, stop being modest," said Jonah.

Liz blushed, but she continued.

"Sandrine doesn't really define herself through healing," she said. "She never cared for high-stress settings and sickness."

"Well, good for her," said Jonah, who completely understood Sandrine's desire to not be defined by her aura. But his feeling of excitement for Sandrine dulled somewhat when he saw he frown on Liz's face.

"You're not happy for her?" he asked.

"Oh, I am," said Liz hastily, "very much so! It's just...I don't want my family scattered, Jonah. Not with the mess we're in. If things had been fair, I would have wanted this job opportunity to come up in a time where Creyton and the Deadfallen disciples were finished. I could see Sandrine going up north then because there would be no cause for worry. I want her to advance, I'm in full support of growth and further learning...just...just now right now. Does that make me sound selfish?"

Liz's jade eyes were pleading, but it wasn't necessary.

"I got you," Jonah assured her. "I don't think you're selfish. But Liz, the point of life is to live it. Creyton's already won if we sit here and hide away. And Sandrine is so mild-mannered and unassuming. I doubt she'll have any worries."

Liz looked down, wanting to believe Jonah so badly, but before she could say anything else, a sharp gust of wind distracted them all.

Jonathan was standing in their midst.

His arrival elicited many a gleeful reaction, and several people surged forward to shake his hand or hug him. He looked at the front door expectantly, and someone knocked.

The new arrivals were Felix and Prodigal.

Prodigal was happy to see them all, particularly his specific group of buddies, and Felix merely stood away, aloof as usual. Jonah might have smiled if he hadn't known where Felix had been.

"It seems we all dropped in the middle of fun and expectation," said Jonathan with a smile. "By all means, keep it going!"

Everyone continued to have fun late into the night, but no one was truly tired, seeing as how the night wouldn't truly begin until midnight. Jonah, Terrence, and Reena were festive, but they had a vested interest in whatever Felix and Prodigal had found out. At about nine-thirty or so, they retreated from the noise, and Reena led them to a barely used room near the kitchen. Reena had deduced that once Felix and Prodigal got done briefing Jonathan, they'd want to get away for a while, too.

"What makes you so sure they'll come in here, though?" wondered Terrence aloud.

"It's near the kitchen, doesn't require much walking, and it's quiet," said Reena. "When it comes to getting away, men aren't that difficult to read. They will probably get there the same time we do."

And, shortly thereafter, and to Jonah's and Terrence's utter surprise, Felix and Prodigal arrived at that room within five minutes of each other. Reena gave them a knowing smile, while Felix gave them a look of thanks.

"We knew you three would want to know what was going on," he said. "And we figured you wouldn't be in the kitchen, as it's too peopled, or the art studio, as it's too far." He gave Reena the usual look of respect. "And I'm guessing that you knew we'd come in here, too," he added. "Are we men that predictable?"

"For the most part," snorted Reena. "We've got time before we're missed. So, what's going on?"

Felix pulled an apple from his pocket and bit into it, which Jonah found odd, as there were appetizers galore out there. Felix also placed the bottle Vintage on the table in front of him. "You go, Prodigal," he muttered, his voice much cooler than minutes prior. "I just want to unwind for a moment or two."

Prodigal didn't speak until he polished off some barbecue chicken. It almost seemed that he wasn't willing to talk until he had at least a small amount of food warming his stomach. "The underground is damn near lost." he murmured.

Jonah saw Terrence wince. Reena shook her head.

"Are you serious?" said Jonah. "How? I know we know some of what's going on, but...that fast?"

Prodigal nodded. "Creyton's promised them the moon," he said. "And it hasn't been fast, Jonah. It's been slow, and that was by design. First, it was the clothes and the blankets. Then it was upgraded to jewels. Then it was food; I'd heard that people were going entire weeks without being hungry. For a sazer, that's a huge deal. Creyton, through that Broreamir guy, has been playing Santa for a good long time. All he has asked in return is for them to do thus and so when he says this and that."

"But that's bullshit!" cried Terrence. "Felix, you could have matched them gift for gift. You could have altered the balance of power—"

"By getting all the sazers goodies and saying, 'Follow my lead?'" demanded Felix. "Terrence, as a former homeless orphan, you know that's not how you deal with people! Sometimes, the last thing a poor sazer needs is money." He grabbed the Vintage and looked it over. His eyes ran over every line and curve of the bottle like he'd done so a million times. "Besides, it's not like anyone in the underground would listen to me."

"What does that mean?" frowned Jonah.

"It means I've been ostracized by them," grunted Felix sharply. "They didn't take my arguments seriously because, as a multi-millionaire, I could never understand their struggles. They don't know the hardships I've faced as well. They don't know what I've lost. They only see my money. Now, anyway."

Jonah didn't understand, but Reena sucked her teeth.

"Creyton putting bugs in their ears, huh?"

Felix grunted his agreement. Prodigal looked at the ceiling.

"The dude is a master," he said. "In another life, he could have been a public speaker, the way he sways people."

"Prodigal," said Terrence tentatively, "I didn't want to breach this subject, but the last time we saw you, you said that Abimilech had taken off. Y'all had had a falling out, or something. Were you able to check on him? Is he alright?"

Prodigal's eyes never left the ceiling. "Didn't you hear me talking about Creyton being able to sway people?" he said in a quiet voice.

Jonah shot up from the chair. There was no way. "Abimilech's been turned?" he demanded. "But... that was your best friend!"

"For a long while," said Prodigal. "Since before I took the name Prodigal, and whoever knew me just called me 'Kid.' If Creyton could turn him, there's no telling who else he can he get. I thought that there might be a way to bring him back. I thought there might be a chance for rehabilitation, as Felix calls it. But then stories reached me about him taking parts in murders and tortures. By all accounts, he's enjoying his role as a Deadfallen disciple."

Prodigal looked at the Vintage like he wanted to drink some himself. "Abimilech is the reason why Felix's safehouse was ambushed."

Jonah looked at Terrence and Reena, and then back at Prodigal. "Are you kidding?" he asked. "So Autumn Rose was not at fault?"

"Not entirely," said Felix, "but less so than I previously thought. She did indeed mess up, but it was Abimilech who put Broreamir on her tail, not the unauthorized *Astralimes*. He was the one that told him that she's looking for Jael. The rest just fell in place for them."

A tear slid down Prodigal's cheek. Reena grabbed his shoulder in a comforting way.

"Do any of you know what it's like to have your best friend in the world do a complete one-eighty?"

Jonah had already made it clear that he didn't believe in one-eighties, but at the moment, he remained silent. Felix remained silent as well, but Jonah thought that it probably had to do with the fact that he did not desire to share experiences that he'd had with his own former best friend.

Which reminded Jonah.

"Felix," he said. "Were you aware that Laban was the one who sold Trip's dad out to Creyton?"

Felix's eyes bulged. "Son of a bitch," he muttered. "He was?"

"Yeah," said Jonah. "He revealed it to me, Laban did. Some of Trip's little biddies bugged the tunnel with Laban's cell, heard it, and told him. Trip came out there and tried to break into the cell to murder him. But that's not all concerning Trip…he'd been acting strange lately. All of his friends, too."

"Trip can burn in hell, and his posse right along with him," spat Felix. "He's turned 'acting strangely' into an artistic expression. I wouldn't worry about it."

Jonah nodded, deciding not to say that something still bothered him. He just didn't know what it was.

"Look at the time!" said Terrence with excitement. "It's almost time for the ball to drop!"

The quintet hurried back into the family room, where a great many people had gathered, some holding wine, some holding soda, and some holding tea. Jonah himself grabbed some apple juice and was ready for the final countdown. Everyone shouted out the numbers, and seconds later, there was a loud rash of applause, whoops, and laughter. Bobby swung Liz around, Douglas and Katarina were laughing themselves silly, Kendall and Reena shared a kiss, Terrence jokingly roughhoused with Alvin and Sterling, and Spader darted here and there, hi-fiving people and crying out, "This is the first time I've seen you this year!"

The whole raucous setting calmed enough for an off-key rendition of Auld Lang Syne. As Jonah joined hands with Nella and Magdalena and sang along, he tried to allow the elation to reign supreme. The momentary joy was bliss. Who knew what this New Year would bring? Would it bring blessings? Triumphs? More shit? Even worse shit?

The singing ended, and Magdalena and Nella wrapped him in a group hug. He hugged them back, and tried hard to hope, trying harder not to doubt.

* * *

The good feelings of the New Year lasted for about a week, which was also the length of many people's resolutions. In Jonah's case, it took that long for much of the positivity he'd mustered to kind of wane and his mind to shift back to all the things Laban had told him. The minute he was off from the library on a Tuesday about nine days into the New Year, he was knocking on the door of Jonathan's study, full of questions and maybe a little annoyance.

"When were you going to tell me how far below Creyton I am?" he demanded before Jonathan had invited him to sit down. "When were you planning on informing me that everything I might be, he already is in spades?"

Jonathan looked impassive. "Sit down, Jonah," he sighed. "I've already had to deal with Titus towering while seething about Daniel not allowing him to break into the cell and murder Creyton. I don't want to deal with it a second time."

Impatiently, Jonah lowered himself to the edge of the seat. This wasn't the type of subject he needed to be comfortable for.

"First of all," said Jonathan, "exactly what did Laban tell you?"

Jonah told him as much as he recalled, which, in regard to the comparisons, was just about all of it. Jonathan looked unmoved.

"Tell me, Jonah," he began quietly, "did you expect anything less from Laban Cooper?"

"Never mind that!" Jonah didn't even hide his frustration. "Is it true?"

"It is true that Creyton is powerful," said Jonathan, "but it is also true that *you* are powerful. Particularly in regard to balance."

"Um, Jonathan," said Jonah, measuring his words, "after what I just told you, I'm afraid you are going to have to do a little better that the balance—"

"Jonah, sooner or later, every extreme bows to balance," interrupted Jonathan, sharpness in his tone. "Every single one. Failure is balanced by success. Fear is balanced by courage. Doubt is balanced by faith. And power is balanced by humility. This is true even for absolute power."

Jonah frowned.

"Creyton has gone through life, and even his brief stint in the afterlife, with complete and utter blindness to anything except power," continued Jonathan. "And power is just like money; it benefits you the most when you appreciate it. Take it for granted, and what once was boon can quickly become a bane when it goes through checks and balances. Creyton lost sight of that decades ago. He took his gift and perverted every aspect of it. His actions have resulted in a check…a callback to balance. That is you. Laban views you as weak only because he cannot comprehend power that is tempered by appreciation, peace, and harmony. His viewpoint is a byproduct of the warped teachings of his former Transcendent. Therefore, he is wrong. So, he gave you a litany of things Creyton is capable of. He can be a bully, three cheers for that! Hardly noteworthy, wouldn't you say?"

Jonah said nothing but allowed himself to be cautiously assured. Those capabilities that Laban touched on were scary, there was no point in lying about it. But Jonathan had a way of helping him to understand that there was more to the Blue Aura than just the ability to destroy. True power wasn't entailed by one's ability to take physical life. It was like Jonathan had said before: Being cold, unfeeling, and dangerous wasn't a mark of strength.

He nodded slowly. "I see where you're coming from," he muttered, which was the best that he could give at the present time.

Jonathan seemed to understand that, but also appeared to be okay with it. Jonah was anxious to move on from it now that he had momentarily compartmentalized it.

"You said that you would be back here around Christmas," he said, "but you were out for another week. Was something wrong?"

"Not at all, Jonah," said Jonathan. "I greatly appreciate your asking."

Jonah didn't exactly know where the boldness to ask came from, but he did it anyway. "What have you been doing, Jonathan?" he asked.

Jonathan simply smiled. "That is personal, Jonah," he said. "I do have a personal life, though it is on a different stage from one you might expect."

With a nod, Jonah rose and headed for the door. He paused at it and turned around. A thought had just occurred to him. "Jonathan," he said, "did you get any information on One? Or Two?"

Jonathan's eyes narrowed very slightly, but Jonah didn't sense any negativity. Truth be told, he didn't know what to read from the expression at all.

"Nothing to say as of yet," was all he said.

"How are you coming with that cipher?"

That was the first question Jonah asked Reena in an undertone when everyone was in the dining room at dinner. Terrence rolled his eyes to show his disapproval, but Reena lifted her eyes from her Caesar salad with frustration.

"Slowly," she grumbled. "I have discovered that it's in Phantom Cipher, which may be a little above my pay-grade."

"Phantom Cipher?" repeated Jonah. "The hell is that?"

"It means that it has been done via the language of Spirit," Reena explained. "We hear spirits speak verbally to accommodate us, but they don't have to speak aloud to each other. Jonathan's got it down to a science; most spirits and spiritesses do. Creyton could have mastered it at any time, and probably polished his skills while he was in Spirit."

"Wait," said Jonah, "you're talking about thinking things to other spirits and people?"

"It's not uncommon, Jonah," Reena reminded him. "That was how spirits and spiritesses communicated to us back when Creyton had them ethereally shackled. And the heralds have to intimate thoughts into our minds, as they have no voice. In this case, Phantom Cipher entails an Eleventh Percenter transferring thoughts to paper, having neither spoken nor written a single word."

"There are no words on those papers?" said Jonah in a rather elevated tone, which prompted Douglas and Nella to break off conversation and look at him, puzzled. He muttered a quick apology, flashed a manufactured grin, and then turned back to Reena. "How exactly is there a message, then?"

"Jonah, haven't you been listening?" said Reena. "There *is* a message, but it's in Phantom Cipher. Language of Spirit. I assumed all that I needed was Spectral Sight and a little ingenuity, but it won't be enough. I did more research and found out that I will also need—"

"A Phantom Key," said Terrence with no emotion.

Both Jonah and Reena looked at him in surprise. Upon seeing this reaction, Terrence rolled his eyes again.

"One day, and one day soon," he grumbled, "you too will stop underestimating me."

"No, no, it's not—you know we don't—how did you know that?" sputtered Reena.

"Dad's old colleagues in Spectral Law," said Terrence. "The ones that were behind desks, like he'd been. They were always going on about Phantom Ciphers. I used to always hear them say that an Eleventh Percenter could crack them with a Phantom Key and the proper know how."

"What is a Phantom Key?" asked Jonah.

"It's a book," answered Terrence. "They're usually about that thick," he held his thumb and forefinger about three inches apart, "you know those big walkthrough manuals that they have for video games? It's kind of like that."

"Yeah, exactly," said Reena, vigor in her tone. "Do you know how to get your hands on one?"

Terrence shrugged. "Maybe," he grunted.

"What's up with you, Terrence?" asked Jonah, taken aback. "Why are you acting like that?"

Terrence dropped down his fork and rose from the table, abandoning his lasagna. Alarmed by this, Jonah and Reena immediately followed. They found him in the gym, seated in a weight bench, eyes on the floor.

"Terrence?"

"I don't know how comfortable I am helping to dig through Jonathan's secrets!" he spat out. "This could be some serious shit! It just ain't right!"

Reena settled next to him, quickly shaking her head at Jonah. She probably read in his essence that he was impatient. She struggled for a moment to curtail her own impatience, and then spoke.

"Terrence, I'm not accusing Jonathan of anything," she said, trying hard to be soothing. "I've been here a while, and Jonathan has never kept information from us. Not like this, anyway. I have to admit, it's got me a little scared. Because it means that either he knows and doesn't know how to proceed, or he's protected us from something. I don't agree with being ignorant, Terrence. I'm not made that way. I think it would do us well to be in the know."

"And on top of that," threw in Jonah, "they aren't Jonathan's secrets. They're Creyton's. Jonathan confiscated them. Maybe we can help. Maybe we can have a leg up on Creyton for a change. Isn't that worth it?"

Terrence's eyes remained on the floor. Jonah saw him swallow, and then take a deep breath. "Jonathan's done a lot for us over the years," he said. "If you think that doing this is some way of giving back, then I'm in."

Jonah felt relief. He saw the vigor revisit Reena's features.

"This is excellent," she said. "So, you can borrow one from your dad's old S.P.G.'s buddies?"

"Ain't possible," said Terrence. "I don't think they still have any. But we won't need one of those guys."

"We won't?"

"Nah," said Terrence as he stood. "Networkers have them, too, and just happen to be on speaking terms with one of the best."

15

Patience, (Once Again) Not the Virtue

With the prospect of Terrence obtaining a Phantom Key from Patience, Jonah was able to get a comfortable night's sleep. He knew that Reena would sleep like a baby as well. Although Terrence had agreed with them, Jonah could tell that he wasn't entirely on board. Partially, he could see Terrence's concern. Terrence, as everyone knew, had been burned by a lot of people in his early years. He wasn't the most trusting person because of that, though that stance had softened somewhat once he got around decent people. And sometimes, not even then: Jonah thought about Terrence's friendship with Reena. they'd lived in the same place for over a decade, but they hadn't actually bonded until Jonah came along.

But Jonah was sure that, in Terrence's mind, the trust he gave out had to be reciprocal, and vice versa. They'd strayed from the beaten track more than a few times, but it hadn't even included stealing from Jonathan. Terrence's biggest problem was that right there. Jonah hoped that he could see past his own qualms for the bigger picture.

As it happened, however, Terrence's doubts weren't tested immediately. They didn't see Patience the next day. Or the next. He didn't even come to Sunday dinner. Or the next Sunday dinner.

In fact, they didn't see Patience until halfway through the first week of February. By that time, emotions were in directions for several reasons.

First, Stella Marie had nearly gone into Red Rage when Karin had wondered aloud why sazers would ever breed and make further mistakes. A brawl had been avoided only when Jonathan had spoken to them privately. Neither woman repeated what had been said, but they never went near each other again if they could help it. Another thing that had happened was that Douglas' grandmother had reduced Katarina to tears when she's said that she didn't know how Douglas put her "weak willed ass." Douglas had viciously told his grandmother off, and she, in turn, got angry at him for "taking sides against his family." Jonah and Terrence prayed that Douglas never argued in public with his grandmother. People from afar would never understand that she was a bitch, they'd simply see a young man being insubordinate to an elder.

Jonah, Terrence, and Reena were tense as well, but the reasons were so different that it wasn't even funny. Reena's patience was held together by a thread. She was angry with herself as well; she was a perfectionist and she'd yet to deliver. The lack of the Phantom Key for the cipher was driving her up the wall.

Terrence hadn't really been all that bothered not seeing Patience, or so it seemed. As his heart wasn't fully in the thing to start with, each day that Patience hadn't shown up was day that he'd been let off the hook. With Jonah, his largest concern only had a small part to do with the lack of the Phantom Key.

It had to do with the fact that it was February.

He had to come to associate the month with bad things. His track record with February had not been a great one. The February before last, Creyton had returned from the grave by achieving Praeterletum, nearly killed Jonah, and almost started a war. Last February, Creyton nearly killed him again, and Jessica murdered Mr. Steverson. The month, in Jonah's mind, brought trouble of the worst kind, and he spent each day of the first week of it hoping to avoid some fresh hell. And if getting this Phantom Key prevented said fresh hell, the sooner they got it, the better.

So, Patience's appearance may not have solved every problem, but it solved a few for Jonah and his brother and sister.

It was a Wednesday, and Patience spoke at length with Jonathan. Then he ate dinner, and then relaxed in the den. Reena was ready to throw Terrence into the room, but then Terrence blindsided both her and Jonah.

"You're doing this with me," he said.

"What now?" said Jonah.

"Are you joking?" said Reena. "And if you know what's good for you, you will answer yes."

Terrence regarded them both with impatience and disbelief. "Did you really think that I was doing this alone? Y'all are the ones that want the damned thing, not me!"

"Terrence, you're the one who knows about them—"

"Reena did too, once she did some research—"

"This is your show, Ter—"

"Not if you want to make this thing happen. I'll be damned if I do your dirty work—"

"Shut up!" roared Reena. "Terrence, I don't know why you made this sudden dash into left field, and at this point, I don't care. Let's just get this fucking book before I burst a blood vessel."

The reluctant unit walked to the den. Terrence conjured a polite look, superimposed it on his annoyed face, and knocked on the open door.

Patience sat in an armchair, eyes closed. He drummed his fingers on the arms of the chair as he rested. When he saw who it was, he gave them a fatigued grin.

"Well, well, well," he murmured warmly, "if it isn't my favorite three the hard way."

Jonah, Terrence, and Reena walked inside, and all sat on the chair opposite patience. Upon further inspection of the Networker, Jonah could see that the man was in bad need of a night of sleep. He needed a shave, his clothes looked so wrinkled and rumpled that it looked like they should be atop a dirty clothes pile, and the bags under his eyes would hold groceries.

"You look like hell, sir," he said without thinking.

"Jonah!" hissed Reena, but Patience just laughed.

"It's fine, Reena," he said. "Because it's the truth, after all. As for what you said, Jonah, I feel as though I've been through hell."

"What have you been through, sir?"

Patience put his hands to his eyes. "Vampire activity had increased," he said. "I'm sure that Felix and Prodigal have filled you in about the sazers—"

"Yeah," said the three of them.

"Well, because of the sazer situation, Engagah has outlawed any liaisons with sazers," said Patience. "We are not to get their help with fighting vampires. She's made it an Eighth Chapter crime."

"Seriously?" said Jonah. "Not even sazers with whom you've collaborated in the past? Not even Felix?"

"No sazers." Patience shook his head. "She has already made examples of Witherspoon, Hershey, and Myers for trying to contact sazer friends they've worked with in days past. Shame, really, because we need all the manpower... and woman power—" he nodded at Reena, "—that we can get."

Jonah shook his head in disgust. Felix's words about how the sazers that Creyton had successfully seduced would make all sazers look bad. It was beyond unfair.

"Anyway, with so many sazers now out of the mix, the vampires feel as though they have a carte blanche," continued Patience. "They've been terrorizing spirits and spiritesses, Tenths, and Elevenths. Networker-in-charge Spaulding, my boss, was told by Engagah to create anti-vampire units. A great many of us were assigned lifeblood looter duty while the rest deal with Deadfallen disciples. There are six units, and Engagah put me in charge of all of them."

"Are you kidding?" said Terrence. "You got saddled with anti-vampire duty?"

"Uh-huh?" said Patience. "And there was another part, too. Everyone whose services got volunteered for this, myself included? They have all been people who have a strong relationship with Jonathan. Supporting Jonathan got us this garbage job, while everyone else is business as usual. That's not to say that they have it easy. I mean to say that they get to be home every night, while we are all out all night patrolling for vampires."

"That's fu— I mean, that's just wrong!" said Reena. "So, people have an opinion, and they're given such a duty? And you're really out all night?"

"Pretty much," said Patience, too tired to put coldness in his voice. "That's why you haven't seen me here these past few weeks, or at the Sunday dinners. They've even given us a nickname... we're called The Midnight Children."

As angry for Patience as Jonah was, a strange ripple in his mind noted that the nickname was kind of cool. He filed the distraction away.

"Let me see if I'm getting this," said Terrence. "Creyton, out of one side of his mouth, is spoiling the sazers rotten, and getting them to cater to his every whim. And out of the other side of his mouth, he's telling the vampires to romp and be merry. Why is he collaborating with natural enemies?"

"They have their uses," muttered Jonah. "Creyton will use anyone or anything till they are no longer useful."

Reena must have thought that this was a good time to get to the point. She whacked Terrence's arm, and he flashed her a dirty look.

"Patience," he said steadily, "in light of everything you are dealing with, I truly hate to ask a favor. But at least it's not a hard one."

"What do you need?" asked Patience.

"I wanted to know if you had a Phantom Key," said Terrence, whose words dripped with reluctance.

Patience frowned. "Why do you need one of those?" he asked.

"Um," said Terrence, who looked as though he'd gone blank, "um, well, see—"

"We're interested in Phantom cipher," interrupted Reena.

Now Patience's eyebrows inclined. "You've come across Phantom Cipher" he asked. "Why haven't you taken it to Jonathan? Language of Spirit is his primary language, after all."

"We didn't want to bother him at the moment—"

"Understood," said Patience instantly. "Go get it and bring it to me. As a Networker, I'm pretty good at it—"

"No!" said Reena a little forcefully.

Now, Patience looked suspicious. Jonah could have kicked Reena's foot.

Reena sighed. "Look, Patience," she said, sounding much more composed, "what I mean to say is that while we're greatly appreciative of your desire to aid us, but you have a whole bunch on your plate as it is. You don't need to be exerting what little energy you've managed to regain on us. Besides, if you interpret the Phantom Cipher for us, we will only be knowledgeable of a few things. But if we teach ourselves, we'll have our knowledge, and also acquired a new skill at the same time. It's a win-win."

Jonah had to give Reena credit. She had both acknowledged Patience's ordeal and accentuated her love for knowledge at the same time. In his personal opinion, she'd fixed the emotional slip perfectly.

Patience sat up straight. "Reena," he said slowly, "I've been a Networker for two campaigns, three years. I'm more than aware of when someone is trying to game me."

Reena swallowed.

"However," he said with a sly smile, "In the midst of your gaming, you made a valid point. Gleaning knowledge is very beneficial."

He reached into his pack and pulled out a leather-bound book. He placed it into Reena's hands, who looked as though she'd just been handed the Holy Grail.

"Study it hard, and do well with whatever you're doing," he said with a yawn. "Now, please leave me be. I'm gonna try to get an hour of sleep, and then it's back into the night I go."

"That blows for Patience," said Terrence minutes later in the art studio. "To be give such a bullshit assignment, just because he works closely with Jonathan! I thought the Curaie would have tightened up, 'specially after they started losing their own."

"And Creyton is eating it up," growled Jonah. "People falling left and right, Deadfallen disciples running around like they own the world, and then, there's this business with sazers and vampires. I'm surprised Felix hasn't reddened out and gone on a vigilante spree. Prodigal, too."

"Stella Marie and Autumn Rose might just do that," muttered Reena. "Especially if Trip doesn't reign in his buddies."

She lowered the Phantom Key on her table, pushed her sketches aside, and laid the papers they'd taken from

Jonathan's study next to it. For several seconds, she simply stared at them.

"Do you know how you are supposed to work them?" asked Jonah.

"I have the gist," she said, "but I don't know how long it will take. That's the thing."

"What time frame are you thinking?" asked Terrence.

Reena narrowed her eyes in thought. "Worst-case scenario, a full month," she said. "Best-case scenario, two and a half weeks."

Jonah heard the tone of her voice sharpen just a little, and he knew her patience stores. He tried a different track.

"Can you give us a little insight on how it works?"

"No problem," said Reena, who sounded more than ready. "Go into Spectral Sight."

Jonah closed his eyes, took a deep breath, and willed the curtain to rise and the stage actors to perform. When he'd opened his eyes, he saw that Terrence and Reena had done the same.

"First thing that you have to understand is that people keep secrets for different reasons," said Reena. "Language of Spirit, to an untrained person, is just silence. To the ones in the know, it's thoughts that are laced with words. To determine those, we are unable to use verbal and written language. At least to start, anyway. So, we use essence and intent. Let me demonstrate."

She took a blank piece of paper, focused intently on it for about two minutes, and then threw it down.

"I've just used Phantom Cipher to place a message on that paper for the both of you," she said. "Now if we go back to what I said about essence and intent, we can decipher the message."

She opened the Phantom Key. Every page was as blank as the files and the drawing paper.

"The pages of the Phantom Key are activated by essence and intent, as I've already said," she told them. "My aura is yellow, and therefore, so is my essence." She placed a few fingers on a page, which now seemed infused with a dull, yellowish glow, "and my intent, emotionally, is a positive one. I want to help you out. Now that my essence is in the pages, along with my good intent, I want you to go through the book and decipher my message."

Reena tossed Jonah a pen. His head swam as he began to look in the pages along with Terrence and began writing down letters as they were illuminated in the yellow of Reena's aura color. It was a little harrowing, but Jonah wanted it to work. He believed with everything in him that decoding this crap would benefit them.

"I'm tapping out," he muttered. "But go on, Jonah! You're doing great!"

"Thank you, Terrence," grumbled Jonah, and he continued on.

Fifteen minutes later, he was done. The page read:

HELLO, TERRENCE AND JONAH. HOW ARE YOU DOING?

Jonah took a breath. That had been mentally exhausting.

"Uh-huh," said Reena, who saw the fatigue in his essence. "It's emotionally tiring, too."

"What do your emotions have to do with anything?" asked Terrence.

Reena rolled her eyes. "Have you not listened to anything I've said? Essence and intent! Intention is emotion-based! The Deadfallen disciples could have been angry, happy, sad, devious, crafty, or all of the above. The pages don't produce a damn thing until the intent matches. So, if it takes anger, I have to manufacture that emotion before I touch the page. Sadness, the same. Deviousness, the same, and so on."

Jonah looked at Reena with newfound respect. She wouldn't get a damn thing until she manufactured the emotions that were in the intentions of the pages? But people's emotions fluctuated, even when there was a primary emotion to begin with! "Now I get why you said it would take time," he said. "That takes a lot of emotion and brainpower."

"That and the fact that I can't shut myself away," said Reena. "Seeing as how I have a job, a fiancée, responsibilities, and everything."

Terrence's eyes were wide. Jonah was right there with him.

"For God's sake, Reena," he said, "let Terrence and me help you. That's a whole lot of work—"

"No," said Reena instantly. "When it comes to something like this, my concentration would suffer if I had help. I appreciated it, but I've got this. Just do me one favor: if you see a tense, wired look in my eyes, just leave me alone. If it is a serious matter, of course, let me know. But if you know it's trivial, just leave me be. I will let you know when I'm finished."

Jonah shook his head slowly. Reena looked at the pages and gave them a cold smile.

"Journey of a thousand miles," she muttered, and then got to work.

Terrence was already near the stairs, looking as though his brain was swelling with just the thoughts of the enormity of Reena's task. When Jonah reached him, he whispered to him once Reena was out of earshot.

"We know that Reena is a badass, but I hope that this isn't the thing that breaks her."

"Me too, brother," said Jonah. "Me too."

16

An Old Friend and an Old Place

Jonah was compliant with Reena's request, and he made a point to see to it that Terrence was as well. He only saw Reena during meals and training and at those times, she looked like a shell-shocked veteran. The mechanics of her body worked, but her mind was in a faraway place. Many people, particularly Liz and Del, were slightly concerned, but Jonah told them (with their promise to remain discreet) that Reena was experiencing a bit of burnout and was detoxifying from her stress on her own.

Terrence accommodated her by making her favorite health-nut meals, which wasn't too hard or taxing because there were other people he had to accommodate like that, too. When Jonah did make contact with Reena, he would raise his eyes and flash a questionable thumbs up. She would always nod and return it.

After a couple of weeks passed, Jonah was feeling a trace of impatience as well. He wished Reena would hurry, that was true, but not as much as he wished February would leave. They'd made it to the twenty-first; there were seven days to go. No tragedies at the estate, none of his friends had been hurt. If only this month would go on and leave.

There were more than enough distractions, though. Liz and Nella happily announced that the rose tattoo was finally gone. Nella was ecstatic, embracing everyone all around, and her sister ten times over.

"And you know the best part?" she gushed to Jonah. "Now I can get my dress! And I can try it on and not have to worry about that tattoo on my body anymore!"

Jonah was very glad of it. Now that the tattoo was gone, that meant all traces of her misadventure with Dylan Firewalker were done. Finding Nella, barely responsive, on the side of the road still revisited his nightmares sometimes, and he had to remind himself that she was okay and whole.

Concerning the prom, though, he was happy letting Simone talk to Nella and Themis about that. He sought out Liz later, who smiled when he brought it up. "I'm glad too," she said. "And I pray that she will continue to make smart choices in the future. Ever get the feeling like you want to protect your family from everything?"

Jonah could have had Liz there all day talking about that one, but he knew that she was still sad about Sandrine's relocation, which had happened the day before Reena had gotten the Phantom Key.

"Liz, you don't have to worry about Sandrine," he told her. "She is the most non-confrontational person ever! All she is interested in is working. Speaking of which, how is that job?"

Liz gave him a small smile. "She is already in love with the job and the pretzels," she said quietly. "I just hope it was too fast, you know? Philadelphia is a long way from Rome, you know?"

At that moment, Bobby thundered to the door, grabbing his coat without even hesitating. "Liz, go to the infirmary and get your stuff ready," he said in a cold voice.

"Bobby?" she said, alarmed. "Bobby, what's wrong?"

"I'm about to kill Spader," he growled. "In his infinite wisdom, he asks Doug to teach him golf. That little scruffy bastard lost his club, and it flew into my windshield. I saw it from my room."

He swung open the door as Spader was just about to open it. His eyes nearly popped out of their sockets when he saw Bobby. Then he turned and fled, throwing a quick "Sorry!" over his shoulder.

"Liz, I don't want you to see this next part," he said as he bellowed, "Come here, you little shit!"

Jonah and Liz laughed themselves silly, wondering what would occur first, Spader's pounding or Bobby's frostbite.

Jonah was at the library the next day, using a small portion of his lunch break to snap twigs, as usual. He figured thirty-nine was a good number. Then he sat in his car and went to work on his sandwich, chips, fruit snacks, and fruit punch. It wasn't the most nutritious lunch, but it sure was good.

Paula walked out, waving sweetly at him en route to a Ford Taurus. He acknowledged her with a nod, but not much else. He wondered if she still talked about him to Wally, wondering what they possibly could be saying now. After that night, his co-workers adored him. Sometimes he would smile about it, but it was a bit cold because adoration had been what he was trying to avoid. Months of work, undone with one performance. He sighed.

Knuckles rapped his passenger side window, making him nearly jump out of his skin.

"Wha-?"

"Hey, boy," said a familiar voice from outside the car. Jonah's jaw dropped.

"Mr. Norris?"

"Yeah, it's me," said Elijah. "Can we talk?"

Jonah hadn't responded, still taking in Elijah's appearance. Jonah had only seen him on The Plane With No Name. With his hard, cantankerous disposition, always ready for attack, he was in his element there. In this quiet little parking lot in front of one of Rome's two libraries, however, he looked like an animal recently unleashed into an unfamiliar habitat. Even his clothes seemed wrong. His slacks seemed dull and poorly ironed, but it was nothing compared to his–

"Tank top?" said Jonah, astounded. "Mr. Norris, aren't you cold?"

"It's Elijah, and nah, I ain't cold," Elijah rasped. "This place is Bermuda compared to winters on The Plane With No Name. Can you talk?"

"Uh...yeah, sure," said Jonah awkwardly, getting out of his car and moving nearer to Elijah.

Elijah pulled out a battered cigarette case. "Mind if I smoke?"

"Yes, I do, actually."

"Pah, you can tolerate it. I'll take one drag."

Elijah lit up a cigarette, blew the smoke from his mouth almost disdainfully, and eyed Jonah. "Spirit world's a mess, ain't it?"

Jonah stared at him.

"Well, uh, that's one way to put it," he answered.

Elijah snorted. "Forgive me, son," he croaked, "but that was my poor attempt at small talk, and I ain't good at it. Been talking to turd stains and miscreants too long. I'll just drive right in."

Jonah frowned at this behavior, but he couldn't really fault him for these antics if his only company was ethereal prisoners. Elijah dusted ashes off of this cigarette and spoke again.

"I need you to relay a message to Jonathan for me," he said. "There's a bit of a problem he needs to know about."

"Really?" said Jonah. "What's that?"

"Dexter City, Maryland," Elijah replied. "'Member that place?"

How could he forget? "Yes, of course I do."

"Well, something might be boiling up there," Elijah hinted.

Jonah's eyes narrowed. His experiences in Dexter City had not been pleasant ones, and if something new was "boiling," as Elijah put it, he was going to wind up hating the place even more than he already did. "What do you mean?" he asked cautiously.

Elijah took a deep breath. "Three S.P.G. practitioners were touring the Plane With No Name," he said. "Good kids, relatively new. A little too bright-eyed and bushy-tailed to be doing Spectral Law if you ask me, but oh well."

"They were exploring the Plan With No Name alone?" said Jonah incredulously. "If they were so brand new, why was that allowed?"

"Do you think I'm stupid?" snapped Elijah. "You think I'd let three wet-behind-the-ears, punk kids barely out of Huggies in there alone? I was with them. Along with two Very-Elect Spirits."

"Then what was your problem?" demanded Jonah, matching him. "And what's it got to do with Dexter City?"

"Dexter City was their point to come out on the other side of their Astralimes travel," said Elijah. "Problem is, when they used the Astralimes to exit where they'd been, they didn't reach their destination."

Jonah frowned. This wasn't making much sense. Truth be told, it wasn't making any sense at all. "Did they screw up the location?" he asked. "Were they Astraliming when they had no business doing so?"

Elijah took a long draw off of his cigarette. "Those kids were fine," he answered, "until the Very Elect Spirits with them were usurped in transit. The kids' path was intercepted at that point and I ain't heard a peep out of 'em since."

Jonah stiffened. *Very Elect* spirits got usurped? But they were so high up in the pecking order! How was that possible?

"Yeah, I wondered how they got usurped, too," said Elijah glumly, prompting Jonah to raise his eyebrows.

"Did you read my essence?"

Elijah scoffed. "Heavens, no," he said. "I can't do that; I ain't got that endowment power. I just assumed that's where you were mentally."

Jonah relaxed, but only a bit. "When did this happen?"

"Week before Christmas."

"What?! And you're just trying to get help now?"

"No, boy!" Elijah snarled. "I tried to go through proper channels! The bunch of S.P.G. practitioners I talked to tried to bump it up, but the Networkers are running ragged. I went directly to the Curaie and requested a meet. I only got to see half of 'em, and they said they would 'sort it out internally' or some garbage. They're so damn scared of their own shadows that they can't even bother themselves to look for their own!"

Elijah had gotten himself riled up; he'd even tossed away the cigarette, which must have been accidental, because when he'd composed himself somewhat, he lit another one. "I get that I'm not more than a Gatekeeper," he murmured through a cloud of acrid smoke, "and in some eyes, just a glorified prison guard. But those kids came through *my* gate, Rowe. They disappeared from the East. If they are still physically alive, they need help."

Elijah's miserly disposition cracked, about as much as it could, anyway. Jonah was angry. The Curaie's name was lower than feces in his mind anyway, and the fact that they were willing to cut their losses like that brought them down even lower. He didn't understand those spirits, he just didn't. Jonathan respected all life; he'd even gotten annoyed with them when they'd shown no remorse over Deadfallen disciples losing physical lives. And how could these Oh-So-Special Spirit Guides be so indifferent?

"Alright, Elijah," said Jonah. "I'll tell Jonathan all about it."

Elijah nodded, looking profoundly grateful. "Thanks, kid," he said. "Give Jonathan my regards. And tell him that their Astraliming point was a Greyhound bus station smack in the middle of the city. He or the heralds would find that as good a place as any to start."

Jonah nodded.

Elijah flung the filter away from him. "You're a great one, boy," he told Jonah. "If I'm still here when Omega descends, rest assured that I'll be fighting by your side."

Jonah swallowed. He didn't know what to say to that one. "Right," he managed. "Thanks for that."

But there was a problem. Jonah couldn't find Jonathan. Anywhere. He looked all around the estate. Not a single peep. He couldn't even find Bast. Funnily enough, *that* was what was odd to him. Bast was usually the one holding the fort down when Jonathan was gone. Or Daniel.

Daniel.

Jonah found him near the training grounds in the Glad, with his usual whitewood bow and quiver of arrows. The bullseye had been pulverized. Daniel looked like a man possessed; Jonah had a distinct feeling that he was visualizing Broreamir with each shot.

Without warning, Daniel's head snapped Jonah's way. Jonah actually jumped.

"Is there anything that I can help you with?"

Daniel asked this question in a tone that clearly said he didn't want to be bothered. Jonah got the hint loud and clear.

"Nope," he said promptly. "Not at all."

"So, the Curaie just abandoned them there?" asked Terrence in utter outrage after Jonah told him the story.

"Yeah, I know," said Jonah coldly. "And Terrence, have you ever met Elijah Norris. He is intense, hard, and cynical eight days a week. He is one rough guy. And *he* was bothered by it. One would think that he only cared about the fact that they were intercepted within his Gate, but he might actually give a damn about their safety and that's all there was to it."

Terrence shook his head. "And you couldn't find Jonathan?"

"Nah. I guess he's Off-plane, doing…whatever the hell he does there."

"Bast?"

"Nope."

"Daniel?"

"For all intents and purposes, no," said Jonah evasively.

Terrence frowned slightly but didn't question. He took a very slow, deliberate breath. "You want to do this yourself," he guessed. "But Jonah, you know everyone wants you to lay low. Stay close. Don't go looking for extra trouble and all that."

"I'm a little fuzzy on the staying out of trouble thing, given that I'm a focal point for a supposedly upcoming spiritual war," Jonah responded. "And I know trying to be a hero, Terrence, it just doesn't seem right to leave people there like that. Even if they are S.P.G. practitioners."

Terrence thought for a moment, then shrugged. "Hey, man, I had to deal with someone pinching a coil in one of the damn urinals," he said. "I'll be damned if *that* will be the highlight of my day."

"Sweet," said Jonah. "But there is just one thing. One more thing."

Terrence blinked. Jonah nodded.

"Reena," they said aloud.

Terrence grabbed his steel knuckles. "We uh…" he began shakily, "we may need these early."

They walked down to the art studio like they were descending into the devil's secret lair. When Jonah thought about it, that's what Reena reminded him of when she was laid bare.

And he thought Bobby was bad when he was bodybuilding. They found her with her back to them, two fingers going over the blank pages while her other hand was jotting down letters. She must have sense presences near her because she turned around rather swiftly.

Although Jonah had been seeing Reena at meals, her appearance was still alarming. She looked dog-tired. Her eyes had a tinge to them that mirrored the scarlet in her hair. The bags under her eyes, while not as pronounced as Elijah's, were still prominent. Reena never cared about how her hair was styled anyway, but now it looked like she had gotten into a fight with a blow dryer, and the blow dryer emerged the victor.

"I distinctly told you," Reena said in a quiet, dangerous voice, "to not bother me–"

"Unless it was important," finished Jonah softly. "Think about it, Reena. Look at how much peace and quiet you've had. It's been weeks now. Would I be bothering you now if it weren't important?"

Humanity stirred in Reena's fatigued face as she frowned. Seemingly on a hunch, she removed her dampener and instantly showed concern. "Jonah, what's the matter?"

Jonah told Reena everything that Elijah had told him. He told her about his inability to find Jonathan or Bast, and how he and Terrence sought her help.

"And it might do you good to get away from the cipher," added Terrence. "When we were teenagers, you always told the Elevenths in high school with you that the best way to study was to step away from the subject from time to time."

Reena's deadened eyes stirred with even more life. "You remember that?"

"Of course," said Terrence. "It was good advice for what it was."

Reena moved away from the table and appeared to be somewhat thankful to do so. At least for now, anyway.

"Before we go," she began, "I'm going to need some coffee, black, and vitamin C. And, oh yeah, a toboggan."

They were ready after about a half an hour. Not too many people were around; Wednesday was an "every man for himself night" and Terrence did no cooking. Reena took some time to savor the coffee, and Jonah even joined her for a cup. It was no problem–he'd always preferred his coffee slightly bitter anyway.

Reena obtained permission from Daniel to use the *Astralimes* (neither Jonah nor Terrence asked how she was able to approach him), and two steps later, they were at the Greyhound bus station in Dexter City.

It was a most unremarkable place, particularly at night. Dexter City was a large enough city that the buses ran until one or two in the morning, but most of the people who would be using the bus were already at home, or work, or wherever.

Terrence sighed and shook his head. "You can always tell the quality of a neighborhood by the buses that run through it," he said. "For example, look at that one there, number two. North Orchard Street, it says? Look at those folks. Happy go lucky, smiling temple to temple. But look at number fifteen over there, East Trade Street. *Those* people look like they could sleep twenty more hours. I promise you they ain't riding to the land of milk and honey on *that* bus, believe me."

"Terrence, I must ask you," said Reena. "As interesting as that information was, how exactly does it pertain to this situation?"

"It doesn't," said Terrence, shrugging. "I was just making an observation."

"Save those for later, brother," said Jonah quickly. "We need to find a nice place for Spectral Sight. We can look for some clues or spirits."

"No need for that," said a voice nearby. "You'll be able to see me just fine without the Sight."

They turned and saw the spirit of a middle-aged black man walking toward them. The man was prim and proper in an old-school business suit. It fit his profile so well, he looked as if suits could've entailed his entire wardrobe if he were physically alive. His expression was friendly as stern underneath a black buzz cut.

"Pleasure to meet you, spirit, sir," said Jonah slowly, "but I'm a little curious as to why we can see you without our Sight."

"The pleasure is mutual, Jonah Rowe," said the spirit "My name is Graham. You can see me because I am a Very Elect Spirit. For that reason, Eleventh Percenters can see me without having to resort to ethereality."

"Huh," said Terrence, intrigued. "I always wondered, what do Elect and Very Elect Spirits do, exactly?"

Graham smiled.

"No harm intended, but don't think that is salient information," he said. "Particularly right now. But you are, undoubtedly, here to seek out those S.P.G. practitioners that were taken."

"Well–" began Jonah, but Reena placed a hand on his arm, regarding the spirit with suspicion.

"I don't intend any harm either," she said slowly, "but why exactly are you here? We have been told that the Curaie has not touched this. Yet you, a Very Elect Spirit, are here to help. Explain."

Graham merely smiled again. "I can forgive the doubt," he said. "In this current state of things, a healthy suspicion wouldn't go amiss. I am of the Curaie, Miss Katoa, but I am not one of the thirteen. I do not agree with everything that is said or done. Particularly this, where Very Elect Spirits are usurped and S.P.G. practitioners are abandoned."

"Why has it happened?" Jonah asked.

"The Curaie have adopted the stance that they knew what they were getting into," said Graham. "That may very well be true, but I don't feel that laying down physical lives is an expectation."

Reena's suspicion evaporated. Jonah could see that.

"Can you give us some information?" he asked.

"I can tell you that they are nearby," he said. "The practitioners were with the Very Elect Spirits long enough to have trace amounts of their essence. That might help you find them before it is too late."

"Too late?" said Terrence hastily. "You mean something specific by that?"

Graham shook his head. "I was merely remarking on the sad fact that when you deal with Deadfallen, all things are possible, and not in a good way. You have all been endowed."

Jonah flinched at the endowment. He had only ever been endowed by regular spirits and spiritesses, never by a Very Elect one. It felt firmer somehow, more resolute. It felt like the endowment was sourced by a stronger vein of Spectral power.

"I wish you success, Elevenths," said Graham. "I wish I had done more, but I hope that what you have is enough."

"Thank you, Graham," said Jonah. "It's appreciated."

The spirit nodded and disappeared.

"It's nice to know people in the Curaie have brains of their own," said Terrence. "That 'collective consciousness' mindset thing really chaps my ass."

"We always knew it wasn't everybody, Terrence," said Jonah.

"It's *never* everybody, Jonah," said Terrence in a bored voice, "but rarely do we see the exceptions. We usually see the idiots."

"Guys," said Reena suddenly, "I can feel the essences Graham was talking about. He was right—we aren't far."

Jonah backed off to let Reena lead the way. He had his baton out, ready for whatever may come, but he kept his gloves on so as to not attract unwanted attention just yet. He knew that Terrence had on his ethereal steel knuckles underneath his gloves, ready to rip them off at any time. Reena had her javelin in dormant form in her pocket, but Jonah knew she carried it for sentimental reasons only. Ever since she'd come across an ethereal steel socket wrench in an underground room early last year, she has fallen in love with it and carried it around ever since. Jonah found the whole thing amusing—when he'd seen her with the javelin, he thought it fit her because she was graceful and athletic. But when he saw her with the wrench, he thought that fit her too because for all of her athleticism, she was as prone to bash someone in the face as he or Terrence. It was just one of the complexities that made up his best friend.

A few blocks from the bus station, the environment was rather unsavory. It was strange how, maybe twenty minutes away, there was more repute; but here, it was clear that life just sucked. It felt as if there were an invisible, yet recognizable, line between the haves and have-nots here. It seemed a little obvious here than in other places. Terrence, in the past, had described this place as Americana. Right.

Reena stopped at a corner, looking up. "Corner of Prinesdale and Stony Island Street," she read. "They're here, in one of these houses."

"Awesome, Reena," said Jonah, looking around. "That narrows it down to about twenty."

Reena looked his way. It was pretty dark, but he could tell the blaze in her eyes. "Don't get smart with me, Jonah," she warned him. "This is *not* the time."

The increasing adrenaline had taken Jonah's mind away from Reena's immense stress as of late. He felt a hint of shame. "My mistake," he said. "Sorry."

"A lot of these houses have been left in disrepair," said Terrence, trying to smooth things over. "I've crashed in houses like them before. If you're keeping hostages, ones you want physically alive, anyway, you want them comfortable enough for health, but not for comfort, if that makes sense. Ragged houses offer either/or, never both. So, what we are looking for is a place that will be small enough for a nefarious need, but big enough that ill activities can go unnoticed."

Jonah didn't waste time with fascination, though that was an interesting insight. "I'll bite," he said. "Which house do you have in mind?"

Terrence looked around. "That one," he said, pointing four houses down. "1003 Stony Island."

Reena looked in the direction of the house and frowned. "I'll be damned," she exclaimed. "You might be right!"

"You'll be damned," Terrence grumbled. "How about you'll be blessed?"

"How about we'll be going?" said Jonah. "Keep gloves on though, in case they have lookouts."

It was a good thing that Jonah made the suggestion because near the porch of Terrence's suggested house sat a lone figure. Jonah's expression sharpened.

"I have a plan," he told Terrence and Reena. "It will have to be precise, but we work well together. I need him to stand up, though."

He told Terrence what to do, and Reena too. She nodded, backing off. Jonah could tell the guy was dozing, but the proper noise would shock him if it was random enough.

Jonah crouched holding a small twig in one hand, one of his batons in the other. He glanced at Terrence, who nodded. He looked over at Reena, who gave him a two-fingered wave.

Just has he suspected, the guy's head jerked up and he shot out of the chair. Jonah grabbed his chance, running straight at the guy. The man's attention shifted to him, utterly confused.

"Catch!" said Jonah sharply, and he threw his baton at his face. The guy succumbed to his natural reaction and raised his hands to catch what had been thrown at him, and Terrence ran in, delivering a vicious, ethereal-steel knuckle powered body jab to the gut that had just been exposed.

Jonah hoped that his expectations were right, and they were; Terrence had tagged the guy in the gut so hard that he knocked the breath out of him, meaning there would be no shouting out or cries of pain. It made this next part that much smoother.

Almost in unison, he and Terrence jumped back. Reena used her speed attack, turning the guy in a full circle before he fell to the ground, out cold.

Jonah grinned.

"Sweet!" he whispered excitedly. "The watchman's out, and we didn't even need to unglove our hands!"

"That was great, Jonah!" said Terrence.

Jonah felt rather proud of himself until he saw the angry look on Reena's face, from where she was inspecting the unconscious watchman.

"What's up, Reena?" he asked softly.

Reena looked up at him. "It's Prodigal's former best friend," she whispered. "Abimilech."

The light faded from Jonah's eyes somewhat as he looked down into the unconscious face of the boy who had been seduced by free gifts and had betrayed his lifelong friends, resulting in the murder of several of them He hadn't known him well enough to be heartbroken by it. But he knew Prodigal well enough to be pissed for him. But there was a task at hand.

"He'd better be glad that Prodigal isn't here," he said. "Or Autumn Rose or Stella Marie. Let's go inside."

The door wasn't locked; the door was so old, it wasn't even capable of being locked. Jonah, Terrence, and Reena walked in, feeling that the time was right for them to unglove, revealing their aura-colored weapons. The place was an abandoned mess, with a single candle burning in one of the back rooms. They could see the flame's light dancing outside the room.

Jonah frowned.

"This seem a little easy to you guys?" he couldn't help asking.

Terrence swore softly. "You think we are too late?" he asked.

"Calm down, boys," said Reena. "If we were too late, Abimilech wouldn't have been keeping watch, however sorry said watch was."

Jonah relaxed. Kind of.

"You're right," he said. "Let's see what's in the candlelit room."

They moved as a unit to the room furthest from the door, and walked in. The room was stripped bare; it was the only room in this ragged house that was kind of clean. Clean of junk, anyway; age and disrepair still made it quite unsightly.

There were three people near the wall, bound, gagged, and blindfolded. The two men were tied to either side of an old-school radiator, stripped down to their boxers. The woman, tied near the corner of the wall, was in nothing but her underwear.

They were all underneath broken windows.

Semi-nude.

In winter.

Jonah gritted his teeth. Motherfuckers.

He mentally viewed the term as all encompassing, meant to include the Deadfallen who did this and the Curaie who left them to whatever fate. Angrily, he motioned Terrence and Reena to assist the men, and he headed to the woman, removing his coat.

He dropped the batons, making her jump, and then removed the blindfold. Unsurprisingly, her teary eyes went wide, and she engaged in a muffled scream. Frantically, he did a cutthroat sign with his free hand.

"Here to help!" he hissed. "I'm Jonah Rowe, those two—" he jutted his chin toward Terrence and Reena, "—are my friends helping out as well. Here."

He draped his jacket across her shoulders and removed the gag. She took her first unencumbered breaths in who knew how long.

"Jonah Rowe?" she said incredulously. "You're the Blue Aura!"

"He knows that," said Terrence from nearby, with an impatient bite in his voice.

"Terrence!" chided Reena. "Can you cut a hostage some slack?"

"Oh yeah... my bad, sorry."

The woman only had eyes for Jonah. "Did our superiors send you?" she asked. "Or the Curaie?"

"No," said Jonah simply, having no desire to go further.

That very second, her eyes went wide. "Behind you!" she gasped.

Jonah whipped around without thought, lifting the blue-glowing baton to intercept whatever. In this instant, it intercepted rather sharp fangs which clamped awkwardly on the ethereal steel.

Out of the corner of his eye, he saw Terrence and Reena fighting too. They got the Deadfallen disciples, he got the vampire.

Why hadn't Reena read the essence?

A snarl brought him back to center.

Jonah raised his other baton to keep the vampire from snatching it. The beast tried snapping at his hand, but Jonah hastily drew it back. He attempted a cheap shot, but that only pissed the vampire off. At that moment, they both tripped over something, and toppled in a heap. Jonah pressed his advantage, and struck with the baton, but he knew that the boon was only temporary—

"Let him up, Jonah!" cried Terrence. "I got your back!"

Jonah wondered what Terrence had in mind but rose. Terrence punched the Deadfallen disciple in the face with his steel knuckles, busting his mouth wide open, and spraying blood. He then immediately backed off, looking smug. The Deadfallen disciple looked at him in bloody, yuck-mouthed rage.

"Seriously?" he murmured. "You think I can't take a punch? You think that will stop me? You've only made it worse for your—"

Terrence whistled loudly to silence him and pointed in Jonah's direction. Jonah, who'd been as confused as the Deadfallen guy, looked around and understood.

The vampire that he'd been fighting had completely lost interest in everything in the room... except for the blood running down the Deadfallen disciple's face. The disciple realized his situation, and his eyes widened.

"Oh no," he mumbled. "No... get away from me, you bloodsucking idiot!"

The vampire's entranced expression faltered for a moment when he processed the insult.

"Idiot?" he whispered as he advanced.

Now the disciple looked scared. "Get away!" he bellowed. "Get away!"

He loosed some swear words as he threw himself out of the window. The vampire did the same without hesitation, and

Jonah could hear the disciple screaming in terror as the vampire gave chase.

"Well, his night's only going to go downhill from here," said Jonah. "Thanks, Terrence."

"Doing what I can with what I got," said Terrence. "Reena?"

"No worries," mumbled Reena. Her opponent at her feet with a nasty bump on his temple, courtesy of her socket wrench. "I'm good."

Jonah had already gone back to helping the woman. He finally succeeded in untying her and helped her to her feet. When her hands were free, she zipped up his jacket for a modicum of decency.

"Thank you," she said, her voice much clearer and stronger now. "My name is Amelia Bennett."

"Hello, Amelia," replied Jonah. "You're safe now."

"Because of you," said Amelia. "How is Jerry?"

"Fine," said Terrence, who turned to the guy. "I'm assuming you're Jerry?"

"Yeah," said the man. He had trouble focusing his eyes. "I'm alright."

They all looked at Reena. She looked deeply troubled.

"This man is in Spirit," she said. "He was already gone before we got here."

"No." Amelia moved to the physically lifeless man's still-bound body. Jerry held a hand to his own head, wincing as he regarded the corpse.

"I was hoping that Rich would make it," he said softly. "That damned vampire had been feeding off of him for weeks."

"Feeding?" said Jonah. "Was he going to be turned?"

"No," said Amelia, who blinked back tears. "He wasn't biting him. He was drawing blood with a syringe. The blood loss and the cold must have been too much."

"Why did they have you guys damn near naked?" demanded Jonah.

"He had planned to feed on us all," answered Amelia. "So, he stripped us, and put us near these broken windows. Our blood started leaving our extremities, and going to our hearts, which was where he had planned to draw the blood. That sick bastard said that our blood doing that was like 'salting the meat' for a vampire."

Reena looked pissed at that. "The whole point of keeping you here was to drink you into oblivion?"

"Yeah," grumbled Jerry. "They took us for fun. They intercepted our *Astralimes* travel, usurped the Very Elect Spirits that were with us, and brought us here. It was all for their fun; the vampire got his bright ideas later. Those other bastards even started placing bets on which one of us would succumb first."

Jonah shook his head. "How long have you been here?"

"Since before Christmas," answered Jerry. "Have our superiors been looking for us?"

"It's hard to say," said Reena before Jonah could say anything else. "Spectral Law is being pulled into so many directions nowadays, and we...we just don't know. But it was Elijah Norris who let us know that you'd been taken—"

"The grimy gatekeeper from the Plane?" said Amelia, flabbergasted. "I thought he hated everyone."

"That's what you get for assuming," chided Jonah. "But let's get out of here."

"Jonah," said Reena, "what about this guy here? And Abimilech outside?"

Jonah sniffed. "When they wake up, they can kill each other for all I give a damn."

* * *

When the group returned to the estate, it was very late. Jonathan and Elijah were waiting, along with Raymond, Felix, and Reverend Abbott. Terrence assisted Jerry, while

Jonah helped Amelia. When they were near the door, Amelia stopped him, which made Jonah look at her, puzzled.

"What's up, Amelia?" he asked. "Aren't you cold?"

"Been naked and cold for weeks," shrugged Amelia. "A few more minutes doesn't matter. I wanted to thank you for helping us, man. The Curaie... they've got their own opinion about you... call you everything but a hero. I bought it. Not proud of it, but there it is. And I'm mature enough to admit that I made a mistake. I apologize for that, and I thank you for what you did."

Jonah stood there for a second. He already knew that the Curaie dragged his name through the mud any chance they got. And a great deal of their employees bought their crap. But, at the end of the day, he couldn't judge them for believing what the people they looked to for order told them. It was bullshit, but if certain people, like Amelia, could see the error of that, then he could give them the benefit of the doubt. It was what it was. "I appreciate that, Amelia," he said. "And I am glad I was able to help. I imagine Terrence will want to feed you guys, and Reena will want to get you some clothes. After that, I'm guessing that Raymond and Elijah will want to take you both to the Spirits of Mercy. How about I come visit you there?"

Amelia nodded. "I'd like that."

Jonah nodded himself. That was that.

When Elijah saw Jonah, he gave him a nod and a half-smile. Jonah was appreciative. It wasn't in Elijah's nature to be sentimental, so that acknowledgement was plenty. Felix asked him, Terrence, and Reena if any sazers or vampires were involved in the ordeal, and they flat-out lied. Jonah didn't even feel any guilt about it, either. Felix was on a warpath, just like Daniel. He didn't even want to think about how Felix would react if he found out that a sazer and a vampire, natural enemies, were working together under the auspices of Creyton. And just to cover all bases, Reena had sworn Amelia and Jerry to secrecy in the event that Felix asked them.

They also decided amongst themselves not to mention to Prodigal that Abimilech was involved. Prodigal was a great kid, and they didn't want to tell him things that might unleash his inner Felix.

Jonathan approached them at the kitchen. Jonah, Terrence, and Reena had resigned themselves to the fact that a lecture was on the way. They braced themselves for it.

But it didn't come.

"I'm proud of you all," he said. "And relieved that you came through it all in one piece. But, for your sakes, I will not ask you to relive it all right now. We will talk about it in the morning. Later on in the morning, I mean to say."

Jonah had just enough energy to frown. "Jonathan, we can't talk later on this morning. We all have work—"

"You aren't going to work tomorrow," said Jonathan. "How in the hell would you function through a workday? I'll handle all of it. Good night."

He rose and went away. Jonah came to his feet.

"Finally, a break!" he said with as much life as possible. "Now let's get to—Alvin?"

Alvin walked into the kitchen. He wasn't good for much at this hour, either.

"What have you been doing?" asked Terrence.

"I had to put food in that bastard's cage," murmured Alvin. "I opted to do it since I was awake, because I didn't feel like doing it later. I think that that cell is making him crazy."

"What was your first clue?" yawned Jonah.

"The way he spouts random things," said Alvin. "I told him the awesome things that you guys did tonight, and he responded by saying, 'Three.' Seriously? Spouting out numbers at random? I think he's been too long without the sun—what? What did I say?"

Jonah's eyes were wide, much of the drowsiness gone. Terrence and Reena were the same, and completely ignored the confusion on Alvin's face.

Reena was hard at work on the cipher, they'd saved a couple lives, and despite that, the bastard had hollered out Three?

So much for February passing without a hitch.

17

Smacks and Cracks

Jonah didn't want sleep, but exhaustion took over. Even so, it took some of Reena's melatonin to quiet his mind. When he fell asleep, his dreams were full of Laban's laughter and a debilitating shower of numbers that consisted of ones, twos, and threes. If he got hit by a 1, it was a low-level discomfort. If he got hit by a 2, it was a stronger, lingering ache. But when he got hit by a 3… that was a pain that felt like a bruise or a sprain. When he sought shelter from the numbers, Creyton's face was always there, muttering the same two words: *Halfway there.*

Hours later, he opened his eyes, feeling that returning to wakefulness was a hard-fought battle. He looked at his clock. 10:23 AM.

A one, two, and a three were all included in the time. If that was someone up there's attempt at humor, it was a poor one.

He went downstairs to the kitchen. Terrence and Reena were already there. Terrence was tucking into a bowl of Fruit Loops, while Reena worked on two grapefruits. He grabbed a bowl and reached for the Cinnamon Toast Crunch.

"Don't eat that," warned Reena. "The cinnamon will put you right back to sleep."

With a grimace, Jonah moved his hand to the left and grabbed the cornflakes.

Breakfast didn't take long at all, probably because no one's mind was really on food. When it became clear that their bodies didn't want any more food, they rose and went to Jonathan's study.

Thankfully, he didn't greet them with a full assault of a morning person, but he was bright enough. Once they'd comfortably seated themselves, Jonathan spoke.

"Amelia and Jerry will make full recoveries," he announced. "They were malnourished and dehydrated, but they are doing better. it is highly unfortunate that Rich passed into Spirit before you got there, but I think it is safe to say that there wouldn't have been anything you could have done, even if you had reached him."

"Why's that, sir?" asked Jonah.

Jonathan's eyes flickered with anger. "In addition to the vampire regularly looting his lifeblood, he'd also been the victim of a Bloodless Sever," he told them. "Remember what that is?"

Jonah took a deep breath and nodded. A Bloodless Sever was a dark ethereality technique where an affliction was placed upon a victim that mimicked the same effects of a stabbing or slashing, all without an actual wound. Jessica had done it to Anders Langton, Jonah's former boss, back before he knew she was a Deadfallen disciple. Whatever Jonah's feelings for the guy had been, he still thought that the way he checked out hadn't been right.

"I wish it hadn't been the case," continued Jonathan, "but at least two lives were saved. Preservation of physical life is always a blessing."

"Jonathan," said Jonah, trying hard to keep frost out of his voice, "Elijah told us some really messed-up things about the Curaie. Stuff that was backed up by a Very Elect Spirit we met last night named Graham."

Jonathan's eyebrows rose a bit. "You were assisted by one of the Very Elect? Is that who endowed you all?"

"Yes, sir," answered Jonah. "Why?"

Jonathan looked relieved. "I'm thankful that your adventure lasted only as long as it did," he said, "because an endowment from a Very Elect Spirit can be tracked by the Curaie. If you'd had that endowment for say, two hours more, the three of you plus that spirit who endowed you would have been in very serious trouble."

"Funny you should come back to the Curaie," grumbled Jonah, "because that's who I was just about to speak on. Elijah and Graham said that they viewed leaving those people behind as 'cutting their losses.' They were actively looking the other way with this situation."

Jonathan gave Jonah a resigned nod. "I am aware of these occurrences," he said. "Sadly, I have to tell you that that was just one. The Curaie have been, as you put it, 'cutting losses' left and right. Elijah spoke to you about the Very Elect Spirits that Creyton had usurped?"

"Yeah," said Jonah. "He said there were two of them."

Jonathan scoffed. "No. Those two brought that number to twenty."

"What!" cried Jonah, Terrence, and Reena together.

"Also, Rich wasn't the first loss among the ranks of the S.P.G. He was the eighth. And Patience has lost two colleagues among the Networkers in this whole vampire-chasing business."

Jonah just stared. Terrence murmured, "Jesus." Reena had tightly clamped the two sides of the chair.

"Why are they doing this, Jonathan?" she asked. "Covering up things?"

Jonathan grabbed the Vitasphera and held it in front of them. Jonah could swear that it had gotten darker since the last time he'd seen it. "To hide the fact that they're crashing and burning. People want to believe that the Earthplane and Astral Plane are safe and strong, and they look to the Curaie for that assurance. Meanwhile, the Curaie, as powerful they are, have deluded themselves. I'm sorry to say it, but there it is. They would like to believe that they have been challenged and tested before, and they have. But not like this. There have always been Spirit Reapers, but none have done the things that Creyton has done. The Curaie send out their troops, and they valiantly make arrests and do what they can, but I will assure you that they haven't arrested a single person of consequence. The Curaie is scared, and they can't afford to show the losses they've experienced. It has to be kept quiet, and all damage must be sorted through internally. Or so they feel, anyway."

"But that's stupid!" Jonah exclaimed. "I know it isn't everyone, but still! Why can't they get their heads out of their asses and realize that they need help?"

"Remember what I told you about Creyton during our very first full conversation, Jonah?" asked Jonathan. "You live a certain number of years, and you get to thinking that your way is the best way. And that's Creyton. He is a hundred and seven years old. The members of the Curaie outstrip that by several centuries. Engagah herself has been Overmistress for half a millennia. But don't dwell on perceived ages and time; the salient point is the process. Centuries of experiences. That's a lot of thinking one way. It is not a surprise, nor is it a coincidence, that most revolutions occur with the younger generations."

Jonah exhaled. "You should head the Curaie, Jonathan," he said bluntly. "See how amazing things would be then."

Jonathan merely smiled. "I've always been content right here," he said. "As a Protector Guide and mentor."

"Why did you choose to stay a Protector Guide, Jonathan?" asked Terrence. "I remember that you said that Engagah said that they offered to make you a Spirit Guide, but you declined."

Jonathan shrugged. "Simply wasn't meant to be," he said. "Being with the Curaie wasn't where my heart was."

Somehow, they all knew that that signaled the end of the conversation. With a nod and a smile, Jonathan began perusing the bookshelf. Behind his back, Terrence looked at Jonah and Reena. He held three fingers and pointed to Jonathan with raised eyebrows. Jonah looked at Reena.

With a deep breath, she shook her head.

"Leave it to me," she mouthed.

Jonah didn't do much that day, and spent most of the time watching Netflix, writing, or in the gym. He and Terrence made a point to keep Reena away from the cipher, for one day, at least. They both knew that she was feeling the pressure to crack it now that Laban said Three, but they also knew that the ethereal world would be just as screwed up the next day as it would be that day. They even pulled the Kendall card, reminding Reena that she hadn't spent time with her in over a week. Alarmed by that fact, she headed upstairs, showered, changed, and headed to LTSU to surprise Kendall for lunch.

A lot of people wanted to hear the story of the previous night, and Jonah and Terrence obliged. Sharing took the load off of them at least. When Jonah got to Amelia, Spader grinned.

"Maybe you should ask her out," he suggested.

That was so random that Jonah raised an eyebrow. "Why do you say that?"

"Oh, come on, man," said Spader, "I mean the job was already halfway done; you've already seen her in nothing but her panties—"

WHACK!

"Ow! Dammit!" Spader shrieked.

He grabbed his head and looked around. Katarina was near him, wide-eyed.

"Sorry!" she exclaimed. "Very sorry! There was a daddy long legs on your head!"

Spader rose and walked off, grumbling. Jonah looked at Douglas, who looked at his girlfriend with surprise and approval. Magdalena and Themis weren't even trying to hide their grins. Terrence snickered.

"Katarina, I've been here a lot of years," he said, "and I have never seen any daddy long legs in the family room."

Katarina looked away, awkward defiance in her violet blue eyes. "Well, there was one this time," she insisted. "That's my story, and I'm sticking to it."

Terrence tried to narrow his eyes, but he couldn't do it. He burst out laughing, along with Jonah and everyone else. Still giggling, Jonah rose.

"I'm in the mood for a club sandwich," he said. "I'll be back."

He went to the kitchen, still snickering at the thought of Katarina smacking Spader in the head. He was sure that would be the last time he said something like that, at least around an old-fashioned girl like her.

When he reached the kitchen, he saw Liz, laughing loudly as she looked at her laptop. Upon seeing him, she waved. He grinned at her.

"What's up, Liz?" he said.

"I'm on Skype," she replied with a grin. "Vera just told me about a prank she played on East. Want to say hi?"

The grin fell right off of Jonah's face. He swallowed and went to the pantry. "Nah," he muttered. "I'm just…gonna make my sandwich."

Jonah's one day from work had been enough to rest him up, and after three hours at the library, he felt pretty content. Lunchtime would be soon, and then he'd probably snap some more twigs that could be used as portals.

"Hey, Jonah!" said Smith a few feet away.

"Yeah?"

"Looking forward to spring?" he asked conversationally.

"A bit," said Jonah, making sure that all the monitors were on the main menu. "But largely, no. I prefer the cooler months. They are the ones that are most peaceful to me."

This fact was less true now than it had been in days gone by, but he chose to keep that to himself.

"You sure?" said Smith. "You don't like warmth, longer days, and pools? I thought that you were a summer baby!"

Jonah snorted. He'd actually heard that before. "I am, Smith. Guess I'm an anomaly."

Smith chuckled and resumed his work. Jonah finished replacing returned books to their proper shelves and checked the clock. Lunchtime.

He headed toward the exit when Victoria bumped into him, headed to lunch herself. For some reason, Victoria regarded him rather strangely.

"Jonah, I left the book you put on hold at the desk," she said.

Jonah looked at her. "What are you talking about?"

"You put a book on hold," said Victoria. "I found it and put it at the desk."

Jonah still stared. He hadn't put any book on hold.

"I never ever would have pegged you as one of those who read cheesy romance novels," continued Victoria. "Unless you were looking for tips."

"Oh that," said Jonah. "Well... well, yeah, you got me there. I was looking for ideas, and figured since I worked in a library, I may as well take an advantage."

Victoria's weird look left her face, but she looked at Jonah in all seriousness. "If you want help," she told him, "talk to a woman. No books, no magazines, no websites. You'll just look like a fool."

Jonah nodded, and she patted his shoulder. He then headed straight for the desk. He hadn't put a book on hold. Half of the old books in this library were ones he wouldn't be caught touching, let alone reading. He didn't want to be paranoid, but he was, anyway.

Smith was still there.

"Hey, Smith," he said. "Vicky said that there was a book here for me?"

"Oh yeah," said Smith, snickering. "You're a better man than me."

He slid the book Jonah's way, and Jonah stopped it with his hands, dumbfounded.

It wasn't because of poorly taped over price. It wasn't because of the hulking Fabio-looking guy with his arms around a scantily clad, slavish-expressioned brunette.

It was the title.

In fancy, cursive script, were the words *Halfway There.*

* * *

Jonah had his "nothing is wrong" mask down to a science nowadays. He was thankful that he spent so much time around Tenths because it allowed him to keep his nuances sharp.

But he flew home when his shift was over. He even kept that infernal book.

He had heard "Halfway There" in a dream. He hadn't said it aloud. Not to anyone. It had just happened a few days ago.

There was no way that it was coincidence that someone had put a book in hold with that title.

No way.

A distraction in the driveway shifted his thoughts when he reached the estate.

Among the cars was a black SUV.

He knew that SUV well, although he hadn't seen it in a long while. What was he doing here?

He hopped out of the car and hurried inside.

Seated in the family room, with Jonathan, Daniel, and many others, was Gabriel Kaine.

He rose with a smile. Facially, he'd aged just a bit, his hair had grown out some, and he had the beginnings of a beard, but otherwise he was the same as Jonah remembered.

"Jonah," he said, and Jonah's eyes narrowed because he'd forgotten that off-putting deep voice, "nice to see in one piece."

"Same here, Gabe," Jonah replied. "What are you doing here?"

"Just passing through," said Gabriel.

"Nope," said Jonah. "Try again."

Jonathan laughed. Gabriel looked a little sheepish when he smiled.

"Alright, then," he said. "I was wondering how you guys have been holding up. It's rough out there, and I wanted to check on you all."

At that moment, Terrence came out of the kitchen.

"Food's ready," he announced. "It's just leftovers, but they'll hit the spot just the same. And yes, Daniel, I made toast."

The people that were present rose and headed for the dining room. Jonah approached Terrence.

"This was a surprise," he mumbled.

"Yeah, it was," Terrence mumbled back. "More of a surprise that he drove all the way from Florida and didn't use the *Astralimes*."

"Where is Reena?"

"Back in the studio, with that damned cipher," Terrence grumbled. "I wonder what will crack first; her, or that code."

Jonah was right there with him, but he knew that when Reena got into her stride, no one could deter her. No one.

Themis attempted to sit near Gabriel, but Nella grabbed her arm.

"Forget it, girl," she said bluntly. "These people are special, and not in a good way."

Daniel regarded Gabriel warily, but he was like that with strangers anyway. He stood near the door, bow and arrow close to him, while he ate buttered toast from a napkin. As Jonathan had no need to eat, he stood nearby, but his guard was down a lot lower than Daniel's.

"Tell me, son," he said to Gabriel, "have things improved at Sanctum Arcist since the sanctions were lifted?"

Gabriel snorted, more derision than humor in it. "Yes and no," he said. "The Curaie didn't officially get off of our backs until Creyton started raising hell. We can at least defend ourselves now, as the weapons and ethereality restrictions are gone. But once the Curaie gave us back our freedoms, a bunch of people just left."

Bobby tilted his head. "Defections to the Creyton's side?"

"A few," said Gabriel, "but mostly people just went home because they weren't willing to follow me."

A collection of groans rippled across the table. Jonathan's brow furrowed. Jonah just shook his head.

"They blame you for what happened to Gamaliel and G.J.?" he asked.

Gabriel snorted again. "If only," he said. "No one took sides with the Network, but they treated me differently. Apparently, being a stool pigeon proved that I couldn't be trusted."

Jonah grimaced. Gabriel's father and brother had gathered several residents of Sanctum Arcist and created a cabal to do some very nasty deeds. Gabriel had gathered evidence against them but had only been able to bring his findings to light after his father and brother had been murdered. A bunch of the idiots at Sanctum probably felt that good names had been besmirched.

"Wow," muttered Liz, "so much for family. Gamaliel said that your counterparts could be trusted to the gates of hell."

"I'm trying not to judge people too harshly," said Gabriel. "Fear is a powerful motivator. Everyone trusted Pop, G.J., Iuris,

Cisor, all of them... then they turned out to be vastly different from what they originally thought. No one really knew what to think. The Curaie cracked down on us, and they still see fit to blame us for the actions of my dad. People didn't know who to trust, and, as Pop and G.J. made a point to belittle me every chance they got, a bunch of folks didn't see the benefit of working under me. Can you blame them? Who'd want to be aligned with a—"

"You are not a failure, Gabriel," said Jonah suddenly, turning many heads his way. "You got beat down all of your life, then you do the right thing, and that makes you a failure? No. It makes you a hero. A far more prominent hero than your dad and brother, no offense. I'm just saying that you're alright in my book. Doesn't matter if what you did wasn't popular in some people's eyes. It needed to be done."

Jonah didn't mean to get worked up, but he'd come to respect Gabriel after everything he'd gone through. It wasn't his fault that half of Sanctum Arcist were a bunch of turds. At the same time, he was thankful that he was an estate resident. None of his friends would abandon the place like that. That knowledge was more contenting than just about anything else.

"Well said, Jonah," said Jonathan, and a murmur of agreement went around the table. Trip shook his head and rose.

"I need a cigarette," he said. "Forgive me if I'm gone awhile."

Gabriel barely registered Trip, looking at Jonah.

"I greatly appreciate that, man," he said, "no wonder Rheadne still talks about you all the time."

Jonah felt heat in his face. He glanced at Terrence, who rolled his eyes. "Does she, now? Is she, uh, she one of the ones who stayed?"

"Of course," said Gabriel. "Penelope, too. And Vaughn, Michael, and Aloisa. A bunch are still around. June Mylteer still shows up sometimes—Reena!"

She had appeared at the top of the stairs from the art studio. Once again, her hair was in shambles, and she looked fatigued. But she had on a welcoming face when she saw Gabriel.

"Hey, Gabriel," she said. "Hadn't even realized you were up here!"

"Reena?" Jonathan looked and sounded concerned. He wasn't the only one looking that way. "Are you alright?"

"Yeah," Gabriel frowned at her, "are you working hard, or hardly working?"

Reena shrugged. "One's hard work is another person's easy task," she said. "It's all about perspective."

Jonah watched her intently. Reena brought up her hands so as to pull back her hair. As he watched, she, very surreptitiously, beckoned with her index finger. Then she turned.

"Just wanted to stretch my legs," she said. "Nice seeing you, Gabriel!"

She headed back downstairs. Jonah glanced at Terrence, making sure they were on the same page. Terrence nodded.

After a few minutes, they both stood up.

"Need to check on something," said Jonah. "Please keep on talking up here."

"Yes, please keep talking," murmured Themis, looking Gabriel's way. "I love the sound of your voice."

Jonah and Terrence walked down the basement stairs as casually as possible, so as not to draw attention. Even so, Jonah felt Jonathan's eyes on his back the whole time. He didn't acknowledge it.

Reena was waiting for them at the base of the stairs.

"Thank God," she said. "I hoped that the two of you caught it."

"Reena, you look terrible," said Terrence, looking worried. "I swear, you would scare Freddy Kruger right now—"

"Shut up, Terrence," said Reena instantly. Her voice was tense and focused. Terrence instantly did so. Jonah looked at her.

"Reena? What's—?"

"I've cracked it," she said. "I've cracked it, and I want you both to come with me. You need to see this."

18

Six

Jonah almost completely forgot about Gabriel and his troubles at Sanctum. He had no doubts that Terrence probably did, too. They followed Reena to her art studio, where she practically resided for the past few weeks.

Reena's painting stood as majestic as ever, but her table was a complete mess of scratch paper, bone-dry ink pens, and pages full of numbers and words. She turned to face them, looking so frazzled that Jonah would have offered her a drink had she been a drinker.

"Right now, I am so taxed emotionally and physically that I don't know what to do," she said. "I have had to mimic essences and intentions full of anger, malice, ambition, deviousness, savage pleasure, and, in some cases, even fear. If I have been a bitch, that's why. But I have what we wanted. I know what we wanted to know."

Jonah knew that Reena had to be handled delicately right now, but he almost couldn't contain his patience. Creyton and the Deadfallen disciples, not to mention Laban, held so much information over their heads. It would be nice to achieve some sort of equal footing somewhere.

Reena went to the mess at the table and shoved it all to the floor. She then reached into a nearby drawer and pulled out the Phantom Key and huge stack of paper that was much neater and more concise than the scratch paper on the floor. She then stretched out several sheets on the now-empty space, including the seemingly blank files. Jonah tried to peer over, but she must have sensed his presence, because she rounded on him.

"Uh-uh," she snapped, "eyes on me. If you take even one thing out of context, you'll be so far behind that you won't even know it."

Terrence looked uncomfortable, and he hadn't even tried to look over Reena's shoulder. "Reena, I still have strong feelings about this," he said. "This feels like we are looking into Pandora's Box, or something."

Reena slowly turned her eyes to Terrence. It was clear to Jonah that she had been recreating emotions for so long, she was trying to remember how to do patience. "I have already told you, Terrence, that I understand your concerns," she said. "Your objection is noted, trust me on that. But if you don't hear what I've discovered, you will regret it. I promise you."

Her tone was so ominous and serious that Terrence raised no more objections. Vocal ones, anyway. Jonah was ready, and his patience was nil. But something told him that Reena wasn't procrastinating for dramatic purposes. She was afraid of what she'd seen. So, behind the impatience, he felt concerned.

Finally, it seemed that Reena was ready. She turned around to face them once more. "I have been working hard, as you both know," she told them. "After Alvin said that Laban said the number Three, I felt a crazy sense of urgency—"

Jonah had half a mind to tell Reena about that crazy dream and the book title, but he had the distinct feeling that if he interrupted her, she'd attack him. He didn't like his chances, given the mood she was in at the moment. These thoughts made him nearly miss what else she said.

"—that would not be sated until I reached my goal. And now, I have."

She reached behind herself and grabbed the blank files. Jonah and Terrence regarded them.

"It turns out that these pages concern something called The Season of Omega," she revealed.

"What do you mean, Season of Omega?" said Jonah. "I've heard that before; Laban said it."

"Yeah," answered Reena. "These pages state that we're in that season now. And before Omega can happen, there are a certain number of events that will occur."

"Yeah?" asked Terrence. "How many?"

Reena took a drink from her water bottle, and then steadied her breath. "Six."

Jonah frowned. Six events, during the "season" of Omega? What, did Creyton feel like he had to unleash just the right amount of drama before he dumped true hell on them?

Reena beckoned them nearer to the table, where her pages were.

"This took a lot of trial and error," she revealed, "because manufacturing the emotions to get the codes and letters was only the first part. Stringing them together to get the messages was another matter. But now, I'm ready to show you."

She pointed to a page where she'd drawn a picture of two tenterhooks linked together. "The first event, according to these pages, is the Allegiance," she said. "The second is the Inquisition, and the third," she pointed to a drawing, "is the Victory."

There was something in Reena's voice that made the aspect of victory sound like anything but. Jonah looked at the symbol, which seemed to be a hand raised in victory, but Reena had outlined it in orange. He raised questionable eyes to her.

"What's the deal with the orange hand?"

"That one was tough," said Reena with a grimace. "The codes wouldn't even register until I manufactured sneakiness and craftiness. So, I took that to mean that the victory was false in some way. So, I colored it orange to signify the 'victor's' ignorance."

"Wait, what?" said Terrence, furious. "Orange means ignorance? What the hell! My own aura is orange!"

"Terrence, colors have all kinds of meanings!" snapped Reena. "It's not like it's a universal truth, it's just an interpretation! It might have even been because someone was lazy and slapped a random color to one meaning! Besides, even if it is an aspect of your aura color, it could be a negative one. Everything has a dark side; my aura color does, and I'm certain Jonah has long since tired of hearing the light and dark aspects of the Blue Aura. It doesn't mean *you're* ignorant. Not at all."

Terrence still looked a little miffed, but also seemed to have gotten the point. Kind of. Jonah was slightly ashamed of himself, but he was more interested in moving on.

"What's Four?" he asked.

"Four carried no discernible symbol," said Reena, "but I decoded the event to mean the Attempts."

"Attempts?" repeated Jonah. "As in, plural?"

"Yes," said Reena. "That one took some time, too. When I decoded the word, the essence I felt—and had to manufacture—was kind of like a vacillation between certitude and doubt."

Jonah's eyes narrowed. "So, whatever these Attempts entail, they can go either way? Success or failure?"

Reena nodded. "I think so."

Terrence lowered himself into a chair. "Well, given that these are Creyton's files, one would think that whatever havoc it is would lead to success. For him, anyway."

"I don't think that it particularly matters either way," said Reena, and, once again, there was something in her voice that bothered Jonah. "Because Five and Six are the ones that really concern me."

She actually touched the next piece of paper, so that the words appeared in addition to the symbol already on it. It was a snake whose head was in the process of being forcibly severed from its body.

"Wait a minute, Reena," said Jonah. "Why do you have to touch the word for it to appear? Will it disappear if you stop touching it?"

"Yes," nodded Reena. "I guess that some of the ethereality used in the cipher transferred over to the decoding. It's powerful stuff, Jonah. Trust me."

Jonah looked at the illustration again, and the word beneath it. "The Cut," he read, and then raised his eyes to Reena.

"The Cut?" Terrence, who'd backed off a bit, moved forward to see it. "I'm guessing that doesn't mean a layoff, huh?"

Both Jonah and Reena looked at him. He grunted in resignation.

"I've said it once, and I'll say it again," he mumbled. "What are we without hope?"

"And last, but not least, this one." Reena touched the last sheet, which had an illustration of bits and pieces of wood. "Six, which is the Splinter."

Jonah's eyes narrowed. "The Splinter."

"The Splinter," said Reena. "These are the events that supposedly will happen before Creyton feels the playing field will be ripe for Omega to descend."

"Well, that's just amazing," said Terrence. "We've looked into Pandora's Box, found numbers, and have no clue what to make of them."

"Jonah?" said Reena suddenly. "What are you thinking?"

Jonah had gone into his mind. His brain was working a little hard, but his face was a mask of calm. He must have looked near catatonic to his friends. "I know what to make of these events," he murmured. "Or some of the numbers, anyway."

Jonah was sure that he was right, but it was both liberating and unnerving at the same time. He looked at his brother and sister.

"Explain," said Terrence unnecessarily.

"One was the Allegiance, right?" said Jonah. "Well, Laban said the number One right after Jonathan brought him here."

"But that ain't an allegiance!" said Terrence. "We didn't team up with Laban; he was a prisoner! Still is!"

"A prisoner that Jonathan pressured to spill information," Jonah reminded Terrence. "That requires some sort of togetherness. It really is an allegiance. Two was the Inquisition, which, in my mind, has to mean the time when I asked Laban about One. It means that I was on the path with my questions, maybe."

"You're grasping now, Jonah," said Terrence, who shook his head. "This Inquisition involved you simply asking Laban a question? That's not a big enough event. Makes zero sense."

"It makes perfect sense, Terrence," said Reena quietly. "Jonah's inquiry meant that he was intrigued. Hooked. And Jonah, when you're hooked, you see things through. And remember, we had to see this one through, because we weren't going to get answers any other way."

Terrence closed his eyes. "Fine, whatever. What about Three, then? This so-called 'ignorant' Victory?"

That was the one that had Jonah a bit curious. "Not pretending to be a paragon of knowledge here," he said, "but the first thought that came to my mind was what we just did in Dexter City. But why would it be false in any way? Was it because we were able to save two out of three?"

Reena shook her head. "I'm going to stab in the dark along with you, Jonah," she told him. "I think it's viewed as false because, at least in the Deadfallen disciple's eyes, we didn't do anything noteworthy. We saved two people, but so many people are falling left and right. Tenths and Elevenths alike. Besides that, the two people we saved were people that the Curaie had already written off. Our thinking is, *we saved two people, great!* and they're thinking, *They saved two physical lives. Meh, whatever.* I could be wrong, but I doubt it."

"I doubt it, too," said Jonah. "It would be just like them to view two lives as insignificant."

"Yeah, it would," said Terrence. "And that leaves those Attempts, the Cut, and the Splinter. Halfway there. I do not like that."

Jonah gritted his teeth. Terrence triggered that memory. "Terrence, Reena, there is something I haven't told you," he announced, and told them about the dream, and the conveniently titled book.

"And before you ask," he said as he concluded, "I know for a fact that none of my co-workers are spies of any kind. They are all about as unremarkable as they come."

Terrence whistled. "Fools messing around your job again," he muttered. "Again. You can't get a break on discount, can you, Jonah?"

"You might want to ask Jonathan to make sure there are protections around the library," suggested Reena. "He'd probably need to do that directly, because being on the Networker's grid nowadays is about as useful as..."

Reena's voice trailed off, and she began to keel forward. If Jonah and Terrence hadn't caught her, she'd have slammed face-first on the floor. She was out like a light. Jonah had no idea how many hours of sleep she'd gotten, but all the work had finally caught up with her. Terrence cracked a smile.

"You know, I'm actually glad," he said. "Maybe all the cogs and bolts inside her will right themselves now."

"Yeah," said Jonah, who placed one of Reena's arms across his shoulder. "I think this discussion is done tonight."

As if in response, Reena began snoring lightly.

"On second thought," he murmured, "the conversation is done for the next few nights."

19

Karma

The problem was, Reena was out. She didn't even move in her sleep. Jonah and Terrence hadn't worried the first day, but after she slept through a full second day, they were a bit concerned, and asked Liz to check on her. Liz did a thorough inspection while spiritually endowed, moving green-gleaming fingers across the entirety of Reena's body. When she straightened, she looked baffled.

"This is the severest case of exhaustion I have ever seen in my physical life," she announced. "I've ascertained that over the past several weeks, Reena's only had twenty-six hours of sleep."

Jonah looked at her, astonished. "Twenty-six hours?" he breathed.

Liz nodded, and splayed her fingers across Reena's head again. "It seems to have been intermittent, too," she revealed. "It's like Reena was going for bunches of time in some kind of forced insomnia."

"What?" frowned Terrence. "But she was going to work and everything! We saw her at meals!"

"I know!" Liz shot back. "I was there! I thought something wasn't right, and that was before you guys went to Maryland.

Then you had to release a spiritual endowment from a Very Elect Spirit, which was probably draining as all get-out—"

"But we all got sleep," said Jonah. "Terrence and I were good—"

"That's you," said Liz who looked troubled, "but Reena wasn't good. She has zero energy. I'm...I'm a little out of my element here. Jonathan needs to see her."

"Huh?" said Jonah without thinking. Terrence's eyes widened.

Liz hadn't noticed, as her attention remained on Reena.

"Yeah," she said, "he'll need to do something. Let me go get him."

Jonah could have mentally summoned Jonathan, but Liz was very disappointed in herself for not knowing how to help Reena. She probably needed to walk off some of the negative feelings she had about herself.

But Jonah had a new issue.

Terrence glared at him, livid. "She did this for you, Jonah!" he whispered angrily. "She has damn near killed herself trying to help you out! I *said* that this was a bad idea!"

Jonah looked at Terrence in disbelief. "You're blaming me?" he demanded. "Terrence, Reena was the one running herself ragged. I tried to stop her!"

"She did this for your situation, Jonah!"

"I didn't want her body to give out!" snapped Jonah. "I was confused as hell, just like you! And you know that's not a lie!"

"I ain't saying it is," said Terrence coldly, "but you have to make this right, Jonah. I told you both that this was foolishness. And you just sat there, convinced me that it was all for the greater good. You said that it wasn't Jonathan that we were spying on, it was Creyton—"

"You need to dial it down, Terrence." Jonah was no longer whispering. "This is not my fault. I'm not trying throw Reena under the bus or anything—"

"Then don't even bother saying what you're about to say, then!" snarled Terrence.

"I will do nothing of the kind!" spat Jonah. "Reena herself was the one who stole those pages from Jonathan's study—"

"I beg your pardon?" demanded a voice.

Jonah froze. Icy tendrils of fear laced the interior of his body. Terrence himself looked as though he'd been encased in stone.

"Turn around and face me, Jonah."

Swearing inwardly, Jonah did as he was told. Jonathan stood there. His face was clear of emotion, but there had been no need for it, because his voice contained it all. Liz was behind the Protector Guide, wide-eyed and fearful. She didn't understand, but she clearly knew that Jonathan was pissed.

"Elizabeth." Liz actually flinched when Jonathan said her name. "Return to your schoolwork. Thank you for hailing me."

"Y-You're welcome, sir," said Liz, and she hurried off.

Jonathan brought his eyes back to Jonah and Terrence. "What was that, Jonah? What did you say just now?"

Jonah closed his eyes. "Reena took some papers from your study, sir," he said.

Jonathan blinked very slowly. "The ones that were confiscated from Bryce Firewalker's tattoo parlor?" he asked quietly.

Jonah hesitated for just a moment. "Yes, sir."

Jonathan closed his eyes and took a leveling breath. "Report to my study," he said, his voice still dangerously quiet. "Do that now. No deviations, and no pit stops. Straight there and wait for me. I will help Reena."

Jonah headed out of Reena's room for the study. Why the hell had he started using his regular voice? He just had to run his fat mouth. If he had had half a brain, he would shut Terrence down, and told him that then was not the time to discuss it. It probably would have been a fail, but he could have tried. Instead, he stood there, allowed himself to get riled, and now they were in trouble.

Jonah hadn't even realized that he'd gotten to his destination so quickly. He opened the door, not even paying attention to Terrence behind him or the Vitasphera. Truth be told, he was kind of afraid. A part of him tried to find that laughable. This wasn't the principal's office, and he wasn't a kid.

So why did he feel fear?

The answer was simple.

Because it was Jonathan. That was all there was to it.

Terrence hadn't said a word the whole time. Jonah didn't know whether or not if that was because he was angry with him, or because he was scared, too.

But what about Reena, though? Liz said some type of forced insomnia. That didn't make sense. Not entirely. Reena was a perfectionist; she would work until she dropped. But she had as much common sense as she did book sense. She had even said that she had a life, fiancée, and responsibilities to attend to. So, for her to run herself straight into the ground like this... something wasn't right. Reena had a strong work ethic, but she had never let it get in the way of her life. Especially now that she had Kendall.

This was in Jonah's head when Jonathan appeared in front of them.

The number of times that he had seen his mentor angry were few, but legendary. But they had never concerned Jonah personally; the most he'd gotten was sternness. But by the look in Jonathan's eyes, sternness wouldn't be the case here. Jonah cleared his throat. Time to man up.

"Jonathan, before you say anything," he began, "Terrence is innocent in all this. He disagreed from the very beginning."

"Don't do that shit, Jonah," said Terrence instantly. "I'm a part of this just as much as you."

Jonah gritted his teeth. Tried to save his ass, and he shot it down. *Fine,* he thought, *you want to be destroyed with me, be my guest.*

Jonathan lowered into his chair, having not even blinked. He carefully placed his hands in front of him on the desk.

"Explain." His voice was clear and cold.

Jonah glanced at Terrence. How the hell could he start? He couldn't very well say that Reena had called him a liar. But he had to say something. "We were still concerned about One," he ventured, "and Two. Jonathan, it was bothering me—"

"So you've said," said Jonathan shortly. "Try again."

Jonah blinked. "Well, we'd asked you about it, and you told us that you didn't know what it meant—"

"—and immediately after that, I said I would obtain more information, and told you not to worry about it," snapped Jonathan. "As I said before, *try again.*"

Jonah swallowed. Two strikes. He had to fight the urge to tell Terrence to feel free to say something at any time, since he wanted to be Billy Badass and stay in here when Jonah tried to cover for him.

"Alvin told us that Laban said 'Three' after we were done in Dexter City—"

"A fact that is immaterial to the matter at hand," dismissed Jonathan, "seeing as how Reena had been working those files for weeks before that."

Jonah stared. "How did you—?"

"Reena's very being was rife with a preternatural fatigue for about that length of time," said Jonathan. "Now, Jonah, Terrence, I will grant you fair warning. You would do well to tell me the whole truth, with no sugar coating or prefacing. Further stalling will piss me off even further."

Why did that sound so frightening? What would be the consequence if the beating around the bush continued? Jonah didn't want to find out. But like he told Terrence before, he didn't want to throw Reena under the bus.

"Jonathan, here is what happened." Terrence finally spoke up, with resignation in his voice. "Jonah asked you about One, and you said you had no idea. And Reena...Reena didn't believe that was truthful. She used her essence reading to find those papers, and was hell bent on cracking the cipher."

Jonah winced, but when he thought about it, he couldn't even be angry at Terrence. Jonathan wanted the truth, and there it was.

Jonathan contemplated Terrence. "That cipher required a Phantom Key, as it was in Phantom Cipher. Where did you acquire one?"

"Patience," both men murmured.

"Was Halloran aware of what the two of you were doing?"

"No," said Jonah.

Jonathan took a deep breath. "How far along did Reena get with it?"

Jonah sighed. "The whole thing," he admitted. "She found out that there are Six events that have to happen that will supposedly precede Omega."

Jonathan looked at them, and then shook his head. "Jonah, Terrence, when I give you a rule, I expect you to abide by it. That is not because I view my role as a dictatorship. It is never my intention to keep you on a leash. It is to protect you. Do you want to know why I took those papers as soon as you all returned here from the tattoo parlor that night? It was because there was a dark ethereal trap affixed to them. A curse, for lack of a better term. The more you handled them, pored over them, riffled through them... the more they drain. The power of the trap could be intensified by the focus and concentration. A victim will begin to become listless and lethargic—begin to lose their sense of self. Large periods of time pass without food, sleep, and personal interaction. If it goes on long enough, the person can literally be drained of their physical life. That is why I lied. That is why I deterred you from pursuing those numbers."

Jonah was suddenly overcome with fresh terror. "Reena...what about her—?"

"Reena is blessed," said Jonathan. "A series of small miracles kept her physical life from ebbing away. When she stopped for meals, however rare and small they were, her essence would rejuvenate her somewhat. Time with Kendall helped as well, as positive feelings such as love can be powerful healing agents. But she benefitted the most by receiving the spiritual endowment from Graham. It was a shot in the arm if you will. I infused her with as much replenishment as she could take. Were she a teacup, she would be overflowing into the saucer right now. She will probably sleep a few more days, but she will make a full recovery."

Jonah closed his eyes, relieved. The mere thought of what might have happened...he shut his mind to it. It was unnecessary to think about it. Reena would survive.

When he opened his eyes, Jonathan looked directly at him.

"Terrence?" Jonathan's eyes remained on Jonah. "Was it true that you disagreed with the plan the entire time?"

"Yes, sir," said Terrence.

"But you still admit to taking part in it?"

"I do, sir."

"Very well," said Jonathan. "You are ethereally grounded, for sixty days. No endowments, no ethereal travel of any kind, and no Spectral Sight."

Terrence's eyes widened. "But sir," he protested, "Alvin, Bobby, and I are going to help Malcolm with repairing houses in Historic Rome for the spring. I like to be endowed for stuff like that, it's tough work—"

"The punishment is non-negotiable, Terrence," said Jonathan. "I suggest you enlist Bobby's assistance in giving you a strength-building plan in the gym, and when the work starts, you had better employ inner reserves and fortitude. Now, leave. I want a private word with Jonah."

Displeased, but not complaining, Terrence left. Jonathan followed him out with his eyes, and once he was gone, he looked at Jonah once more. His gray gaze was penetrating and once again angry.

"Jonah, I understand that Reena undertook the task of her own volition," his voice was heated once again, "but she ventured into those activities for you. Do you understand that?"

Now, Jonah was the one that was furious. Terrence had said that same thing. "Jonathan, this comes back to *you*. None of this would have happened if you'd been on the level with us from minute one. You sat in that very spot and lied to our faces. I find that just a little disturbing."

Jonathan raised an eyebrow. "Jonah, I lied to protect you. You may not agree with it, and you're entitled to feel that way, but it doesn't excuse the wrong that you yourself have done."

"I didn't do a damn thing!" snapped Jonah. "I didn't take those papers! I didn't break the cipher! I don't want to throw Reena under the bus, but I didn't do anything!"

"Reena was indeed the one that did the work," conceded Jonathan. "No one is disputing that. But you were chomping at the bit for her to finish. You were impatient and fit to burst. Do not insult my intelligence by telling me that you weren't."

Jonah chose to ignore that. "Jonathan, I don't mean any harm, but you've known me long enough to know that I don't do well with being kept in the dark, especially when it's supposedly been done for my benefit. I don't function that way. I might have been impatient with Reena near the end there, but I felt like we had every right to answers. If you could lie, why couldn't I dig?"

Jonathan shook his head. "Jonah, you probably don't even realize it, but you just said 'I' five times."

Jonah screwed up his eyes. "What's that got to do with anything?"

Jonathan sat forward, his voice now low and urgent. "Jonah it is vitally important that you understand that it's not just about you," he said. "You are not doing this alone—"

"Are you frickin' serious?" demanded Jonah. "Not once did I ever-say—"

"I'm talking," snapped Jonathan, "so let me finish. You are a beacon of hope, Jonah. An extraordinary individual, and extraordinarily powerful. You may think that you don't influence people, but you do. It doesn't have anything to do with how you wanted things to be, and no, that is not a fair notion. But it is the way things are. As the light Blue Aura, you are an icon, and that is not to be taken lightly. It is a precious, delicate, and almost sacred thing. You have to be very careful with people, Jonah. You may not have done the deed, but you still share the blame."

Jonah was silent for a few moments. The words hit him hard, but he still felt that they were unfair. "You just said it, Jonathan," he said at last. "I'm the light Blue Aura. The damn beacon. I'm the one that can't be blissfully ignorant, because I'm the one that Creyton wants the most. You can't treat me like I'm still a child."

"And I am doing no such thing," said Jonathan. "You are not a child to be sheltered. You are a man to be respected. And trusted. And that trust begets responsibility. You need to be mindful of those things, Jonah. They supersede petty prattles you may be dealing with."

Jonah sat there, breathing heavily. A small part of him (and he resisted it vehemently) could see Jonathan's point. It was rather humbling to hear that he influenced people, directly or otherwise. At the same time, he didn't really care for being held responsible for other people's actions. He didn't feel like he had that power.

But it had been wrong for him to take a part in taking those papers. The papers that nearly killed Reena.

There was a funny thing about it, though. He regretted stealing from Jonathan. He regretted being caught, and most importantly, he regretted what happened to Reena. But he couldn't bring himself to regret what they'd found out. About the Six. Those numbers were a pull, almost like a leash. Knowing about them was a freedom in itself; like a barrier of some kind had been crossed. But if Jonathan wanted to take a restrictive stance before, then he ought to be forthcoming now.

After all, cards were on the table now.

"Jonathan, I think you ought to know something." Jonah told him about the dream and thinking nothing of it until that romantic novel had the same title as the dream's message.

Jonathan frowned slightly. "And this book was on hold for you?" he asked. "None of your colleagues knew that it wasn't you who reserved it?"

"Nope," said Jonah. "Reena suggested that you might need to put some defenses around the library. She suggested that right before...you know." Jonah stood up. "What's my punishment? Go ahead and tell me."

"No ethereality until further notice," answered Jonathan. "Of any kind."

Jonah's eyes narrowed. Terrence got a month, he got indefinite. Swell.

The strange thing was, if Jonah read Jonathan correctly, it seemed as though he thought his punishment might be a little harsh. No, Jonah wasn't innocent, and there'd be consequences. Jonathan was still angry, that was clear, but he seemed...reluctant. Weird.

"There is one more thing, Jonathan," said Jonah.

"Enlighten me," said Jonathan.

"Terrence, Reena, and I figured some things out," he revealed. "About the Six. Since you lied to us, I imagine you already know, but I'll say them anyway. One was the Allegiance, and that was when you got Laban off the Plane with No Name.

Two, the Inquisition, was when we started having questions about One, asking you and Laban, and searching on our own. Three was a Victory that Creyton and the Deadfallen disciples view as false, because so few people were saved against how many people were losing their physical lives." He took a deep breath. "That leaves Four, the Attempts, Five, the Cut, and finally, Six, the Splinter. After that whole 'halfway there' thing, I pray that the situation is handled quickly. Especially the Cut. That's the one that bothers me the most."

Jonathan glanced at the Vitasphera, and then back at Jonah. "Thank you for that information, Jonah," he said. "You've given me a great deal to think about."

Jonah nodded stiffly and left the study to go to his room. Terrence was at the door when he got there. He looked at Jonah without words, but Jonah got the silent gist.

"Nah," he muttered, "I ain't mad at you. But why didn't you let me get you off the hook?"

Terrence scoffed. "I wasn't going to abandon my brother," he said. "Even if I'm pissed at him."

Jonah nodded. "Good to know."

Terrence looked away. "I'm a little ashamed that I said I was glad that Reena was asleep," he said, "knowing what I know now and all."

"Sorry for a lot of things," Jonah mumbled.

Terrence half-smiled. That was that.

"So, are you worried about the Cut, too?" he asked.

"More than you know," nodded Jonah.

Now, Terrence frowned. "What's that mean?"

With a huge intake of air, Jonah looked Terrence right in the eye. "I think the Cut is a murder," he admitted. "And I think the Cut is me."

20

March Madness

As fate would have it, though, the beginning of March didn't allow Jonah much time to pore over the Cut. Not at first, anyway.

Reena still hadn't awakened yet, but color was steadily returning to her face, and Jonathan told him and Terrence that her body had strengthened to the point where it didn't have to be regularly bolstered by his essence. Glorious news.

What wasn't glorious news was the fact that several people around the estate began to treat him differently.

Somehow, what he, Terrence, and Reena had been doing had gotten out. Initially, Jonah was unaware of it, but started to figure it out pretty quickly when people here and there would mutter things like, "I'm glad I'm not close to Jonah," or "I thought Blue Aura meant balance, not batter." First, Jonah was uncomfortable, then he got pissed off. These were people who didn't have a clue and made like the entire thing had been his idea.

"It doesn't make sense, though," said Terrence one morning after weights. "How did it get out like that?"

Jonah closed his eyes at the question. He'd thought about that very thing since he'd started hearing the snarky comments and could only come to one logical conclusion.

And it was a conclusion that he didn't want to believe.

"Terrence, there was only one person who overheard what we said," he muttered.

Terrence looked at him with a frown, and then his eyes widened. "No," he said. "Liz? Jonah, you know she wouldn't do that!"

"Do I?" said Jonah quietly. "World is changing, brother. Maybe people are changing with it."

"Do you really believe that, Jonah?" said Terrence.

"I don't know what to believe, Terrence," said Jonah a little tersely.

"Well, you need to figure things out," said Terrence, who matched Jonah's terseness, "because we need to be more concerned with the three things left of the Six."

Jonah looked at Terrence with a silent question. Terrence caught it and shook his head.

"Don't look at me like that," he murmured. "I'm still not a fan of any of it, but the way I see it, we're already falling down the rabbit-hole anyway. May as well see it through to the end because Jonathan is concerned as hell."

Jonah was temporarily distracted. Not only because he was relieved that he had support, but because he suddenly recalled something else. "Funny that you mention Jonathan being worried," he said. "I caught that, too. Along with another thing." Jonah was busy removing his left weight glove. It took some effort because his left wrist was a little sore. He used the extra effort's time to gather his thoughts. "Jonathan is more concerned than I think he's letting us know," he said when he was done. "You know that day when Jonathan gave us our punishments? When he made mine indefinite…I don't know…it seemed like he thought it was overboard."

"Really?" said Terrence with a frown.

"Yeah," said Jonah, a little confused himself. "He kind of got over his anger, too. He was still pissed at me—no doubt about that—but the more we spoke, it was like he wanted to stress the need to look out for people. It was like he wasn't as mad as he probably should have been. He went to some serious lengths to deter from looking into that shit. I was ready to have my head ripped off, but it didn't happen."

Terrence shrugged. "Well, we've seen how angry Jonathan can get," he said, "back during that thing with Gamaliel, and that time he got into a fight with Creyton. Since the only thing that happened concerning us was ethereal grounding, I'm good with it."

Jonah attempted to convince himself that the mutterings were nothing. He also attempted to remind himself of his childhood when he went through stuff like this and more. But those justifications simply didn't work anymore. He didn't know what had changed; maybe he'd grown accustomed to having so many friends for once (or acquaintances, at least), or maybe he thought the ignorance that he'd dealt with in the past would fade now that he was an adult. Obviously, that was farce. He saw that now.

He just couldn't believe that Liz was the reason he could see that again.

He didn't know how to feel towards her. Did he hate her? Absolutely not. Liz was his little sister. He adored her. Was he angry? Strangely enough, he couldn't actually say yes to that, either.

Maybe it was disappointment. Yeah, that might be it.

As the family room was no longer the welcoming place it had been in the past, Jonah spent more time away from the estate. That meant many more nights with Lola, which was never a bad thing, and staying late into the night at the library. Even in the midst of doing that, he was a grown man. He'd have to deal eventually. It wasn't a necessary thing, though it wasn't fun at all.

Of course, most of the people that made up his core, like Terrence, Alvin, Bobby, Douglas, Malcolm, Spader, and Magdalena didn't treat him any differently. He and Katarina were friends now, and she wasn't so keen on believing the worst of him anymore (man, wasn't *that* a change from the past). Akshara, like most of Jonah's friends, thought that the notion of Jonah being a bad omen was absurd. And Maxine could be counted on for the nerdiest conversations at any time. Nella and Themis weren't particularly sociable at the present time, but Jonah knew that was only because they were agonizing over prom dresses. But there were many other people whose energy had shifted in regard to him. Even people he'd made progress with over the years, like Ben-Israel, Barry, Benjamin, and Noah. And he still couldn't bring himself to speak to Liz.

But the most challenging thing was when he finally had to face Kendall. Jonathan had been delicate when he explained things to her, but when she sought out Jonah, there was fury in her eyes.

"Did this have to do with…with whatever it is you guys do?" was the first thing she demanded of him when she saw him.

Reluctantly, Jonah nodded. Kendall stood there silently, taking very heavy breaths.

"What happened?" she asked him.

Jonah didn't know what Jonathan had told her exactly, and he sure as hell didn't want to contradict. "Reena—um—overexerted herself mentally and physically while trying to help us out," he said, which was generic without being totally vague. "The strain of it all was too much."

Kendall looked away for a second. "Did you have anything to do with how hard she pushed herself?"

Jonah swallowed. "Indirectly, yes. But Kendall, you're the one that's going to marry her soon. You've been with Reena long enough to know that she's too goddamned stubborn to hold back when she starts something, no matter what it is."

"I know that, Jonah," said Kendall, "but I'm still pissed at you. Reena worships you. She talks about you all the time, and she'd do anything for you. If she ran herself ragged like this, it was because she didn't want to let you down."

Jonah ran impatient hands over his face. There it was again. First Terrence said it. Then Jonathan. And now, Kendall, the Tenth Percenter who didn't live at the estate with them, but apparently thought along the same lines.

"Tell me this, Jonah," said Kendall after a few moments, "and for your sake, the answer had better be yes. Whatever Reena was doing—was it worth it? Did she at least make a dent in what she was trying to accomplish?"

That, Jonah could answer with no shame. "Oh, she accomplished it." He didn't miss the note of pride in his own voice. "Dent? She busted it wide open."

Kendall didn't smile, but her face wasn't so full of anger anymore. "Jonathan told me that she was going to be alright," she said. "I'm relieved as hell to hear that… you would have had to deal with me if she didn't recover."

It was a funny thing. Jonah was a powerful Eleventh Percenter, and he'd seen and been through shit most people couldn't imagine. And yet, the notion of having to deal with one angry woman was more frightening than all of that. Seriously. "I understand that, Kendall," he said. "But fortunately, we don't have to entertain that. Reena will make a full recovery."

Kendall sighed in relief and nodded. "I just wish she would hurry it along and wake up."

"Me too," said Jonah. "In the meantime, I hope that you can forgive me. However indirect my involvement in this was."

Kendall looked away. "It's an easier thing to work on now that I know she will be alright," she admitted. "But a part of me understands your dilemma. I'm well aware of the fact that once Reena gets on to something, you can't pry her away. Her tenacity is one of the reasons why I love her."

Jonah nodded. Being on the path to forgiveness was better than nothing at all. Kendall stood.

"Excuse me," she told him. "I'm going to sit with her for a few more minutes."

Jonah noticed a small tube in her hands.

"What is that, Kendall?"

"Oh, nothing," Kendall answered a little too quickly. "It's just that Reena's lips have gotten really chapped and dry..."

Jonah's straightened. "Lip balm? Kendall, you know Reena would never wear that!"

"Well, this is a special circumstance," said Kendall rather evasively. "I'm helping her out for health reasons."

Unfortunately for Jonah, Liz wasn't stupid. She figured out that Jonah was avoiding her. When that happened was anyone's guess, but she did.

And she cornered him at the earliest convenience, which happened to be a Saturday evening, after he'd gotten done with helping Spader, Melvin, and Douglas with a new fence, and then later helping Nella till soil for the new season. It was rough work made rougher by the fact that Jonah couldn't take on any spiritual endowments. He'd just gotten to his room, wondering what poor Terrence was going through repairing houses with Malcolm, Alvin, and Bobby when she spoke from his door.

"Did you really think I wouldn't figure out why you've stopped talking to me, Jonah?"

Startled, Jonah turned. Liz stood there, arms folded, and looking tense as hell. Her jade eyes were blazing.

"And don't you dare play dumb and say 'Huh?' " she warned as she walked into the room. "It'll make things worse, because I know full well that you heard every word I said."

Jonah had to look away from Liz. In certain moods, her eyes were scary. "Liz, you overheard what we had done, and then it magically became estate news."

"So, you automatically assume that I'm a gossip?" Liz demanded. "It never occurred to you, not once, to ask me? To check your facts? Reena's been asleep for almost two weeks, Jonah. Do you actually think that I was even focused enough to snitch on you?"

Jonah's eyes narrowed. "You're saying it wasn't you?"

Liz rolled her eyes. "No, it wasn't me, Jonah! Haven't you been listening?"

Jonah was floored. Seriously? Yeah, all he had was Liz's words, but something about it made him believe her. He had trouble believing that Liz had said anything in the very beginning; now he knew he should have gone with his gut then. He'd been focused on the wrong person.

But who did it, then?

Liz brought his attention back to her by snapping her fingers. "Don't start sleuthing just yet," she told him. "I've got an idea about it, which we will get to in a second. But we aren't finished yet, Jonah."

She seated herself on Jonah's bed without invitation.

"When did it become your M.O. to just ignore people who care about you, Jonah?" she asked. "Here lately, you've been making a bunch of decisions based on partial information, and then judging people accordingly. You've done it with Vera, and now, you've done it with me."

Jonah looked at her, incredulous. Where the hell did that come from? "Where are you going with this, Liz? And how did Vera get into it?"

Liz cleared her throat. "You've treated Vera like the town leper since she's started repairing her life."

Jonah's expression soured. "Vera has made it clear—" he began heatedly, but Liz cut him off.

"Vera's made *nothing* clear, because you've hardly spoken to her since November!" she exclaimed. "She's been almost a non-entity to you since the moment you found out she had a new man in her life, Jonah, and don't you dare say that's not true!"

Jonah looked up at the ceiling and sucked in air through his nostrils. "Liz, Reena is in the infirmary right now—"

"Recovering a steady pace," interrupted Liz. "You will not trade on Reena's plight to get out of this. You didn't even thank Vera for returning your class ring!"

"What? How do you—?"

"You think my best friend in the world doesn't tell me everything?" said Liz with impatience.

"I was very appreciative of what she did!" said Jonah, defensiveness in his voice. "I didn't say anything to her because I wanted to respect her wishes—"

"You hurt her, Jonah," said Liz. "She was really bothered by that. And the way you shot down speaking to her a while back to make a damned sandwich? Really, Jonah?"

Jonah sat down in his computer chair because he needed to get off of his feet. Hearing Liz say that Vera had been hurt by his distance served to take some of the strength from his legs. Still.

"Liz, there is something you need to know," he said. "The night Vera left here—" Jonah decided to skate over the night's events, "—she left me a note, telling me to live my life, because she was going to live hers. She even suggested that I seek out Rheadne. Basically, she said that it couldn't happen."

Now Liz's expression went from aggravated to piteous. "And you decided to forget her, did you?" she said. "Forget the Time Item...the woman whose physical life you saved, the woman you saved from being burnt out like a candle. The woman that you had so much consideration for that you bought her *Wicked* merchandise, a playwright anthology, and a *Les Misérables* poster. The woman you went to The Maiden on the Rose with and spent night after night in her house. She fought with us in that tattoo dungeon. Jonah, you slept with her, for God's sakes! How in the world would you forget that?"

Jonah stared at her. "How the—?"

"I said it once, and I will say it again, Jonah," said Liz, her impatient face back on, "you think my best friend in the world doesn't tell me everything?"

Jonah shook his head. Whatever.

"Jonah, look," said Liz, whose voice sounded more contemplative than irritated now, "you're a grown man, and Vera is a grown woman. She's in a relationship, and you've got your friend with benefits. It's all cool. You're living your own lives and making your own choices. But Jonah, Vera is your friend. Our friend. The fact that she's touring with her play doesn't change that. The fact that she is the baby sister of a murderer doesn't change it, either. She is a still human being with feelings, Jonah. She told you to live your life and forget her, yeah. But emotions...they make us say some really dumb things. She didn't mean it; she can't have. And you simply stopped talking to her. Just like you stopped talking to me."

Jonah said nothing. Jonathan's words rattled around his head once again.

It's not just you. You aren't doing this alone.

"I'm sorry, Liz," he said. "I screwed up. I just got caught up in my own mind, in my own thoughts. You know I would never voluntarily hurt you, or anyone else."

Liz looked irritated for several more moments, and then her expression softened. She hugged Jonah tightly, which took him by surprise.

"Liz, I'm a sweaty mess—"

"Me, too," dismissed Liz. "I was out pulling weeds in the other gardens while you and Nella were tilling."

Jonah snorted, and hugged her back.

"I need a shower," she said, "and then Bobby and I are going bowling."

Liz headed to the door, and then paused. When she looked at Jonah again, her face was serious once more.

"Talk to Vera, Jonah," she said flat-out. "Not right now, because you need to gather your thoughts. And I don't mean email, Facebook, or texting. There is too much room for error and misinterpretation when things are in writing. Call, or Skype her."

Jonah sighed, and nodded. Just like with the fair-weather imbeciles at the estate, he'd have to deal eventually.

"Liz, wait," he said suddenly. "You said you had an idea about who blabbed on me and twisted everything."

"Oh yeah," said Liz. "Think hard and clear, Jonah. I heard the whole conversation, but I wasn't the one who told the world. Never said anything. No one else was around. Who at this estate would have the ability to manipulate sound so as to hear things when they were a safe distance away?"

Jonah's face hardened instantly. Of course. Of damned course!

Liz saw the change in his face and nodded. "I figured that it couldn't be anyone else," she said. "Jonathan isn't loose-lipped, and I never told anyone. Not even Bobby."

Jonah nodded again, furious. "Thank you again, Liz," he said in a carefully measured voice. "I should have spoken to you right away."

"Yes, you should have," Liz agreed. "But it's under the bridge now. See you later."

"Uh-huh." Jonah almost toppled her as he stepped out of his room.

Time for another conversation.

And there'd be no hugging or soul-searching this time.

Jonah had never been on the top level of the estate before, as most of the rooms weren't occupied, and the ones that were belonged to a collection of people that no one cared for.

And they especially didn't care for their leader.

Jonah reached the right door and banged on it viciously.

"What the hell?" a voice said from inside.

Jonah sneered. Although that voice wasn't a surprise, it wasn't the one he wanted. He banged again.

"Who the hell is banging on my door like that?" another voice demanded.

Jonah braced himself. That was the one. "Open this door, Trip!" he snarled. "Do it now, or I swear to God I'll kick it down!"

The door flew open, and suddenly Jonah and Trip were face to face. Trip was shirtless but wore athletic shorts. When Jonah looked him over, he couldn't help but frown. Trip had more tattoos than he did. Did he cut a deal with an artist, or something?

But he filed away the distraction.

"Put on a shirt, dude," he snapped. "You ain't impressing anyone, believe me."

Trip looked at Jonah with such abject fury that Jonah was temporarily grateful that looks couldn't kill. "What do you want?" he whispered.

"Why'd you do it?" Jonah shot back. "Why did you run all around the estate, telling some bullshit half-cocked story that you didn't understand?"

Trip's eyes narrowed. "Rowe, I'm occupied at the moment, so if you could kindly fuck off—"

"You told me something once, Trip, and now I'm telling you the same," said Jonah in a nasty tone. "I'm sure I don't care."

Trip made a growling sound somewhere in the back of his throat, and then he backed up a step, looking at a point somewhere behind his door.

"Give me a moment," he said, and then he stepped out, pulling the door shut.

"Hate to break it to you, Trippy," said Jonah, "but if your answers aren't satisfactory, Karin's going to have to wait for much longer than one moment. Now, why did you have to cause discord? Isn't there enough going on out there without you scurrying about, being Mouth Almighty, Tongue-Everlasting?"

Trip folded his arms. "So, this is why you're cock-blocking me, Rowe? Because you and Aldercy, in your infinite wisdom, damn near killed Katoa, yet again? You're mad at me for *your* poor judgment?"

"Spare me, Trip," hissed Jonah. "I'm pissed because you were spying on the infirmary and then flew off, spewing lies and half-truths about me. I didn't 'damn near kill' anyone. You ain't got a clue. And then you had the audacity to go and spread shit—"

"That's where you're wrong, Rowe," interrupted Trip, who actually pointed in Jonah's face. "The time for these barely developed upstarts to learn the truth about you has long since come. Every adventure you've ever had has gone your way due to dumb luck, chance, coincidence, accidents, or because Katoa had the right amount of intelligence to bail you out. And what's the thanks she gets? You nearly drained away her physical life."

Jonah felt his eye begin to twitch. Not a good sign. "Reena mistakenly pored over booby-trapped papers," he barked. "My only mistake was not helping her out. I would have gladly traded places with her—"

"And no one wishes you had done so more than me," interrupted Trip.

Jonah's eyes widened in horror and anger. Trip pressed on.

"Yeah, I said it," he whispered. "I don't regret what I did in the slightest little bit, Rowe. You ought to thank me."

"Say what?!" cried Jonah.

"I did you a favor." Trip's voice was wintry. "For far too long, you've been looking at the ethereal world from the ivory tower everyone's placed you in. They treat you like royalty, like some Hollywood superstar, and that's how you behave. You're not an icon; you're just a screw-up who can turn things blue. You needed to be brought back to Earthplane, Rowe. Hard way if necessary. I have always said that you'd lead us to ruin…forget anything that Creyton does. People need to know that their faith in the 'light Blue Aura' is misplaced. You need humility, bitch. And there is nothing more humbling than having someone throw shade on your game."

Jonah felt like his blood would explode in his veins. Was this guy serious? Jonah didn't know what was more twisted; the words Trip said, to the fact that he believed them. "You ain't playing with a full deck, Trip," he whispered. "I don't know if it's drugs you're taking, or drugs you *need* to be taking, but you're crossing a line. I never wanted this life, but that's what happened. Never once have I acted with an inflated head, but I'm damn proud of the times I've helped people. You run around all the over the place like the world owes you something, and you need to let that shit go. It's nobody's fault that your daddy didn't hug you, and that his daddy didn't hug him—"

Trip stepped away from the door. He and Jonah were literally nose to nose. "You better mind yourself, Rowe. I warn you. Stay clear of things that don't concern you. I've told Jonathan time and again about you, and he just will not listen. That's cool; if he won't do something about you, I'll be happy to."

Jonah regarded the bastard. "Was that a threat?"

"No, it was a bookshelf," snapped Trip.

Jonah took a very small step back. "Alright then, smartass. Take care of me. By all means. Nothing in your way here."

Trip's eyes narrowed, like he was tempted, but then a strange thing happened.

He smiled.

"What could you possibly do to me?" he asked quietly. "You are ethereally grounded until who knows when. Now run along, write in your little notebook, and pray to your God that your ideas don't wither and die, like everything else you touch."

Somewhere in Jonah's mind, the words surprised him. "Death isn't real."

"With you, it is," murmured Trip.

And with that, he was back in his room with Karin and had closed the door, leaving Jonah in the hallway, pissed off and rife with violent tendencies.

Jonah couldn't return to his room. He'd break something. Trip set fire to his insides with those words. He tried to file it away. Didn't work. He tried the anger management techniques that Felix taught him. Nope. He was so angry that it scared him.

And that was bad. Bad was an oversimplification, but it was the only word that came to mind.

He went downstairs to the gym and headed for the punching bag. His left wrist was still sore, but he taped it up and decided to make himself as oblivious to it as possible. He did make sure that the tape and gloves were done properly, though. His anger had gotten him into trouble in the past, and he wasn't about to get injured down here. Not for Trip.

He got to work. And his thoughts did, as well.

How messed up was it that Trip was locked away, banging that stupid skank Karin, while he was down here beating the hell out of a punching bag?

That made no sense.

Jonah was no boxer, but a strange thing happened. He began to envision Trip's face with each punch. Suddenly, each one seemed to get more accurate. More intense.

What the hell did Trip know? All that shit he said, and then he topped it off by saying that Jonah's dreams would wither and die. That was really something, coming from a musician whose band couldn't even get arrested.

What was Trip's deal?

You needed to be brought back to Earthplane, Rowe. Hard way, if necessary.

Jonah never thought he was better than anyone. Not even those bastards at Sanctum. Not even Trip himself. He'd even saved the bastard's life once.

Ungrateful degenerate. Had the nerve to say that he'd rather it was Jonah up there in the infirmary than Reena...

A cracking noise made Jonah's head shoot upward.

The chain holding the bag to the ceiling had partly detached.

Then fully detached.

It crashed in an undignified heap in front of him. Jonah stood there, still visualizing Trip.

"Want to deal with me, do you?" he whispered. "I'm a screw-up, right? Just give me a one on one, Trip. It's been a long time coming anyway. Just one. I'd be more than happy to see you 'do something' about me..."

"Jonah? Who are you talking to?"

Jonah spun around. It was Terrence. He had been busy today as well, but he hadn't had the distractions Jonah had. He, unlike Jonah, was freshly showered, clad in a red T-shirt and cotton shorts. Jonah was an even nastier mess than he'd been before. And on top of that, he'd just destroyed one of the punching bags.

"No one," murmured Jonah. "I just needed to blow off some steam. I'm a little on edge."

"Well, you can let it go, man," said Terrence gleefully. "Reena's awake!"

Jonah stared at him for a moment longer, and then they both dashed out of the gym and up the stairs, with a whole bunch of playful shoving and laughing the entire way. When they reached the infirmary, Reena was sitting up, looking slightly disoriented, but otherwise quite well. Jonah didn't think he'd ever seen a better sight in his life.

"How are you feeling?" asked Terrence.

Reena sighed. "Like I never, ever want to sleep again." She pursed her lips, and then frowned. She ran a finger across them, examined it, and then she snapped their way.

"How long has Kendall been putting lip balm on me?" she demanded.

Jonah almost smirked. "Couple days, really," he confessed.

Silence.

Then Jonah and Terrence pounced on her, both of them giving her the tightest hug conceivable. Reena wasn't even deterred, grabbing them back.

"What have I missed?" she asked.

Jonah and Terrence looked at each other. *Here we go,* thought Jonah.

"We've got a lot to talk about," he said. "But let's get you some grilled chicken and Caesar salad up here. God only knows how hungry you are."

21

Madness, Continued

The greatest thing was that once Reena was awake, the rest of her recovery went like nothing. She was eating almost immediately after waking up and was up and walking shortly after that. The first thing she did when she was strong enough to stand prolonged was take the world's longest shower, and then promptly ate more salad. Then she went to visit Kendall. No one was surprised that they didn't see her for a couple days. But when she returned, Jonah laughed at the fact that Reena had decided to humor Kendall by continuously applying the lip balm.

There was one snag. Liz gave Reena a Green Deal, which prohibited her from any ethereality of any kind. Jonah shrugged when he found that out.

"Look at it this way," he told her, "Terrence isn't done with his grounding yet, and I'm grounded forever, it's looking like now. We can be the Unendowed Three, or something."

Reena smirked at that, but it slid off of her face shortly thereafter. There was no doubt in Jonah's mind that her thoughts wandered to all the information that he and Terrence had shared with her. Jonah couldn't know Reena's mind, and just this once, he wished he had her gift of essence reading so as to figure out where her head was. He hadn't forgotten how, a long time back, Creyton, in disguise, had disrupted Jonah's cleansing of Reena's dampener after she'd been generous to let him use it. Her own stressors, compounded by Jonah's, had hit her hard, resulting in unconsciousness and short-term memory loss. Several months after that, she, Jonah, Terrence, and Douglas had experienced a Haunting, which turned one's emotional baggage into bile in their systems. That event had rocked his sister to the point that she had contemplated trying to purge herself of her ethereality.

And then this happened.

Jonah had already been enlightened that sometimes he could be selfish, but he didn't want Reena contemplating the abdication of her powers again. They needed to keep their unit as tight as possible, especially now.

Very slowly, Jonah realized that Reena had eyes on him. She shook her head.

"Jonah, you can save your concern," she told him. "I'm not going anywhere."

Jonah frowned. "I thought you'd been Green Dealt. Isn't reading my essence—?"

"I didn't have to read your essence, Jonah," grinned Reena. "You were as obvious as all get-out just now."

"I'm wondering something, Reena," said Terrence. "You were full throttle using that Phantom Cipher stuff. With all the emotions that you had to manufacture, why couldn't you ascertain that it was hurting you?"

Reena drank some water. "The odd thing is that I probably did, Terrence," she said. "But I probably didn't think anything about it because there was so much negative activity already. That essence could have been masked by everything else."

Jonah's eyes narrowed. That sounded like something Creyton would do; bombard someone with so much negativity that they couldn't figure out that one or two things were a little more malignant than the rest. And Jonah was supposedly equal to such tactics?

"And there is still Four, Five, and Six," said Terrence.

"The Attempts, The Cut, and The Splinter," Reena ticked off her fingers as she said them. "I think the first three were just appetizers. These next three are the meal."

"I disagree," said Terrence. "I think Four and Five are the meal. Six is the tasty treat at the end."

Jonah decided not to contemplate that one too much and took a deep breath as he regarded Reena. "Reena, I'm thankful that you are free of that cipher's pull," he told her, "but I'm a little sorry that we can't do any more digging."

"And who said that?" asked Reena, surprised.

Jonah looked at her, equally surprised. "Reena, you can't go anywhere near that cipher again, it's too dangerous. Plus, Jonathan confiscated everything you had down there, and returned the Phantom Key back to Patience—"

"I duplicated the notes," said Reena.

"You did what?" cried Terrence.

Reena nodded. "It was a Plan B," she explained. "Of course, I wasn't expecting the physical life drainage thing, but I wanted a backup in case we got caught." She turned to Jonah. "Jonah, I don't want to put this in your consciousness, but that the Cut—"

"—is me," finished Jonah. "Yeah, Terrence and I got that far, too."

Reena's eyes widened for a second, and then she looked determined. "Well, that's not going to happen. We won't let it, right, Terrence?"

Terrence swallowed, and then sighed. "Like I said to Jonah before," he murmured, "we're already down the rabbit hole now. But Jonah, we can't be sure that it's you. Last year, you thought that the red in the Vitasphera was meant for Prodigal, but it wasn't. It was—"

Terrence paused, unthinkingly reaching the sore spot. Jonah closed his eyes.

But the awkward moment was interrupted by noise in the hallway. Alecksander and Obadiah came into the door, dragging a rattled and disoriented Douglas between them. Spader, Katarina, and Autumn Rose brought up the rear.

"What the hell?" said Jonah, alarmed.

"I told him not to do it!" exclaimed Katarina, who looked horrified.

"I did, too!" cried Autumn Rose.

"Not to do what?" demanded Terrence.

"It felt so good outside, we wanted to play some basketball," Alecksander explained. "We had a pick-up game going on. Me, Spader, and Stella Marie against Doug here, Autumn Rose, and Obadiah."

"Alecksander was powering inside the key, and Mr. Gladiator there decides to try to take a charge," grumbled Autumn Rose.

Jonah winced. Douglas took a running charge from a sazer?

"I told him not to do it!" whimpered Katarina. "But he convinced him!"

She jabbed a finger at Spader. Reena leapt from her seat and got in Spader's face. He tensed, which made her look at him curiously.

"Really, Royal?" she demanded. "I'm not back to full strength yet, and you're flinching? What did you tell Doug?"

"Nothing much!" evaded Spader. "All I said was that he might like basketball!"

"You're a damn liar!" snapped Obadiah. "You said that basketball was more kick-ass than golf and playing a pick-up would impress Katarina!"

Reena glared at Spader. But then, she focused on Douglas.

"Doug," she said in a soothing tone, "are you okay? How are you feeling right now?"

Douglas raised his gaze to Reena's face. "Grandma Dine," he said groggily, "can you find me a concussion? I think I have a Green Aura."

Katarina whimpered again, but Reena's eyes widened in shock.

"Go get Ben-Israel," she grumbled. "He needs to fix that concussion right now. I'll be damned if Doug calls me that crusty old bat again!"

Jonah and Terrence couldn't help it. They laughed their heads off.

* * *

By the time Reena was at full strength and Liz lifted the Green Deal, it was the middle of March. Reena's full release from Liz's care was a huge bright spot in a week that included several Hauntings near the county line. This was a major cause for concern, as sazers usually aided in vanquishing Haunts. Since they'd been made pariahs, however, and the Networkers were spread thin dealing with other Eight Chapter crimes, poorly equipped S.P.G practitioners had had to deal with them. Patience, who was the one recounting the story as Sunday dinner, stopped at that point.

"The less I say about the end result, the better," he told them.

Jonah believed him.

"What about that brawl at the office complex near Dad's garage?" asked Bobby. "Was that that Jessica woman's influence? I remember that she could make people do crazy things."

"She can indeed do that," said Patience, "but I think that mess at the office complex was the shifts in essences affecting the Tenth population."

"You don't think Jessica's done anything?" asked Jonah. "We know that she's been back in the game since last November."

Patience munched on some lettuce before answering. "I'm not saying she's innocent, and since I was so lovingly coerced into this vampire business, my info is sketchy. But the Networkers who are still working the Deadfallen disciple cases have told me that Jessica Hale is on a tighter leash than the rest of Creyton's people."

"Why is that?" asked Magdalena.

"Because of Jonah," said Patience, with approval and pride in his voice.

Jonah, who hadn't expected to hear his name, raised his eyes in surprise. "Me? What did I have to do with anything?"

"Before you, Jonah, Hale had been batting a thousand with her C.P.V., so I've heard," said Patience. "When you proved that it could be broken, well, the luster of Inimicus was a little lost. I've heard that, among the Deadfallen disciples, her star has begun to fade somewhat."

"I find that ironic," smiled Nella.

"Why's that, Nella?" asked Jonah.

"Jessica's had a bit of a fall from grace," she said. "Her star is fading, while Vera's star is rising."

That elicited some positive thoughts and laughter, but Jonah glanced down at his short ribs and vegetables. He hadn't yet followed Liz's advice and gotten in contact with Vera. He'd justified it with a laundry list of excuses. The first was that he was worried about Reena, but as fate would have it, Reena awoke the very day that Liz advised him. Next, he had used work, beleaguering the point about the creepy coincidence of that book. Further inquiries yielded nothing at the library. Then, he'd made up in his mind that Vera was busy. She was touring with a play after all. When would she have time to talk?

But the more the justifications mounted, the sorrier they became. He didn't want to talk to Vera because of East. He might have been a quintessential prick, but he was who Vera had chosen.

And he was filthy rich. He could probably buy her the South of France if he wanted.

Liz had been wrong. Vera wasn't a non-entity.

She was an off-limits entity.

"Focus, Jonah!" hissed Reena. "You need to hear this!"

Jonah glanced up the table, and saw that Trip was talking. He frowned. Rarely did he eat dinner with everyone. Besides, he'd just as soon not hear anything he said.

"—contingencies regarding the estate's well-being, sir," he was saying to Jonathan. "And of course, the residents," he added as an afterthought.

For some reason, Daniel, who'd been eating buttered toast near the door, moved to the table.

Jonathan was at the head of the table, and of course, had no food. He joined his fingers and sighed. Jonah tensed, and straightened. That was that 'boss about to lay off people' pose. But this wasn't a job! What did it signify here?

"It's not a secret to anyone," Jonathan began, "that I have always had the utmost regard for everyone's well-being. There is an old, outdated idea passed down from Overseer to Overseer of this House that, while I disagree with it, you need to be aware of."

Jonah and everyone else looked at him. He hated to say it, but Jonathan didn't have to let the silence spiral.

"It involves an exodus," Jonathan said.

Daniel rolled his eyes. Alvin, the nearest to Jonathan, was the first to ask.

"Exodus? From the estate?"

With another sigh, Jonathan nodded.

The silence could almost be felt. It was as if someone had taken a high-pressure washer, put it on the highest dial, and hit Jonah's brain with it. "Leave the estate?" he blurted out. "Why in God's name would we do that?"

Trip looked murderously at Jonah as usual, but because of Jonathan's presence, he answered. "The estate is stronger without so many people fouling up its essence," he murmured.

Daniel looked outraged, but Jonathan raised a hand to stop him, looking at Trip in an irritated fashion.

"That is an oversimplification is the highest order, Titus," he said as he turned to Jonah. "Jonah, it is true that the estate has a strength all its own that's affected by our presence. But that is only because the estate stretches its strength to protect us with it. We are included in its scope."

"But Jonathan," said Karin, who shocked people by speaking, "is there something to what Trip said? Is our inclusion in the scope making the estate weaker?"

Jonathan's expression was shrewd when he looked at Karin. "Let me answer your question with a question, Karin," he said. "When you take a tonic into yourself for healing, and that tonic spreads throughout your body, does that make its healing potency weak? No. It means that it's doing its job. It didn't get weaker, it simply moved to begin work in several functions. This estate is no different. Our presence does not weaken it. It just changes the focuses of its function."

Karin looked disarmed. Magdalena giggled.

"Looks like you dropped something, Karin," she said, "your face."

Jonathan sighed. "I will be the first to admit that I am not fond of the exodus idea." He threw Trip an angry look. "But you need to know that you have the choice to do whatever you wish. Eleventh Percenters have lived, crashed, recovered, and rested at this place since before your or even my time. You are welcome to do as you see fit. But I would much rather that all of you stay on."

Jonah stood up. Trip mumbled, "Oh great." With effort, he ignored him.

"I don't speak for everyone, obviously," he said, "but personally, I elect to stay here at the estate. This is the place where I feel safest, no matter what. The way I see it, as long as you're here, Jonathan, this is the safest place in the world."

Trip looked angry. Jonathan grinned, looking touched. Daniel stepped away from the table.

"Well said, Rowe," he told him. "No one thrives scattered all over the damn place, following a thousand different trains of thought. That's why anything that involves the Curaie nowadays falls flat. It's not an accident that the word united begins with *unit*."

And then, Daniel resumed his trademark silence. Patience cleared his throat.

"What Daniel said," he murmured, and many folks laughed. Then people began to disperse. Jonah saw Trip and Karin leave for outside. When he went into the family room, Terrence and Reena followed.

"What the hell was that about?" he demanded of them both. Jonathan was not cool with that suggestion at all. How was it even brought up?

"Trip," said Reena. "He started talking about it while your mind was wandering."

"Why would he suggest leaving his home?" said Terrence, bewildered. "He's been longer than anybody, save Jonathan! Why this sudden one-eighty?"

"You know how I feel about one-eighties," said Jonah. "I think he's been giving it serious thought. He probably threw it out there to see what Jonathan thought about it."

"Well, Jonathan made his thoughts as clear as a bright and sunny day," said Terrence.

"Uh-huh, so why is it that I feel like that wasn't the end of it?"

Slowly, Terrence and Reena looked at Jonah.

"Not it," said Terrence.

"Not it," said Reena.

Jonah gave them both a sour look. "You never *were* it," he muttered.

He dragged himself out of the chair, through the door, and into the night.

Jonah's initial reaction to seeing Laban again was shock. When he'd reached the cell, he saw that Laban had completely disassembled the bookshelf. When he raised his head and saw the look on Jonah's face, he smiled.

"Bring it down a thousand, boy," he said. "It's just a time killer. I enjoy seeing things built up, and then torn down. It lets you know what to tweak and prone when it comes time to rebuild."

There was a hidden meaning in that statement somewhere, but Jonah only had eyes for the bookshelf. "How did you do it?"

"What? This?" He indicated the bookshelf. "Screwdriver, of course."

He waved it for Jonah to see.

"How in the hell did you get that?" demanded Jonah.

"I asked that lanky boy… Alvin, I think his name is—to ask Jonathan," answered Laban. "He approved, but it had to be ordinary steel."

He tossed it among the pieces of the bookshelf, rose, and walked to the glass. "How may I be of service?"

"I want to know something," said Jonah readily. He felt that cutting to the chase wouldn't give Laban enough time to manipulate. "About Trip's dad."

Laban raised an eyebrow. "You want to know about T.J.? Why?"

"Because I want to know how much of him is in his son," spat Jonah. "What was he like? And nutshell it. I'm not interested in a monologue."

Laban looked intrigued. "Huh. Wonder what's got you so turned 'round,'" he mused. "But if it's a nutshell you want, it's a nutshell you shall have. T.J. Rivers was sharp, ruthless, great at torture and strong-arming, proficient with five musical instruments if I recall correctly, and a womanizer."

Jonah's attention sharpened at that. "What, now?"

"You heard what I said," said Laban. "T.J. Rivers was a wanton philanderer. His cheating is one of the reasons why Trip's mother is in the nuthouse."

Jonah's mouth fell open. "So, she actually is insane!"

"Uh-huh," said Laban. "Here is something that you'll never hear from Trip because he's...Trip. But he is of Haitian descent, through his mother's side. When T.J. brought her to the U.S., she had menial skills, and spoke very little English. Her first language is French. That's why Trip is so fluent."

"Trip speaks French?" asked Jonah, grudgingly impressed. He didn't know that Trip spoke anything other than douche.

"He wouldn't have been able to speak with his mama otherwise," said Laban. "Anyway, as his mother was an immigrant, she didn't have a lot of access to things, didn't know anyone, and was pretty much under T.J.'s thumb. He did whatever he wanted; what was she going to do, go back to Haiti? But T.J. didn't even bother to hide what he was doing, and that took a toll on her eventually. She'd been losing her touch for years. I suppose that all of T.J.'s running around made her feel less and less like a woman. The man's dead and buried, and Trip hates him still."

"Really," said Jonah. "Then why was he so mad at you for betraying his dad?"

"That's an easy one to explain." Laban folded his arms and smirked. "Trip hated his dad, but he adores his mother.

And she loved T.J. Despite everything, she loved him. Despite messing with her psyche, she forgave him time and time again. Stupid bitch. Trip put up with it because his mother loved his father. And when I betrayed him, and he got killed, that was the last straw of her sanity. And all that time, he thought Felix was the one who killed his father. It's all so pathetic."

Jonah was horrified. Laban regarded the look with shrewd eyes.

"You're feeling sorry for Trip, now?"

"Hell no," said Jonah instantly. "I feel sorry for his mother."

Laban shook his head. "Why are you going to pity a little twit who has spent the past two decades being cuckoo for a certain cereal? I've already warned you that your compassion is going to come back and bite you in the ass. That day might be coming sooner than you think."

Jonah fastened onto that. "What do you mean by that?"

"All I'm saying is that this is a wild and crazy time to be alive," shrugged Laban. "And caring, loving…all of that horseshit? It won't get you through it. As for Trip, he is his daddy incarnate. He just doesn't want to admit it. And you?" He gave Jonah a serious look. "Until you learn to disregard everyone and everything, Creyton will be your superior. I say that with certainty. As long as you put others before yourself, and continue being all noble, you might as well hold up a neon sign that says, '*HERE I AM, CREYTON! COME RIP MY HEAD OFF!*'"

Jonah shook his head. "Which of us is in a cell?"

"Which of us is a slave to the madness of decency?" countered Laban.

Jonah turned his back on Laban. "Get back to your building blocks," he grumbled.

He was back in the clean air within minutes. He couldn't believe those things that he heard about Trip. Or more accurately, his mother.

And Jonah thought his own parents were screwed up. Trip's situation was madness.

Still, personal responsibility had to play into the equation somewhere. Trip was a grown man, with his own mind and opinions. He had based his entire life view on past experiences. The people around him now were not the guilty ones. His father was.

Laban said that Trip was his father incarnate. Besides the womanizing, Jonah could almost see that.

And it bothered him.

He certainly didn't want to disregard people for perceived wrongs. That was neither right nor fair.

Speaking of disregarding people...

Jonah shot off a text, and then headed to his room. When he brought up Skype, he was surprised to see that she was online. Remembering Liz's admonitions, he opted for video chat. Seconds later, Vera's face was on his screen. Her hair was pulled back into a ponytail, which threw her facial scar into full relief. She looked tired, but alert enough to have a curious face.

"Hello, Vera," said Jonah.

"Hey, Jonah," she said. "What's up?"

"Is this a bad time?"

"If it was, you wouldn't be looking at me," said Vera.

Jonah nearly rolled his eyes, but caught himself, and took a heavy breath. "First and foremost, I never thanked you for returning my class ring," he said. "I'd given up on finding it. It made my day, seeing it on Christmas."

Vera looked at Jonah intently. "You're more than welcome, Jonah."

Jonah nodded. Now, it was time to man up. "We need to talk, Vera."

Vera looked at him for several seconds, and then left the screen. Jonah was puzzled until he thought he heard a door close. Then she returned.

"Yeah, Jonah," she said. "We do."

* * *

"So how did it go?" asked Terrence a few hours later.

"Wasn't pretty at first," admitted Jonah. "But we hashed things out. Cleaned out the negativity. It took some doing—Vera is stubborn as hell—but she eventually admitted that just leaving a note was kind of fucked up."

Terrence looked at Jonah in disbelief. "You actually got her to admit that she was wrong? You are my hero! No disrespect, but there aren't a lot of women in this world who would have admitted that. Just saying."

Jonah grunted. "I know that. And I'm savoring the victory. Why do you think that I conveniently left Reena out of this conversation?"

Terrence laughed. "Smart man!"

22

Prom Nights Present, Prom Nights Past

March faded unremarkably, which was definitely worth something. April had had the oxymoronic effect of being a dragging blur. By the time May rolled around, most folks had tired of being on edge. More people were spending time outside, because inside was the place where it was too easy to be engulfed in thought. At least outside in nature, there was a picturesque backdrop. It was easy for negative thoughts to fade away.

On principle, Jonah, Terrence, and Reena didn't obsess over the final three of the Six. Between them, there was a fear that the trap in those papers might have transferred itself somehow. Reena had duplicated the notes on scratch paper—ordinary rag—but the apprehension was still there. When they *did* speak on the matter, they were never around those notes. And Reena remained confident about Jonah's safety.

"Jonah, I've gone over in my head about a hundred times," she told him. "I just don't see how the Cut can come to fruition—how Creyton can get you—while Jonathan is here."

"And Daniel," added Terrence. "He's always chomping at the bit to shoot something with an arrow. If his first chance happens to be Creyton and a bunch of Deadfallen disciples, so be it!"

Terrence's overt heartiness was a giveaway; he was still very worried. So was Reena. Jonah was, too, if he were honest with himself. But there was something just a little odd about it.

And that was the fact that his old, unwelcome friend had settled into his consciousness.

That old feeling that he was missing something.

The difference this time was that it didn't seem to be obvious. He didn't feel like there was a piece staring him in the face. It felt clandestine, devious... shrouded in shadows, as though the Inimicus situation was on them all over again...

Jonah did all he could on his end. He trained hard, if for no other reason than to prevent being caught unawares. He kept the lines of communication open with Jonathan. And he kept a closer eye on Trip. Even after a month and some change, he still couldn't shake what Laban had said about Trip out of his mind.

Trip is his father incarnate; he just won't admit it.

Jonah had already thought about it. Except for the womanizing, he could see it—

Or hell, Trip might be a womanizer, Jonah didn't know. He didn't know everything that went on in Trip's life—Karin could be one of several—

Jonah hadn't spoken to Laban anymore, but he had spoken to Jonathan about his concerns over the guy continuously disassembling the bookshelf (Alvin, Malcolm, and Bast had all told him that the activity was a regular occurrence). Jonathan attempted to put him at ease.

"Jonah, if that is the most annoying thing he's doing, it's of no concern," he said. "Rest assured that that screwdriver and that bookshelf, disassembled or not, are not powerful enough instruments to incite a panic."

Still, Jonah was unnerved. He told Alvin, Malcolm, and Bast to keep an even keener eye on Laban. He had a feeling that Laban's time as a cooperative prisoner was drawing to a close. He didn't know where the feeling came from, but he trusted it. And it unnerved him.

Jonah felt a little strange, delegating things like that. He would have gladly kept watch himself, but he felt pretty useless, as Jonathan still hadn't lifted his ethereal grounding. He found this to be annoying because his punishment had been ongoing since February. Terrence was free of his punishment, and Reena, who was the one who had the idea to take the files in the first place, hadn't been punished at all. Yeah, she'd been out for a couple of weeks afterward, but that was beside the point. At times, Jonah found himself wondering if Jonathan had forgotten.

But somehow, he doubted that.

As the first week of May came to a close, however, there was a distraction.

Nella's and Themis' prom.

That had been a struggle in itself. Mr. and Mrs. Manville had been cool on the idea for the longest time, but Liz, who shared their concern, helped Nella work on them, nonetheless. It took a long while, but Nella had prevailed with an approach that had impressed even Liz.

"You let Sandrine move all the way to Philadelphia, despite all of this mess," she'd argued, "and you won't let me go to the middle of town for my prom for just a couple hours?"

"This is different," her father had contested. "Sandrine is a twenty-eight-year-old woman. You are only seventeen—"

"Family is family," Nella had stubbornly responded. "Whether you're eight or eighty. I'm smarter than I was last year, and more cautious. Even my ethereality has improved!"

In the end, her parents relented. Jonah was glad of that. It'd been World War III if Nella had missed her prom.

Nella and Themis had slaved over finding the right dresses for months. Themis had even jokingly lamented that, of all the various skills possessed by estate residents, not a single one of them was a seamstress or dressmaker. Finally, they'd found two perfect dresses, which they revealed to everyone hours before the prom.

Themis, the only lilac-colored aura Jonah knew, wore a dress of that same color that was rather full in the skirts and the sleeves, but somewhat snug at the waist and cuffs. She had gotten Reena-who else?-to darken her honey blonde hair, so that her skin would be thoroughly flattered by the color of the dress. Magdalena had braided pearls into her hair as well.

Themis was beautiful, Jonah gave her that approbation. But Nella was nothing short of ravishing.

Her dress was a stark scarlet and complimented her figure which almost matched Themis'. There was a kind of checkerboard pattern that repeated around her midsection, which made her waistline seem smaller than it actually was. At her throat were some of her mother's finest pearls. She'd wanted to wear star ruby, her birthstone, but it was Jonah's understanding that the stone would clash with the dress. In his opinion, the pearls suited her just fine.

Everyone in the family room broke into applause when both young women walked carefully down the stairs. Even Reena, who felt that girls and older women expended far too much money, sanity, and time on such affairs. But she'd chosen to humor them, at least for tonight.

Jonathan, who was near the front door, smiled widely when he saw them.

"How resplendent and alluring the both of you are," he said with fondness. "Bona fide belles."

Jonah was a bit puzzled by Jonathan's expression. It was a nostalgic look, a look that seemed to be invoked by past memories. It seemed that Nella and Themis, at least in Jonathan's mind, were sentimental replicas of an event or time long since past. He looked melancholy for the slightest of seconds, and then his mirth was as evident as everyone else's.

"Everyone take pictures of them now," said Jonathan. "I estimate that their dates will be arriving in a matter of minutes."

At that, Jonah and Terrence immediately turned to Reena, who had instant responses.

"Themis' date is named Lyle Bennett-Barker," she told them. "He's in the top ten percent of their senior class, and he was an outfielder on the baseball team. Nella's date is named Jacob Devereaux. He's in her Language Arts and U.S. History classes and has been in JROTC for three semesters."

"Great," said Jonah. "Do you trust them?"

"Only qualm I have with them is that they're typical, teenage hormonal boys," said Reena. "But they're both great kids."

"How nice," said Terrence. "Now are you coming with us to watch their prom?"

Reena scoffed. "Is this a question?"

* * *

Jonah, Terrence, and Reena actually beat many of the kids to the venue where the prom was held, which was the community center in the heart of town. Jonah was entertained by the turnout: the happy couples not fettered with a curfew, the less than ecstatic couples that were, the people who came with relatives to save face, and the ones who had no other choice but to go "stag."

"There is another high school in Rome, right?" he asked Terrence.

"Yeah," mumbled Terrence. "Trand High. Their prom is next weekend. I'll be one of the janitors on hand."

"Look," pointed Reena. "They're right there."

Jonah and Terrence did so. Amongst the kids were Nella, Themis, and their dates. It was obvious that Themis' date was an athlete of some kind, but Nella's date was slight, a little uncoordinated, and—

"Short!" Jonah exclaimed. "Shorter than Nella! Why would he do that to himself?"

"Do what to himself?" grinned Terrence. "If anything, the other guys might be impressed!"

"Not likely," said Jonah. "If anything, they'll make quips about him needing a damned high chair, or something."

At that point, Reena gave Jonah a narrow-eyed look. "Why do I detect personal experience?" she asked.

Jonah sighed. Reena Katoa, ever the observant one. "When I was in undergrad, my roommate thought that it would be cool to set me up on a date with this girl in the university's chamber orchestra," he recounted. "Beautiful girl named Khadijah Dandridge. He told me that she sang tenor and showed me a picture of her and everything."

"So, what was the issue?" said Reena. "it's not like you're stumpy, Jonah."

"I'm not finished," Jonah told her. "What he didn't tell me, and what the picture did not show, was the fact that this girl was six foot-eight."

Terrence mouthed, *"Wow."* Reena's eyes widened.

"Uh-huh," said Jonah in response to their reactions. "I got to the meeting spot, and Dee Dee took one look at me, laughed, and said, I'm sorry, short stuff, but you have to be this tall," he raised his hand over his head, "to ride this ride."

"Ouch," muttered Terrence.

Reena was still distracted. "Great God Almighty," she breathed. "Six-eight?"

Jonah rolled his eyes. "Yes, Reena," he laughed. "A real modern-day Amazon. Well, I can't really say modern since I was like nineteen at the time."

"Well, how 'bout this," said Terrence, "since we're at this prom, why don't you tell us about yours?"

Jonah snorted. "You just got a story from me. You first."

Terrence relaxed in the passenger seat. "I didn't actually go to high school, you know," he said. "Between my parents and Jonathan, it was pretty much a kind of home-school deal. I got my G.E.D. and everything, but no high school. Anyway, Mama set me up as a prom date with this girl that was in her contra dance class named Sue Cullipher." Terrence gnawed on a Twizzler. "She was a nice enough girl, I guess, but a little too backwater for me. Since I was biracial, she viewed me as exotic."

Jonah, who'd been drinking water at the time, choked. "What?" he sputtered. "Exotic?"

"Hey, I said she was backwater," said Terrence.

Jonah laughed hard at that. Reena joined in, and Terrence soon after. When they piped down, Terrence finished.

"The night was fun," he said. "I figured if I was going to be arm candy, I'd make the most of it."

Jonah raised an eyebrow. "You had sex with her, didn't you?"

Terrence shrugged. "It was prom night, brother!"

Jonah shook his head and turned to Reena. "How about you?"

"Yeah, how about you, Reena?" Terrence sounds intrigued. "I never knew…you were in your own little world back then."

"I thought the same thing about you back then, Terrence," said Reena with a chuckle, "but my story is easily told. Julia was still in the closet, so we weren't about to go to the prom together. But the time that we were trying to figure something out was the same time that her father found out about us and went batshit. He forced her to go to the prom with some guy that ran track with her. There was no way in hell that I was going to the prom with any guy, so I skipped it, went to the movies, and watched *The Matrix Reloaded.*"

Jonah and Terrence stared at her. She waved a hand.

"Don't pity me," she told them. "It's ancient history. Now it's your turn, Jonah."

Jonah wasn't stupid. Reena regretted not going to her prom, even if that regret was slight. But he obliged her, for one reason only. "Well, I think I can top you both," he said. "P.J. Denim, my best friend at the time, and I had dates lined up. He'd set me up with a distant relative of his, and she was pretty cute. Meanwhile, he had set up a date with this girl in Maryland that he called himself dating. Anyway, two days before the prom, my date backed out because her great-aunt passed into Spirit, which I understood. P.J.'s date ultimately couldn't make the trip. We'd already gotten the corsages and everything."

Terrence and Reena looked bemused, but Jonah shook his head.

"Don't react too early," he warned. "You're going to want to save that for the next part."

"Do tell," said Terrence.

Jonah grabbed one of Terrence's Twizzlers. "As it happened, we managed to scrounge up two last-minute dates. Sabrina Deloatche for P.J., and Regina Tyler for me."

"Well, that's good, right?" said Terrence. "Plan B to the rescue!"

"Plan B, he says," grumbled Jonah. "Unbeknownst to us at the time, Sabrina was an undiagnosed bulimic, and Regina was the campus drunk."

They stared at him.

"A drunk?" said Terrence.

"A bulimic?" said Reena.

"Mmm hmm, to both of you," said Jonah, chewing on his snack. "I suspected something was wrong when Regina started laughing at things that weren't funny and Sabrina had chicken grease stains on her dress. But we finally got to the prom, and I took pictures with Regina. How she remained steady for those poses, I'll never know. But within an hour or so, Sabrina had made plans to go to a motel with another dude, and Regina was in some other guy's car, lit on Southern Comfort. P.J. and I said screw it, got with a bunch of friends, and had a late dinner at Ruby Tuesday's. I was home by 2:30 in the morning."

Reena sat back in her seat, while Terrence looked forward.

"Damn," said Terrence, "so you mean to tell me that between the three of us, my prom night was the best?"

"Well, I wouldn't say that," said Reena. "*The Matrix Reloaded* was pretty awesome."

"And if I knew you back then, Reena, I would have gone to watch it right along with you," said Jonah.

They all shared a good laugh about that. Terrence sobered somewhat after that.

"I'm going to miss this," he said out of the blue.

"Miss what?" frowned Jonah.

"This," he said, spreading his hands. "I feel like whatever hell is coming sooner rather than later. And when it hits, there won't be any more time for fun, for great food and great times, for things as simple as...as sitting here in a car, shootin' the breeze about corny proms and whatnot..."

Terrence's voice trailed off.

Jonah almost smiled. Almost. It wasn't a heartening notion at all, but it was nice to know that he wasn't alone. He thought that thinking about good times and hanging out with friends was at best selfish, at worst blithe. But knowing that his brother and sister shared the same thoughts also meant that everyone else probably felt similar. There was a feeling of universality.

Why was he inspired by that?

"I'm right there with you, brother," said Jonah, who made his voice hearty. "But be content in the knowledge that hell isn't here just yet. Tonight, worrying isn't your job."

"No," said Reena, "tonight, your job is to sit here with us and make spiteful comments about these brainless gala affairs."

Terrence laughed, nodded, and soon enough, they were all conversing about a whole bunch of nothing again. The lighthearted banter continued for the next few hours, until they saw people begin to file out of the community center, Nella, Themis, and their dates among them. Not a single hitch, and not a single concern. Those two girls got to have to have their evening of simplistic frivolity, just like everyone else. Satisfied, Jonah, Terrence, and Reena headed back to the estate, grateful for the night of fun and peace, while Jonah, in a compartmentalized box in his mind, still wondered how much longer the fun times would last.

23

Biblio-Informant

Jonah had awakened the next morning after having a weird dream where he had been the one tasked with coordinating a new prom, since the one that Nella and Themis had just attended was declared a fail. What was even crazier was the fact that Vera was the one who had been ordered to help him do it.

Well, that dream pertained to nothing, and made no sense.

He got up, showered, and went downstairs to make eggs and grits. He couldn't help but laugh when he thought about the debate that he and Terrence had had forever concerning grits; Terrence preferred his cheesy and with salt, while Jonah preferred his sweet, with brown sugar and cinnamon. They both viewed the other as strange.

Being that Jonah awakened at such an early hour, it was quiet. Reena hadn't even gotten up to run yet.

Why was he awake this early, though?

There was a possibility that it was no big deal, and he was overreacting. After all, that feeling that he was missing something had been there for the past couple weeks.

And, truth be told, maybe Jonah wasn't even missing anything. He hadn't found anything out of the ordinary. Not even with Terrence's and Reena's help. When they spoke on Four, Five, and Six, they agreed that subtlety would be a factor, maybe even subterfuge as well. They had agreed that it would be a seemingly insignificant event, a random event, that would be the sign they'd been looking for. What they needed to do when they saw that sign, however, was a different matter. They'd just have to cross that bridge when they reached it.

He finished his breakfast and sat for a moment. It was five in the morning. The library wouldn't be open for another three hours.

What the hell was he supposed to do?

He decided that fresh air might assist him. TV was out of the question. And besides, the only thing on at this time of the morning was damnable news.

The grounds were quiet. A couple heralds walked about as though they owned the place, which made him smile. The gazebo was resplendent with flora all around it once more—he could wait to get home from work later on that day and write some out there. The courtyard looked great, with Jonathan standing there—

Wait.

Jonathan?

Jonah hid behind some bushes, but after several seconds, he no longer thought that hiding was necessary. Jonathan wasn't actually doing anything suspicious. He simply walked around the courtyard, taking in the sights of the morning. It was no different than what Jonah was doing. Everything the Protector Guide saw, he regarded with a smile: Liz and Nella's gardens, the wooden gnomes that Malcolm had created and placed everywhere—everything. He just stood there, drinking it all in. It was about as peaceful a scene as could be.

Jonah shrugged. For all he knew, this could be Jonathan's ritual. Lord knows he wouldn't know; he was never up at this time of morning.

He decided not to engage him in conversation and went back inside. There'd be nothing good on TV, but that wasn't the case with Netflix.

When Jonah arrived at the library, he'd already been awake for almost five hours. That just wasn't right. He laughed about it as he walked in.

Once he actually got into the swing of things, it was no big deal. Smith was as chipper as ever, going on and on about how today, May 12th, was such a "good day to be alive." Jonah actually snorted, because in Smith's eyes, nearly every day was a "good day to be alive." This was just the latest.

Victoria was in good spirits because she had finally mastered her allergies. Wally was enjoyable to be around because he was quiet, which Jonah always thought was due to the fact that he couldn't ever get a word in edgewise due to Paula.

"The warmth makes me smile," she said for the millionth time. "I cannot wait to hit my mother's timeshare in Wrightsville Beach! I will bask forever!"

Jonah glanced at her. The woman had already soaked up so much sun over the years that she resembled a bruised peach.

"Well, hey!" said Wally, who jumped at the opening, "maybe you can read this, provided Jonah doesn't mind, of course."

He slid *Halfway There* Paula's way, smiling devilishly at Jonah. Jonah felt his lip curl, but he paused when he saw Paula's reaction.

Under normal circumstances, she'd have laughed out loud with Wally. But this time, she looked a bit puzzled. Jonah frowned. Was dense in addition to being unsightly? Did she not get the joke, as stupid as it was?

But it didn't seem to have anything to do with idiocy. She seemed to be trying to put something together. Apparently, there was some connection between Jonah and that book that she couldn't grasp.

But what would she know about it? Victoria had been the one who told Jonah about the hold, and Smith had been the one who'd given it to him. Paula had had nothing to do with it.

Unless—

Jonah approached her, casually and smoothly. Alarming her wasn't necessary. It was clear that she wasn't used to concentrating; her head looked as though it might explode. "Paula? Is something wrong? Did that book trigger a memory, or something?"

Paula turned her frown Jonah's way. "It—it did," she murmured. "I don't... something odd..."

"Does it involve the book?" persisted Jonah. "And me?"

Wally even looked concerned at the way Paula was acting. But Jonah was so focused, he didn't mind the nosiness.

"Yeah," said Paula. "I put that book on hold for you."

With effort, Jonah forced his eyes not to widen. When he spoke, it was as calm as he could muster. "Why did you leave it on hold?" he asked. "It was kinda silly, and I've never shown a minute's interest in romance novels."

"I—I know," sputtered Paula, "and I didn't even want to! Some woman told me to do it."

Jonah remained cool, but now he was internally more alert than ever. "A woman told you to?" he repeated.

"Yeah," said Paula, still quite puzzled. "She told me to do it and forget it, and I *had* forgotten it... until now."

Jonah nodded, fighting the impulse to grab Paula's shoulders and shake her. "Describe her, please."

Paula's brow furrowed further. "She might've been your age or couple years older, but just a couple. Blonde hair, but it wasn't like mine. And, for some reason, she had on a choker."

Jonah closed his eyes. This was precisely why he didn't want to get close to these people. They could be used, hurt, or manipulated... just like last time...

But why had Paula been the one that Jessica had chosen? He couldn't stand the orange, overbearing woman.

But it didn't matter. Whatever her fallacies, and there were many to consider, she was an innocent Tenth. As were Victoria, Wally, Smith, and everyone else.

"I have to go," he said.

They all looked at him in surprise.

"But, Jonah," said Victoria, "you've only got an hour and a half left, and you're off for the entire weekend!"

"Too true," said Jonah, his mind already a million miles away. "Later."

24

Ai

Jonah didn't bother to call Terrence or Reena. At the moment, he didn't have enough proof to incite a panic. He needed Jonathan.

Would it be expecting too much for him to still be surveying the grounds?

The minute Jonah pulled up onto the estate grounds, he saw that it was indeed too much to expect. Jonathan was nowhere in sight, and he wouldn't be in the daylight. It was hard for spirits and spiritesses to maintain strength while in the sun.

But Jonah had to ignore that right now. It sucked, but he had to ignore it.

He looked around, hoping to find Bast, but the only herald he saw was Naphtali. She'd been Vera's favorite herald.

And she'd do wonderfully now.

"Naphtali," he called, "come here, please."

She bounded toward him, and her amber eyes were as intense as ever. *"Yes, Jonah?"* she intimated.

"I need you to summon, Jonathan," he said. "I can't do it myself; I still can't use any ethereality. Tell him—"

"Done," intimated Naphtali. *"He's on his way."*

Sure enough, Jonathan was in front of Jonah seconds later, seemingly shrouded in light. Jonah felt guilty as hell when he saw that, but he filed it away.

"Jonathan, I'm sorry," he said. "I know that forming in direct sunlight requires a lot of effort. Had I been thinking, I would have asked to meet you in your study, but—"

"Don't worry about it, son," said Jonathan. "My strength is sufficient enough for conversation. What's the matter?"

Jonah told him all about Jessica using C.P.V. on his fellow employee to put the library book on hold for him. Jonathan sighed.

"I figured as much," he said. "When I gave the matter further thought, I figured as much."

"Jonathan, there is something that I don't get," said Jonah. "Jessica told Paula to forget it. Forget everything about it. How did Paula break it?"

"I think that it's a combination of two things," said Jonathan. "I think that when you powered through Jessica's C.P.V. last year was the first that had ever happened. It may very well have had an effect on her resolve and confidence. Dark ethereality like the kind she uses requires immense focus, and she had never failed at it. Until you. So now, when she does it, there is that doubt. The second thing is this: when you told me about that book being reserved in the library, I provided some protection there, in addition to the measures you take every day. I got to see your colleagues; feel their essences and gauge their personalities. The one you speak of—Paula—has an astute proclivity for gossip. And she can't keep a secret worth a damn. So, when Jessica told her to forget something? She may as well have told a Protector Guide not to protect, or a vampire not to desire lifeblood. It was a lose-lose situation for Jessica, using that particular woman as a pawn."

Jonah could hardly believe it. There weren't too many situations in life where being a gossiping snitch was a good thing.

He shook his head. "One more thing, sir," he said. "It concerns the remaining three of six. The Attempts, the Cut, and the Splinter."

Jonathan regarded him. "Yes?"

Jonah sighed. Here goes. "I haven't even given the Attempts any thought," he admitted, "but I think—I think the Cut is me."

Jonathan's expression didn't change. "Jonah," he said, his voice deliberate and clear, "you are protected. I cannot stress that enough. And if you were in a situation where your physical life was in the balance, I have no doubts that you would give a superb accounting of yourself. You are incapable of doing any less. You've grown into a powerful man, and I have full faith in your abilities."

Jonah felt a bit awkward. That was high praise. But one thing stuck out to him. "With all due respect, sir," he murmured, "I was already a man when we first met—"

Jonathan chuckled. "A grown man can still be a baby, Jonah," he told him. "Decisions and experiences determine maturation, not age."

Jonah nodded. Answers like that were classic Jonathan, after all.

"I must attend to some things," said Jonathan, "and also get out of the daylight. Thank you for this information, Jonah. I will see to it that the defenses around your job remain reinforced."

"Jonathan, hold up," said Jonah hastily. "I was wondering if you were willing to lift my punishment now."

Jonathan smiled. "No. Nice try, though."

He disappeared, leaving Jonah a bit perturbed. And still unnerved.

He decided to check on Laban. Had to see what that weasel was up to. He headed for the garage.

"So, you're making him appear in broad daylight now."

It wasn't a question. But it was definitely a voice that Jonah had zero interest in hearing.

Trip leaned against the side of the garage, smoking the usual cigarette.

"Why aren't you at work?" frowned Jonah.

Trip pulled on his cigarette. "My schedule is none of your business, Rowe."

"Man, whatever."

Jonah shook his head, was about to walk inside when Trip blocked him with an arm.

Jonah closed his eyes. Anger is a tool. He had to remind himself of that. "Trip," he said quietly. "Maybe you didn't get it. When I said whatever, that was when the conversation was over—"

"Rowe," Trip rasped, "one day soon, everything I've said about you will happen, and you will ruin everything. When you screw up, irreparably so, I will be there. And, at long last, I will beat your ass."

Jonah employed the deep belly breathing that Felix had taught him during those anti-Haunt lessons. It helped. Kind of. "As I told you that night, I found out you were a damn snitch," he grumbled, "all I need is to know where and when. But just so you know, me irreparably screwing things up is never going to happen. And what about you? Who's to say that it won't be *your* dumb ass messing everything up?"

"I'm well aware of what I'm doing," sneered Trip.

Jonah laughed with no mirth. "Yeah. I'm sure your Daddy said that same thing, right before the 49er handed him his throat."

Trip was so shocked and infuriated that he dropped his arm. Jonah wasted no further time. He was proud of himself. If only he could own Laban every once in a while.

When he reached the cell, Laban was seated on his bed, staring straight ahead at the bookshelf, which he had reconstructed. When he saw Jonah, he smiled.

"Pleasure to see you, boy," he said.

Jonah didn't answer immediately, enjoying the sense of relief he had about the shelf being back together again. It felt wrong as hell when the thing was in pieces. It felt like Laban had several tools. Several weapons. "Just wanted to see if you were behaving yourself," he said finally.

Laban raised his eyebrows. "Even entombed in this cage, you still view me as a threat. For that, I congratulate you."

Jonah's eyes narrowed. "Come again?"

"You heard," said Laban, his voice terse. Once again, there was that changeability.

"Why the hell is that cause for congratulations?" demanded Jonah.

"Because it shows that you are making forays beyond the things that you can see," said Laban. "That is all."

Jonah left him. He found out what he needed, and that was that. Thankfully, Trip was no longer outside. He decided to punch the bag a bit and wait for Terrence and Reena to get home. This very strange day would pass a lot more quickly with company.

Jonah was considerate enough to let his friends settle and relax before he gave them information. Before he could do so, however, they informed him that they too felt a sense of oddness.

"I don't know," said Reena, "maybe I got up on the wrong side of the bed this morning. But I can't shake it. It's something in the air."

"It's just been a weird day," concurred Terrence. "It's like the feeling you have when your supervisor wants a private meeting."

"I'm on the level with you," Jonah told them. "I woke up right after five, yet I haven't felt tired at all today. I get to work, and lo and behold, I discover that Jessica had used C.P.V. on Paula to get her to reserve that book for me. She told her to forget it, but it didn't work."

Reena, who'd been alarmed at Jonah's words when he revealed that a Deadfallen disciple had been at his job, looked baffled at the last part. "Why didn't her C.P.V. work?"

"According to Jonathan, her faith in the ability was shaken after I broke through it that time," Jonah replied. "And also, she made the mistake of choosing the gossip girl, and—also according to Jonathan—something about Paula's mind for gossip being too sharp to be vulnerable for long."

At that moment, Bobby approached them, looking confused.

"What's up?" he asked. "Is something wrong?"

Initially, Jonah thought that he'd overheard their conversation, but his mind seemed elsewhere.

"Why do you ask that?" asked Terrence.

"Jonathan," responded Bobby. "Usually, he gets Malcolm, Bast, and Alvin to give Laban his food and watch him. Tonight, though, he's got Prodigal and Raymond helping them out. That brings it up to five. I don't get why he would double up for such a boring job. All the guy ever does is meditates, reads, and breaks down that shelf."

"Has he broken it down lately?" asked Jonah.

"Nope," said Bobby. "He hasn't done it for a couple of weeks now. As a matter of fact, he hasn't done anything, or so Alvin says."

"I still don't trust him." Spader, who had been unrepentantly eavesdropping, moved their way. "Then again, I guess I just don't trust people in general. All I want to know is…what's been the point?"

Jonah frowned at him. "The point of what?"

"The point of having Laban Cooper here," said Spader. "I remember that Jonathan said that Laban was turning snitch on Creyton or whatever, but has he done that? Has he told anyone anything noteworthy?"

Jonah glanced at Terrence and Reena. Was Spader serious? "You don't think he's said anything?" he asked.

Bobby now looked as intrigued as Spader. "We don't know anything about anything he's said," he murmured. "I was just talking to Alvin about that this morning."

Jonah's eyes narrowed. "When Trip was badmouthing me some months ago," he said slowly, "what exactly did he say? I knew that he was running his mouth, but I never bothered to figure out the specifics because it was so stupid to me."

"Oh, that." Bobby scoffed. "It was something about Reena stealing something out of Jonathan's office, and you pressuring her to figure out what it meant. He claimed that was what put Reena in a coma; you overtaxing her, or something. A bunch of folks took it like it was the gospel, but I thought it was bullshit."

Jonah was too shocked to register the fact that Trip had spread drama based on an outright lie. He was more focused on the information itself.

Trip hadn't told them everything? Did that mean that Jonah, Terrence, and Reena were the only ones who knew about the Six? Alvin had even heard Laban spout one of the numbers but had written it off as the mutterings of a lonely prisoner.

Jonah was almost reeling. Terrence and Reena didn't look so hot, either.

Spader and Bobby seemed to realize that their words had had a curious effect with their words.

"Are we missing something here?" asked Bobby.

"Not at all." Reena said it quickly enough to have not shown hesitation, but not slowly enough to seem evasive. "We just hadn't been aware of the immensity of Trip's embellishment. That was all."

Bobby bought it. Spader looked suspicious but said nothing.

"Trip's a douche, man," said Bobby. "All there is to it."

"But there's no need to talk about him," said Spader. "Who's up for Pizza Pit? It's 'Every man for himself' night, and personally, I'm not interested in leftovers."

Sometime later, two delivery guys showed up, toting an armload of greasy pizzas between them. When they saw the group, they assumed it was a party. As they were thanked kindly and generously tipped, neither of them asked any questions. Jonah had to admit that the combination of food and positive atmosphere elevated his mood. It brought about a nice sense of normalcy, especially when Terrence held a paper plate with two huge slices of Supreme pizza under Reena's nose, saying, "Live a little!"

Suddenly, Jonah shot up. "The guys watching Laban," he said, grabbing a couple boxes. "Almost forgot them!"

As he went outside, he was pleasantly surprised to see that Grayson was once again among them, talking it up with Maxine and Magdalena. With everything that Jonah had been going through with Trip, it did him a world of good to know that someone in their group had a mind of their own. Maybe it was possible that some of the others would catch a clue, too.

The guys regarded the pizza excitedly when Jonah brought it to them. One would have thought they hadn't had a decent meal in all of their lives.

"What, is there a shindig going on up there?" joked Malcolm.

"Nope," laughed Jonah, "everyone was just feeling lazy, and didn't want to prepare leftovers. I wanted to make sure you guys got some because it was fading fast."

The guys took it with great relish. Bast positioned herself in Jonah's line of sight.

"*I know that you haven't forgotten me, Jonah,*" she intimated. "*I can smell the tuna.*"

Grinning, Jonah lowered the Tupperware bowl of tuna to Bast's level.

"This is all so wonderful," said Laban, mirth in his voice. "I'm touched. But you aren't the only ones here. Slide me a few slices, all the exertion has gotten me quite famished."

The grin faded from Ray's face as he knelt, tapped the ethereal steel, and muttered, "Food." He then slid a few slices through the opening. Laban cleared his throat and moved forward to retrieve it, but otherwise did nothing else as he seated himself to eat.

"You're far too kind, Raymond," he said softly.

Jonah ignored the niceties and looked at Raymond. "Exertions? He's doing pushups all hours again?"

"Yeah," said Raymond. "He's been working off and on all day. I thought Dad was durable for this age, but this man is crazy."

"Tell me about it," said Prodigal, "I've been here since before Ray, Malcolm, and Alvin showed up. That guy started off with, like, a hundred sit-ups, then some Hindu squats. Then it was push-ups and jumping jacks."

"Huh." Jonah looked over at Laban. "Sounds like an old-school football workout. I knew about his affinity for pushups. Is all the other crap new?"

"I can hear you, you know." Laban sounded bored. "Rowe, I keep my strength up as best I can. It's a good practice for any man, particularly one over fifty, like myself. Today, I did more than pushups, because I felt looser, and compensated for that. End of story."

"Uh-huh," murmured Jonah. "Right." He looked at his friends. "See you later, guys. When is Jonathan letting you free?"

"Bout forty-five more minutes," said Malcolm. "Can't wait for that."

"I bet," snorted Jonah. "See you guys soon."

Everyone was full of pizza, and probably near a food coma when Jonah got back into the estate. It was a few minutes after ten, and no one had anywhere to go in the morning except for Bobby, who had decided to touch up on fundamentals with his athletic instructor. Alvin would love that because it meant that he didn't have to tag along.

Reena hadn't retreated to her studio, choosing to assist Stella Marie and Autumn Rose with something involving wrist strength. He didn't see Terrence, but that wasn't a surprise. He was probably upstairs watching some B-movie action film of some kind or reading WWE spoilers. He headed upstairs himself, thinking of a long shower and heading to bed early.

He passed Doug's open room door, where he saw him inattentively watching something on his laptop.

"Hey, Doug," he said. "What are you trying so hard to get through?"

Douglas seemed to be relieved for a distraction. "It's a bible documentary," he answered. "Katarina lent it to me."

"Really?" said Jonah. "I thought Katarina was agnostic."

"She is," said Douglas. "She only gave it to me because it deals with battles in the Bible, and she knows I have a thing for strategy because of my love for chess."

"Bible battles?" queried Jonah.

"Yeah," said Douglas with a small smile. "And this one is talking about Ai."

Jonah walked further into the room, glancing at the place where Douglas had paused it. "Ai," he repeated. "What happened there? Can you nutshell it?"

"Oh yeah," said Douglas. "The Israelites suckered the soldiers of Ai into chasing them until they were out of the city. When all of the defenders of Ai left the city, a hidden unit of

Israelites went into the wide-open city and besieged it. The men of Ai turned around and saw their city in flames."

"Damn," said Jonah. "Sounds epic."

"It's the oldest strategy in the book," said Douglas. "Although, just to be fair, it was probably revolutionary at that time."

Jonah chortled. "Thanks for that, Doug," he said. "Don't think I've ever heard that bible story. Is it the Old Testament?"

"I'd expect so," said Douglas. "That's where most of the fighting was."

With a laugh, Jonah bade Douglas goodnight, and went to his room, where he flopped on the bed without even taking off his shoes. The shower could wait for the morning.

He was thankful. The day had started off oddly and strangely, but had transformed into a pleasant and relaxing thing, full of laughs and calories.

He wasn't worried about Jessica. He had her number now, and he trusted Jonathan whole-heartedly. All concerns could wait for a different day.

Jonah closed his eyes, laughing to himself about how he'd have to walk in to work on Monday morning and gloss over his abrupt exit. But he wasn't worried. He had faith in himself to handle that situation. He'd won them all over already, so damage control should be no problem.

Right now, all that was on his mind was resting after being awake for almost fifteen hours. He was like a kid almost, looking forward to Saturday morning.

2:10 AM

That was what the clock said when Jonah's eyes flew open.

Something wasn't right. At all.

The wrongness that mildly peppered his thoughts the previous morning had now enveloped him.

He leapt out of bed, wrenched open the door, and threw himself out of it—

To find that he was one of many. It seemed like everyone was out of their beds, running for the stairs. Within seconds, he was shoulder to shoulder with Terrence.

"So, you felt it, too," he said breathlessly.

"Like a fire under my ass." Terrence's nod was jerky. "What do you think—?"

"No idea and I'm not assuming," said Jonah flatly. "Let's just get downstairs!"

They practically led the mad dash to the family room, where the rest of the estate residents were congregated. There was a small collection of people in the center of the crowd, which plainly meant that they'd been there already: Jonathan, Daniel, Felix, Patience, and Reverend Abbott.

"What was that?" demanded Terrence. "That feeling. Was it a Ghost Wave?"

"No, Terrence," said Jonathan. "It was an Eris Effect."

The words silenced the entire room. Jonah didn't know what to think. And Eris Effect was the feeling that preceded a truly catastrophic occurrence, one that would result in things getting a whole hell of a lot worse before they got better. Jonah had experienced the feeling three times now, and the worst feeling one was the one that happened before Creyton achieved Praeterletum. This one felt like that.

So, what was the deal now?

"We all felt it, too," said Reverend Abbott, looking worried as hell. "I used the *Astralimes* straight here."

"Same here," said Patience. "I'm probably going to be a reprimand for abandoning my post, not that I give a—"

Then, for the first time in over a year, Jonah felt a painful buzz at the back of his skull. He grabbed his head with both hands, vaguely realizing that everyone else had done the same thing.

Now's not the time, he thought to himself. *Now is not the time to black out...*

But he didn't. No one did. The Mindscope hadn't knocked them out this time. The only thing that seemed to be different was that his sense of hearing was more sensitive than it had ever been in his life. What was that about? Had the Mindscope jostled a switch in his mind and made him ultrasonic, or something?

But then, words were spoken in his head. It was the one voice that he hadn't heard in a year, but he'd never forget it. Not in a million lifetimes.

"Per Mortem, Vitam."

Everyone froze. Jonah saw the horror in every eye and was right there along with them. Jonathan had said to him that when you heard that phrase, then someone's time was up.

The Cut was coming. They were coming for him.

"You're safe, Jonah," hissed Jonathan when he caught Jonah's expression.

"Like hell I am—!"

Jonathan raised both his hands to the residents. "You have all been endowed," he announced. "Go to your rooms, the armory, wherever you keep weapons, and get outside! Don't let them surround you!"

Movements almost shook the floor as everyone went to obey Jonathan's command. Jonah hadn't moved a muscle for two reasons.

One, he didn't need to go anywhere for weapons, as his batons were always in his pocket. Second, he didn't feel the exhilaration that everyone else did. Jonathan hadn't endowed him!

"Jonathan!" he shouted over the noise. "Your endowment missed me!"

"Indeed, it did," said Jonathan.

Jonah's eyes bulged. "What the hell, Jonathan!" he snarled. "I've learned my damned lesson! Let the punishment be over and done with! They are coming for *me!*"

"It is not about punishment, Jonah!" Jonathan shot back. "You don't understand, and I don't have the time to explain it! Get outside and stay close to Terrence and Reena! They'll watch your back!"

With a roar of fury, Jonah hurried outside, pulled out his batons, and flicked the switch at the bottoms to bring them to full size. To hell with being handheld in a fight. The bastards had weak spots.

Still, he looked here and there for Terrence and Reena, as allies. Not to be protected.

He couldn't get a bead on anything, because everyone ran in all different directions, and it wasn't like Terrence and Reena were the only yellow and orange auras at the estate—

A savage shout hijacked his attention, and he looked near the gravel driveway. Several Deadfallen disciples advanced from that way. Jonah didn't see any weapons, but as their auras were black, it didn't make much difference. He ran forward with a plan to join a group of residents who had charged forward to defend against them, but strong hands grabbed him and swung him around.

"What in the name of hell are you doing?" demanded Felix. "You're unendowed and wide open!"

"I'm no one's bitch, Felix!" snapped Jonah. "I can fight! Weren't you the one that said we relied on ethereality too much, anyway?"

"Jonah, you get your ass—!"

A Deadfallen disciple clotheslined Felix, but with a nip-up, Felix was right back on his feet. He grabbed the man, looped his arm, and proceeded to beat the holy hell out of him. Jonah backed away just in case Felix lost it.

Where the hell were Terrence and Reena?

And then someone grabbed him at the throat. Jonah gurgled in surprise and clutched at the hands. The person was strong; their hands were like iron. Going on instinct alone, Jonah allowed himself, full weight, to fall to the ground. His momentum brought the guy with him, and Jonah felt the man's jaw crash into the top of his head. The man roared as he let go of Jonah, even spitting out a couple of teeth. Jonah grabbed his batons, struck the guy in the back, and then rammed a knee up to his already bloody mouth. The guy fell back, and Jonah left him.

He couldn't focus on fighting because he'd noticed something. Just noticed it.

All around him, friends were fighting Deadfallen disciples. They were fighting for their physical lives. But Creyton's followers, while hardcore, no disputing that—seemed to be phoning it in...

And also, at the same time, making the residents fan out further and further from the estate...

Jonah's eyes widened. They were employing the Ai strategy. Douglas had just explained it to Jonah hours earlier. What kind of sick, coincidental mess was this?

Wait.

Why would they pull everyone away from the estate? Surely, they weren't going to burn it down.

About ten yards from where Jonah stood, a Deadfallen disciple had dodged away as a golden arrow from Daniel's bow nearly pierced his skull. Seeing the blaze of gold made Jonah realize it. Daniel wasn't the only gold aura. The other one wasn't out here with them.

"Jonathan," Jonah breathed.

He tore off towards the estate, and nearly broke down the door when he got there.

Jonathan stood in the center of the room; eyes closed. But when Jonah barged in, they shot open.

"Jonah!" he exclaimed. "Why are you in here? I told you to stay close to Terrence and Reena!"

"I couldn't find them, and I was trying to!" said Jonah, which was the truth. "But you're the one that needs help. You're completely alone!"

"I don't need your help, boy, I can take care of myself—"

"Don't bullshit me, Jonathan!" snapped Jonah. "I don't know what their plan is exactly, but right now, they're doing some strategy that was used in some bible city named Ai. They're pulling people away from the estate! But no one's here with you, man! It's necessary to protect our leader."

With that, he turned his back on Jonathan and got near a window so that he could see. He gripped his batons tighter. Unendowed or not—hell, Cut or not—they weren't reaching his mentor.

Suddenly, Jonah was completely shrouded in some kind of vapor. He could breathe just fine, but he was completely encased. He dropped the batons in surprise.

"What the hell?" he cried and whirled around. "What—?"

His voice ceased. For some reason, Jonathan had a hand raised his way. He was the one that had done it.

"You're absolutely right, Jonah," he said in a carefully leveled voice. "We have to protect our leader. By sending you outside with everyone else, that's what I was doing."

The air began to shimmer a few feet from Jonathan, and there was no wind. A twig portal. Jonathan glanced at it, but looked neither surprised nor scared.

"Words cannot describe the honor it had been to know and teach you, Jonah," he told him.

Jonah saw the hugest Haunt he'd ever laid eyes on emerge from the shimmering space. It was as big as a damn horse. His eyes nearly popped out of their sockets.

But Jonathan just smiled.

"I'll give your grandmother your love, son," said Jonathan. "Take care of everyone for me."

Jonah shook his head. "Jonathan, no..."

Jonathan removed something from his pocket as the massive Haunt wrested itself from the portal and gave Jonah a smile.

"Goodbye."

He threw something at Jonah just as the Haunt launched itself at him. Though the object was small, it hit him with the force of a wrecking ball and knocked him clear out of the window and on to the front lawn. But Jonah felt neither the impact of the object nor the crashing through the window and hitting the ground. Whatever Jonathan had done to him had left him completely unscathed.

Jonah didn't register any of that. He looked at the broken window he'd just flown out of as the horror in him reached a crescendo.

"Jonathan," he whispered. "No...God, No!"

He stuffed the object into his pocket and ran back into the estate's family room.

The only trace of Jonathan was the Infinity medallion, which was in a golden pile on the floor.

25

Six-Fruition

Jonah stared at the medallion, shaking his head. Reality was what a person made it, and Jonathan being gone was not reality. He didn't accept it; he wouldn't accept it—

It was at that moment that Jonah realized that he was being watched. He slowly raised incredulous eyes.

Jessica stood at the place where the portal had been created. She was dressed in a black short skirt, blank tank top, and oddly, a black fedora. Her grin was radiant.

"The black outfit is for the sad occasion," she murmured. "But the Transcendent sends his regards."

Something like a lightning bolt of pure rage tore through Jonah at the sight of her. He charged, grabbed Jessica by her skimpy shirt, and slammed her against the wall, which caused her to cry out in surprise and pain.

"Bitch!" he bellowed. "I'll kill you! I swear to God, I'll fucking kill you!"

Jessica's eyes were slightly reddened from hitting the wall, but she regarded Jonah with frost. "You'll be dead long before me."

Jonah howled in rage, and meant to strike her, but with the snap of a twig that he hadn't noticed, Jessica faded into the shadows and was gone. Jonah's hands were empty.

He stumbled to the medallion on the floor and collapsed to his knees. Tears of every emotion poured from his eyes: shock, horror, anger, grief... every single one of them was present in those tears.

"No," he whispered. "I could've done something... I could've helped... why didn't you endow me?"

Jonah spoke to the infinity medallion. The infinity of life. At this moment in time, that notion was a joke. A sick joke. An idle side note compared to the medallion on the floor in front of him, which no longer had an owner.

He heard footsteps behind him but didn't bother turning around. He'd know who it was soon enough. He was sure of it.

"Jonah!" It was Reena. "Thank God. Terrence and I were looking for you—"

Reena stopped speaking, and Jonah knew why. Her eyes had fallen on the object on the floor where he knelt. She was smart; she'd figure out the truth in a second.

There it was. The dreadful gasp followed by sobs. Jonah never imagined that badass Reena was capable of sounds like that. But one learned something new every day.

Then there were the others. So many others. Just when he thought everyone was there, there was always a new set of footsteps. A new set of exclamations. A new set of sobs. And he could identify each and every one without even glancing their way. But through all of the hell coursing through his head, a new emotion emerged.

New, but by no means foreign.

Fear.

No, not fear. Terror.

Jonah had only felt it on this level once before when he'd lost Nana. She was beyond reach. And when Jonah found out about The Eleventh Percent's limitation of not being able to see the spirits of other Eleventh Percenters or the spirits of people they were close to, he'd felt like he'd lost her all over again.

But this was *Jonathan*.

He had already been in Spirit, became a Protector Guide, and had become even more powerful because of that. But now he'd been vanquished. He'd been forcibly sent to the Other Side. Another indomitable source of light, forever beyond Jonah's reach.

The two words that were at the forefront of Jonah's mind when he lost Nana were back again at this time, with the loss of Jonathan.

Now what?

A powerfully strong hand touched Jonah's shoulder, but the grasp was one that soothing and reassuring.

"Get up, son." It was Reverend Abbott.

Jonah didn't protest, but it was rather laborious, because he'd been on his knees a while, and they were killing him. But with effort, he stood and looked around.

And wished he hadn't.

Reena was sobbing. Terrence sat in his favorite chair, hands at his temples, while silent tears pooled at the tip of his nose before they fell. Liz, Maxine, Magdalena, Nella, and Themis. All in tears. Bobby, Spader, Douglas, Ben-Israel, Benjamin, and Akshara weren't in tears, but the expressions on their faces clearly stated that they weren't faring much better than the crying ones. There were so many people there. So many tears, so much helplessness.

It was impossible to believe that, mere hours earlier, they were all laughing over pizza, popcorn, and drinks…

Pizza…

"Malcolm," he said suddenly, "Alvin, Prodigal, Raymond, Bast…they were down there guarding Laban. Where—"

"I'll check it out." Felix hopped up. "I'm probably the strongest of you all right now."

"What are you talking about, Felix?" said Bobby.

"The spirit that we received our spiritual endowments from has been vanquished," said Felix, his voice measured. Controlled. "Our endowments have been ripped away as a result. You haven't experienced it yet, but the fatigue will be crazy. It will kick in for me, but I can manage because I'm a sazer. For those of you who are standing, sit down. I'm not as good with estimates as Jonathan—" Felix closed his eyes. Speaking about Jonathan was that commonplace. "All of you just sit down, damn it."

Felix left. No one was offended. Everyone could see through his grief.

"Jonah," said Daniel in a voice so frigid that it was frightening, "tell us what happened."

Jonah closed his eyes, having no desire to see anyone's face. He told them everything except the part about Jonathan throwing the object at him. He hadn't really gotten a good look at the thing he'd caught and pocketed, but he was pretty sure what it was.

And it terrified him more than he was willing to admit, or handle, at the moment.

The story had about the effect that Jonah had expected, but Terrence shook his head.

"A damned *Haunt* took Jonathan out?" he demanded. "Are you shitting me? We've seen Jonathan handle Haunts! Bunches of 'em at a time!"

"You didn't see this Haunt, man," said Jonah in a hollow voice. "It was...it looked 'roided. It was big as a fuckin' horse—"

"A War Haunt," said Daniel with no emotion. "Specially bred to destroy Guides. The Curaie had them hunted to extinction in the seventeenth century. The only one who would have had the knowledge to create a new one—" Daniel's eyes flashed, and he glared at Jonah. "Broreamir sent that thing, didn't he? Did you see him, Jonah?"

Daniel's expression was so scary and off-putting that Jonah was almost afraid to answer. "No, I saw Jessica," he said. "Broreamir wasn't anywhere around."

Daniel glared at him for several more seconds. "The girl was sent in his stead to do her little pretty-talk and control the mindless thing," he said. "But Broreamir is the one who created it. The girl was but a tool. He was the one." He stood up. "I'm heading out."

"Like hell you are," said Patience, who barred the way to the door. "Plotting fratricide, are you? That's not the way we do things, Daniel."

"Speak for yourself, Halloran," growled Daniel.

"I'm trying to speak for Jonathan," said Patience.

That stopped Daniel cold. Swallowing heavily, he slowly returned to his spot by the fireplace.

"What we need right now is to occupy our minds," said Patience to the group at large. "Let's assess injuries from the skirmish we just had. How many Greens are there—?"

Jonah's phone rang, which made everyone jump. It took Jonah a few moments for it to register to him that it was his cell phone, even though he recognized his standard ringtone. He answered it on autopilot.

"Yeah?"

"Put me on the speaker." It was Felix, and he sounded furious.

"What? Why?"

"Put me on the speaker now."

Jonah was too numb to be fazed by Felix's temper. He doubted he'd ever feel another emotion again in his life. "There. You're on speaker. Now, what is it?"

"Laban's escaped."

Jonah had spoken too soon. Emotions found him again, fear being the first.

"WHAT!" shouted Daniel. "How? Did Jonathan's ethereality cease with the cell—"

"Never mind that!" spat Bobby. "What about my brothers?"

"They're all here," said Felix. "Unconscious, but still physically alive. Now, some of you go wrangle up some spiritual endowments, 'cause I need some help."

A motley crew answered Felix's call, consisting of Jonah, Terrence, Bobby, and, since Liz was beyond distraught, Akshara. Neither Jonah nor Terrence were mad at Reena for staying behind. Even after all of her crying, she was still in bad shape. They went to the Glade, obtained spiritual endowments, and went to the chthonic place that had contained Laban's cell. It almost looked normal.

It was the outside of it that was a mess.

Everything—chairs, card table, supply chest—had been destroyed. Felix had gotten everyone awake, and Akshara began to assess them, waving green-tipped fingers over their forms.

"Malcolm's jaw is dislocated," she announced. "Prodigal has injured ribs; three are bruised, and another three are broken. Alvin has a sprained wrist, but nothing further. Raymond has—"

"I already know, Akshara," said Raymond angrily, but it didn't seem that his anger was so much directed at her as the situation. "A laceration right at my hairline, two back teeth broken out, and I've torn the shit out of some ligaments in my left arm."

"What the hell happened down here?" Terrence demanded.

"Stupidity, and carelessness," murmured Raymond. "When you brought that pizza in here, we gave Laban some, like we were instructed to. I thought his sneezing when I made the opening was random, but he'd slid something into the opening before it was fully closed. I don't know what it was exactly—"

"It was a part of that damned bookshelf," mumbled Jonah. "I *said* that it was a bad idea to have it in there with him. That's probably why he stopped disassembling it; he had what he needed. So, what did he do?"

"Well, we didn't know the piece of bookshelf was there," said Alvin, who winced every few minutes. "I had always thought this was boring and mind-numbing, so I might have dozed off. Then there was that Eris Effect, and we didn't know whether to come up and see what was going on or keep with the watch. Then, it was like the ethereality of the glass...I don't know...it dimmed, or something."

"And that Laban dude went to work," muttered Prodigal. "All I remember is him grabbing at the small hole he made and ripping it wide enough for him to jump out. We tried to rush him, but he started using ethereality I've never seen in my life. Don't ask where or how he got a spiritual endowment; I couldn't tell you. It was a blur. Bast ran off, I don't know where. God, Jonathan is gonna kick our asses when he finds out how bad we screwed up."

Felix looked at Jonah, Terrence, and the other members of the rescue crew. Akshara, who'd been assisting Malcolm with his jaw, lowered her hands, and closed her eyes. Terrence decided to drop the anvil.

"You guys didn't mess up," he said. "The ethereality of the glass dimmed because...the spirit who created it got vanquished."

Malcolm's brow furrowed. "Vanquished? But Jonathan was the one who made the cell—" his eyes bulged. "NO!"

"Malcolm," warned Akshara, "your jaw—"

"I won't believe it!" said Malcolm loudly, jaw injury be damned. "Not until I see it! I refuse to believe it without proof!"

He ran down the tunnel towards the stairs. Raymond, Alvin, and Prodigal hadn't moved. Alvin didn't even look capable of moving. Prodigal looked as if he'd awakened from a nightmare, only to realize that the waking world was worse. Raymond's eyes were slits. It was like he planned to fight the tears as soon as they came.

"When Malcolm gets inside," he said in a quiet voice, "what is he going to find?"

Jonah had walked inside the cell, where he'd begun to inspect that infernal bookshelf. But he regarded Raymond with sadness. "He's going to see Jonathan's medallion in a heap on the floor," he answered. "Creyton got Daniel's brother to create some big, badass, Guide-killing Haunt, and set it loose on Jonathan. Jessica led it here, controlled by her C.P.V. It took Jonathan out, but Jonathan took it with him. Our mentor went out in a blaze of glory."

It was clear that Raymond took no pleasure in Jonah's last words. "But he still *went out*," he murmured, dipping his bleeding head between his knees as he said the words.

Bobby, who hadn't said anything to this point, walked to the sides of his older brothers. "I don't have a problem in the world with you guys' grieving," he said, "but I think you need to do it above ground. Let's go on back up."

Felix assisted Raymond, while Bobby assisted Alvin. Prodigal pulled himself off of the ground, but he walked at a deliberate, careful pace.

"Ain't lookin' forward to those stairs," he grumbled.

Akshara returned her equipment to her healing satchel and glanced at Jonah. "You coming?"

"You go ahead, Akshara," said Jonah. "I—I just want to collect my thoughts."

Akshara nodded and left. Terrence remained behind and regarded Jonah.

"You found something, didn't you?" he asked.

"Hell yeah," said Jonah, who pulled a folded piece of paper from a book and lifted it for Terrence to see. "That bastard left a message."

Terrence's eyebrows flew up. "How the hell did you know that was in there?"

"Laban might flip-flip through moods," said Jonah, "but the one thing that was always consistent was his inane need to be an attention whore. He is a little bit too far up his own ass to have simply escaped and have that be the end of it."

Terrence shook his head. "You're becoming like Reena, man."

"I wouldn't go that far," said Jonah, "but I knew that Laban couldn't leave without rubbing it in. Now, let's see here…"

He unfolded the paper once Terrence was nearer to him and slipped on his reading glasses. They read together:

Rowe.

I know, beyond a shadow of a doubt, that you will find this. You have more smarts than I initially thought. Not too much more, but more than I thought.

Count your blessings, boy. I didn't kill your little buddies, and you have no idea how badly I wanted to. Your daddy went to hell owing me, and now you owe me, too. I'll be cashing in on when you least expect it.

I'll give credit where it's due—Jonathan wasn't an easy target. But now, Ghost Man is gone. And that REALLY sucks for you, Blue Number 2.

I was out of commission on The Plane with No Name, but I wasn't out of the loop. When Creyton failed to make you embrace the dark, Omega was the next logical step. Sorry to break it to you, boy, but now that Jonathan's on the Other Side, the only chance you have is no chance in hell.

I warned you so many times to disregard your fetters and run for it, but you didn't. So, when the fires of Omega rain down, your ass will burn, and your little friends will, too.

Just don't die before I cash in on what you owe.

Laban

Oh, P.S.: Let me put your mind at ease, assuming you haven't already figured it out. Since I doubt that you have, here you are:

FOUR, The Attempts, involved your Amazon friend cracking the Cipher and damn near dying, and your attempts to save Jonathan. Which leads me to FIVE, the Cut.

The Cut was always Jonathan. Creyton wants your demise on a grander scale. Jonathan's? Not so much.

So, there you are. Five.

Jonah and Terrence finished around the same time and stared at each other. Terrence was the one who voiced the question burning in Jonah's mind.

"If vanquishing Jonathan was Five, then what on God's green earth is *Six*?"

In the following days, Jonah was glad to just have something on his mind other than the obvious. People were at a loss concerning how to hold a funeral for a man that had already been in Spirit for decades. At the same time, though, everyone agreed that even though Jonathan had passed from physical life at thirty-five, his seven-plus decades as a spirit mentor and Protector Guide were just as valuable, maybe even more. To not acknowledge the contributions that he made as a spiritual being would be a monumental disservice. So, they planned a memorial service. Felix and Prodigal left to break the news to their friends among the sazers.

The date was set for the week after Nella's and Themis' graduation. A lot of people hemmed and hawed about having the service follow so closely after their big day, but Nella, of all people, was the one who didn't care at all.

"You think it isn't a good time," she said. "When it comes down to it, is there ever a good time for a memorial service?"

Jonah and Terrence brought Reena up to speed about Four and Five, as well as their lack of knowledge on what Six, the Splinter, might be. Reena didn't give it a great deal of thought because her mind was where everyone else's was. She still, however, admitted to being concerned.

"It will probably be no different from all the rest," she said with heavy pessimism, "and blindside the hell out of us."

But the subject that weighed as heavily on Jonah's mind as Jonathan's vanquishing came on a Tuesday, five days before Jonathan's memorial service. Everyone was seated in the family room, largely in silence. That silence was broken by Patience, who'd been conversing with Elijah Norris.

"I can't help but wonder about the new Overseer of the Estate?" he said. "I've been in Jonathan's study—Bast still refuses to leave it—but I didn't see the Vitasphera. Did it go with him?"

Jonah closed his eyes tightly. He hadn't even told Terrence and Reena. But he couldn't avoid it any longer. He rose.

"No, Patience," he said softly, "it didn't."

He reached into his pocket and pulled out the Vitasphera.

People gasped, eyes bulged, and there may have even been a few people who choked on drinks. Jonah paid none of those things any mind.

"He threw it to me before he and the War Haunt took each other out," he said to the room at large. "I had come in here to have his back. When I said that it was necessary to protect our leader, he told me I was right, and threw the Vitasphera at me. I've been carrying it ever since."

Silence. Ever Terrence and Reena didn't know what to make of it. But Jonah didn't expect them to. He didn't know what to make of it himself.

"I think I like this," said Elijah, who looked pensive. "A new element. Creyton grew up with Jonathan. Knew everything about him. But he don't know everything 'bout you. You might do great at it, Rowe. You just need to learn how get nasty. Learn to be more hard knocks."

Jonah looked at Elijah. "I appreciate that," he said, "But the thing is I'm not entirely sure—"

"Fuck you, you son of a bitch! I'll be Goddamned if I call you my Overseer!"

Jonah wheeled around. It was the one person that no one had seen for days—Trip. He was armed with a hunting knife that was red with the color of his aura, and anger didn't describe the look on his face. He was deranged. Irascible.

"Trip?" said Jonah. "What—?"

"You will be as quiet as humanly possible," Trip rasped. "Or the first place on you that I jam this will be your balls."

Patience stepped forward. "What are you doing, boy?"

"What should have been done a long time ago," whispered Trip. "And I don't need your interference."

Patience pulled out his weapon. "I know you're upset, Trip," he said slowly, "but I will put you down hard and give you some time on the Plane to calm down."

"No, you won't," said Trip simply.

He snapped his fingers, which caused a red spark. When that happened, Patience, Reverend Abbott, and Elijah passed out. Residents looked at them, stunned.

"Nice," grumbled Trip, "and oh yeah...Karin?"

Karin bulleted through the *Astralimes,* slamming Reena against the wall in the process. The impact knocked the breath of Reena, and she fell to her knees, disoriented and dazed. Karin shoved Reena to the floor, where she bound her legs with ethereal fetters. Terrence roared and rushed forward, but Ian, another of Trip's buddies, came through the *Astralimes,* a spiked club aimed at Terrence's throat. At that moment, all of Trip's friends came into view, all armed, and all spiritually endowed. All estate residents shot up in alarm, but they didn't dare go near those endowed weapons.

"Sharp," said Trip, unfazed by the resident's alarm or Jonah's horrified face. "None of you have to worry about anything. They'll only attack you if necessary."

Grayson, who'd been near the fireplace, looked at Trip with wide eyes. "Trip, come on, man—"

"You made your choice, Gray," said Trip. "Now shut up."

Jonah finally found his voice, though his eyes were on the collapsed forms of Patience, Elijah, Reverend Abbott, and Reena. "What the fuck, man?"

"Necessary," said Trip. "They were the biggest threats to my goal. And Katoa, well—couldn't have her being Sonic the Hedgehog, fucking things up."

"Goal?" Jonah was still in disbelief. "You've done a damn insurrection!"

"Read a dictionary, Rowe," snapped Trip, whose eyes grew colder by the second. "No wonder you have no books released. An insurrection is a revolt against an established regime; you are merely the turd stain that's had the Vitasphera for a handful of days. This is an *intervention*."

Jonah looked at Trip in confusion. "Intervention? No one here is an addict!"

"They are!" snarled Trip. "They are, and the drug is *your* destructive ass!"

Many baffled eyes were on Trip as he neared Jonah. Jonah felt like he should back up, but his knees were buckled in place. He was having trouble wrapping his head around this.

"Let me start at the beginning," said Trip, "so that even the dumbest of you will understand. See, my daddy couldn't keep his pants zipped to save his life. He was all over, running around on my mother—women in church, women a few towns over, women at school... well, Charlotte Daynard, to be specific—"

There were gasps of shock. Jonah's mouth was wide open that he thought he might not be able to close it again. Trip never spoke about his personal life, much less his past. He'd even warned people about asking questions about it. Now it was him that was spilling things like an upturned washbasin. His dad had an affair with Charlotte Daynard? Did he have relationships with other women among the Deadfallen disciples?

But Trip was far from done. He was down the stairs now, with a tunnel-vision for Jonah.

"He made Mama's life near hell," he growled. "But she still loved him. That's the only reason why I didn't kill him. I was fed up with him trying to mold me into a Deadfallen disciple. Tired of him cheating on Mama almost every day. But I didn't kill him, for her. And then he died anyway, which resulted in her final mental break."

Jonah blinked. Trip said the word *die*. Yet again. He knew better.

"Mama was all I had, and now she's wasting away in a sanatorium in Orangeburg," he said. "And I was ready to end it all. But Jonathan saved me."

People's faces seemed to vacillate between pity for the terrible story, and fear of Trip, who looked as though he would explode. Jonah didn't know what to think. Trip had had it as bad as some of the rest of them, but pity was the furthest thing from his mind as he watched the man slowly approach him.

"He told me that I could be a worthwhile man," said Trip. "He showed me that I didn't have to be the man my father was. Or the man my grandfather was. All I had to do was make a different choice. I believed him. Believed every word. It was refreshing to have a positive male influence in my life, for once... then you came along."

A murderous, frightful look was in Trip's eyes by that time. Jonah still couldn't get his legs to move.

"The big, blue problem. And suddenly, Jonathan changed. He had this blind spot for you. Because you were the Blue Aura, you had this hold over him. Stupid, useless, and volatile as you are, you had a hold over him. You sank your claws into everybody, but Jonathan most of all."

Jonah's eyes narrowed. "Trip, you need to calm down—"

"You need to shut the fuck up." Trip's voice was reminiscent of the calm before the storm. "He green-lit so much bullshit for you, Rowe. And I told him, time and again, that you were dangerous. I told him you'd fail. I told him that everything you touched would turn to garbage. And I told him what I'm telling you now: that you are a disease... a cancerous parasite that would rise and choke out everything around him."

Jonah's own anger grew. He had tried to give Trip a slight benefit of the doubt, because they were all grieving. But that was out of the window now. Trip knew exactly what he was saying. The emotions were but a crutch. "Funny that you talk of cancer," he said quietly, "when you're the one who is always outside, sucking away at a cancer stick with each passing emotion—"

"I said that you would destroy everything." Trip cut him off with a whisper, yet everyone clearly heard the words. "And I told you that when that happened, I'd beat your ass into the ground. I should have done it before you took Jonathan away from me, but fuck it all, I didn't. But the last straw is seeing you here, defiling the Vitasphera with your thoughts of a takeover. Given that you had such a hold over Jonathan, I had a feeling that you wound up with it when he got vanquished. Jonathan didn't understand that you had that hold over him, and everybody else. But I did. My friends here did. Therefore, it's up to me to open everyone's eyes. It's up to me to right all of your wrongs. It's up to me to take over. My friends and I will fix all of this. First, I'll need that Vitasphera."

"Don't you dare give it to him, Jonah!" snarled Terrence.

"Shut up!" Ian decked Terrence across the face.

That was when the true fight broke out.

Terrence tackled Ian around the waist and pulled him down to the floor. Markus ran to intercept, but Malcolm swung a massive forearm across his face, knocking him on his ass. Trip's other friends dropped their weapons and got into full on hand-to-hand brawls with the other residents. Jonah distinctly saw Spader raise a hand at Reena's legs, and the ethereal fetters came unlocked. Roderick Rivers, Trip's cousin, kicked Spader in the groin from behind, yelling, "You greasy bastard!" Spader bellowed in pain and collapsed to his knees.

"Spader!" Jonah tried to go for him, but Trip grabbed him by the throat.

"Oh no, bitch," he barked. "Your ass is mine."

He threw Jonah down to the floor, and, quick as a flash, threw something red into the air. Seconds later, a sheer red box caged the two of them. No one could interfere with this fight. Jonah also realized that he couldn't hear the chaos going on outside the red box. He saw Liz bang ineffectual fists on the thing until another Trip crony named Melissa Mitchell yanked her away.

Jonah's momentary distraction by the fighting outside the box cost him.

Trip hit him in the face so hard that he thought bones had been smashed. He fell back to the floor, and the Vitasphera rolled out of his hands. Of course, it didn't break, but the interior of it was black as night. He saw no amber, and no glint of the golden infinity symbol within. He rose to his hands and knees, but Trip punted his side. That whole area of Jonah's body exploded with pain as he rolled over from the force of Trip's kick. Groggily, he noticed that Trip had ripped off his shirt, and tossed it to the side. His sable-brown skin seemed to radiate with rage, and his every muscle bunched and deadly.

"YOU SEE THAT?" he bellowed, pointing at the Vitasphera. "Pitch-black! No hope! No way out! And THAT'S BECAUSE OF YOU!"

Trip lifted Jonah up and body-dropped him over his back. It was a miracle that Jonah didn't land on his head. As it was, he slammed on his already-injured side, and roared in pain through gritted teeth. How could he fight Trip? The man outstripped Jonah's experience by years, and all that knowledge was backed by a spiritual endowment and unbridled rage. Jonah didn't like his chances. He didn't like his lack of strength.

He stood and threw a left punch. Trip parried it lazily and tagged Jonah in the abdomen. The second Jonah doubled over, Trip hit him with a knee to the face. Jonah gurgled, and fell to a knee. Jonathan had always said that they weren't fighters, but that obviously hadn't registered with Trip.

Trip moved in, and grabbed Jonah's shoulder vice-like, so as to yank him upwards. Somehow, Jonah had sensed that particular move, and allowed the momentum to work for him, swinging his right fist in a backhand punch. The blow staggered Trip, and Jonah followed it with his own kick to Trip's gut. Trip bowled over, and Jonah tried to kick him again. Unfortunately, Trip wasn't in as much pain as he'd let on. He'd feigned, grabbed Jonah's leg, and yanked him down. Now his back and side were both hurting. Great.

"I'll save all these useless bastards, for Jonathan, if nothing else," spat Trip. "They're up your ass, too, but I will *make* them see."

There was a copper taste in Jonah's mouth, and red in his eyes. He blinked rapidly; he couldn't afford to be blinded. But hell—he wasn't doing so hot when he could see, either. He got a glimpse of Nella. She'd shoved one of Trip's friends away, and banged her fists on the red blockade, tears of frustration in her eyes...

Trip knelt down next to Jonah. Jonah's feeble attempts at offense hadn't even bruised him. His rage allowed his face to morph into disgust as he regarded the man he'd just beat down.

"You're nothing, Rowe," he said as he spat in Jonah's face. "You're lower than the shit in the herald's little box. If I could only travel back in time, I'd have stopped your sorry ass daddy from giving your mother a second look. Or, better yet, I'd go back further, and stop your grandma from even having the bitch. Retroactive abortion would have been a blessing in your case."

Those words did it.

Trip rose, and actually turned his back on Jonah, seething over a bleeding fist. Jonah rose, suddenly feeling no pain. But he felt Trip's spit on his face. Felt the blood from his mouth running down his chin. He felt what blood was left in his face begin to throb in his ears. And he felt a guttural, bestial, roar build in his diaphragm and burst forth from his mouth as he hurled himself at Trip's back.

They slammed into the red barrier when their bodies collided, and both of them crashed onto the floor. Before Trip even knew what had hit him, Jonah was on him, pummeling his face.

It was at that moment that something scary happened.

Dangerously scary.

Some type of dam broke in Jonah's mind. Suddenly, all he could see was every bully from his childhood, every toxic boss, everything that had hurt him in his life. He saw Nana's white casket, saw Jessica slitting Mr. Steverson's throat... all of it. He could see it all in Trip's face, which was becoming more and more bruised, battered, and bloodied.

He didn't register the fact that he could hear voices again...hear shouts all around. They didn't matter. He wasn't finished...he couldn't hurt Trip enough...

Suddenly, hands were all over him, trying to pull him off. He remained steadfast. The strength that had eluded him earlier was there in spades now. He would not be denied...Trip was the one who started this little rebellion, he was merely finishing it...

An electrical charge pierced his neck, and then surged through his entire body. He could have laughed. A taser? Really? He was a Blue Aura! Electricity was something he regulated and controlled, even when he didn't have an endowment!

He was amused by the taser.

He was not amused by the educated and lithe arms that wrapped around his neck and pressed on his carotid artery just enough for his brain to send a new signal to his body besides blood rage. He couldn't breathe.

The punching stopped as his hands clawed at arms smaller than his own, but expertly clamping all the right places.

He wondered if Reena was the culprit, but he happened to see her on the edge of his vision as she Superman-punched Karin to the floor. Who else was an expert at chokes?

"Forgive me, Jonah," said an apologetic voice, "but you were going to kill him."

"L-Liz?" gasped Jonah. "Get—off—me!"

"No," said Liz, "I will not watch my big brother become a murderer."

"Damn it," Jonah managed, "I said, get off—"

There was a dull boom, and what felt like an ocean wave—sans the ocean—knocked everyone down. Jonah and Liz were already on the ground, but the wave hit them hard, nonetheless. Liz cried out and turned Jonah loose, but it didn't matter. Jonah was good for nothing after that blast. Everyone was.

"That. Is. ENOUGH."

It was Elijah who'd done it. He must have awakened during the fighting; done some crowd control trick that must have come in handy on the Plane with No Name a time or two. But he looked angry as hell. "Look at y'all! Fighting among yourselves in the place that Jonathan himself consecrated for you! You should be ashamed! This is disgraceful conduct! You two—" he pointed at Liz and Nella, "fix up Jonah. You two—" he pointed at Ben-Israel and Barry, "fix up this boy..."

His voice trailed off. Trip was not a pretty sight. His face looked beyond terrible. And Jonah wasn't in the slightest bit sorry.

"Better yet, every Green Aura here—except the two I told to help Jonah—fix up that boy," said Elijah. "He's bad off. But fix them up and do it quick. We have a huge problem here, and we *will* settle it...in a civilized way."

Jonah was taken to the infirmary, while Trip was taken to a makeshift medical spot near Reena's art studio. No one imagined that the two of them convalescing in the same place was a good idea, so those arrangements were made.

Liz and Nella sat Jonah down, and began inspecting him with their green-gleaming fingers. Jonah's head was throbbing, but it paled in comparison to his anger. The *nerve* of Trip...freaking bastard...

"Are you mad at me, Jonah?" asked Liz.

Jonah made eye contact with her and took a heavy breath through his nostrils. "No, Liz," he said, and he meant it. "I understand why you did what you did. I don't agree with it, but I understand."

Liz nodded. "I can accept that. Now, Nella and I need to get to work."

Terrence and Reena walked into the infirmary. Jonah leered at them, but the emotion wasn't aimed at them at all.

"What has happened with Trip's group of ass-kissers?" he demanded.

Terrence scoffed. "Patience and Reverend Abbott said that they are family, and on equal footing with us," he said. "Therefore, no arrests would be made, unless they were necessary."

Jonah's eyes narrowed. "But he and Elijah have them all together where they can watch them, right?"

"Hell yeah," said Terrence. "Old Man Norris is prepared to do that crowd-control thing again if need be."

Jonah looked at Reena. "Are you alright?"

"Fine," she snapped. "Bruised up, but fine. More than I can say for Karin."

Jonah frowned. "I saw you Superman-punch her. Did you mess her up?"

"Uh-huh," said Reena with indifference. "Deviated septum, and I cracked her jaw. Unfortunately, that's all being repaired now. But how are you, Jonah?"

Jonah growled, ignoring the question and the pains. "How in the hell could Trip do that?" he demanded. "He organized his little buddies and planned a hostile takeover…planned to take the Vitasphera away from me by force! And then he proceeds to beat the living shit out of me. I just didn't know he was capable of that."

"With all due respect, Jonah," said Reena, who looked a bit calmer, "look who's talking."

Jonah opened his mouth but had no response. Now that he was back in his right mind, he felt a bit of concern for Trip. The sanctimonious son of a bitch had no right to do what he did. None at all. But Jonah lost all control of himself when he went to that dark place. His fists were battered, sore, and bleeding. He knew, in that moment, that the damage to himself might have been nothing in comparison to what happened to Trip.

"You're probably wondering what you did to Trip," said Nella. "I did a quick scan before we all got separated." She sighed. "You fractured his left eye socket, knocked out eight teeth, broke his jaw and nose, cracked his skull, and lacerated his tongue."

Jonah winced. Reena even looked discomfited, while Terrence vacillated between indifference and concern. Liz nodded.

"You did that damage without an endowment, Jonah," she said. "And to think, you spend most of your time doubting how powerful you are."

Jonah winced as he shifted his aching torso. "Can they—Akshara, Ben-Israel, Barry, all of them—can they fix him up?"

"Yeah," said Terrence. "But he's gonna be in pain for a while. Before Reena and I came up here, we saw Reverend Abbott going downstairs with a black bag. I'm guessing he'll have to do some old-school Tenth surgery before they can wrap things up with ethereal healing."

Jonah closed his eyes. "Trip went too far," he attempted.

"And you paid him back in kind," said Reena. "Jonah, as pissed as I am right now—and you don't even know—it has to be said. You took it to a really scary level. We all have our dark sides, but what I saw down there—before Liz put you in that chokehold—it frightened me, Jonah. Trip took it too far, hell yeah, he did. But you took it just a little farther. You realize that, right?"

Jonah looked at Terrence, whose eyes betrayed him. He was just as unnerved as Reena was. Liz had already made her point known, and he hadn't forgotten how Nella had been a bit leery of him when they began to administer treatments. A part of him still wasn't sorry; only a fool would lay down and be beaten to hell. But there was another part of him—the rational part of him—that felt shame. He sighed. "Yeah," he mumbled. "Yeah, Reena, I do."

Reena nodded, and then her features hardened somewhat. "Be that as it may," she said, "you can rest assured that there aren't many people who wouldn't have done what you did. A lot of folks have never seen Trip owned. He was asking for it."

"Begging for it," corrected Terrence.

"It was badass, Jonah," said Nella. "Disproportionately so, but badass nonetheless."

Jonah snorted, despite everything. "And you, Liz?"

Liz had just completed taping Jonah's injured fists. She stood up and untied her hair. "When the need arises to pummel someone," she said at last, "I...I'm not saying don't fight back. In the future, just...just scale it back a few levels, okay?"

Jonah nodded. "Got it. So, what happens now? Elijah said that we are going to settle this problem in a civilized manner...what did he mean?"

"Your guess is as good as mine—" began Reena, but just then, the man himself rapped on the infirmary door.

"You doing alright, boy?" he demanded. "Have these little girls here done their jobs?"

"These little girls have names," snapped Nella.

"Shut up, Nella," said Liz. "Now isn't the time."

Jonah ignored them and focused on the grizzled prison guard. "I'm good," he muttered. "I'm hurting, but I'm good."

Elijah nodded. "Good man," he said. "In about forty-five minutes, head down to the Family Court room."

"Oh no," said Jonah. "Family Court isn't a good idea right now. We just had some infighting in case you forgot."

"Who said anything about having Family Court?" snapped Elijah. "What good would that do at this point? I said come to the room itself."

"Why?"

Elijah crammed some tobacco into his mouth. "Because that's a wide enough space for my plan."

"Why do you have to wait forty-five minutes?" asked Reena. "Why can't we just get…whatever this is, over with right now?"

Elijah regarded her. "Because that is the time it will take for Rivers' dental healing to take hold. He can't talk if his teeth ain't right."

Forty-five minutes later, Jonah, Terrence, Reena, Liz, and Nella walked to the Family Court room. Everyone else was there, some people sporting bruises and cuts, while others had bloody lips and blackened eyes. The segregation was stark. Trip's supporters were tucked on one side and looked as though they had no intention of even breathing the same air as everyone else, let alone share the same space. The other estate residents looked just as disinclined to go anywhere near them.

"What is this?" Jonah asked Elijah.

Elijah raised a hand. "The Vitasphera, please."

Jonah glared at him, but the man shook his head impatiently.

"I don't want to take it," he said. "It's a symbol. It needs to be in the forefront right now."

Jonah wondered, but handed it over. The way the sphere was pitch-black dark within really troubled him.

Elijah took it with reverence and respect and placed it on a table in the middle of the room, where everyone could see.

"You four," Elijah pointed at Terrence, Reena, Liz, and Nella, "sit down. Jonah, you stay right here."

They complied, and Jonah eyed the man.

"What are you—?"

Elijah snapped his fingers, and Jonah fell back into a chair that had not been behind him seconds before. Ethereal binds clamped his wrists.

"What the hell!" he snarled.

"I can't have you going savage again when you see him," said Elijah.

Trip walked in—or had been forced in, it was hard to tell—with Patience and Reverend Abbott at his side. Even after the painstaking treatments of the Green Auras, he was a mess. The entire top of his head was bandaged, and gauzes were on either side of his face. His visage was swollen and stitched, but he looked as deadly as ever.

"It's about time someone bound that bastard the way he needs to be." Trip's mouth injuries may have been on the mend, but his voice still sounded like talking was a labor.

"Here, Trip," Akshara rose from her seat and pulled a vial from her satchel, "drink some more of this—"

"Keep that shit, girl." Trip swatted the vial away from Akshara's hand, and it broke as soon as it hit the floor. "I don't need any more of your damn coddling."

Some people gasped in surprise and shock, but Elijah just nodded.

"Behaviors such as that are precisely the reason why *this* will happen for you, too, boy."

He snapped his fingers again, and Trip, like Jonah, got thrown back into a recently conjured chair. He also had his own set of ethereal binds.

"You bastard!" he snarled at Elijah.

"I am nothing of the kind," spat Elijah. "My parents were quite married when I came along. Now, then," he addressed the room at large. "This Vitasphera here—" he pointed to it, "is supposed to be a symbol of hope. Faith. Inspiration. But everything it stood for when it was in Jonathan's possession was soundly besmirched tonight, by an insurrection that occurred within these very walls."

"For the last damn time," snapped Trip, "it was not an insurrection! Those only happen when a system or regime is strong, and dissidents rage against it. This little crusade Rowe here has going on is anything but that."

"Pound it up your ass, Trip!" responded Jonah. "I've heard you for months! You were organizing your little buddies over there...you were planning this even before Jonathan got vanquished! What were you going to do? Vanquish Jonathan yourself, and become the Rivers family man you were always destined to be?"

Trip glared at Jonah from across the room. Even though one eye was red from the recently repaired eye socket, the expression was still somehow murderous. "If you ever say that again, Rowe, I will kill you."

"Go fuck yourself," muttered Jonah. "You'll kill me? That plan would fail almost as spectacularly as your little rebellion."

"That is quite enough of that," said Patience. "Both of you have responsibilities to this estate, and both of you have failed in them. Trip, you have been a mainstay at this estate for the better part of twenty years. You've defeated Spirit Reapers, flouted your father's wishes to be a disciple of Creyton, and made differences in the lives of the children you've taught, and the people who have heard your music. You were even instrumental in foiling the plans of Sanctum Arcist some time ago!"

"That's what I do, Patience," said Trip. "And the only thing I ever asked for in return was respect. And evidently, that was too much. How am I wrong for understanding that I don't need to be a celebrity to get things done? I don't need to be admired, like this fool here."

"Admired!" cried Jonah. "You think I *wanted* these things that have happened to me? You think I wanted to be attacked all the time? Spend my life looking over my shoulder? You think I wanted to lose friends—?"

"Ix-nay on the pity party, fucker," grumbled Trip. "People drop every day; it's a fact of life. Or were you not listening to anything Jonathan ever told you?"

"Shut up, Trip," said Patience. "Jonah, you are the light Blue Aura. The beacon of hope in the abyss of things Creyton has created. How many times have you been a hero, unwanted or no? And Jonathan saw fit to bequeath the Vitasphera to you—"

"Which was a damn mistake," Trip burst out. "Rowe had Jonathan and all of you fooled! He loves being at the point of it all. He feels like he is the centerpiece of the show! And he manipulated Jonathan into giving him center stage! The fact that he could manipulate a spirit is mind-boggling. He is just as much a threat to the ethereal world as Creyton!"

"How dare you?" Jonah's voice went quiet. A sure sign that his temper was on the outs. "How dare you compare me to Creyton? That man has screwed up my life in more ways than I can count. He had Mr. Steverson killed. He had your damn father killed. He had Jonathan killed! How could you ever lump me in with that monster?"

Trip didn't answer. Instead, he took a deep breath, and slowly let it free. Seconds later, a sound wave reverberated through the room, and his ethereal bonds fell away. He rose and kicked the chair away.

"Much better," he said.

Some people in the crowd looked at him in alarm. Elijah stepped forward, as did Reverend Abbott. But Patience was the one who drew a weapon.

"Boy, if you try anything," he warned. "I will summon a dozen Networkers here and place you on The Plane with No Name. If you think I'm posturing, try me."

Trip rolled his eyes. "Trust me, there is no need for that."

"Trust ain't really high up on the list of things I feel for you, Rivers," said Patience. "You've already knocked me out once."

"True," said Trip. "It won't happen again. It only happened in the first place… my whole plan only happened in the first place… because people wouldn't give me a platform for change. So, yeah, I tried to wrest it by force. And now, since you've got everyone here, you will now know why."

Before things went any further, Jonah drained half of the electrical power in the estate and willed it to his hands. His own ethereal bonds exploded, and he, too, was free. Some people jumped, but Jonah simply stood up. Trip regarded him, cautiously.

"I'll be damned if I sit on my ass while you stand," he grumbled. "You want to talk so badly? Speak your piece."

"As though I needed your permission," said Trip coldly as he turned to the crowd. "You people. I do not speak to my friends; they already get it. You, on the other hand, do not. Allow me to break it down. When the Decimation happened, years and years ago, how did Creyton lay waste to so much? Because Jonathan and everyone else here back then was caught unawares. He straight massacred them because they were unprepared. Never in my life will I ever support Creyton, but the man attacked them intelligently. The superior opponent only goes into a fight after he knows it's already won. Creyton did that. So many lives lost. So many things destroyed. Jonathan stayed behind to teach us, but he taught us defense. Not enough. As awesome as he was, that was woefully not enough. Patience here is a Networker; he can attest to the fact that when you're out there on a limb, you need a little bit more than defense. And Prison Guard Norris? You're a veteran on the Plane. You know that it takes more than defense to keep those lunatics in line."

Neither man said anything. But Jonah didn't like the expressions on their faces. They looked as though Trip had a point.

"Yeah, I tried to take the Vitasphera by force," Trip continued. "You may not have agreed with my methods, but whatever. A lot of you have known me for years, and don't like me. Whatever to that, too. I am who I am, and I'm not here to be loved. You may not agree with me or my friends, but it's because I'm real. I'm blunt. Sometimes the truth, the brutal truth, is the only thing that can break down the wall. And here is the brutal truth: You cannot beat Creyton. Not like this."

Everyone looked around. Jonah looked at Trip in dislike and wonder. Trip let his words hang for just a second, and then went on.

"You cannot beat him," Trip repeated. "Why? Because none of you are willing to cross the line. Creyton is the textbook definition of madness. He kills, he manipulates, he betrays, he uses, he usurps. And what are you guys? You go to the back of the Glade, and practice. Practice, practice, practice. I assure you, if you come across a Deadfallen disciple, he or she ain't gonna check to see how many ducks and dodges you can do. They're just going to kill you."

There was a shudder among the group. Jonah wanted to attack Trip so badly, but how would it look if he did that right now? He was in a bona fide rock and hard place.

"A lot of you think I hate Rowe, and you're not wrong," said Trip, who cut his eye at Jonah for only a second. "He is bad for business. He is bad for everything."

"What in the actual fu—"

"I'm not finished, Rowe," snapped Trip without looking at him. "Since Rowe has been here, look at things that have happened. The estate was attacked mere weeks after Jonathan discovered him. Weeks. I attempted to fix things then, tried to protect people, but Rowe's meddling ruined that. Then, the Time Item woman. Tenths and Elevenths both lost their lives on that one. Jonah made unauthorized trips to the Astral Plane, said nothing about why, and got away with it. Why? Because he conveniently corrected what he sabotaged, and Jonathan looked the other way. Reena—the woman he calls his older sister—has come to grief *twice* because of him."

Reena, surprised by Trip's naming her specifically, focused on Trip in alarm.

"The night he didn't properly cleanse her dampener left her comatose," said Trip. "And then she got Haunted, because she followed behind him."

"Neither of those things were my fault!" argued Jonah. "Everyone here knows the truth of how things went down!"

"Look at my face," said Trip as though there were no interruption. "Yeah, I started the fight, but there was a problem that needed handling. I've no regrets. But Rowe—your new Overseer—nearly killed me. He cracked my skull… one of those bones could have easily punctured my brain. He is willing to beat the hell out of me, allow his best friends to experience misfortunes on many occasions—"

"Okay, stop," said Reena, who stood up. "Trip, Jonah is my brother, and I love him with everything in me. You will not sit here and slander him with half-truths and contextual stories. This is wrong; everything about it is wrong. And I need you to keep my name out of your mouth."

"I'm with you, Reena," said Terrence, who stood as well, glaring at Trip. "You don't speak for me, dumbass."

"I speak for no one," said Trip. "I'm simply opening these people's eyes for the first time in ever." He returned his focus to the group at large. "If I had taken the Vitasphera, I would have put us on the path to victory. Would I have committed some acts that you all didn't agree with? If the situation called for it, hell yes. But, as I said, beating Creyton will involve crossing the line. Jonathan thought we could be decent people… keep our hands clean. And he got vanquished, protecting Rowe. Volatile, defiant, rebellious, non-compliant Jonah Rowe is the reason why Jonathan is gone. My chance to take control—make things right—is now over. Rowe will lead you all to your ruin. And I won't be ruined with you."

He gave a signal, and all of his friends, which amounted to over thirty people, stood up. Residents looked at them. Jonah stepped forward.

"What the hell does that mean?" he demanded.

"It means that we're out of here," said Trip, whose voice returned to the usual wintry tone that he reserved only for Jonah. "As long as you are the Overseer of this estate, we will be elsewhere. We will be where things can get done. That can't happen here, with you in the backyard, teaching people defense. We will protect ourselves our way. Because of you, Jonathan is no longer here to try to convince me to tolerate your inadequacies. We're gone."

"You can't leave—!" Jonah moved closer to Trip, but Trip shook knives from under his sleeves. They glowed the red of his aura.

"Are you going to stop me?" he asked. "Because one, that's an abuse of your new power, and two, I will have the right to defend myself against you, by any means I deem necessary."

Jonah stopped. If he attacked Trip, then he would be the one who was the bad guy. He hated the man with every fiber of his being. He found himself half-wishing that Liz hadn't put him in that chokehold earlier.

"Fuck off," he grumbled.

Trip flicked him off and returned his eyes to the residents. "The choice is yours," he said. "But if you stay here...enjoy dying. If the word bothers you, tough shit. Because it's exactly what will happen if you remain here under the supervision of Rowe. It's going to happen to your loved ones, too. You might not want to hear it, but like I said, sometimes, the brutal truth is the only thing that cracks the wall. And Gray...get your ass over here. *Now.*"

Gray swallowed, hard but left the group and went to Trip's side. "Yeah, man," he grumbled. "I'm here."

Trip and all of his supporters—plus Grayson—took one step backwards into nothingness. It was amazing how crisply and precisely they did it. They were gone.

The silence they left in their wake was deafening. Trip had always been a man of few words; not quite as taciturn as Malcolm, but not loquacious, either. But, son of a bitch, when he chose to be an orator, he had some serious power. He left Jonah with nary a clue of what to do, think, or say as he looked over all the stunned, baffled faces in the group.

Suddenly, someone stood up. It was Maria Vidal. Jonah didn't know her well; they'd exchanged pleasantries here and there. He wondered what she was doing, but then she headed for the door.

"Maria!" said Magdalena. "What are you doing?"

"I'm leaving," said Maria. "Trip had a point. It makes me sick to my stomach to agree with him, but I do. I've got to think about my family. I can't be here, while they're out there exposed. Maybe I can use some of what Jonathan taught us to help them. I'm sorry, Jonah. But I have to go."

She left. Jonah looked at the door in shock, and then looked back at the residents. The looks he got back made him realize, in that moment, the true damage that Trip had inflicted. It was probably his plan all along, but he left Jonah holding the bag. Anger began to rise in him, like steadily increasing rainwater. That bastard. That filthy, conniving bastard.

"I have the Vitasphera," he said in a quiet tone so as to keep from shouting, "but I have no right to stop you. If you want to stay, stay. If you want to go…go."

For almost two full minutes, there was silence. Then, people rose and began to leave. Ben-Israel. Barry. Sherman. Noah. Tony. Melvin. Maxine. So many others. After struggling with himself, Alecksander stood up, followed by Stella Marie.

"Alecksander?" said Autumn Rose. "Stella Marie? After everything we've been through? After what Abimilech did?"

"It ain't about that," said Alecksander, who looked at Autumn Rose with genuine sadness. "I'm still not over losing all of our friends last winter. I don't want to go through that anymore. I can't. We don't have enough stuff to lose things all the time. That includes our friends."

"Your friends?" said Autumn Rose, who let tears fall. "What am I? What is Prodigal?"

"We'll always be family," said Stella Marie. "But... you know we've always done better on our own, on the road. Cooped up in this fancy house? It ain't our gig, Autumn Rose. It just ain't. Tell Prodigal that it isn't personal. We'd just rather go back to the way things were on the road than watch another friend join Creyton or get killed."

The two sazers left the room, leaving Autumn Rose looking almost shell-shocked. Jonah watched all of it in barely contained silence.

When all was done, over fifty people had left. Trip and his buddies were an additional thirty.

Nearly eighty-one people had just abandoned the estate. And Jonah had only been Overseer for six days. Numbly, he looked to see who had remained.

Terrence, Reena, Liz, Bobby, and Malcolm, the first friends he ever made at the estate, were still there. The others who remained were Spader, Nella, Autumn Rose, Magdalena, Themis, Douglas, Akshara, Alvin, Raymond, and literally four other people. Reverend Abbott, Elijah, and Patience seated themselves, looking as stunned as Jonah felt.

Numbly, Jonah approached one of the remainders he wasn't really familiar with, a light-skinned black woman with braids down her back. He extended a hand, and she took it.

"What is your name, friend?" he asked.

"Xenia Pryce," she responded.

Jonah snorted, annoyed with himself. "Xenia, I've seen you around here for a few years, and I think we've exchanged maybe twenty words," he said. "Why did you stay?"

Xenia snorted, much like Jonah had. "Trip had a point, sure," she conceded. "But do you know how many assholes make a good point from time to time? The hell with that fool."

Jonah shook his head. Just like that, he'd made a new lifelong friend. "Thank you, Xenia," he said, and he turned to Spader. "Spader, you wanted to leave two years ago, and I stopped that. Made you give away all your money. I was in no position to stop you this time, yet you stayed."

Shame crossed Spader's face, but he shut it down. "That's the past," he muttered. "I didn't understand some of the things then that I understand now. I'm not going anywhere."

Jonah nodded. Spader had just elevated himself many notches with those words. "Thank you all," he said in a louder voice. "You really can't put a price on loyalty. You all are the best in the world. The ones that wanted to back out? Fuck 'em—"

"Jonah, no." Liz's voice was so stern and strong that it was off-putting. "You don't mean that."

"He can mean it if he wants to," snapped Spader. "How the hell can you respect someone who abandons the table so early in the game—"

"I wasn't talking to you, Spader," said Liz, whose eyes were on Jonah's face. "Jonah, you love those guys, all of them! And in Maxine's case, her mother forced her to leave; she'd been here texting back and forth with her the whole time. They're still our friends, Jonah, and you've gone to bat for them before. More than once! I'm leaving Trip and his posse out of this because they were dirtbags anyway. But the others? Don't you dare act like you don't care about them. I understand their situations. I'm hurt and sad by the way they bailed, but I understand. They want to be with their families. Want to know that they are okay. We all do. They just chose to do that with their presence, not by phone or Skype. Gray didn't even want to leave. Yes, Trip twisted things, and that was crap, but please don't disregard your friends. Your family. Don't judge them, just wish them the best."

Jonah sighed. Of course, that came from Liz. The similarities between her words just now and a few months ago were jarring. But she was right. As much as he wanted to agree with Spader, he didn't hate them. He wasn't indifferent towards them. If he had blood relations that he was close to, maybe he'd have been on the first thing smoking, too. But he didn't have to make that choice. Not for blood relations, anyway. "You're right, Liz," he said. "I didn't mean it." He looked at everyone else. "Five was the bullet," he told them, "and Six was the knife. Creyton had it all planned. But it was at the very end that he got us. Vanquished Jonathan, knowing that it would divide us... splinter our forces. It was almost psychic—"

"Nope," said Reena at once. "We may be privy to preternatural things, Jonah, but that wasn't the case with the Six. Creyton is a master strategist. He studies people; learns how they think. When one knows how people think, then one knows how people will act. He simply planned things accordingly and nursed them along when necessary."

Jonah didn't even look Reena's way. There was more truth in what she'd just said than he cared to admit. "I wonder what Trip's plan had been if Jonathan hadn't been destroyed," was what he said instead. "He had that plan to leave beforehand. He had to have had it already planned; their exit was too smooth."

"Just guessing here," said Reverend Abbott, "but, knowing what I know now, I would guess that Trip's idea was to try to force Jonathan into re-thinking his stance on an exodus, with his plan being the threat of him and his friends leaving the estate if Jonathan didn't agree. I truly believe that he thought that he could bully Jonathan!" He sighed. "But when Jonathan got vanquished, in a very sick way, Trip probably thought he'd been handed gold. And he used it masterfully when he tried to take this place over."

There was silence for several moments, which was broken by Liz.

"Sitting here deliberating won't help much, if anything," she said. "It looks like all of you guys have some injuries from the fight with Trip and everyone else. Come on to the infirmary. Nella, Akshara, and I can address all of you there."

Everyone rose. There was a bit more conversation, during which Jonah got a little more acquainted with Xenia and his three other new friends, whom he discovered were named Jada Yancey, Sebastian Torgas, and R.J. Holley. Soon enough, though, he was alone with Terrence and Reena.

"What a night," grumbled Terrence. "What a frickin' night. So, what happens now, Jonah?"

Jonah suddenly became interested in the wall. "I don't know how we are gonna get through this," he said.

Reena placed a hand on Jonah's shoulder. "It's okay to not know what to do," she said.

Jonah looked at the darkened Vitasphera in his hand. "Not when you're the one in charge."

26

Time-Honored

After the majority of the estate residents abandoned the estate, Jonah spent three days outside by himself. He didn't even go into the estate, as he didn't need to see it for a little bit, so he brought a tent and a sleeping bag out near the Glade. He didn't want to talk yet, and he wanted to be away from prying eyes so that he could train. And he trained from morning well into the night. He hadn't eaten, and he didn't care. He just trained. Not defense, not ethereality. He just focused on one thing, and one thing only.

And that one thing had to be perfect.

On the morning after that second night, Terrence and Reena sought him out. It was 4:45 AM, but he was already up training. He sensed their presence and hid the baton behind his back.

"We left you out here because we understand that everyone deals with things differently," said Terrence, "but they're calling for thunderstorms all day today. I didn't want you to get caught up in that."

"Uh-huh," said Jonah with narrowed eyes. "Like that's the reason you got up at 4 something in the morning to come find me."

Reena shook her head at Terrence, who threw his hands in the air.

"Okay, I lied," he snapped. "We were worried about you. I know you needed to grieve, but you're my brother. I was still worried."

"I could read your essence from the estate," said Reena. "You have a wildly strong determination about something, Jonah. What's up? And don't think that I didn't see you hide something behind your back when we got here."

"You think you were alone?" scoffed Terrence. "Stevie Wonder could have seen that."

Jonah sighed. He loved his brother and sister, dearly. But shit... couldn't they have just let this one go?

"Fine," he conceded.

He pulled his left baton from behind his back and showed it to them. As it was still dark, they had to crowd in. Jonah didn't even look at them as they inspected.

On the baton was a knife, with a black blade. It had a serrated edge on one side, and a filet-style blade on the other. The handle had a square peg affixed to it, so that Jonah could remove it from his baton and add it on as he saw fit.

Terrence looked up from the knife to him. "Where did you get this?"

"Not important," said Jonah. "Let it go."

Terrence looked as though he still wondered but asked another question. "Why does it have a black blade?"

"I thought it'd be poetic," murmured Jonah.

"I thought you didn't do blades," said Reena.

"This one time, I will," said Jonah.

At that point, Terrence and Reena both regarded him. Jonah swallowed, not out of apprehension, but resolve.

"It's for Jessica," he revealed. "That bitch has been there for the destruction of two very important people to me, and she laughed both times. Well, I'm going to wipe that grin off of her face permanently. The next time I see her, I will kill her."

Terrence blinked. Reena looked away.

"Jonah, what about the thing about giving way to darkness?"

"I thought about it," admitted Jonah, "and I've decided that I don't care."

"What!" demanded Reena.

"I don't care," repeated Jonah. "I am in control of me. Light and Dark are about choice. The only thing that matters is what I choose. I won't become evil or *Dark* unless I choose to do those things. And I have no intention of becoming evil...I know my role."

Reena looked at Jonah straight in the eye. "Does this have anything to do with Trip saying we need to cross the line?"

"Fuck Trip," snapped Jonah. "This has nothing in the world to do with his dumb ass, and everything to do with a self-infatuated bitch that saw fit to have fun helping her master fuck up my life. That is done. She has screwed with me for the last time. Jessica Hale is not long for this world. I have no idea what will happen the next time I see Creyton. But the next time I see Jessica, her physical life is over. End of story."

Jonah's mind was made up, but he still braced himself for all the fruitless convincing about to come his way. He hated to tear them down, but he was ready to do so.

"Okay," said Terrence.

"I feel the same," said Reena. "That bitch needs to go."

Jonah frowned. "Seriously?"

"Yeah," said Terrence. "I can't believe I'm saying it, but yeah."

"Jonah, listen," said Reena. "Make no mistake, I'm not comfortable with this. But Jessica...that bitch...she needs to go. Wherever she goes, a chain of calamity follows. If this is what it takes to break that chain, then so be it."

Jonah couldn't help but be surprised. Truly, his brother and sister had just surprised the hell out of him.

And he loved them for it.

Now he hoped that he'd see Jessica soon. Maybe the next time they saw each other, *he'd* be the one that laughed.

The family room was lovely.

The art was symmetrical and pristine. The pottery and flora were all beautifully placed as well.

These things were complimented but the always comfortable furniture, entertainment center and flat screen. No one could have asked for a more welcoming place. It was the ideal mash-up of old-school aesthetic and new-school creature comforts.

But at the moment, it may as well have been a war-torn shack.

So vivid were the looks of denial. So fragile were the resolves. So fearful and tense were the minds, at least when they thought of the future.

And so heavy—so sagging—were the hearts.

It was Saturday morning, four minutes to ten.

Everyone waited, with an unstable patience, for the final four minutes to pass.

The front door opened, and Felix walked in. Jonah regarded him. His beard was the usual pencil-thin precision that it was when he wasn't on the job. He was wearing a sharp black suit with an ash-colored shirt and black tie. For the first time that Jonah had known him, Felix actually looked like the multi-millionaire he was.

And it didn't mean a damn thing.

"Reverend Abbott says it's time," he told them.

Everyone rose and followed him outside to the Glade. Jonah couldn't help but think about the first night he'd been there, when he still had misinformed, incorrect views about "death" and "dying." Jonathan had sent him straight soon enough, using that spinning circle as a metaphor for life never actually ending. That thought was assisting him at the moment.

Sort of.

Jonah wondered about the curious habits of himself, and fellow human beings. They were smart enough to know that people in their lives would not always be there, at least not in the same form. They all knew that. Yet they still got used to people being around. Things changing became the notion that was possible, but was rarely, if ever, spoken of. And when that change happened, they always rebuked themselves for not being prepared.

Death wasn't real. Jonah got that. But there were still components to the Eleventh Percent that still made it feel real at times. Like the facts that Elevenths couldn't see the spirits of other Elevenths, nor could they see the spirits of Tenths that they'd been close to. As knowledgeable about the truth of life as Ethereal humans were, there were still times when they were just as limited and constricted as the Tenths.

Jonah had gotten used to Jonathan. He'd grown accustomed to those blazing gray eyes that could see through just about anything. That welcoming smile that let you know that being near him, and under his protection, was the only place you wanted to be on the planet. The cryptic words that may as well have been a foreign language one day, then make perfect sense the next. He'd grown used to thinking that, no matter what, that was one spirit who would always be right there.

Until that fucking War Haunt, big as a damn moose and specially bred to kill Guides, tore his essence to shreds and forced it to the Other Side.

Jonah thought about the Masonic bible on Jonathan's desk. Had he been a Mason when he was physically alive? Jonah hadn't ever asked. There were a whole bunch of questions he'd never asked.

It still stung him that so many people left the estate. Six. The Splinter. But he had hoped that they would have shown up for the memorial.

They weren't there. Not a single one.

And Trip and his lackeys weren't, either.

Jonah knew that, beyond a shadow of a doubt, he and Trip would be enemies for life. And a part of him still very much enjoyed beating the shit out of him. But the things he'd said about Jonathan making him feel like a worthwhile man, and showing him a different, and better way than what he'd known...Jonah felt the same way. It was quite a thing to behold; two men permanently gulfed by mutual hatred of each other yet synchronized by the positive effect that the Protector Guide had had on them.

Again, it was quite a thing.

Despite their absence, there was still a turnout that Jonah never imagined. There were Elevenths that he had never met before; either past estate residents, or simply those who'd had no dealings with the estate but had good relationships with Jonathan. He saw a smattering of Tenths who had Elevenths for relatives and had had the honor of hearing stories about Jonathan. Then he saw his family. There were all of the Decessios, and Terrence was with them. There was Reena, in Kendall's embrace, her shoulders quaking. There was Spader in black slacks and dress shirt, complete with a long black coat and black top hat. It was the first that he was in formal dress and not complaining about it. Magdalena was there with her entire family. Liz and Nella were with the rest of the Manvilles; even Sandrine was with them. Douglas and Katarina were there. Bobby had placed a comforting hand on his mother's shoulder, while Sterling was between Alvin and Raymond, both of whom looked to be hanging on by a thread. And, of course, Malcolm was there, sharply dressed, and solemn.

Then there were the members of Jonah's extended family. Felix, looking so earnest in that suit. Prodigal, in a black golf shirt, charcoal chinos, and loafers. Autumn Rose in a neat blouse and black pants, which was about as feminine as she was going to get. Obadiah was with them. There was Akshara, next to Jonah's new friends Xenia Pryce, Jada Yancey, Sebastian Torgas, and R.J. Holley. There was Patience, in his full Networker uniform of burgundy (he had already explained that anyone involved in Spectral Law had dress uniforms to match their auras). Elijah Norris stood next to them, in an ancient silver dress uniform. To Jonah's mild surprise, Amelia Bennett and Jerry Bladen stood next to them, in S.P.G. dress uniforms of plum and white, respectively. Gabriel Kaine was there, with Rheadne, Aloisa Chavis, and Michael Pruitt. That was it for Sanctum.

With anger, Jonah saw the entire Phasmastis Curaie seated at the front. They were wearing ominous looking hoods, but no one was put off by it. Forming in daylight was taxing for spirits and spiritesses, even ones as powerful as the Spirit Guides. So, they were hooded to maintain some modicum of shade. When Jonah looked around, he saw many other hoods, but he only recognized a few of the Spectral beings, like Graham, Samantha Lockman, Ruthie the nurse spiritess who had helped him once, and his favorite World War 2 soldier, who used to always endow him when he'd first gotten to the estate.

Finally, there were the heralds. Jonah never was fully aware of how many cats there were on the premises, but there were dozens, and they represented, just like the auras, every color of the spectrum. Bast was at the head. It was at that moment that a figure, which was kneeling near Naphtali, rose to find a seat, and Jonah's eyes widened.

It was Vera.

She had darkened her hair somewhat, but she had since stopped putting makeup on the scar on her jaw. As a matter of fact, save for her eyelids, she wore very little makeup at all. She was still the woman that she always was, despite now being a successful stage actress having to deal with so much phoniness. She must have felt Jonah's eyes on her at that point. Noticing that there was an empty seat next to her, he raised his eyebrows with a silent question. She nodded without hesitation. He came forward and settled down next to her.

"You look nice, Jonah," she said quietly.

"Likewise, friend," said Jonah back.

Reverend Abbott walked to a podium, next to a wonderful picture of Jonathan that Reena completed after five hours of work. It was so life-like that Jonah caught himself half-expecting Jonathan to speak from it. But that was wishful thinking.

"You know," he began, "some of you probably wondered how to have a eulogistic service for a spirit. The answer is easy. We simply don't view Jonathan as a spirit."

He looked at Reena's sketch, steeled himself, and continued.

"Jonathan was always the first one to tell you that life never ends. So, with that in mind, I don't see a spirit. I see a Protector Guide who aided many but was never a harsh taskmaster. He embodied everlasting life more than anyone I can think of, and no matter what the endeavor, he took every facet, every moment, every idea, and squeezed it for every single drop there was to be had. I didn't see a spirit. I saw a man who was full of life, and I don't view that as being vanquished."

Reverend Abbott had been doing well, but his voice broke there. He closed his eyes, and let the tears fall without shame.

"I see him not as vanquished, but as a being that was released from the Earth and Astral Planes and is now simply continuing his journey."

He then nodded to his left and seated himself. Nella and Themis walked up, both holding their guitars.

"The first song that I ever mastered on guitar was 'Wonderwall,'" said Nella, red-eyed. "For whatever reason, Jonathan absolutely loved to hear me play that song, and sing the words with it. I thought it'd be nice to play it for him, one last time. Themis will help me."

Themis had come along nicely under Nella's tutelage, it seemed, and she held up her end with no trouble. Nella cried the whole time, but she powered through, and did the song justice for Jonathan. It was a beautiful cover. If Nella decided to pursue music in addition to healing, she'd go very far.

After that, several people got up and made remarks. Jonah closed his eyes, willing them to just let it be.

But that was a fail.

He opened his eyes to find that just about every eye in the crowd was in him. He could have scowled. In this moment, in this particular moment, he envied Trip's ability to will himself to not be seen.

Stop looking at me, he silently begged everyone. *Stop frickin' looking at me!*

Then soft, familiar fingers wrapped around his hand.

"You've got this, Jonah," said Vera. "I believe in you, always have. And we need you right now."

Jonah was still nervous but raised the hand Vera just grabbed to his face and sighed. There were actually traces of rose oil on his hand from Vera. God, if it wasn't one of the nicest scents in the world.

He rose and began the walk. The podium seemed miles away. The distance between the chair rows may as well have been mile markers on I-40. He glanced at Reena, who tried to smile, but her heart wasn't in it. He looked at Terrence, who nodded encouragingly.

Finally, he reached the damned podium. He straightened as much as he could, as he was still dealing with soreness from his and Trip's fight. Purposely, he ignored the Curaie. He hated everything about them right now.

He looked out to the many faces, and then looked at Jonathan's sketch. Jonathan had told him that he'd evolved into a powerful man. He wanted so badly to do him proud. The tears began again. It had been a mistake focusing on that sketch.

Way with words, he thought.

"How crazy is it?" He chuckled through the tears. "How crazy is it that the closest thing that I had to a father was a spirit?"

People shook their heads. No one thought it was crazy. A fair few of them probably thought the same.

"Some of you might not know the whole story," Jonah continued, "but I'll try to paraphrase it. The day that Jonathan kick-started my aura and my vision went blue, it was one of the most terrifying moments of my life. Jonathan appeared, and looked me over, like he truly had his work cut out for him with me."

That got a few laughs.

"But the one thing that I took from that very first exchange was that Jonathan meant me no harm," said Jonah. "He was always stalwart and steadfast. So unshakeable. As I said, I was terrified. But there was something about him that calmed me somewhat."

Jonah gripped the podium, and the soreness in his fists made him think of Trip again. What he had done. The things he'd said that had swayed people so dramatically. He'd had no fear or reservations. He wasn't shy about it when it rocked the boat.

And now Jonah was supposed to be afraid right now?

Oh, hell no.

Before he knew it, he was in front of the podium. Damn the discomforts. He didn't need that thing at all.

"The thing that Jonathan always had was peace of mind." The tears faded as he said the words. "And he always made a point to pass that on to everyone. Creyton knew that. They grew up together, so I'm sure that Creyton would like to think that he knew exactly how Jonathan ticked. He's probably sitting real pretty right now, thinking that taking Jonathan away from us makes triumph absolute. That line of thinking was his first failure."

Some of the sad faces looked at Jonah in confusion.

"Creyton is of the mentality that, now that Jonathan is gone, everything is completely lost," Jonah told them all. "But that mentality is one of the biggest lies on all of Earthplane. Just look."

He raised his arm, soreness and all, and pointed in a wide arc. People eyed his action, still confused, but Jonah wasn't worried. He was a bard; he'd get them back soon enough.

"The world didn't turn dark," he said. "The estate is still there, as majestic and proud as ever. Jonathan saw to it that everything was safe, taken care of, and whole. What Creyton doesn't realize—*can't* realize—is that he didn't take Jonathan from us. Malcolm, stand up, please."

Jonah was unsurprised by the puzzlement on Malcolm's face as he rose.

"Malcolm, I know that you will remember, but I never knew," said Jonah. "What was the first thing that Jonathan ever told you when he saw your woodwork?"

Malcolm was taken aback by the question, but he answered it at once. "It was an eagle. He said that the true artist's talent wasn't creating the eagle, but seeing the eagle inside the wood itself, and having the know-how to reach it."

Jonah nodded. "Sounds like something he'd say," he murmured. "And tell us, Malcolm, the feeling of elation that you had when Jonathan told you that...will Creyton ever be able to take that from you?"

"Well, no, I—"

Then Malcolm realized Jonah's point. Jonah smiled when he saw the realization.

"No," said Malcolm, with a stronger assurance in his voice than there had previously been. "No, he can't."

"Thanks man," said Jonah and he nodded to denote that he could return to his seat.

"Reena." This one was a risk because she could burst out in tears again at any moment. "The first time you painted in that studio, what did Jonathan say?"

Reena rose, swallowed, and sniffed. "He said that the painting was amazing only because I was the masterpiece first."

"And those words... what did they do for you?"

"I was so angry and negative then," said Reena quietly. "But Jonathan, with those words, began to crack through. It was nice to be loved. Nice to be praised and accepted."

Jonah nodded, but he saw that Reena was losing it. So, he bade her sit back down.

"Spader," he said, "let me ask you. When you were ordered to donate your getaway money, you were pissed, weren't you? And be for real, please."

Spader blinked. "Yeah, I was pissed," he admitted. "More than a little bit."

"But after you funded Nella's club's trip to Valentania York, what did Jonathan tell you?"

Spader laughed to himself. "He said that performing that blessing for those young women made me a blessing in the flesh."

"Right," nodded Jonah, "another thing that sounds like him talking. And that didn't suck at all, did it?"

"Well, I hadn't appreciated having to give up my money," shrugged Spader, "but after Jonathan said what he said, nah... it didn't suck. To be honest, I didn't even mind helping the girls out so much after that."

"So, I take that to mean that you're never going to forget that?" asked Jonah.

"Highly unlikely!" snorted Spader.

People smiled. Many of the other grieving faces achieved mirth.

"I'll even bring myself into this," said Jonah. "Anyone who knows me knows that I was a bored accountant in a loser job. Then I found out that I was not only an Eleventh Percenter, but one that was supposedly a big deal. I'll be the first to admit that I felt less than useless. But Jonathan told me, even before I'd had a lick of training, that I could give a superb accounting of myself in whatever I do. Those were his words, verbatim. I didn't want to call him a liar, but I didn't believe that. Even so, Jonathan still had this…this *thing* that made you feel proud of yourself. Malcolm, Reena, Spader, and I are only four people he did that for. Jonathan was on Earthplane for a hundred and ten years. I'll bet everything I've got that he touched way more than four people. That's obvious by looking at all of you right here."

People were catching on. The stirring had caught on.

"As long as you have your hearts, minds, and spirits, Jonathan will never be gone," insisted Jonah. "As long as his influence is in the world, he is still in the world, too. All of you know that Jonathan could take the lowliest person, and within one conversation, make them feel like the most intriguing, complex, and valuable person in existence. Creyton took his essence away. But he did not take away his teachings."

There were some whoops in the crowd. Some rigorous nods.

"Omega is coming," said Jonah. He still felt apprehension about that word, and what it meant. But he was flying high, and the adrenaline allowed him to power through. "Let it come."

His voice had such conviction that people looked at him in alarm. "Creyton doesn't know what he's done. He had no earthly idea what he's done."

Jonah looked at the Spirit Guides from the Curaie, and then at Jonathan's sketch. There was no doubt in his mind that Jonathan outstripped all thirteen of them. Not a single doubt.

"Jonathan said that in life, the valleys strengthen, and peaks allow appreciation," he said. "Well, we are undoubtedly in a valley right now. But if valleys strengthen, then we have a chance and a choice. We can take this chance to rebuild and rise with newfound strength, and we have the choice to apply that strength when the need arises. That's why I say let Omega come. Let Creyton bring it on. Because when he shows up, he won't meet a group of people grieving in a pool of pity. Hell no, he won't. He will be meeting badasses wearing every lesson that Jonathan ever taught them like a frickin' banner. LIFE NEVER ENDS!"

His words received a standing ovation. People were out of their seats, applauding raucously. Spirits were applauding. People were shouting.

And the Phasmastis Curaie looked extremely uncomfortable.

Jonah wasn't surprised about any of it. He had done, with one speech, what they had failed to do for months. For these precious moments, mourners were inspired and determined. For these precious moments, Jonathan was with them again, in the form of the wisdom, love, honor, knowledge, and understanding that he gave to everyone present. Jonah decided to leave the podium on that note. He felt it best to leave them with the precious moments that they cherished the most.

The memorial began to disperse shortly thereafter. Engagah and the rest of the Spirit Guides left without a word to anyone. Jonah didn't really give it much thought, as he was mobbed as soon as he left the podium.

The zillions of conversations were more taxing than his speech. He talked briefly with Rheadne, who just couldn't leave the conversation without kissing the side of his face. But then Gabriel ushered her away from him, which was no biggie.

Then Vera caught his eye and beckoned to him. As she didn't look displeased or angry, Jonah guessed that she hadn't noticed Rheadne.

"You missed your calling, Jonah," she said when he reached her. "I swear, when all eyes were on you, you did wonderfully. Why were you so nervous?"

Jonah half-smiled. "I don't know where all that came from, Vera," he replied. "Guess I was channeling deep emotion, or something. But you already know that once I get going, the butterflies just fade. I felt like I owed it to Jonathan to do him proud."

"That you did, Jonah," said Vera. "That you did."

Jonah smiled and nodded. "Vera, I need to tell you something," he said, "or... do you need to head out soon? Is East waiting for you in town?"

"No," said Vera. "We've got plans later, in Seattle, I mean."

"What? But you could be late—?"

"Ethereal human, Jonah?" Vera raised her eyebrows. "Who happens to be the Time Item?"

Jonah paused, and then shook his head. "Duh."

He then took a deep breath. "Vera, I'm proud of you," he told her. "You're an amazing actress—you control every aspect of that stage when you're on it. I'm so happy that not only have you gotten the chance to do what you love, but you're a hit, and you're only getting higher and higher. As far as I'm concerned, there is no more heat or negativity between us. I hope that you believe that because I'm not going to try to convince you. I hope and pray that you and East are going strong. I mean that."

Jonah had to give himself a compliment on a job well done. He almost believed that last part himself.

Vera nodded. "Fair enough, Jonah," she said. "I accept that and thank you for your praise."

It was at that moment that Jonah realized he was in Vera's personal space. He immediately backed away.

"Sorry about that," he said.

Then his eyes narrowed slightly. Unless his sense of sight fooled him, Vera looked disappointed. Seriously? Why would that be? All he was doing was respecting her, and her relationship. He didn't want her to think that he was putting her in a position that was awkward or improper. He respected her that much.

And she was disappointed.

"May I have a hug, at least?" she asked quietly.

Jonah raised his eyebrows. Vera rolled her eyes.

"I did just lose my mentor, Jonah," she told him. "You might not see it, but I am saddened, and seriously bummed out right now. I'm not cheating on my boyfriend if I give one of my closest friends a damned hug."

And, almost defiantly, she threw her arms around Jonah's neck. Mentally saying *What the hell* to himself, he obliged her and hugged her back.

* * *

Jonah had hoped to sleep in the next morning. Exhaustion had finally taken over. But there was scratching at the door.

Quite insistent scratching.

He pulled himself up and opened the door. It was Anakaris. Jonah recognized him because he was the only herald that was Abyssinian.

"Mornin', Anakaris," he mumbled as he curtailed a yawn. "What's up?"

Anakaris looked him in the eye. "*Hi, Jonah,*" he intimated. "*Meet Reena in Jonathan's study.*"

"Why?" frowned Jonah.

"*You, Terrence, and Reena have more to do,*" intimated Anakaris.

"More to—?"

But Anakaris scampered off. Jonah stood there for a few moments, and then headed to the study.

It was amazing how... normal it seemed. Everything was in order, as always. Jonathan could have been Offplane, due back at any minute. All seemed as it was.

Except for the absence of the Vitasphera. It wasn't here anymore; it was in Jonah's room, reverently placed in a wooden jewelry box that Malcolm had made forever ago, but never had a use for. Jonah kept the box closed, so that he couldn't see the Vitasphera. He still couldn't process it yet.

Terrence and Reena were already there. Reena almost cracked a smile when she saw him.

"What's up?" he asked them.

"Jonathan left us a letter," said Reena without preamble.

All drowsiness inside Jonah faded as he stepped in and closed the door.

"For us?" he asked. "Just us?"

"Yep," said Terrence. "Reena just deciphered it."

Jonah looked at Reena. "I didn't think you'd ever do that again," he said.

Reena almost smiled again. "This wasn't a trap," she said. "And it was one of the simplest, most benign experiences ever."

Jonah seated himself. Terrence extended a hand to Reena.

"I can read it, Reena," he offered.

"I'm good." Reena shook her head. "I got it."

She moved the Phantom Key to the side, smoothed out her scratch paper, and read:

Dearest Jonah, Terrence, and Reena,

If you are reading this, then I am now on the Other Side.

I know that all of you are saddened, and likely feel abandoned, but I have faith in you, and the entirety of our unit.

I know that you have the components for victory, but it was not meant for me to walk that victory road with you. I made my peace with that long ago.

There are a few things that you all need to know.

I always knew about the Six. The skeleton of the plan, anyway. And I knew that the Cut was me. Creyton views Jonah as such a non-entity that he thinks by eliminating me, he can now power his way to Omega. That's the reason why I was angry with you when I discovered your investigation. I didn't want you to discover that they were gunning for me. That is also why I forbade you from taking spiritual endowments for such a prolonged time, Jonah. I knew that the Cut was coming, but I didn't know how Creyton would go about implementing it. Whatever was coming was going to go for the most powerful Eleventh Percenter at the estate. That was not me. It was always you. And if you had a spiritual endowment, or did any ethereality, whatever Creyton unleashed would zero in on you. To protect you, I forbade endowments. That way, all the heat would be on me.

Reena stopped when she saw Jonah's face. Tears spilled out of his eyes that he had no energy to wipe away. He had been so angry with Jonathan for not endowing him. But what he thought had been punishment had been protection. When he nodded, she continued:

Jonah, you are a magnificent Eleventh, and an even better man. Do not be afraid to be powerful. Ever. You are Creyton's better, and you always have been.

Jonah closed his eyes. To the point, but profound. Reena read on:

> *Reena, I never told you this to your face because I respected you and knew that it wasn't your way to be overly sentimental. But I've always viewed you as my precious daughter. From the day I met, this was true. Always be proud of yourself. Every little thing that makes you who you are is a blessing to the world. The entire world, not just the ethereal. That was true before I met you, true when I met you, and it is still true now.*

Reena began to cry again. Terrence clamped her shoulder, pulled the letter from her hands, and continued himself:

> *Terrence, pay attention to this. Stop doubting yourself. You are worth so much more than you give yourself credit for. You have more common sense than anybody, you provide the lifeline for any place you go, and your actions are those of one equal to his team, not a sidekick. I ask that you trust yourself, because your knowledge is always beneficial, whether you are aware of it or not.*

Terrence paused, and took a huge deep breath. Then he powered through:

> *Now, this is where I implore you to follow my directions this one final time, without question. I gave Daniel strict orders to place my medallion in my drawer, should anything happen to me.*

Reena opened the drawer and lifted the Infinity medallion out of it. Jonah looked at Terrence and motioned for him to continue. He didn't want to look at the medallion in a golden heap. If it wasn't around Jonathan's neck, it was out of place. Plain and simple.

Terrence took the hint:

I knew the Cut was coming soon, but I didn't know when. But the central point is this: I was ready.

Terrence paused again, raising his head in shock.

"He was ready?" he demanded. "But why—?"

"Keep reading, man, and we'll find out," said Jonah.

Terrence returned to it:

Take my medallion to Trinity Cove Road. You will understand when you get there. Thank you, and I love you. I love you all.

If you find yourself getting down and sad about me, don't.

Life never, ever ends.

Jonathan

Jonah sat there in silence. Terrence placed the letter on the table and stared off into space. Reena, however, looked pensive. Jonah caught her expression and frowned.

"What is it?" he asked.

"I know that address," she said. "That's Miss Mott's house."

Jonah remembered the house from last November when they did Butterball or Bust. It was a nice little house, just one story, and rather engulfed by slightly overgrown hedges.

"Why would we need to go to Miss Mott's place?" questioned Terrence. "What can she do to help us?"

"Jonathan said do this for him," said Jonah. "And we won't find out a damn thing here."

They walked to the door, and Reena knocked. The door was almost immediately opened by a hard-faced, middle-aged woman who wore an apron covered with flour. She'd have looked comical if she didn't look so menacing.

"What?" she snapped.

Jonah's eyebrows flew up in surprise, but Reena tapped his arm.

"Good morning, ma'am," she said kindly. "We need to speak to Miss Mott."

"Why?" demanded the lady.

Jonah leveled his breath. This woman right here was a ray of sunshine. "We were thinking that she could help us with something."

"Like what?"

"Like—"

Jonah faltered. He didn't even know what he was about to say, but it would have worsened things considerably. Terrence spoke up.

"Ma'am," he said slowly, "tell me what went wrong this morning."

Jonah frowned, but the woman's expression grew darker.

"Damn transmission started sticking," she grumbled. "I don't have money to repair it. It doesn't even seem like it'll take a lot of work, but fools are gonna charge me so much labor—"

"I'm pretty good at auto mechanics, ma'am," interrupted Terrence, who now understood why the woman had such a foul mood. "No need to be humble; I'm a whiz. My father runs a shop, and he taught me everything he knows. I can help you. I'll even do it for free."

The lady's eyes brightened, but she looked like she had trouble believing in such good fortune. "Free, eh? What's the catch?"

"Catch is," Reena joined in, "you allow us to talk Miss Mott without interruption."

The women contemplated them for a few moments, turning it over in her mind. She made a decision. "Give me two minutes," she said, and closed the door. Jonah looked at Terrence, puzzled and impressed.

"How did you know that?" he whispered.

"No one is that angry this early in the morning unless they got hurt, got a speeding ticket, or something was up with their car," said Terrence. "One of the three."

The minutes passed, and the lady was back at the door.

"Don't speak too fast," she said. "Or too loud. She might be over a hundred, but her hearing's still pretty good. My name's Mabel, I'm her nurse."

"I'm Jonah, this is Terrence, and that's Reena."

Mabel nodded to each one of them. "Walk straight through there," she instructed. "She's sitting in her chair."

They walked down the narrow hall in a single file, and the hall opened to a wide room, full of old possessions, pictures, and old sofa and recliner, where Miss Mott sat.

She was a thin, very slight-framed woman. Her iron-colored hair was pulled back into a ponytail, which slightly pulled back the wrinkled skin of her forehead. Her face was further lined, and her skin seemed slightly translucent. But Jonah could tell that her blue eyes still held within them the locked treasures of a long past but far from forgotten youth. There was such a vibrant smile in her eyes that Jonah wondered how lively and adventurous a woman she was in her younger years.

She looked them over with warm interest.

"You are all such beautiful children," she commented. "And you," she pointed at Terrence, "I think I know you already! You've cut my grass a bunch of times!"

"Yes ma'am," grinned Terrence. "My name is Terrence."

Jonah smiled. It was hard not to be pleasant in this woman's presence. "My name is Jonah, Miss Mott, and this is Reena. I see that you already know Terrence. We need to speak with you for just a couple minutes."

"That's fine, darlin'!" she said in a low yet excited voice. "It's just Mabel and me, so visitors are always welcome."

Jonah nodded, and looked at Reena.

"Miss Mott," she said, "something came into our possession. It's our understanding that you might like to have it."

Jonah saw Mabel raise her eyebrow. Miss Mott tilted her head to the side, curious.

"What would that be, darlin'?" she asked.

Reena pulled out Jonathan's Infinity medallion. Both Miss Mott and Mabel gasped so dramatically that Jonah, Terrence, and Reena jumped.

"Give it to me!" exclaimed Miss Mott. "Let me hold it!"

Reena handed it over, and Miss Mott took it, looking utterly delighted.

"Oh, thank you." The elderly woman looked livelier than she'd been in years. "Thank you, thank you!"

Jonah's eyes were wide. What the hell? He looked at Terrence and Reena, but they were confused, too.

"Mabel!" cried Miss Mott. "You know where it is! Do it! And show them!"

"Yes ma'am!" Mabel looked as ecstatic as Miss Mott did as she took the medallion and motioned to Jonah, Terrence, and Reena.

"Y'all come with me!" she said.

Perplexed, they followed her outside, headed toward a shed.

"How'd you kids get this?" she asked en route.

"It wasn't ours," said Terrence. "It got handed down."

"Lordy Jesus!" said Mabel, but she was smiling. "You three are a mysterious bunch! But I'm glad you did this. Y'all have done Miss Francine a *blessed* favor."

She got to the shed, unlocked the door, and invited them inside. Mabel led them to a table overloaded with pictures.

"That's her," said Mable, pointing to a bunch of pictures. "Miss Francine."

Jonah looked at them. Most were black and white, but very well maintained. They showed a Francine Mott that was young, vivacious, and strong, in all types of settings. She was in several pictures with horses. In one, she stood next to an ancient (but probably modern at the time) Chevy. In several others, she stood with a bunch of children, arms laden with baked goods. Though he couldn't see the blue of her eyes in the black and white pictures, there was no mistaking the joy and happiness that this lady had in those days.

They were sweet pictures, but Jonah didn't get the point of looking at them. He was just about to ask that when Reena gasped.

"Jonah," she whispered, "Terrence. Come here."

Jonah and Terrence were at her side in seconds. It was Francine, probably in her early twenties, standing in front of a lodge of some kind.

And she was wearing an Infinity medallion.

They looked at Mabel, who smiled and nodded.

"Where did she get that?" breathed Jonah.

Mabel pulled a photograph from behind several others and showed it to them. In unison, their mouths dropped.

It was Francine and Jonathan.

"She got it from the man she was going to marry," answered Mabel.

Jonah took the picture. He had seen Jonathan smile before, but never as happily as he looked next to this woman. His beam practically glowed through the black and white picture. "*Was* going to marry, you said?"

"Yes," said Mabel, "she's told me all about him. His name was Jonathan Grannison."

They all froze. It had never occurred to Jonah that Jonathan had had a last name. It seemed to humanize him somehow. And his last name was Grannison? One of the names attached to the estate?

"She says them met each other and knew that they were the ones for each other from the very beginning," said Mabel fondly. "She said that people thought that he was so mysterious, but she understood him perfectly. He wanted to do something more for her than just a ring, so he made this—" she held up the Infinity medallion they brought, "—for himself, as well as this one."

Mabel reached into a jewelry box and pulled out a second, thinner Infinity medallion.

"The two of them together do this."

She clamped the thinner one inside Jonathan's, the larger one. When they were clasped together, they formed a perfect, synchronous symbol.

"She told me that he said it meant they were infinite," Mabel continued. "She said that he wasn't fond of the word death, and never said that things died. According to her, one of his favorite things to say was life never ends. Said it all the time."

Jonah just stared at the picture. He couldn't believe it.

"But then he died himself, though," said Mabel, who shook her head. "While they were still 'courting,' as she put it. She never knew how it happened. Never got over him, and never married anyone else."

"Really?" said Reena. "She stayed unmarried all of her phy—I mean, all of her life?"

"Sure did," said Mabel. "She was hopelessly devoted to Jonathan, even after he was dead. She spent her life doing a whole lot of other things besides getting married...you can see that in the pictures there. But she never forgot that man. She said that he was always helping folks out, so after he died, she did a bunch of humanitarian work, did UNICEF and all that. Been all over the world, but she retired back here. What y'all just did? This might have been that one more miracle."

Jonah frowned. "One more miracle?"

"Miss Francine said that she's felt Jonathan with her for her whole life," said Mable. "She said that he always gave her strength, always gave her hope, that kind of thing. For that reason, or so she claims, her life has been 'full of miracles,' and she kept saying that she was waiting for one more. I think this might've been it."

Jonah and Terrence looked at Reena, who nodded.

"Miss Mabel," she said, "this is my number. Please call me...you know...if..."

Mabel nodded. She probably felt the same way. She took the paper that had Reena's number on it and pocketed it. "I don't think she's much longer for this world, either. Clearly, she has more days behind her than she does in front of her. Which is why I'm glad y'all came when you did. Miss Francine's a happy woman by nature, but I haven't seen her that happy in a long while. Thank you again, so much."

Jonah shook her hand, as did Terrence and Reena. Terrence passed over his number as well.

"For when you want your car fixed," he smiled.

"Give Miss Mott our best," said Jonah. "I hope that she enjoys seeing them together again. Both together like that, I mean."

"Oh, she will," said Mabel. "One more time, thank you."

* * *

Jonah finally did get his late sleep the next morning. He'd taken a leave of absence from the library. Maybe he'd go back. Maybe.

He looked at the clock next to the bed. Nearly noon. He got up, stretched, and opened his door.

Where Terrence and Reena stood. It looked as though Reena was about to knock.

"What's up now?" he asked them.

Reena lowered her hand and pulled out her cell phone. "Mabel called."

Jonah stared. "Last night?"

"Nah, man," said Terrence, "this morning. Mabel said that Miss Mott spent all last night calling us angels."

"And Mabel was with her," said Reena. "She said that right before she passed into Spirit, she said that she saw 'her Jonathan, smiling with his hand held out.'"

Jonah backed into his bedroom and lowered himself on his bed. Jonathan had been right in the letter. He *did* understand about the medallion. Jonathan hadn't just stayed behind to mentor upcoming Elevenths. He'd stayed behind to look after the woman he loved as well, Francine. He'd probably given her kind impressions, gentle breezes on hot days, or subtle feelings of strength when she was down. He'd probably done all those things, without fail, for years. And, as a spirit, he'd probably sensed that her time as a physical being was coming to a close. She'd waited for "one more miracle," and Jonathan had provided that through them. He'd faced his inevitable vanquishing with a smile on his face, because not only had he saved Jonah and believed his students to be ready, but he would also be reunited with his true love shortly after he was in Spirit.

"I don't know how things work on the Other Side," said Reena, "none of us do. But I believe that when Miss Mott passed into Spirit, Jonathan was indeed right there, arms outstretched, waiting for her. You know I'm not one for sappiness, but this time only, I will say that that is the sweetest thing ever."

Terrence nodded. "Yeah. It was cool as hell."

"I agree," said Jonah, "but damn. She never wanted anyone else. Never married. That's a lot of dedication to one love."

"Jonah," said Reena, "trust me on this: When you meet that one—that great, perfect one—no one else measures up. No one."

Jonah thought that there might be a hidden message in there that had nothing to do with Jonathan and Francine. But his mind shifted once again. To Creyton. To Omega. To a leadership position that he now had but wasn't sure he wanted.

"I've got to ask you a question, man," said Terrence suddenly. "In light of this—this sweet gestures and good feelings and all of that—have you changed your mind about taking out Jessica?"

"Hell no, I haven't changed my mind," said Jonah. "This matter with Jonathan and Miss Mott was a sweet, beautiful thing, I grant you that. But it doesn't change anything. That bitch's days are numbered. If I'm lucky, Creyton's are, too. But Jessica? It's a definite that she ain't long for this world."

Terrence and Reena said nothing. Jonah was glad of that. They weren't going to change his mind, anyway.

He went to the jewelry box Malcolm made and finally opened it to remove The Vitasphera.

It was his now.

The thing was black as night. Not even a hint of the gold within was visible. Jonah just stared at it.

Omega was coming. There was no stopping that. Jonathan, in that letter, had advised Jonah not to be afraid to be powerful. Jonah didn't know the extent of his powers. Even though he'd gotten stronger and better, he still didn't know the full scope of his powers. Creyton, on the other hand, was well versed in his own.

Jonah's responsibilities weighed on him much like one of Bobby's adjustable weighed athletic shirts.

"I don't know what you're thinking, Jonah," said Terrence from behind him, "but I promise you, you don't have to figure out everything today."

"And another thing, Jonah," Reena's voice was oddly stern. "The only way we do this is together. You will not attempt that Lone Wolf bullshit you've pulled in the past. Got me?"

Jonah sighed, his eyes still on the Vitasphera. "I'm not going anywhere, Reena."

"Good." Terrence tried to be stern, but he couldn't hide the relief in his voice.

Jonah finally turned to his brother and sister. "I don't know what's going to happen," he said quietly. "I know that I spoke a good pitch at Jonathan's memorial, but I don't feel that way one hundred percent. Creyton's batting a thousand right now, and Jonathan's gone. Over seventy people have left here, and our numbers are the shits. Last but not least, Laban's free, and out doing God knows what. How we're going to win all of this, with me as the leader? I...I just don't know what will happen."

"Jonah," said Reena, "none of us do."

"And don't worry," said Terrence, a trace of a grin on his face, "we'll get through it."

Jonah looked at him. "How, man?"

Terrence looked seriously at him. Even the trace of smile was gone. "The same way we get through everything else around here," he said. "Somehow."

Jonah stared for a second, and then extended his hand. Terrence got the hint and placed his hand on top of it. Reena stood and placed her hand atop theirs.

Jonah didn't know how he felt about everything, but he knew three things for sure.

One, Omega was coming.

Two, even if he couldn't bring himself to say it aloud just yet, he was the Overseer of the Grannison-Morris Estate.

And three, when Omega finally did hit, he'd face it with his family.

"Yeah," he said to Terrence with a nod. "Somehow."

Dear reader,

We hope you enjoyed reading *Six*. Please take a moment to leave a review, even if it's a short one. Your opinion is important to us.

Discover more books by T.H. Morris at
https://www.nextchapter.pub/authors/th-morris

Want to know when one of our books is free or discounted? Join the newsletter at
http://eepurl.com/bqqB3H

Best regards,
T.H. Morris and the Next Chapter Team

Acknowledgements

The 11th Percent Series, Book Six. *Six.*

Wow. Just looking at that sentence boggles my mind. To say that it has been a journey reaching this point is an understatement, and in no way did I make this trek alone. Over the course of my writing career, I've forged invaluable bonds for which words cannot convey my gratitude. Though some of the names have changed over the years, the levels of support have remained the same. And I'd be remiss if I didn't give thanks. To my family—thank you. You're the best in the world, and I wouldn't be the writer I am without you. My beautiful wife, Candace, thank you for being just as ardent a fan and just as staunch a supporter of me as you when I wrote the first manuscript. Hell, the first *word*. It makes me misty-eyed when I think of all the strides and assistance you extended to me on the path as my first fan, cheerleader, inspiration, and confidante. Without you, none of these books would've gone beyond a weird collection of ideas in my head. I love you genuinely and thank you a million times over for pushing and motivating me. Miika Hanilla and Next Chapter, thank you for taking a chance on me. Thank you for breathing fresh life into my projects and transmogrifying them into bigger gems than I could have ever imagined. I'm still so excited and humbled to be a member of the team, and my gratitude is boundless. Cynthia Witherspoon, my informal sister and collaborator in the Gods and Ghosts series, thank you for helping me keep my irons sharp with boundless ideas and new lore. You embody the notion of iron sharpening iron. Sarah Mann, thank you for being the best damn PA under the sun. Whether it's teasers, blurbs, insights, edits, online takeovers, or just a kind word or compliment, you're in a class by yourself and I'm overjoyed you're on my team. Dani Black, Mallory Kent, Mo Day, Annie Smith, Lily Luchesi, Brandy Martin, Amanda Hoey, Jared Mingia...you guys are diamonds. Each of you have played a part on my journey that has been integral to my success and progression as an author, and I truly do not know where I would be without each and every one of you.

As I have said in the acknowledgments of every book in this series, if I named everyone who's aided me on this path, it'd be a book unto itself. So, I will just say thank you. With every fiber of my being, I'm grateful, appreciative, and blessed to have you all with me. I know beyond a shadow of a doubt that I wouldn't be here without all of you. Once again, my eternal thanks to you all.

About The Author

T.H. Morris was born in Colerain, North Carolina in 1984, and has been writing in some way, shape, or form ever since he was able to hold a pen or pencil. He relocated to Greensboro, North Carolina in 2002 for undergraduate education.

He is an avid reader, mainly in the genre of science fiction and fantasy, along with the occasional mystery or thriller. He is also a gamer and loves to exercise, Netflix binge, and meet new people. He began to write *The 11th Percent* series in 2011, and published book 1, *The 11th Percent,* in 2014, and book 2, *Item and Time,* in May of 2015. Book 3, *Lifeblood,* was published next in November of that same year, and book 4, *Inimicus,* followed in August of 2016, and book 5, *Gaslighter,* in spring 2017.

He now resides in Denver, Colorado with his wife, Candace.

Connect Online!

Twitter: @terrick_j
Facebook: https://www.facebook.com/groups/705132030260044
Email: terrick.heckstall@gmail.com

Also by T.H. Morris:

The 11th Percent (The 11th Percent Series, Book 1)
Item and Time (The 11th Percent Series, Book 2)
Lifeblood (The 11th Percent Series, Book 3)
Inimicus (The 11th Percent Series, Book 4)
Gaslighter (The 11th Percent Series, Book 5)

Coming Soon

Omega (The 11th Percent Series, Book 7)

With Cynthia D. Witherspoon

Gods and Ghosts (Gods and Ghosts, Book 1)

Coming Soon

Gods and Thieves (Gods and Ghosts, Book 2
Gods and Reapers (Gods and Ghosts, Book 3)
Gods and Monsters (Gods and Ghosts, Book 4)
Gods and Vipers (Gods and Ghosts, Book 5)

CPSIA information can be obtained
at www.ICGtesting.com
Printed in the USA
BVHW041150180321
602887BV00007B/1036